PENGUIN BOOKS

Sincerely Yours, Anna Sherwood

Sincerely Yours, Anna Sherwood

BETH REEKLES

PENGUIN BOOKS

PENGUIN BOOKS

UK | USA | Canada | Ireland | Australia
India | New Zealand | South Africa

Penguin Books is part of the Penguin Random House group of companies
whose addresses can be found at global.penguinrandomhouse.com.

www.penguin.co.uk
www.puffin.co.uk
www.ladybird.co.uk

First published 2023

001

Set in 11/17pt Palatino LT Std
Typeset by Jouve (UK), Milton Keynes
Printed and bound in Great Britain by Clays Ltd, Elcograf S.p.A.

The authorized representative in the EEA is Penguin Random House Ireland,
Morrison Chambers, 32 Nassau Street, Dublin D02 YH68

A CIP catalogue record for this book is available from the British Library

ISBN: 978–0–241–63115–7

All correspondence to:
Penguin Books
Penguin Random House Children's
One Embassy Gardens, 8 Viaduct Gardens, London SW11 7BW

For Becca – my fellow romance trope fan-girl!
I think you would've loved this one.

Chapter 1

The club flashes blue, acid green, lilac and back to bright electric blue again. The bass thrums through my chest, my bones, and all the way to my fingertips, lifting me onto the balls of my feet with my hands in the air. Everyone's swaying, shimmying and singing at the top of their lungs to a Harry Styles song that slides seamlessly into a remix of Olivia Rodrigo's 'good 4 u'.

For an icebreaker evening, this isn't half bad.

And this place is definitely a lot better than the Pizza Express where we spent an awkward, stilted two hours earlier this evening, swapping details of our A levels and uni courses and our preferred pizza toppings. (A necessary evil, given that the restaurant had been booked for us by our new employer so we could all 'get to know' one another ahead of working together on the Arrowmile internship programme this summer.)

Tonight is about anything *but* the impending internship.

Which is really saying a lot, because it's taken over my life for *months* between the application process and the agony of waiting to hear if, out of five thousand applicants, I would be one of the fifteen who made it.

As of tonight, I am officially one of those fifteen. Tonight, we enjoy a taste of freedom and excitement before starting one of the most coveted, prestigious internship programmes there is on Monday morning.

Tonight, I let my hair down for once.

For me, that involves some rum and Coke, half a glass of prosecco, and dancing on the sticky floor of a too-loud club with fourteen relative strangers. Four of whom have double-barrelled names, and three of whom are students at Cambridge. All of whom seemed pretty okay at Pizza Express, and right now feel like my new favourite people in the whole world.

There are hands on my hips, the brush of a body behind mine. Broad, masculine. One of my new flatmates and fellow Arrowmile intern for the summer, Elaine, a tall, bony girl with long blonde hair, catches my eye and wiggles her eyebrows, apparently in approval of my new dancing partner. I glance over my shoulder, staring for a moment in the flashing lights before deciding I don't recognize him; he's not part of our group.

I turn back to Elaine and shrug, not minding the hands on my hips or the attention until I'm grabbed by one of the interns who, laughing, pulls me away from my dance partner and into a ramshackle conga line back to the bar. By the time I'm jostled to the front of the group, someone's bought a round of tequila shots and Elaine is pressing one into my hand, a lime wedge balanced on top. Someone else holds out a salt shaker to me. I follow their lead and lick the back of my hand holding the shot, spill some salt there, and pass it on to the next person.

Across the room at the other end of the bar, there's a guy.

And, God, but he's a *cute* guy. Dark, curly hair and chiselled cheekbones accented by a light scruff of stubble, and full lips. He's sat on one of the few barstools, his elbows on the counter (which, in that light-blue shirt and in a place like this, is a risky move) and both hands clasped around a drink.

In spite of all the people packed in here tonight, it's like he can tell that I'm looking at him, because he lifts his head and turns in the direction of our group.

Not our group.

Me. *My direction*. He's looking at *me*.

My brain short-circuits in a way that has nothing to do with the alcohol and everything to do with the fact that a cute guy is looking right at me, and – and he's

3

smiling, too, and all I'm doing is staring back at him with my drink poised.

I only break eye contact because I realize everyone's ready with their shots.

Burnley, a guy who just about clears five foot four, grabs all our attention and booms, 'Arrowmile interns on three! One! Two!'

'Three!' we all scream in unison. 'Arrowmile!'

It's all I can do not to choke on the tequila; the taste is horrible. I suck on the lime wedge along with everyone else and my stomach roils, a clear sign that I need to ease off.

Maybe if I'd gone *out*-out more often during my first year of uni, I'd have a bit more stamina for this kind of thing. Or at least for shots.

Why, *why*, with the shots?

Everything feels very loud and very bright; the music is jarring, my skin crawling where some stranger's arm brushes against me. I'm overwhelmed by the sudden urge to go home where I can crawl into bed and have the soothing tones of an audiobook playing through my headphones. I watch with a weird sense of detachment as the others crush together, hands grasping at one another as they spill back towards the dance floor – completely unaware that I'm not following until Elaine turns back to reach for me.

'Anna, come on! They're playing "About Damn Time"!' she shrieks, like I can't tell.

Actually – I didn't notice until she pointed it out. But I stay put, shouting back, 'I need some water. I'm just feeling a little . . .'

I sift through the noise that's crowding my brain for the right word, worried I'll sound drab and dull for saying I want to sit out and take a breather, but Elaine must mistake my hesitation for borderline blackout-drunkenness.

Her plain, freckled face puckers into a concerned frown. 'Are you okay? Do you want me to stay with you?'

'No! No, go have fun! I'll catch up in a bit.'

Reassured, she nods, gives me a thumbs up and yells, 'Okay, don't go too far!' before diving into the crowd after the others to find them on the dance floor.

I turn away, leaning over the bar. Immediately, my forearm lands in something wet and sticky – *ugh*. I think it's lemonade. I *hope* it's lemonade.

There's a mirror set behind the bar. It reflects a colourful collection of liquor bottles and the rainbow lights of the club – and a pale girl with flushed cheeks and smudged makeup, loose strands of bright orange hair limp and sticking to the sides of her face, a dribble of spilled rum and Coke staining a white blouse that belongs in an office, not on a night out.

I hardly recognize myself, and tear my eyes away.

A few songs later, I've had no luck getting the bartender's attention, always interrupted by someone louder and pushier and then having to wait my turn again, but somehow missing it each time.

An elbow knocks into mine. I glance over on instinct, then do a double take.

It's him. It's Cute Guy From Across The Bar.

Oh, God.

He looks even more attractive up close. He's even got the little Clark Kent curl lying across his forehead and everything. I look at his sleeves, which somehow seem to have made it through leaning on the bar unscathed, which is, just . . . witchcraft.

He's staring at me.

Me.

Although, I suppose, that is probably only because I'm staring at him. I'd probably try to stare down a weird stranger to call their bluff, too.

But then he opens his beautiful, Cupid's bow mouth and leans in close enough to speak near my ear so he doesn't have to yell over the music and he says, 'You know, the secret is a little patience. Here.'

Cute Guy stands up straight. He's a couple of inches

taller than me and ooh, those cheekbones. Those curls, too. The kind you want to run your fingers through – the kind *I* want to run my fingers through. His hair looks inky blue in the lighting, shining like liquid moonlight.

A moment passes, then two, then he catches the bartender's eye and gestures with his index and middle finger, lifting his hand slightly. He nods, but when I look back at the bartender, they're serving drinks to someone else.

I twist around to scowl at him. 'What the hell was that supposed to be?'

'Excuse me?'

'Is this your way of picking up girls?' I ask him, the words tumbling out before I can second-guess them. 'You swan in with this failed attempt at chivalry to order their drinks for them? Emphasis on *failed* attempt.'

He quirks one eyebrow up, his mouth sliding into a bemused smile.

'You know your shirt's wet,' he tells me, a pointed look at my soggy, sticky sleeve.

And then the bartender is standing opposite us asking, 'What can I get you guys?'

I shoot Cute Guy a glower – it's not lost on me that he's smirking to himself and smug as anything right now – and ask the bartender for three cups of water. I'm parched.

My new friend gets himself a Heineken, and after he's paid for it and we've got all our drinks, he nods at my collection of waters in plastic cups.

'Enjoy. Have fun with your friends.'

'Huh? Oh, no. These are for me.'

I neck each of them, chugging it down, and I feel *human* again. The effect is much better than any booze.

Cute Guy laughs at me when, horrifyingly, I knock all three empty cups over as I put the last one down. His hands brush mine as he takes over from me and sets them back upright for the bartender to collect, and something electric rushes through me from the contact. I suddenly become all too aware of my body, feeling awkward and unsure in a way I'm not used to. I can't remember what I'd normally do with my hands, or how I usually stand, and it has everything to do with *him*, not some alcohol-induced clumsiness.

When he speaks, it's once again with his mouth close to my face. He doesn't shout, and it feels like we're in a bubble all of our own, where the music becomes muted and distant, oddly intimate in a way that sends a shiver down my spine.

'Successful attempt, then.'

'What?'

Cute Guy gestures with his beer bottle at the cups. 'My attempt at "chivalry",' he adds air quotes around the word, 'in helping you get the bartender's attention. It was successful.'

'Hmmph. Sure. *Yes*.' And then, because I suppose I owe him that much, I add through my teeth, 'Thank you.'

'You're welcome,' he tells me, his words slow like honey, his voice smooth. His mouth tilts up again with another halfway smile.

Before I can drown in that smile – or do something ridiculous like kiss this complete stranger, because he makes it look so tempting – I turn away from him to face the dance floor again, eyes scouring the room for my new friends and soon-to-be colleagues. I spot Burnley standing on a table by a booth, slut-dropping his heart out. He's acquired a lurid pink feather boa from somewhere – I can only assume there's a hen party nearby – and a security guard is shouting to him, trying to politely coax him back down.

Clearly, it's not working, because three more of the group clamber up to join Burnley. The security guard sighs and kneads his knuckles to his forehead before trying again.

Cute Boy follows my gaze and says, 'Your friends look like real party animals. That not your style?'

I shrug. This would be my opportunity to say something enigmatic and flirty, but my mouth is working faster than my brain so what I actually say is, 'I don't know what my style is. I don't get out very much.'

He laughs again and even though I don't have a drink, he lifts his bottle in a toast. 'Wow. Brutal honesty. I like it.'

'It wasn't for your benefit,' I point out. 'Clearly *your* style is creepy loner lurking at bars and trying to play the hero.'

'*Ha-ha*. Not a loner, for the record – my friends are over there,' he tells me, pointing to a group of boys near the DJ booth, who look about my own age – still younger than most of the twenty-somethings in the club. They're all singing along loudly, moving in a way that's more jumping and punching the air than it is *dancing*. Boisterous, rowdy, and clearly having a great time.

'They look . . . fun.'

'It's not really my style, either,' Cute Guy tells me, and it feels like a secret. Then he gestures back towards the gang of interns on the table. 'Although they're not as much fun as *your* friends, from the looks of it.'

Burnley is, somehow, on the security guard's shoulders now, whipping the feather boa around like a lasso. I don't know whether to laugh, cringe, or go over there and try to help. Two of the girls on the table intervene before I can decide what to do, grabbing at Burnley to pull him back and starting to climb back down themselves. They all seem to be apologizing now. One of the boys who was dancing up there with them has collapsed on the tabletop in fits of laughter, clutching his ribs and rolling from side to side.

Part of me wishes I was over there with them, part of this moment. There's an all-too familiar sting of being left out – of being *cut out*, not included – and I have to remind myself that's not what's happening tonight, and that it's all in my head.

A much larger part of me is happy to have both feet on the floor, watching from a distance. Whatever my 'style' is, I think it's not quite as wild as that.

But still ... There's that little piece of me ... The little voice in the back of my mind that makes me say, 'I wish I was more like that. I wish I was the kind of person who did things like that.' Or, I guess, there's the stupid, tipsy voice in my mouth that says it very loudly, to be heard over the noise of the club.

Cute Guy looks at me and shrugs one shoulder. 'Then go for it. Nobody's stopping you. Well, the bouncer kind of is, but I reckon you could get a good thirty seconds up there before you're carted off and banned forever.'

I crack a smile and lean a bit closer so I don't have to shout so much. My arm presses into his and I get a whiff of cologne that's so intoxicating, so sultry, it makes me dizzy. I don't think I've ever met a guy who smells *sultry* before, but this one does. I tap his wrist with my fingertips absently, trying to ignore the way I can feel the muscles in his arm as I lean against him.

'No, I mean, I wish I could let go like that. Not worry about what other people think. Be myself. Go a little crazy. No inhibitions, you know?'

I feel silly even as I say it out loud, heat creeping over my cheeks and down my neck.

'It's not like I don't ever have fun, but . . . But, you know,' I try to explain, trailing off uncertainly. I look down at the floor and scuff the toe of my sandal against it.

It's just that there are bigger, more important things to focus on. That this time in my life feels so make-or-break, and I can't let myself miss out on that. What would I regret more – missing a night out, or missing out on an opportunity that could change the trajectory of my future career, potentially my whole *life*, for the better? It's a no-brainer.

It's just that I'm not always included much, anyway, and it's a little easier to ignore that fact when there's a

12

twenty-four-hour library on campus to hide out in and coursework or exams to concentrate on.

'Work hard, play later. Focus on the big stuff and let the rest fall into place afterwards. But at the same time, it'd be nice not to take yourself so seriously, sometimes,' my mystery guy from across the bar says, and my eyes flash up to his.

But this time, he's not looking at me. He's looking over at his friends with a wistful expression and something else I recognize, too – resignation. Acceptance, of being an outsider.

There's something so serious about him, a weight suddenly on his shoulders, and even though I never really finished explaining myself, I just know. He *gets* it.

He's lonely, too.

Cute Guy offers me a small, strangely reassuring smile. I return it, even as I look out at the dance floor again; there's something in his features, in his words, that feels too heavy, too *real*, for casual conversation at the bar of a club.

My stomach roils again, sending a rumble through my body that's completely out of time with the bass pounding throughout the club. I regret the fact that I left a couple of slices of pizza earlier, trying to look 'polite'. (Which, what? What was so bloody polite about depriving myself of some food I wanted, just because some of the others did? I got way too in my head about trying to make a good impression, clearly.)

I definitely need some fresh air. Maybe some food. Possibly my bed, too.

Icebreaker evening has been fun, but I think it's time for me to call it a night. As far as good impressions go, I don't think trying to keep up with the others and ultimately having Elaine hold my hair in a toilet stall while I throw up is exactly the way to go about that.

I swing my bag around from where it's sitting against my bum to root through it for my ticket for the cloakroom.

'Somewhere to be?' Cute Guy asks me.

Is he still here?

'Are you still here?'

He looks down at himself like he needs to confirm it. 'Apparently.'

'Well, I won't be for much longer. I need carbs.' I blink at him, stare at the curls of his hair and his thick eyelashes. 'Do you want to come with me?'

Wait. What? Did I really just invite this total stranger to leave with me? I know I had a couple of drinks, but I'm definitely not *that* far gone. His good looks must be way more mesmerizing than I realized.

'For carbs?' he asks, and then grins. 'Sure. I know a place.'

I press my cloakroom ticket into his hand. 'Meet me outside. I'll just be a sec.'

Leaving him, and possibly also abandoning the promise of ever collecting my coat, I wriggle my way back onto the dance floor, shimmying over to the others. I manage to grab hold of Elaine, seeing her first, both my hands wrapping around her arm as she turns to look at me, her eyes clear and sober.

'I'm heading off.'

'Are you okay? Some of us might head home soon, if you wanted to wait and share a cab.'

'Aw, leave her be!' crows one of the guys – Dylan, I remember, with a double-barrelled surname. There are huge sweat patches on his salmon-pink shirt, but I don't shove him off when he throws an arm around my shoulder and gives me a friendly shake. 'She met a guy! I saw her talking to someone at the bar. D'you need a condom? I have condoms.'

He reaches for his wallet even as I laugh at the idea of me picking up a guy in a bar; it's not something I've ever done. I don't get a chance to correct him because Elaine shoves Dylan's hands back to his sides.

'Ohmigod, she doesn't need your weird wallet condoms. Text us when you get home safe, Anna?'

'Will do. Have fun, everyone!' I yell to the group.

Some of them wave me off. Dylan jokes, 'Not as much fun as you!' and Elaine says, '*Ohmigod*,' again and pulls him back into the fray, leaving me to my night with a cute mystery guy.

Chapter 2

I don't know why I'm surprised to see Cute Guy actually waiting outside for me.

But there he is in his pale blue shirt and dark jeans, both hands tucked into his pockets and my denim jacket tucked neatly through the crook of his elbow.

My stomach lurches and, once again, it's a reaction that has everything to do with him and nothing to do with the alcohol I've been drinking. Whatever possessed me a few minutes ago at the bar, it's long gone now. The music is so loud I can feel the beat of it out here on the street. The air is cool against my hot, sweaty skin and suddenly all I can focus on is the gross, wet sleeve of my blouse and the way it's plastered to my arm.

'Listen,' I tell Cute Guy, before he's even noticed I'm outside. He starts, looking around. My mouth is dry; I peel my tongue away from the roof of my mouth and try again. 'Listen, I don't . . . I don't *do* this kind of thing. And, like, I wasn't trying to, you know. Invite you home. Hook up with you, I mean.'

He scoffs, and just when I brace myself for a slew of derogatory cuss words and him storming back inside, he says, 'Well, that's good, because I was really looking forward to some cheesy chips. No offence. I'm sure that would've been fun, but . . .'

Now it's my turn to make a scornful noise. I snatch my coat from him and fold it over my arm, covering my stomach. 'And the charm just continues. I *really* hope this isn't how you try to flirt.'

'I mean, normally I start by introducing myself, and complimenting the girl.'

I wait.

Cute Guy laughs, almost in disbelief, but squares his shoulders and shrugs, his hands open at his sides, palms facing me. His eyes crinkle a little at the corners. They're such a nice green. Like the first leaves in springtime.

'I'm Lloyd.'

'Lloyd.' I don't know why I repeat it, but I like the way it rolls off my tongue. That's like honey, too. 'I'm Annalise. I like that your shirt isn't wet. That's an impressive feat.'

'Is that *your* attempt of flirting with me, Annalise?'

he teases, then puts his hands back in his pockets and jerks his head to one side. 'Come on. Like I said, I know a place. And there's a portion of cheesy chips with my name on it.'

Lloyd begins walking down the street in slow, steady strides, even as his body tilts to one side ever so slightly. I hurry after him, stumbling a little. My right hand slips around his left arm as I steady myself, his skin warm through his shirt. I hang on for a few steps, and he gives me a sidelong look.

'Don't flatter yourself,' I tell him, wondering if he can see me blush in the dark, or if it'll just look like a trick of the light under the street lamps. This whole situation is so unlike *me* that I blurt out exactly what's on my mind. 'I'm not usually much of a drinker. But I am sobering up enough now to realize that walking off with some guy I don't know is not my finest moment.'

'What is your finest moment, then?'

I don't even have to think about it. 'I got a spot on a really prestigious internship this summer. I worked really hard for it. Too hard, probably, but . . .'

'Congratulations.'

'Thanks.'

'Wait, that wasn't a bit of a farewell party, was it? I haven't lured you away from your own "goodbye and good luck" celebrations with the mere promise of cheesy chips, have I?'

I burst out laughing, my hand tightening around his arm reflexively.

I'm sure the girls in my uni halls would have thrown a party for me when I moved out a few weeks ago. *Goodbye and good riddance!* they probably thought.

'No,' I say. 'Tonight was more of a "hello" thing. Meeting the other interns. I'm at Leeds for uni, so I'm just in London for the summer.'

'Ah. Obligated fun. I get it.'

'Is that why you were out tonight?'

'Yeah – a friend's birthday.' He tosses me a smile. 'They won't miss me, I'm sure.'

'You guys aren't close?'

He hums, unsure, and instead of giving me a direct answer just says, 'Everyone heading different places for uni and figuring their lives out was always going to change things, I guess.'

'Has it changed you? I – I mean . . .' I don't even know if he goes to uni. I don't even know how old he is. For all I feel Lloyd is a kindred spirit, I also don't know the first thing about him.

'I've never been much for a night out. Family stuff, you know? Between my dad and working with him through the summers and . . .' He draws a sharp breath, making a visible effort to relax before smiling at me again. 'But I guess I don't need to explain that kind of thing to you, if you're spending your summer on an internship programme that you worked too hard to get.'

I know he's trying to distract me before I pry into something he doesn't want to talk about, but it works. I've been bursting with pride ever since I got that 'Congratulations!' email, wanting to tell anyone and everyone about it.

'They take a really small proportion of applicants,' I find myself saying, 'so it was kind of a long shot, but I really thought I had a chance, you know? I ticked every box on their list. I did *so* much research, prepping for all their rounds of interviews. I had all these extra-curriculars from school and I even took on an extra module at uni studying computer science just to try and build out my CV, and let me tell you, I *suck* at computer science. It was a real slog.'

'But you did it,' Lloyd says, sounding impressed. Or maybe I'm imagining that, and he's doing a good job of hiding his real reaction and he thinks I'm a try-hard dork who needs to get a life. I'd like to think he is impressed, though.

'I did it. Out of everyone who applied, they picked *me*. Even if I had to lie on my application that I was a second-year, but it's not like I lied about anything *important*. So . . .'

He laughs. '*So*. Why lie, though? Why not just wait till next year?'

'This way, I can do another internship next summer. Plus, if I hadn't got in this year, I would've had another shot at applying next year. It's all going to help me be in a better position when I apply for jobs after I graduate.'

And it's not like I had plans for the summer anyway. At least a full-time job, however temporary, will help cover up that fact so my family don't worry about me being too much on my own.

Aloud, I add, 'And it was obviously really worth all that extra effort this year, because now I'm on the internship programme.'

'How do you know it's worth it if you haven't started it yet?'

I blink, not understanding the question.

Of course it's *worth it*. Arrowmile are famous for making electric vehicles; they have a rent-a-scooter initiative near my university, and in the last couple of years they've won numerous industry awards. This internship will help my CV stand out, and it's a good networking opportunity. They even pay their interns a decent salary *and* cover our accommodation, which is why there's so much competition for a place on their programme. And at the end of the summer, all the interns give a presentation on their work over the last twelve weeks to senior managers and board members; if you impress them, you get fast-tracked for an *actual* job with them when you graduate. This internship could be a total gamechanger for me.

Lloyd stares back for a moment before shaking his head and saying, 'So you lied to get your dream job, you don't get out much, you don't – normally – leave your friends behind to go for food with some random guy . . . Tell me something true about you, Annalise.'

Annalise. I like the way my name sounds, when he says it.

I always go by Anna. Everyone always shortens my name anyway, and at some point, I defaulted to it, too. I don't know why I told him my full name instead of 'Anna', like I'd normally do.

I'm glad I did.

I consider his question for a moment. *Tell me something true about you.*

We've turned down another, busier street. This one is narrower, but the buildings are brighter, with lights pouring out from shop-front windows and smells mingling in the air: kebabs, burgers, pad thai. Lloyd walks past them all. I follow.

And I tell him: 'I don't believe in love.'

He makes a funny choking sound before stopping dead and turning to me in disbelief. 'You don't believe in love? What does that even mean?'

'I think it's . . . overrated. Commercialized. I think that relationships are something that you have to work at and put effort into, and I'm not saying that you can't have *feelings* for someone, but I think the whole "love conquers all" thing is just . . . fake.'

I know it is. I *thought*, maybe, I was in love with my ex-boyfriend. We started dating after A levels. He was the first guy who'd ever really shown much interest in me, and when he said 'I love you' I said it back because I knew I should, and thought I probably *did* love him, I just didn't know it yet. It was something I'd have to work on, like everything else in my life, I figured.

I didn't love that spending weekends with him meant I missed a deadline for an assignment, or failed a midterm. I didn't love that I was jeopardizing my entire future over a guy I didn't picture that same future with. I couldn't fathom a feeling where I would be willing to pack away pieces of myself to make space for somebody else.

So, no, I don't believe in love.

'Well. That's . . .' Lloyd scoffs to himself, blinking dazedly. 'That's one way to put it.'

I'm still holding onto his bicep, and use it as leverage to swing myself around in front of him, holding him at arm's length.

'Oh, what,' I guess, 'you're a love-at-first-sight kind of guy?'

'Maybe I am.'

'I bet you fall for a new girl every week.'

He gives me a dry smile. 'Lucky for me, there's still a couple of days left this week for me to find her.' Then Lloyd glances over my shoulder and starts walking again, gesturing for me to follow. 'Almost there. Come on. I promised you cheesy chips, didn't I?'

He did, and I soon find I'm not disappointed.

Lloyd has taken us to a small, cramped takeaway with blue-and-white chequered tile flooring. A queue wraps down the street. Thirty-ish minutes later, we're each holding a polystyrene container of the most delicious chips I've ever smelled – Lloyd's are stuck together with gooey, melted cheese, and mine are doused in gravy.

'A proper Northerner, then,' he remarks, watching me dig in with a little wooden fork the moment we're out of the shop.

'Did you think the accent was just for show?' I take a mouthful of chips and groan; nothing has ever tasted so delicious. The fresh air has helped mitigate the after-effects of the tequila, but the chips settle my stomach. I wave another chip at Lloyd, flicking drops of gravy onto the pavement. 'Your turn. Tell me something true about you.'

He smiles to himself, the kind of smile like there are a thousand secrets on the tip of his tongue just waiting to be told. The kind of smile that's only halfway there, just begging to be kissed at the corner of his lips.

'Well, I believe in love, for starters. Not just the one great love that they boast about in movies and stuff. I think if the right people meet at the right time, under the right circumstances . . . I think you could fall in love with just about anyone.'

'That's sounds more like fate, if you ask me.' This guy really *is* a romantic at heart – and, I think, I'd be silly to think of this connection we have as anything special, if that's how he sees the world. There's a lump in my throat and I swallow it down to say, 'What about some other things about you? Fun, silly stuff.'

His grin this time is a lightning strike, flooring me in its brilliance. 'I tried to teach myself to sew after the Andrew Garfield *Spider-Man* came out, because I thought it was cool that Spider-Man made his own costume. My mum used to make all the costumes for me and my brother for school concerts and stuff, so she showed me a bit.'

'That's adorable. Dorky, but adorable.'

'Were you looking for something more tough-guy? Hate to disappoint you there, but I'm an established failure on that front. Like – I almost got a tattoo when I was eighteen. It was a group thing on a holiday with some mates. My brother went first, and then I chickened out and then everyone else got bored or backed out as well, so now he's the only one stuck with this stupid little SpongeBob on his arse. It's been almost two years but he still brings it up constantly.'

'Your poor brother,' I lament. 'Oh, man. That is *cruel*. Were you supposed to get SpongeBob, too?'

'Patrick. We all drew lots for which character we'd get.'

I laugh. 'I can't believe you let him do that and then bailed on him. You could've at least had the decency not to let him go through with it if you were going to back out.'

'Hey! I had *every* intention of getting Patrick on my left arse cheek until I saw that needle. It could've been worse. Will could've ended up with Plankton, or something. How about you – any siblings you bailed out of matching tattoos with?'

'Two half-brothers, but no matching tattoos. They're a lot younger than me. We get on great, though. Mostly.

27

When they're not leaving honey in my shoes or making me be goalie when they play football.'

'Oh, *no*. Not the honey shoes.'

'I mean, it happened *once*,' I grant, 'but that is one more time than anybody should have to put their shoes on and find them full of honey.'

'It really is,' Lloyd agrees, his face gravely serious as he nods.

I cut him a look, not sure if he's teasing or not, but it's me who cracks into a smile first. I knock my shoulder into his and mutter to him, 'Shut up,' but I hope he knows I don't mean it. The last thing I want is for him to shut up right now.

He doesn't feel like such a stranger anymore. Nothing about this feels strange, actually. It feels . . . *nice*. Right. Like this is exactly where I'm supposed to be right now, and this is exactly how my night was supposed to go. Maybe he was on to something, believing in fate . . .

We emerge onto the riverside, the pathways wide. The street lights bounce amber ripples on the ink-dark water; a small boat cuts through, gleaming white in the dark. Up ahead, the lights of the London Eye are glinting, replacing the stars on a cloudless summer night in the city.

My arm bumps into Lloyd's again as we walk and

eat our chips and tell each other all sorts of true things about ourselves. Inconsequential, miscellaneous things like what kind of movies we like watching or the last thing we listened to on Spotify. Big secrets, like how he's on a gap year from a Law and Economics degree right now and isn't sure he wants to go back to it at the end of the summer, and how I hate that my mum got back in touch with me again three years ago, acting like she never left when I was little and like everything was fine, never stopping to consider if *I* wanted a relationship with her again. Lloyd tells me how his dad used to smile when his mum was still alive.

'You mean, used to smile more?'

The look on Lloyd's face is so lost, so sad, it's heartbreaking.

'No,' he says. 'I mean, he never smiles anymore at all. I miss that, almost as much as I miss her.'

We talk about our star signs because he believes in horoscopes. I confess how glad I am to have a break from the catty people I've lived with at uni and that next year I'll be living with more like-minded people from my course instead. He bemoans the Japanese classes his dad made him take, but is more upbeat when he tells me he speaks a little Hindi; his mum taught him what she could remember.

I laugh when I hear he writes poetry, because of course he does, this boy with his quick heart and kiss-me lips, and he tells me he's sorry that my ex-boyfriend and I couldn't manage to make things work after we went away to different universities, and broke up over Christmas break.

'It can't have been easy,' he tells me, full of sympathy. 'I had a rough breakup at the end of last summer, so I get it. It sucks when someone breaks your heart.'

'*I* was the one who broke up with him,' I point out, but then find myself admitting, 'The hard part was when he said he shouldn't have been so surprised, and it was no wonder I didn't have many friends at school, because I'm cold and unlikeable.'

'Jeez. He said that?'

I bite my lip, feeling like I've gone too far. I've never told anybody he said that.

I'm too scared if I do, people will only tell me it's true.

With our chippy takeaways now long-since finished and the wrapping discarded, Lloyd's hand slips into mine.

'I don't think you're cold or unlikeable, for the record. And that's something true.'

Somehow I can believe it, coming from him.

We talk, and talk, and the city doesn't sleep and neither do we.

Sometime way past midnight, we lean against the wall by the river, watching another boat go by, and people walking along the opposite bank, all of us wrapped up in our own little worlds.

It's nice. Comfortable, and steady.

And none of it is real. Not really, not in any way that matters, because once I get home, I won't see Lloyd again after tonight. He's beautiful. He's charming, a romantic at heart, with an easy smile and ready laugh. He's a dream guy, but that's all he is: a dream.

Still. It's nice to enjoy it, for a little while. To pretend it is real.

I know that it could be. That I could ask for his number, say I want to see him again, suggest we go on a real date – but that's not what I'm in the city for, and not what this summer is about. All that matters for the next twelve weeks is my internship at Arrowmile. I have to give it my all. I *want* to give it my all. I don't need some silly summer fling to distract me.

But still.

It's nice to pretend for just one night.

So when the conversation trails off, and I feel Lloyd shift closer, hear him murmur my name in a soft, heady voice, and his hand comes up to ghost along my cheek, I don't stop him. I twist to face him and let my eyelids flutter shut, enjoying the sensation of his fingertips along my skin, and then brushing back the loose hair around my face. I tilt my face towards his, relishing the way his lips feel against mine.

He tastes of beer and chips, like summers at the seaside with my friends.

This isn't the sloppy, drunken kiss of a random boy on a night out. This is firm; confident. Grown-up and sobered up, a tongue teasing at my lower lip and a shiver running down my spine.

My hand runs over the firm planes of his chest and down to his hip, settling there. Lloyd's other hand finds its way to the small of my back to anchor me close against him and I'm hit once more by the spiced, earthy smell of his cologne as it mingles with the mild, smoggy summer air. I swear he's so close I can feel his heart thundering, or maybe that's mine. Maybe both.

We kiss for seconds, for aeons, and finally, all too soon, draw apart to catch our breath. He lifts his head, lips grazing against my temple, and my breath catches in my throat again.

My heart hammers against my chest, beating a tattoo of *take him home, take him home*, but I know I can't do that. Much as I'd like to. Much as it feels like *he'd* like to, too. This is as far as it goes.

I can't afford to get swept up in some fleeting romance, or even just a one-night stand. My brain weighs up the cost of short-term fun against my long-term ambitions, and comes to the conclusion it always does: *It's not worth it.*

I'll just be the girl he fell for this week. He'll just be a fun story, a sweet memory.

I take a step back before I can forget why it isn't worth it and be too tempted to ask him to come home with me. Lloyd is breathing heavily, his hands falling to his sides as I move away.

'I should be getting home,' I say, and then clarify in a very deliberate, exaggerated tone, '*alone.*'

'Yeah.' He clears his throat, though stutters a little when he continues to speak. 'Yeah. Me, too. I'll, um . . . I'll wait with you, while you call an Uber?'

'Thanks,' I say, not rejecting the offer because it's late and I don't know this city well. I can tell he's offering because it's the polite thing to do, not because he's angling for an invitation to join me.

We wait quietly, two feet apart, for my driver to show up. I try not to pay too much attention to the fare back to Clapham, writing it off as a one-time necessity.

Before long, a Prius idles on the kerb at my pick-up point and Lloyd stands with his hands in his pockets again.

'Well, it was nice to meet you, Annalise.'

'It was nice to meet you too, Lloyd.'

He seems to chew over his next words, but eventually flashes me a quicksilver smile and says, 'I'll see you around, maybe.'

'Yeah. See you around.'

He closes the car door behind me, all chivalry and charm. My lips tingle with the imprint of his kiss. I almost feel a little sorry that I never got his number, and that I'll never see him again.

Chapter 3

The first Monday of June rolls around after months of anticipation, bringing with it the first official day of the Arrowmile internship. After all the build-up, the entire morning is so overwhelming it becomes a blur. Somehow, I get from sharing a commute with a group of equally nervous interns to the large, clinical reception of a shared office building in Victoria. We huddle together like lost ducklings, trying not to get swept up in the tide of people swiping key cards and striding through waist-high glass barriers.

I hadn't been sure what to expect of the other interns, but most everyone seems to have formed a quick camaraderie. I'd been terrified to meet my new flatmates in the accommodation Arrowmile had organized for us all, worried they might be like the girls from my uni halls. I'd been terrified to meet *everyone*.

I guess I also had the idea that they'd be . . . better than me, somehow. Cooler, more worldly. High-flying achievers that put all *my* efforts to shame. Intimidating.

But our collective anxiety about what to do now we're actually *here* reminds me that they're all . . . normal. Just doing our best, with varying levels of self-confidence. I'm not a huge fan of Monty, an Exeter student with a very 'rah' sort of posh accent, who spent the icebreaker dinner talking almost exclusively about himself – very loudly, very brashly – and implying that he was entitled, somehow, to this spot on the internship. But I won't hold it against him; there's a good chance it was just nerves.

In spite of the fact I hardly know these people, the uncertain glances we give each other right now helps me feel hopeful about the rest of the summer. Like we'll have each other's backs, help each other out. Not shun each other if someone hits 'reply all' on a mass email by mistake.

Oh, God, I think suddenly. How do you even write an email? Can you start 'hi', or is that too informal? What's the most appropriate sign-off? How many exclamation marks are too many?????

While I stand paralysed with the knowledge that I've forgotten how to do something so basic, one of the girls, Tasha, takes the lead and goes up to the reception desk. The rest of us follow, and soon enough have signed ourselves in at a guest book and collected bright red lanyards with temporary guest passes hanging from them, with instructions to take the lift up to the twelfth floor and wait in the boardroom.

For a moment, as I wait for someone to swipe their way through the glass barriers before I can follow, an intense paranoia seizes me. What if my pass doesn't work? What if some security guard comes over to stop me because there's been a mistake and I'm *not* on the internship because they've decided I'm not cut out for it after all? I desperately want to go back in time and ask Annalise from five months ago what the ever-loving fuck she thought she was doing applying for this internship.

It'll be too tough. Too demanding. I won't keep up. I'll be bad at that water-cooler small talk and for the rest of the summer everyone will ask, 'Who's that weird ginger girl who can barely string a sentence together?' I'll do everything wrong or not know what I'm doing at all, and they'll find out I'm a fraud . . .

The barrier makes a cheerful little *blip!* sound when I press my pass against the sensor, and opens for me to go through. I remember to breathe, and try to shake off the irrational, intrusive thoughts of failure.

Waiting for the lift, I smooth my hands over my dress. It's a bubblegum-pink, knee-length wrap dress with a modest neckline in a flattering-but-professional cut. When I first tried it on, it made me feel like I was channelling fictional feminist icon Elle Woods – and I could definitely do with her kind of energy and self-belief today.

Up on the twelfth floor, the boardroom is everything I expected: a large, rectangular table, a projector set up at one end, and along the back wall, canisters of tea and coffee we all help ourselves to before finding seats. Windows on one side offer a view of the street and on the other, a wall made up entirely of glass panels emblazoned with the cobalt-blue Arrowmile logo looks onto an open-plan office teeming with people who peer in on us like animals at the zoo, all curious about this new exhibit. I mean, cohort of interns.

Some of them wave, when they see us catching them looking.

One woman strides right up to the room, hand outstretched, staring at us so brazenly I think she's about to tap on the glass wall and see if she can make us move, but instead she opens the door and steps into the room, and our murmured conversations are swallowed all at once by silence.

The woman, despite being slim and petite, dressed in a tailored pair of black trousers and a high-necked black sleeveless blouse, cuts an imposing figure as she comes to a stop near the projector, her hands on her hips. Her ash-blonde hair is cut into a short and severe bob that adds angles to her face. Her lips are painted deep red, and her only other makeup appears to be a precise flick of gold eyeliner.

She looks like she would tear you to pieces with a wave of her hand.

'Alright, then,' she announces. 'Looks like everybody's here, so let's get started! Welcome to Arrowmile! My name is Nadja. I'll put you all through some completely humiliating exercises later to learn all your names – the "hi, my name is—, and these are my three biggest goals for my time here" kind of thing. But first, I'm going to make the most of your undivided attention and talk all about myself.

'My role here is Senior Client Partner, meaning I work a lot with our customers in the B2B area, listen to feedback from focus groups, do the graft when it comes to outreach and new contracts . . . A couple of you will actually be working with me this summer, you lucky ducks.'

Nadja winks, which looks totally menacing, and there's a polite ripple of laughter. I notice a few people shift in their seats like they're praying they're not one of her 'lucky ducks'.

She continues, 'But outside of that role, I've taken a special interest in our internship programme – I think it's one of our best initiatives, and I'm not just saying that because I was one of the people who spearheaded its creation a few years ago. I love seeing all the talent that comes through our doors each summer that we can foster. We take only the best and brightest. You've all worked hard to get to this point – and we expect that same attitude from you while you're here. I want to see you all going above and beyond; don't think that you can sit back and take it easy now you're here. With any luck, some of you might even do a good enough job that we'll see you back here again after you graduate. So don't let me down!'

A pause, for dramatic effect, and another deadly smile. This time when Nadja looks around the room, she locks eyes with each of us individually, as if to really drive home her 'it could be you!' point. It feels more like an 'it won't be you!' threat, but I sit up straighter and weather her gaze when it lands on me.

Tension thickens in the room, and I hardly dare look at any of the others. The Arrowmile internship is tough to get onto, but their graduate placements are even more like gold dust. They only take on about ten people each year – and very few interns make the cut. But they have one of the most competitive salaries going, an impressive rate of graduates-turned-senior managers, and Arrowmile itself is so widely respected as a company that I've heard if you've worked there, you'll waltz into any other job afterwards.

Life-changing – as long as it all goes to plan.

Nadja carries on her introductory speech, telling us that our placements here have been selected based on our applications and interviews – roles where they believe we'll thrive, be challenged, get the most out of this experience. The scheme is designed to push us outside of our comfort zones. We'll have a 'buddy' allocated in our department to be a regular point of contact outside of our managers, and no question is too small or too silly – although, as Nadja says it, some of the interns look around haughtily as if wondering who will be the first to have a terrible question, like it will be a nail in our coffin. Tasha and Monty exchange self-confident smirks, while Elaine turns so pale she looks almost grey.

By the time Nadja wraps up telling us about the company's history and departmental structure, she announces that it's time to find out what our placements are.

And just as she brings out a sheaf of papers with the details on, there's a knock at the door. Next to me, goes-by-his-last-name, table-dancing Burnley lets out a quiet, frustrated groan. His leg is bouncing wildly under the table; he catches my eye long enough to huff at the interruption. I pull a face back, on the same page.

But it turns out we have no right to be annoyed at the delay, because then Nadja declares, 'Ah! Our illustrious leader! Topher, come in, come in – I was *just* about to put this cohort out of their misery and let them know where they'll be working.'

The interloper in the doorway laughs good-naturedly. 'Ah, let them stew a little while longer, eh? Hi, folks. Topher Fletcher. CEO and founder of Arrowmile Inc.'

Heads spin, the room turning as one to gawp.

Tasha and two of the boys shoot to their feet, reminding me of being at school and having to stand up when another teacher came into the classroom. A few others (me included) start to follow suit but Illustrious Leader/CEO Topher Fletcher laughs again and waves us down.

He looks like any other guy. His brown hair is thinning, greying around the temples; wrinkles around his eyes and mouth give away his age. He's wearing a suit, but it's dressed-down, casual, with a tie but no cufflinks, the top button undone. He takes off his glasses and balances them on top of his head as he smiles around us.

He's ordinary, and unremarkable. Somehow, it's disappointing.

What did I expect, though? That he'd have a town crier go before him, ring a bell and announce his presence, or maybe that he'd be surrounded by some glowing white light and that just *seeing* him would make me feel inspired, driven, awed?

'Which one of you is Freya?' he asks, and a tentative hand creeps into the air. 'Ah – brilliant. You'll be shadowing me, Freya. Attending meetings, reviewing reports, all that jazz.'

Again, heads turn as one, this time pinning a stout brunette girl to the spot, a few seats down from me. Her cheeks turn bright red but she nods enthusiastically, all at once honoured and horrified. A couple of people look jealous; some look relieved.

'Well, don't let me keep you!' booms Topher Fletcher. 'Best of luck for your first week, everybody – I'm sure I'll see you around and about the office. My door is always open!'

He raises a hand in farewell and strolls out. Whispers start to circulate – Burnley mumbles to me,

'God, that guy is *so cool*,' – before Nadja claps her hands together to motion for quiet.

'Now! On to the good stuff . . .'

In a spacious, corner section of the eleventh floor, I join the ranks of the Project Development team as a Junior Coordinator. My new boss, Michaela, Senior Project Development Partner, left me a shiny new HP laptop and vanished into a meeting.

It's been six hours since I walked through the doors of Arrowmile Inc., and I am . . .

Still terrified, but also raring to go. Even if the only thing I've done so far is log on, change my password, painstakingly craft my new email signature, and scroll through a few documents Michaela left in my inbox for me.

I'm excited about my role – the team is basically responsible for reviewing ongoing projects for new products and initiatives; they make sure everything is on track, 'value-adding', shut down anything that *isn't* working, and act as a bit of a go-between among all the other teams involved in making things happen at Arrowmile. My role is going to involve a lot of reading documents, chasing people for information, checking over financials, and pulling together slide decks for the more senior members of my team to present at meetings.

Except, obviously, *I* intend to be presenting those slide decks before the summer's over. I'm sure once I find my feet and get the hang of things, I'll be able to ask Michaela if I can step up and give it a go. We *are* supposed to be going above and beyond to prove ourselves, after all.

This is what the summer's about: working my butt off, doing a good job, and getting a glowing recommendation at the end of it – or, even better, a job offer for after I graduate.

In my final interview, they asked me, 'Where do you see yourself in five years, Anna?'

And I said, 'Running a department here. In ten, I'll be running the whole show.'

Which had made them laugh, so I'd smiled along like it was kind of a joke, but I'd been deadly serious. I've always had ambition in spades. Dad says I get it from my mother, which I know should be a compliment but always makes me feel icky. Mum's ambition was more like a poison than a positive trait. Before now, *my* ambition has been channelled into hockey, tennis, cello and piano lessons, school plays . . . basically any extra-curricular I could get my hands on to beef up my university application. But things are different now.

Now, the end goal isn't just the next three years. It's the entire rest of my life.

And right now, that means doing the best I can at this internship. *Being* the best.

And *nothing* is going to get in my way.

'Oh, hello, stranger!' Laurie – my designated buddy – calls out. She was the kind (read: only) person who took pity on me and showed me how to adjust the height on my desk chair when I couldn't find the right lever. She's sitting opposite me, and waves at someone behind me. 'Didn't expect to see you around today, I thought you were in client meetings to help cover for Nadja!'

Behind me, a guy chuckles and says, 'Ah, you know me, Laur. Can't resist scouting out the new recruits, and I had a little time between calls. How're they looking so far? I heard you got one.'

Laurie grins and then cuts a look at me – amiable, like this is a joke I'm in on, not the butt of. I'd guess she's in her thirties. There's a large sapphire engagement ring on her left hand. She seems nice so far, so I smile back, then turn to look at the newcomer and make myself part of the conversation.

Before I can quite spin around on my chair, though, a hand settles warm and heavy on my shoulder and twirls me around. Between the two of us, I have enough momentum to do a full rotation. Startled, I throw my legs out to catch myself.

46

My knees bump into the newcomer's when he doesn't quite move out of the way in time, making him stumble backwards and a mortified apology spill out of my lips (even though it was absolutely *not* my fault). My cheeks begin to burn; wouldn't it be just my luck if I'd almost knocked Topher Fletcher himself on his arse on my first day?

The guy standing a mere few inches away, laughing and apologizing with a broad smile on his face, is cute. He's not much older than me and tall, wearing a crisp blue shirt with the sleeves rolled up to his elbows, a halfway smile on his face. He's got curling, dark hair and bright green eyes, and . . .

The blood drains from my face – from my whole *body*. I turn cold all over, goosebumps prickling across my skin, heart thundering so hard it's about to tear its way right out of my chest. I think I see something flicker across his face for the moment – surprise, maybe, or uncertainty – but it's gone so quickly that I must have imagined it.

His smile stretches a little wider, eyes dancing with mischief and the memory of a kiss by a river, and he sticks his hand out towards me.

'Hi there,' he says, as if we're complete strangers. 'I'm Lloyd Fletcher.'

Chapter 4

There's a ringing in my ears, and I barely hear him introduce himself. I barely hear *myself* when I reply, 'Hi, I'm Anna. Anna Sherwood.'

His hand is still outstretched.

I take it. My best interview handshake – a single firm, quick pump. But when I loosen my grip, he doesn't – his hand stays there, light against mine, his touch dragging along my fingers and sending a jolt of electricity all the way up my arm, right to the bottom of my chest. It makes me gasp. I hope to hell nobody hears it.

But Lloyd smirks, just a little, and I know *he* heard it.

'So, Anna, how're you settling in?'

Anna. Does he really not remember?

'Uh, y-yes, good, thanks. Looking forward to getting stuck in,' I stammer, my voice working quicker than my brain. And then, like it's not obvious, I gesture to

Laurie and the others and say, 'I'm in the Project Development team.'

'The worst,' he drawls, and behind me, Laurie laughs.

She clicks her tongue. 'Don't scare her off too early. At least let me rope her into doing some financial analysis first. Which reminds me – how good are you with Excel, Anna? Michaela said you did some coding at uni?'

'Oh, I'm sure she's a whizz. She'll probably write you a program to run it all for you.'

I cut Lloyd a glower nobody else sees, my brain having finally stopped reeling and caught up. He looks so totally innocent that even I start to doubt if we have actually met before. I can feel thunderclouds gathering over my head.

'I'm not too bad,' I tell Laurie, and then shoot out of my chair, shoving it under the desk and keeping my head down as I skirt around Lloyd, giving him a wide berth. 'Sorry, I just, um, I – I need to pop to the bathroom.'

It takes every ounce of my willpower not to bolt.

'Nice to meet you!' he calls after me.

Hopefully, I'm far enough away that he doesn't see how that makes me cringe.

Once I'm around the corner and in an empty stretch

of corridor, I break into a run, throwing myself into the bathroom and locking myself into a stall where I can finally let myself fall apart, hands tearing at my hair and breathing heavily as I try to make sense of what just happened.

How is he here? *Why?* Is he some hotshot intern who got invited back for a summer job, or something? Was he so good he works here part-time, maybe?

And . . . why is he acting like he doesn't know me?

Maybe he's embarrassed by me in some way, or was disappointed by our kiss.

Or maybe he does that kind of thing all the time, falling for a new girl every week like we joked about, and the night we spent together was so wholly *un*-spectacular for him that he's simply . . . forgotten.

I know it shouldn't matter. That it *doesn't*.

But . . .

Unbidden, the memories of the time we spent together a few nights ago spring to mind, playing out before me. The laughter turns sour on my tongue; the dizzying press of his lips to mine, mocking and cold. The things I told him . . .

Oh, God. The things I told him.

He knows I lied about my age on my application. Is he going to tell anybody? He could get me kicked out. Maybe there's even some kind of rule about inter-office relationships or something, and I'd be fired because I kissed him.

I want to be happy that fate is kind enough to let our paths cross again, but that's a joke. If things like fate do exist, then this is a blatant display of its cruelty.

Something prickles at the back of my eyes and – *no, please, don't let me be the girl who cries on her first day.*

Don't let me be the girl who cries over a boy she barely knows.

Breathe, Annalise.

I do, somehow. Raggedly. It hitches in my throat, tightens in my chest, so I try again a few more times until I've got a little more control over myself. I have no idea how long I've been gone, which almost sends me into a whole new panic spiral – I do *not* want to become the girl who spent half her first day in the toilets – so I smooth my hands over my hair, take a few more deep breaths, and stride out.

Walk tall, shoulders back. Don't let them see. It's fine. Nobody will know.

If he wants to pretend not to know me, fine. Two can play at that game.

But when I get back to my desk, Lloyd is long gone.

The first week at Arrowmile is every bit as overwhelming as that first morning. My new inbox is overflowing with things to read and tasks to complete. I attend meetings with people whose names I instantly forget as they discuss things I can't keep up with, feeling the fool when I agree to write up the minutes. I have to start a glossary in the back of my notebook of all the corporate jargon and acronyms everyone uses, which feels like I might as well have to learn a completely new language from scratch.

I catch sight of the other interns darting about the office, too, occasionally crossing paths with them in the lift or on the way to meetings. Once, I'm stopped on my way back from the toilets by my other new flatmate, Louis, when his manager sends him to speak to someone on my floor; he holds up a LinkedIn profile on his phone and points at someone a few desks over as he whispers to me, 'Do you think that's him? He has more hair in this photo, but . . . How embarrassing d'you think it will be if it's not him?'

We're all out of our depth, but some people do a better job of hiding it. Monty, for one, makes sure to tell any of us unlucky enough to get stuck commuting with him just *how* sure he is that being on Nadja's team is the ideal role for him, and how great he'll be at schmoozing clients. Freya, who already struck me as quiet and is working alongside Topher Fletcher's PA, becomes even more mousy – squeaky and jumpy, afraid of being reduced to nothing more than fetching coffees.

I also see Lloyd around the office.

It's hard not to.

He's everywhere.

Each time I notice him, I can't help but stare. He's only a year older than I am, but he stands around joking with people like they're old friends, talking to senior members of staff as they nod along seriously and hang off his every word. He strides around the office with a sense of purpose and belonging. There's a confidence about him that makes me think that actually, he *struts* – like a peacock. Commanding attention with a hundred-watt smile and a glint in his eyes just daring people to suggest they know better than him.

It's a more self-assured, over-the-top version of the guy I met on Friday night, who didn't think his friends would miss him if he slipped away. This version of him is still open, emotive, with that easy humour, but ... *more*. Other, somehow. There's something off about it, but the more I think that, the more I convince myself that this is what Lloyd is like normally. Who he was with me was the outlier. A lie.

He waves whenever he sees me. Then he'll smile and ask how I'm doing, with exactly the same friendly, casual tone he uses with everybody else. In response, I'll grit my teeth and try to smile back before hurrying away, determined to ignore how much it stings that he's clearly forgotten all about me.

I'm mad at him for not remembering. I'm mad at myself, for making such a big deal out of it when I never thought I'd see *him* again, anyway.

I'm mad, because everybody seems to love him. He's the golden boy of the office. Nobody looks irritated if he interrupts, or sits in on meetings he isn't invited to. I overhear people twice his age thanking him for feedback he gave them on some report or presentation and wonder why they value *his* opinion so damn much – and feel a strange flare of jealousy; *I* want to be that person people go to and rely on one day. I see him in so many places, involved with so many teams, I can't tell what he actually does around here – just that I know it seems important, somehow.

I desperately try to reframe the thought. I tell myself that he's obviously a hot-shot intern who was invited back and that could be me next summer, so I should aspire to be more like Lloyd – whatever it is exactly he's doing here.

But any time I see him, or hear his name, I don't feel inspired: only small and stupid. Maybe it's because

I let him in – or worse, believed he might actually have liked me.

It's Friday afternoon before I run into Lloyd at the eleventh-floor kitchen area with nobody else around to act as a buffer or distraction.

The Arrowmile offices take up the top few floors of the building, and lend themselves towards being open-plan. Hardly any of the managers have their own office, hot-desking with the rest of us. A few partition walls painted with bright splashes of blue offer some separation and a bit of sound-proofing, and the kitchen area has been sectioned off neatly near the toilets and lifts. From here, you can't see out into the rest of the office.

Meaning nobody can see me stop in my tracks when I go to the kitchen to make a cup of tea, only to find Lloyd absently stirring a coffee while concentrating on some documents in a file.

My heart jolts to see him again, but it's not the kind of thrilled little somersault it should be when re-meeting a guy I shared a wonderful time with. If anything, it makes me feel a bit queasy. To think I was so pleased when he said he didn't think I was unlikeable . . . Turns out, I'm just so spectacularly *un*remarkable, he doesn't remember me at all.

I retreat quickly, hoping to make a quick escape before he sees me. I don't think I can face an entire one-on-one conversation pretending we're total strangers – but I must make enough noise that he looks up before I can run for it. He closes the file he was just reading, his hand braced on top of it almost like he's afraid I'll run over and steal it. Maybe it's confidential? Somehow, I wouldn't be surprised if he is trusted with top-secret stuff.

'Oh, hey.' His tone is casual – playful – and it has no right to be. He smiles, which drives the knife in a little deeper. 'Fancy seeing you here.'

'Is that supposed to be funny?' I blurt, frowning.

His smile falters a little – though it may not be from guilt. If he really has forgotten me, I probably just come off rude. Cold and unlikeable.

Deciding it would look even more rude if I left, empty mug still in hand, I give him my best attempt at a polite smile, brace myself, and move further into the kitchen. Still an arm's reach away from Lloyd, but acutely aware of just *how* close he is. Close enough to catch the scent of his cologne, and –

Don't think about how good he smells. Dear God, don't think about how good he smells.

(But he smells so good. Deep and rich and spiced. It's the same intoxicating smell that I noticed last Friday

56

night, only now, away from the stickiness of the club and the cool riverside air, I can pick out some of the notes in it more clearly.)

Not, of course, that I'm *noticing*.

I go through the motions of filling the kettle and fetching some milk and a teaspoon, hoping he'll leave first.

But he doesn't.

He just stands there, too close and still impossibly far away, and says cheerfully, 'So how's your first week been? Coping alright so far?'

'Yep. Doing just fine, thanks.'

'Great! They really chuck you in at the deep end, don't they? You'll get the hang of it all, though – everyone does, before long.'

'Uh-huh.'

'And Michaela's team are great. They juggle a lot of stuff so it probably feels pretty hectic right now, huh? One of them actually got signed off on long-term sick just before you started, so they'll be grateful to have someone to pick up the slack. I'm sure you'll fit right in.'

'Right. Thanks.'

'And, obviously, I'm around a lot, so if you ever need anything, just give me a shout. I'm happy to help.'

Happy to make me feel like a total idiot, more like.

'Cool,' is all the reply I can muster. The kettle finally boiled, I finish making my tea and decide that surely, now, I'm allowed to leave without looking rude.

I give Lloyd another lacklustre attempt at a smile, pick up my tea, and . . . don't leave.

I just stand there, like an idiot, grimacing at him and clutching my mug of tea to myself, desperately trying not to ask him if our night together *really* meant so little to him that he's forgotten me. The longer I stand there, the thicker the air gets, threatening to swallow me whole. It almost crackles, electric. Like if I move, I'll get a shock. Something tells me that the moment I leave, that's when this is well and truly over, and Friday night never happened.

His own casual smile fades, replaced by something confused and unsure. A maddening, fleeting impulse makes me want to reach and smooth the expression out with my fingertips.

It's not a good look on him. It's too serious. Not at all right for the light-hearted, quippy boy with his easy laughter and stories of a golden childhood. It makes him look like a stranger.

Which, I suppose, he is.

I grip my mug a little tighter, gathering the willpower to leave, and knowing that he probably just looks like that because *I'm* the stranger to him, and I think it's obvious I'm one wrong move away from crying.

'Annalise –'

He starts towards me, one hand outstretched.

And the moment's gone when a small group of people walk into the kitchen, mid-conversation and chattering animatedly. They toss us friendly smiles and one says, 'Hi, Lloyd,' which is when I realize he's not just lowered his hand but taken an extra step back. The tension clogging the air has cleared, the electricity long gone, making me wonder if it was ever there at all if these people are so completely oblivious to it.

Lloyd collects his things as I gather the last fractures of hope that we might be able to rekindle last Friday night somehow, and we fall into step as we leave the kitchen.

He clears his throat. 'So, um, any plans for the weekend?'

He's not asking me if I have plans because he wants to ask me out. This, I've learned, is just office small talk; that must be the eighteenth time I've been asked this question today by someone who doesn't really care about the answer but is being polite.

So I give him the same answer I've given anybody else who's asked: 'A bunch of us are going out tonight, a bit of a catch-up on our first week. Celebratory or conciliatory drinks, as required.'

'Oh, right. Of course.' We come to a stop near the lifts and Lloyd hesitates, rubbing the back of his neck, hand shifting up to tousle his hair. A shiver runs down my spine, remembering how it felt when that was my hand at the nape of his neck, his silk-soft curls between my fingers.

'See you around,' I tell him, like I did last Friday night, but this time it's less sorry, less hopeful, and comes out sounding bitter – *brittle*.

Something flickers across his face, but only for a moment, making me wonder if I imagined that too. I turn to leave, but not before I see the smile on his face doesn't quite reach his eyes.

'Yeah. See you around.'

Chapter 5

At the pub after work that evening, the drinks don't flow as quickly as they did last week, which is a relief. Our table is crowded, noisy, with everybody talking over each other and calling down the table to one another, full of good food and the adrenaline of our first week.

Despite sharing apartments in the same building, commuting together and passing one another in the office, this is the first chance we've all really had to catch up as a group since the icebreaker night.

And just like then, we all work a little too hard to sell ourselves: everyone swaps details of our roles and responsibilities, competing over whose sounds the most impressive. I'm no exception: I get swept up in the unspoken challenge, just like everyone else.

I learn that Dylan, who offered me his wallet-condoms last week and is studying towards an

Engineering degree, is working in Research and Development, and Tasha and a couple of others have been given project management roles, so I'll probably work with them a bit, which is . . . nice. At least it'll be easier to reach out to other teams when I can use the other interns as a point of contact – even if that point of contact is Tasha. She reminds me a little too much of the girls from my uni halls – sharp and lofty, with a cruel edge you don't want to be on the wrong side of.

The mood relaxes as we bond over the highs and lows of our weeks. We tease Elaine about getting locked out of her computer first thing on Tuesday and having to do a walk of shame to the IT helpdesk to get them to reset it for her, and sympathize with Freya who spilled coffee on Topher Fletcher's PA when she went to introduce herself.

Nobody else ran into a boy they kissed and never thought they'd see again, though.

If anybody notices I'm a bit too loud and talk too fast when they ask about my team and my week, they don't call me out on it. And if they notice my glass of wine after dinner goes down a bit too easily, they let that slide, too.

Somewhere around nine o'clock, a few of us volunteer to get the next round in, collecting drinks orders. I volunteer to get one for my new flatmates

Elaine and Louis; this, I've learned, is what you do when you want to be part of the group and endear people to you.

I catch up with the others at the bar just in time to overhear Monty, the annoying 'rah' guy, saying, 'She's fit, but seems like a right stuck-up cow.'

'Who's that?' I ask, butting in. I wonder if he's talking about Tasha, then scold myself. I hardly know her; I should at least *try* to give her a chance before judging her as a stuck-up cow.

'Nadja,' Burnley explains for me, laughing. 'Monty's in her team.'

'I don't know if you heard earlier but I'll be working on contracts and proposals,' he tells me, with all the pomp and authority as if he'd just declared he was ending world hunger, and as if he hadn't already announced it loud enough for the whole pub to hear.

'Sounds great,' I reply. 'I thought she seemed nice though. Nadja. You know, quite cool. I bet she'd be really interesting to work with.'

Monty rolls his eyes. He's a lanky guy with coiffed, dark brown hair and a smarmy smirk that seems to be a near-permanent feature on his face. He'd be quite good-looking, if not for his haughty resting-face. 'Don't tell me – next, you're gonna ask if I'd call her stuck-up if she was a man.'

'Next,' Burnley interrupts, voice dry, 'I'm gonna ask if you really want to be *that* guy. Don't be a dick, Monty.'

He shrugs, holding up his hands. 'Alright, chill out. It was just a joke. It's not just me, you know – the rest of the team said she's tough. Ruthless. Apparently, she made some intern last year *cry*. Can you believe it?'

'Better make sure you bring your Kleenex, then,' I say. Monty's cheeks colour, but Burley snort-laughs so hard he chokes, coughing, which sends me into a peal of giggles too.

'Ah, chill out, Monty,' Burnley tells him once he's caught his breath. He reaches up to clasp Monty's shoulder, giving him a friendly shake. '*It was just a joke.*'

Somewhere to my left, Dylan shouts, 'Hey! You made it! Guys – guys,' he says, grabbing for us. His other hand is on someone's arm, pulling them through the cluster of people queuing behind us for drinks.

No.

No.

This is *not* happening.

'You guys all know Lloyd, right?' Dylan asks, as a familiar face appears beside him.

What the hell does he think he's doing here? Did he take my mention of the pub earlier as an invitation?

And if he did – how did he know where to find us? Did he go around every pub in Victoria searching?

'Alright, mate?' Burnley's saying to him, not missing a beat. Friendly, because of course they are. If there's one thing my first week at Arrowmile has taught me, it's that everybody loves Lloyd. 'What're you drinking? Pint?'

Lloyd laughs. 'Shouldn't I get the round in if I'm gatecrashing?'

'Now, now.' Dylan slings an arm around his shoulder. 'Can't have the boss's son thinking we're only using him for his money.'

Lloyd laughs at that, too, but the sound is swallowed by static as the world pitches around me, sliding out of focus as I digest Dylan's words.

Boss's son.

Hi there, he'd said the other day, *I'm Lloyd Fletcher*.

Fletcher, like Topher Fletcher, Illustrious Leader/ CEO and . . .

Shit.

How did I not realize sooner? No wonder I can't work out which team he's on when he's always everywhere, or why the managers show him so much respect. Of course they all fawn over him when his dad owns the company.

This is *not* good.

It's only when I hear my name that I realize they're talking to me, about me – introducing me to Lloyd.

My eyes shift to his, my mouth dry. Surely he must remember me now, surrounded by everyone else? Can't he remember Burnley making a spectacle of himself dancing on the table? Hasn't he connected the dots by now?

'Yeah,' I say. 'We've met.'

Lloyd's smile doesn't falter. 'On Monday. I thought I'd try get around and meet a couple of the new interns – which was a good plan until I got waylaid talking to *you* about the new engine we're working on.' He cuffs Dylan around the shoulder, and they both laugh. 'Thanks for the invite tonight, by the way.'

'Yeah, of course, mate. It's no big deal.'

Did I say I was happy I might get to work with Dylan this summer? I take it back. I've never had an enemy before, but he's just made the list.

'Gotta stay on the boss's good side,' Monty says with a brash laugh, but it's clear that particular brand of joke doesn't go down quite as well coming from him. Noticing, he clears his throat, and is saved by the bartender and the fact it's his turn to order.

Somehow, I end up standing just behind the boys – and next to Lloyd.

He gives me a warm smile. 'Well, hey. Fancy seeing you here. Wait – didn't we already do this?' He laughs at his own joke, not looking at all bothered when I'm not charmed by it. My mouth pinches into a thin, sour line and I can feel my hands shaking.

'What are you *doing* here?' I demand of him.

'Hanging out. Having fun – or, that's the plan, anyway.' He grins. 'After we spoke, Dylan mentioned you guys were all out tonight and invited me along for a drink. Felt rude to say no, you know?'

No ruder than giving a girl the best kiss of her life and then forgetting all about her, I think, and out loud I say, 'Uh-huh.'

Sensing I'm not in a chatty mood, Lloyd falls quiet. As he turns to face forward, I notice the smile slip from his face and feel a pang in my chest. *Cold and unlikeable.* That must surely be what he thinks of me now – and I hate the idea that the guy I met last week might believe that.

I'm not, as a rule, very good at making friends. I never have been. I've always been too serious, too studious. I don't say the right thing, I don't make people laugh, I'm not good at being a shoulder to cry on. It wasn't so bad at school, when I could hide it in a wide collection of extra-curriculars that gave me some common ground to bond with classmates. It was harder at university – suddenly living away from home and with five total strangers, three of whom were clique-y girls who immediately dismissed me as 'not their kind of person' and went out of their way to make sure I knew it.

It's hard to admit that the kindred spirit I thought I'd found in Lloyd doesn't exist after all, and might have been a facade to win me over for the night.

It's hard to reconcile this Lloyd with the one I met last week.

After Burnley, Monty and Dylan collect drinks and head back to our table, Lloyd gestures for me to go ahead.

'Can't be accused of cutting the line *and* gate-crashing, can I?' he jokes.

'Right,' I mumble, and give the bartender my order. Then, feeling all too aware of Lloyd just inches away, and not wanting him to think of me as stand-offish, I gesture for him to add his drink to the order too.

'I'll get it,' he says then, taking his wallet out.

'No, I've got it.'

'Annalise, c'mon – let me get the drinks. I was only going to stay for one anyway.'

'I said, *it's fine*. It's my round, so, I have to get them.'

He sighs, more playful than exasperated, slipping a card out of his wallet and braced as if he's going to race me to reach for the machine to pay, but just as I cut him a glare and prepare to shove his arm out of the way, something clicks.

Annalise.

He knows my name.

He does remember, after all.

Fury explodes inside me, bleeding through my body until I'm vibrating with it. He remembers, and he's just been pretending all this time.

Somehow, that's worse.

I stare at him, horrified and devastated. I know why I didn't ask for his number ... But he never asked for mine, either – was he relieved when the night finally ended, and too polite to say so at the time? Maybe it *was* all an act.

The bartender tells us the total and Lloyd reaches to pay. I catch his wrist to stop him and then drop it like his skin burns to touch. I tap my own card to the reader, doing my best not to mentally track what my bank balance must be right now, and decline Lloyd's help when he tries to take some of the drinks to carry back to the table.

With three glasses balanced precariously in my hands, I turn to Lloyd. I can't manage to meet his eyes, but tell him in the steadiest voice I can muster: 'You know, if you were embarrassed about me and didn't want people to know we kissed last week, you only had to say. You didn't need to act like I was a total stranger all week.'

'That's not – I wasn't . . .'

'It's fine.' It's not. My voice shakes, giving me away. I start to leave – the sooner I can disappear into the crowd among the others, the better.

But Lloyd's fingers graze my elbow, the barest touch, and I can't move away.

'I thought I was doing us both a favour. I didn't mean to . . .' He sighs sharply, dragging his free hand through his curls. 'Can we talk about it? Away from the others. Meet you out the front in ten minutes?'

There's a sinking feeling in my stomach, another flare of anger that he did this *on purpose*, but I agree. And I think: let's see the office golden boy talk his way out of this one.

Chapter 6

Without my jacket, it's surprisingly chilly outside, but given that I told the others I was popping to the loo, I could hardly bring it with me. I wrap my arms around myself, shifting from foot to foot, too hurt and angry to form a single coherent thought, until finally, Lloyd joins me.

I must give him a pretty fierce glare, because he immediately holds his hands up and approaches slowly.

'So, obviously I didn't handle this very well, but hear me out. I panicked when I saw you on Monday. It was a snap decision. It's . . . not a good idea, for me to get romantically involved with the interns when it's my dad's company.'

'That's not my fault!' I exclaim. 'You could have *told* me before you kissed me – instead of just ignoring me for the entire week, acting like it never happened.'

'I didn't know your job was at Arrowmile! You never said. There must be dozens of corporate summer internships in London. How was I supposed to know? If anything, *you* should've known who *I* was.'

The laugh that tears out of my mouth is bitter. I thought, seeing him around the office this week, that he must be pretty full of himself – but this really takes the cake.

'*Excuse me?*'

'Well – I mean, all the research you would've had to do on the company to get the job ... There's a ton of pictures of me with my dad and at company events and stuff. I've grown up with Arrowmile. My dad's mentioned me in a bunch of profiles people have written about him. I'm used to people – especially the interns – recognizing me.'

'I don't remember you being this big-headed last week, you know.'

Lloyd huffs, but looks more embarrassed – admonished – than annoyed. '*Anyway.* I thought I was doing us both a favour, pretending we hadn't already met. We'd only have had to explain to everyone how we knew each other ... and then if people knew we had some kind of ...'

'Connection?' I suggest, when he trails off, although I'm not sure what to call it either. 'Fling' doesn't do it justice, but 'history' feels too expansive for only a single night.

'Right,' he says quickly. 'If they knew that, then there'd probably be rumours that we slept together – and, let's face it, you don't want to end up with a reputation that you're sleeping with me to get ahead, do you?'

I flinch back, speechless.

Because, oh, God, he's right. As hurtful as his words are, *he's right.* If people knew we'd kissed . . . I don't want to be associated *that* closely with Lloyd, not now I know he's the boss's son. Otherwise it won't matter how hard I work this summer, or what I achieve; nobody will think I've earned it, not if they can say he was around to help me out. If they know we met before the internship started, they might even think he helped me get here in the first place. One kiss could undermine my entire internship, derail my whole future, just like that.

Lloyd doesn't say it like any kind of threat, though – more like he really, honestly believes he was doing me a favour by ignoring me. (Which, in hindsight, I suppose he was.)

'And,' he continues, 'I don't want to just be the guy who fools around with the interns, you know?'

A cold sense of dread creeps up my spine.

'Not *just* the guy who fools around with the interns,' I repeat slowly. 'Has it happened before?'

Lloyd starts to say something, then cuts himself off and tears his gaze away, frowning at the floor. A muscle jumps in his jaw, and his silence tells me everything I need to know.

But I must be a glutton for punishment, because I find myself snapping at him, 'Do you do that every year, see how many interns you can hook up with before the summer's over? Is it all some kind of sick joke for you? A game?'

A dark look passes over his face, his green eyes dangerous, his gaze so heavy that this time, it's me who has to look away. My arms wrap a little tighter around myself and I shuffle backwards.

He is *not* the guy I thought I met on Friday night. Not in the slightest. This guy is callous, pompous, full of himself and his own sense of self-importance.

My spine pulls taut as I straighten up. There's a lump in my throat and I swallow it down; I think it's pride.

'So let me get this straight,' I say. 'It's *my* fault I didn't recognize *you*, and you pretended not to know me rather than just talking to me about any of this because, really, you're just worried about your *own* reputation. Did I get that right?'

Lloyd's shoulders sag. And all he has to say for himself is: 'Can you not tell anybody that stuff I told you about not wanting to go back to uni, and not liking my course? And I won't tell anyone you lied about your age on your application, obviously. I mean, I wouldn't tell them anyway, but –'

'Wow. *Thank you*, Lloyd Fletcher, for being so thoughtful. There's that oh-so-charming display of chivalry you were so keen to show off last week.'

'I just meant –'

'I know exactly what you meant. You know what? You were right, pretending like we've never met before. You are the last guy on Earth I'd want to be associated with – boss's son, or not.'

'Annalise –'

No, I think, gritting my teeth, *he doesn't get to have this*. However well-intentioned he's convinced himself that he's being, I'm not stomaching this. He must be so used to people fawning over him, having everything go his way . . .

Not this time, buddy.

I step up to him, arms falling to my sides. I hope

he can't see the way my hands shake, and I hope he doesn't notice that I ball them into fists to try to hide it.

'Here's the deal, *Fletcher*. We both pretend last Friday night never happened, and like we don't know each other. You don't tell anybody I lied about my age on my application, and I won't tell anybody you're thinking about dropping out of your degree. If I see you around the office, I will be nice to you. We will be civil. We will be polite. And *don't* think you're doing me any favours. You're not. Got it?'

I can hear my pulse thrumming in my ears after my little tirade and I'm itching to storm off, but I force myself to wait for his response. I need him to acknowledge it, to know that he heard me.

Lloyd searches my face for a moment, and there's something so familiar about it that it cuts right through me, setting me on the back foot. Then he swallows, his Adam's apple bobbing agitatedly, and nods.

'Got it.'

We go inside separately, an unspoken agreement so the rest of the group don't notice we were together. I hate to admit it but he's right – the last thing I want are rumours going around that I've been sneaking off for any kind of alone time with the boss's son. I got this internship on my own merits, and I won't let anything, not even the boy with the quicksilver smile, take that away from me.

It's only later, home in my bed, that I realize why that look he gave me at the end of our chat got to me so badly.

It's because he was searching my face, looking for the girl he met last week, and clearly he couldn't find her anywhere either.

Chapter 7

'So, how's it all going?' my dad wants to know on Saturday afternoon, eyes shining with excitement even through the phone screen as we FaceTime. 'First week done! Are you settling in okay? Getting on alright with the others? Your new flatmates can't be any worse than the last lot – the *state* of that kitchen sink in your uni halls when we visited to pick you up for summer, honestly . . . Are they being nice to you? Inviting you to things, including you? What about your team – is your new manager giving you enough guidance?'

'Dad, *breathe*.'

He does, taking an exaggerated, melodramatic breath so big it makes his cheeks puff out like a chipmunk, and comes sputtering back out of him in a laugh that's warm and familiar. I'm exhausted, but that laugh revives me a little. I readjust my hold on the phone, tucking my knees up to my chest, and answer his questions in order.

Summer is creeping in lazily this year, filtering in at the very edges: a too-brief golden hour, and sudden and vibrant splashes of lush green leaves appearing on trees where they hadn't been the day before, pale but bright dawns creeping earlier and earlier into the morning.

I've made an escape to St James's Park for a little while. As I explain to my dad now over FaceTime, it's not that I don't like the other interns – but between seeing each other at work and sharing commutes and accommodation, it's nice to have a little breathing space for a while.

Plus, I've been on edge all day, frazzled from a sleepless night replaying my confrontation with Lloyd and cursing myself for falling for his act last week and believing he could genuinely have liked me, when he obviously doesn't want much to do with me at all. Which I must be making obvious because Elaine keeps asking if I'm okay, and I think if she does it one more time, I might break down and tell her everything. She seems lovely, but I've only known her a week – what if she blabs to everyone else?

Besides, I have to be better than this. I promised myself I'd get through this summer and not fall at the first hurdle – I just didn't expect that hurdle to be a cute guy.

Obviously, I don't mention the boy drama to my dad. Instead, I focus on the work stuff, pleased that I can give a good report there. I've started to get to work reviewing some projects alongside Laurie as a bit of a 'practice run' before I take the reins myself next week. So far, it's been like learning to ride a bike with the stabilizers on.

When I say that, Dad laughs again. 'And knowing you, you're itching to get them off already. I'm sure you'll have found your footing there before you know it, Anna, I wouldn't stress too much.'

'I know. I'm trying.'

Although what I actually want to tell him is that it's not as easy as he seems to think. Sure, the Project Development team have taken on four interns over the past couple of summers so they must be used to having an amateur around, and sure, they gave me a thirty-nine slide PowerPoint of information explaining the sorts of tasks I'll be doing with step-by-step flow diagrams . . . But they're also currently a team-member down, run off their feet, and so used to having an intern around that the novelty has apparently worn off. I've noticed more than a couple of eyerolls if I ask them to explain something they deem obvious and basic. I want to prove that I'm useful, that I can handle it – not sit around asking silly questions, a total inconvenience to everybody.

Plus – none of their previous interns made the cut for a graduate job afterwards. My manager, Michaela, joked to me that maybe I'll be the first.

I *may* have taken it as a challenge.

I do tell Dad something that's made it a little tricky to settle in – that, at random intervals throughout the week, we're all corralled back into a single group and introduced to various teams or managers. It's supposed to help us build a better understanding of all the cogs in the machine that is Arrowmile.

'Let me guess,' Dad tells me, his bushy eyebrows twisting upwards. 'You'd rather just get your head down with a list of tasks.'

He's not wrong, but I say, 'Some of it's been quite interesting. Like, the Senior Partner for the Marketing department was an intern five years ago. Five years ago! And now she's leading the department! That's *amazing*. Her name's Molly, and she's agreed to get lunch with me next week so I can pick her brains, and –'

'And see how that can be you, next?'

I don't deny it, and Dad gives a small, affectionate chuckle as he shakes his head. My stomach knots as

I think he's about to make another comment about how like my mum I am, but all he says is, 'There'll be no stopping you, Annalise. Watch out, world.'

I smile, but I should've known it was too good to be true.

'Your mum would be so proud of you,' he says, and it takes all my willpower not to hang up the phone there and then.

Like I want her to be proud of me. Like it matters. Like I *care*.

She forfeited any right to be proud of me when she picked her career over us, and walked out of our lives almost thirteen years ago. Who needs to be there for their daughter when they have a shiny, impressive, high-flying job that's much more interesting to spend time with?

'Have you told her about the internship?' Dad presses, in a way that suggests he already knows the answer.

'So that we finally have some common ground to talk about? No, thanks.'

Dad inclines his head in surrender and, thankfully, lets it drop.

He doesn't need to know that part of me secretly hopes Mum might see the update on my LinkedIn profile about how I'm doing a prestigious internship this summer. I'm aware how pathetic it sounds that the only communication I might have with my own mother would be via *LinkedIn*, of all things.

We chat a little while longer. I tell him a bit more about my week, then ask how my brothers are doing. Dad flips the camera around and takes me to the dining table, where my half-brothers Oliver and Christian are doing homework, so they can say hi.

They're *supposed* to be doing homework, anyway. Oliver, who's slightly older at nine, shoves a red Nintendo Switch under a sheaf of papers hastily. I try to smother a laugh, and hear Dad sigh. He rummages under some half-filled-in maths worksheets for it, prompting Oliver to mutter, 'Thanks a *lot*, Annie,' because it's apparently my fault (it usually is, but I know he never really means it).

Christian throws a plastic ruler at his brother. 'I *told* you you'd get caught. Dad, can *I* play on the Switch later?'

'We'll see.' Which usually means 'yes'.

Christian pokes his tongue out and Oliver throws the ruler back at him, reluctantly going back to his homework.

'So, everything's normal and nobody's missing me too much yet?' I ask Dad.

'Everything's normal and we're all missing you

plenty,' he tells me. He takes me into the kitchen next, where Gina's in the middle of sorting out dinner, holding the phone out so my stepmum can say hi and get a run-down of my week before they have to go. I say goodbye, stomach grumbling like I can smell the casserole Gina was cooking, and I feel a pang that I'm not back at home with them.

At uni, home was only an hour's train ride away, so I had my fair share of weekends back there, enjoying some proper home-cooked meals and a washing machine I didn't have to pay to use … And with everybody politely not mentioning that I was only home because once again, I didn't have plans with either old friends from school *or* the girls in my halls. After the failed midterm and breaking up with my boyfriend, I abandoned the social clubs I'd joined purely in an attempt to make some friends, unwilling to risk my future just so I could look back and say, 'Sure, I didn't get the grades I wanted and missed out on those jobs, but you know what? I played a *ton* of netball.'

I didn't get homesick. I visited too often, and if I stayed at uni it was because I was so busy studying, focused only on the day when all of this would be behind me and I'd be a successful, independent grown-up. Then, I wouldn't waste time worrying over why the girls suddenly went quiet when I came into the kitchen, or burst out giggling as I left the room. I'd be capable, and put-together, and unfazed by such things.

I guess I haven't had chance to feel homesick since coming to London for the internship yet, either – not until now, when it hits hard. I think about spending the next three months here, far away and probably hardly going home at all. Will my brothers look all grown up by the time I can visit next? Will they miss me over summer, or forget all about me? I'll miss them when they go to Spain next month – the first family holiday I won't be part of.

A shiver runs through me, and I hug my knees to me a little tighter – but it's not from the chill of an early summer breeze; it's the uneasy realization that *this* is what growing up means, and all of a sudden I'm barrelling towards it with the brakes cut. I've been so focused on what my future is going to look like that I forgot some of what I'm leaving behind.

It's all for the best though.

It has to be.

Chapter 8

From: nadja.sideris@arrowmile.co.uk
To: anna.sherwood@arrowmile.co.uk, dylan.thurgood-jones@arrowmile.co.uk, & four others
cc: elaine.parker@arrowmile.co.uk, edward.burnley@arrowmile.co.uk, & seven others

Subject: VISIT TO LABS – THIS WEDNESDAY

Hello, interns!

Hope this email finds you well – or at the very least, not crying in the toilets because we've scared you off already.

I've arranged a trip to the Arrowmile labs and factory this week to meet with some of our product development, testing and research teams and to get a first-hand look at some of our products. If you're lucky, you'll get to test-drive something. If you're unlucky, you'll end up breaking it and live in shame for the rest of the summer.

The minibus will collect you all from the office at 9 a.m. – please be prompt. To those of you cc'd, we encourage you to come along, but as your roles don't directly interface with the work in the labs, it's not mandatory. If you are interested in joining, <u>please let me know by end of day TODAY</u>.

KR,
N.

Not two minutes after I finish reading Nadja's email late on Monday morning, I get a 'reply all' from intern Freya with a profuse apology that she won't be able to make it but to please let her know of any future opportunities.

The group WhatsApp lights up on my phone immediately as Monty calls her out for being the first 'reply all' of the summer with a string of laughing faces. I snort, then look back at the email, then type 'KR email sign off' into Google to find out that it stands for 'kind regards', which – duh, of course it does.

My own email sign-off has gone through a few turns, seeing what other people are using and what feels right for me. Apparently, this is a mark of my personality *and* professionalism in one fell swoop. I know it will form part of people's first impressions of me this summer, so it matters.

'Cheers' doesn't feel very like me, and 'best wishes' seems cringey and cutesy.

I'm not bold enough for Nadja's 'KR' and single initial, which I think must require a certain degree of daring that I definitely do not possess.

'Sincerely Yours' has a nice ring to it, though. That's what I've settled on.

I drag the attachment Nadja sent through with her email into my calendar, wincing when I realize it clashes with a few things – including my lunch with Molly (the previous Marketing intern who is now running the department). I know it's not a big deal in the grand scheme of things, but she's the person *I* want to be. She's someone I could learn from – maybe even ask to mentor me, if I'm lucky.

Dejected, I send her a cancellation with a note explaining, and ask as politely as I can to let me know another time she might be available. When she pops up in the bottom corner of my laptop screen with a message on Teams a few minutes later, my heart actually skips a beat.

Molly Phelps
Hey, Anna! I'm free for the next hour if you are?

Anna Sherwood
I am – sounds good! Thank you so much.
Sorry again for the inconvenience.

No worries. See you at the twelfth-floor break-out area in five?

It's only after agreeing that I think I should double-check with my boss, Michaela, if she minds, so I walk over to her desk, nervousness gnawing at me. It feels like being in school and asking the teacher if I can go use the toilet in the middle of a lesson, which only makes me feel younger and more out of place than I already am.

But she nods aggressively in a way that makes me think I've done something right. 'Of course! Excellent stuff, Anna – Molly was one of the best in her cohort of interns, and she's made some great strides here. I think you'll really learn a lot from her. It's so good to see you taking initiative! Before you go though – did you get the chance to go through that spreadsheet I sent you this morning?'

'Yes! I made all those updates you asked for, so it's ready for your meeting this afternoon.' It was a hard few hours battling through spreadsheets, but I got there in the end.

'Great. Thanks, Anna – I know it's a bit of lackey work, but it's *so* annoying to have to update it every week, especially with the formatting issues . . .'

'Can't you automate it? Have the data pull through from the master file and set the calculations to run each time you refresh it, rather than having to plug it all in manually every time?'

Michaela's eyes light up. 'Brilliant! That would be *so* helpful. You can sort that out, can't you? Shouldn't be too tricky, I'm sure.'

Shit. Did I volunteer? I definitely didn't. I limped through my extra computing module at uni, and it didn't even cover Excel formulae. My abilities there begin and end at summing up some cells. The work Michaela asked me to do today, mainly filtering out values based on dates and calculating how much they've changed compared to a budget, took the *entire* morning. I wouldn't even know where to begin to automate that.

But for some reason, I tell her, 'Absolutely! I'll have it finished by this time next week.'

'Excellent. Thanks, Anna. Enjoy your meeting with Molly!'

I hurry off before I sign myself up to something else I don't actually know how to do.

Upstairs, I find Molly at one of the tall, small, circular tables in the little break-out area near the kitchenette. There are a couple of sofas and a few other tall tables with seats, and while there's a TV screen and a bowl of free snacks (including KitKats), there's no pool table or anything. I'm kind of relieved. I'd almost had visions of trying to ask questions over ping-pong serves.

Molly, dressed in a chic pair of beige trousers and plain black top, waves me over with a broad smile. She's wearing a full face of makeup and her hair is in a pretty, effortless updo, with an orange marker pen sticking out of it. I wonder if she knows it's there.

She sets her phone screen-down on the table as I take a seat opposite her. 'Hi! Lucky you messaged when you did, I was *just* about to deal with some admin stuff.'

'Oh, God, I'm sorry. Please don't feel like you have to – I mean, it's . . . we can do this some other time.'

'Nah, it's just some expense claims and stuff. It'll keep. So! One week down, eleven to go! How's life in PD treating you so far?'

I don't bore her with the novel-length report I offered Dad on Saturday afternoon, but as I go through what are probably pretty rote responses, I'm busy reminding myself of the things I want to ask her.

After a little small talk, Molly dives right in. 'You wanted to do a little Q&A about how I got this role and how I found my internship and stuff, right? Well, weirdly, even though my degree was in Marketing, I got put into the B2B team – you know, business-to-business, client-facing – with Nadja. Obviously, you've met Nadja already, yeah? Great, well . . .'

I already looked Molly up on LinkedIn, so I know most of the back story she gives me. She got a first in her degree from Leeds (it's nice to have some common ground in attending the same uni) then went on to do the Arrowmile internship before getting her master's at St Andrew's – where she graduated with distinction. She speaks three languages, and worked freelance doing graphic design, copy writing, and as an SEO specialist alongside her studies. Her CV must be bursting at the seams. She's got more endorsements on LinkedIn than anybody I've ever seen.

And she made head of department (sorry, 'Senior Partner') by twenty-five.

And, as I discovered on a quick stalk of her Instagram, she's just bought a house with her partner and has two cats. Her life looks like a dream. It's picture-perfect, completely intimidating ... and exactly the kind of thing I want for myself when I'm her age.

I need to know all her secrets.

'I need to know all your secrets,' I blurt out at one point, interrupting her mid-sentence, so in awe that I can't contain myself. I'm even a bit jealous, which is ridiculous. There's no reason I *couldn't* have her kind of life one day.

Molly laughs, looking flattered but also like that isn't the first time she's heard that.

'I wish I could give you some kind of how-to handbook, but I don't know what to tell you. Some of it is sheer dumb luck. Some of it's just that I'm good at what I do. I have a flair for this, and some things, you just can't teach,' she tells me – not arrogant, only self-assured. She gives a small shrug. 'I can tell you how the sausage gets made, but after that, it's up to you. No guarantees, you know?'

'I know,' I say, trying to hide my disappointment. It was naïve of me to think there really *was* some kind of secret.

'I will say that one of the best things I did on this internship was push myself outside of my comfort zone. *Way* outside of it. Working in Nadja's team gave me such a good view of what the customer is seeing that it ultimately helped me sort of reverse-engineer my way through stuff in Marketing. But you know when I was on the internship, I *actually* asked HR if I could move teams in my first week. I think I asked every week for the first month, actually.' Molly laughs again, this time punctuating it with a self-deprecating eyeroll. 'I thought I knew everything, but – that's rule number one, Anna. You might have a super-crazy-awesome-cool CV and be a whizz-kid at uni, but here, you don't know jack shit.'

Molly stares at me so hard that I lean back in my chair.

I resist the urge to wipe my hands on my skirt and

instead very slowly, very deliberately, pick up my pen and say aloud as I pretend to write in my notebook: 'I don't know jack shit. Got it.'

She lets out another peal of laughter, which gives me a warm glow in my chest, and I relax a bit. For all her impressive background, Molly seems like the most easy-going, down-to-earth person I've met at Arrowmile. Friendly in a way that makes me feel like, if we'd met at uni, we might actually be friends. 'Seriously, I mean it – learn as much as you can about everything, from everyone. You might want to carve out your niche and focus only on what your manager tells you to do, but make the most of this experience. Even if you don't end up here afterwards, it'll give you some perspective to take with you. Oh – and pro tip, if Nadja sends out one of her invites for shadowing opportunities or visits to the lab or whatever, even if she says it's not mandatory, *do it anyway*. If you want to get a job here after you graduate, showing enthusiasm really gets you in her good books.'

'I kind of guessed. We're going to the labs this week, and her email didn't make it sound very *optional*.'

'She's a real force of nature, believe me – but she's also amazing to have in your corner. She really knows her stuff. Don't take it personally if she's a little blunt though.'

'Or if she makes me cry in the toilets?' I joke.

'Or that,' she says, and then stage-whispers, 'I was one of those. I thought I'd ruined this huge contract renewal worth three million pounds. I mean, obviously, I messed up big time, so of course Nadja wasn't happy about it, and she was only criticizing me to teach me how to do it better next time. But, you know, I was this fresh-faced intern thinking I was single-handedly destroying the company and my manager hated me and was going to give me the sack, so I had a complete breakdown in the toilets.'

'Oh my God. I'd die if that was me.'

'I wanted to, believe me. But Nadja came in to find me when I didn't come back to my desk after a few minutes, and talked some sense into me. She was really nice about it, actually. Although, don't let her know I told you that – I think she likes the whole hard, scary exterior vibe she's got going. It'd totally undermine her to the interns if you all knew she was a major softie underneath it all.'

'My lips are sealed.' And then I find myself wondering what her opinion is of the CEO, since she's being so upfront, unprompted. So I say, 'We met Mr Fletcher the other day, too.'

'Topher?'

'Right. Yeah. Sorry, I'm just – it still feels weird calling adults by their first names, you know?'

For a second, there's a blank look on Molly's face before she remembers what it was like to be a teenager. 'He's pretty cool. Amateur science geek with good business sense and solid people skills. Approachable, but always busy, so good luck catching *him* for one of these little Q&As.'

Good to know, I think, already forming a plan of attack. (Should I email him? Maybe I should try to drop by Freya's desk a couple of times first, suss things out from her and maybe bump into him in person . . .)

'But hey, if you can't grab Topher for a chat, his son Lloyd's always around. Have you met him yet?'

I've done a whole lot more than 'meet' him, Molly, believe me.

'Um. Uh, y-yeah. He came out for drinks with everybody the other night.'

'And?'

Molly's eyes bug and she leans towards me, head bobbling side to side as she waits, eager for *my* opinions this time. I stammer for a moment before managing, 'It's interesting how much he wants to be involved and get to know the interns. Does he . . . make a regular thing out of that?'

I'm fishing for gossip. So sue me.

If anybody is going to spill the tea, I figure it's probably someone like Molly.

'Oh, sure. Wouldn't you? He must've only been – what . . . fifteen, I guess – when I was doing my internship, so he wasn't exactly meeting us for after-work drinks or anything, but wouldn't *you* gravitate towards the only people in the office who are remotely close to you in age? He always seemed . . .' She pulls a face, debating over it for a minute.

'Self-important?' I guess, and instantly regret that I said it out loud.

She shakes her head, still considering – luckily for me, too preoccupied trying to pick the right word to judge me for the one I suggested. Then she shrugs and says, 'Mature for his age. Kind of lonely, I guess.'

Yeah, well, being an arrogant toad will do that to you.

'Poor guy,' I say instead, and then risk adding, 'I heard some rumours he got a little *too* friendly with one of the interns last year.'

Molly's eyes bug wide – delightedly scandalized. 'You could say that! He dated one of the girls. Totally head over heels for her. They called it off at the end of the summer, though. I think it was the long distance, or something, what with her going back to uni . . . Poor kid was *heartbroken*. He was majorly on the rebound for a while, went on a *bunch* of dates. Double-booked himself one night, I heard. Got in a whole *heap* of trouble with the two girls who both showed up at the restaurant!'

I must pull a very judgemental face because Molly laughs.

'Right? I think he's over all that now, though, so don't hold that against him. He's a real cutie.'

Cutie? Could she be underselling his good looks any more? He's almost deliriously good-looking. Not, obviously, that I care. But I can tell it's my turn to talk, and I have to say *something*, so I shrug and reply, 'He's quite attractive, I suppose.'

Confusion flickers over Molly's face before she gives a small breath of laughter. 'Sure, but I meant he's just a sweet guy. I forget he's, like, a fully-grown adult now. I still think of him as a kid.'

Shit. Idiot, idiot. Of course that's what she meant!

'He's been here basically full-time over the last year, though,' Molly adds as an aside – either not noticing my embarrassment, or polite enough to ignore it. 'So he's probably, like, *the* go-to guy for any questions you have. Even my cohort relied on him, although it was a little weird having to ask a kid to explain the intricate dynamics of certain client relationships and stuff.'

Great. That's just what I need: to have the go-to guy be the one person I'm determined to avoid.

'He spends a lot of time around the office though, so he'll be much easier to catch than his dad,' Molly is telling me.

'Oh, right. Cool. Um – sorry, you . . . Quick question. You said he's here full-time? Like, he has a job here? Right now?'

'I mean, "job" is probably stretching it. He kind of floats around everywhere, you know? As much as I *hate* this phrase because I think it's super gross – he really does have his finger in a lot of pies. Like, every pie Arrowmile's got to offer.'

'You're right. That is a . . . super gross phrase.'

Then Molly's distracted by her frantically-buzzing phone. 'Shit, that's my next meeting. I've gotta go, sorry, Anna. But this has been fun! Don't be afraid to reach out if there's ever anything I can help with, or if you want to spend some time shadowing us in Marketing. And seriously – Lloyd's your guy. Make use of him!'

'Thanks, I will!' I call after her as she hurries towards the lifts, hoping she doesn't see that I've crossed my fingers.

Lloyd is anything *but* 'my guy'.

NEW EMAIL DRAFT

Dear Lloyd,

I don't know how you've done it, but you've got them all fooled. You've got everyone thinking you're some stand-up guy, with that winning smile and oodles of charm. You just radiate it, and they've all fallen for it.

I did, too.

You fooled me, worse than anyone. How am I supposed to forgive you for that?

Never mind forgive you. How am I supposed to move past it, pretend it doesn't bother me? It does. I'll never admit it to you, but it bothers the hell out of me. I liked you. And now I very much the opposite of like you. Would it have killed you to just talk to me when you saw me here last week?

I just wish I'd known who you really were, before you kissed me.

Sincerely Yours,
Anna Sherwood

Chapter 9

The Arrowmile labs are out near Canary Wharf, so it takes us a little while to get across the city in the minibus Nadja organized from the office. The labs are housed in an old renovated factory near the river and walking in, it takes my breath away.

The front doors are seven feet tall and open into a light, airy space with a small, single reception desk and a well-organized collection of products and prototypes. A series of podiums with glass cases on top boast a display of Arrowmile's EV engines through the years. Four of their scooters-for-hire are lined up: three are painted and branded to match the city they're already in and the fourth is dark grey, the base simply reading COMING SOON. The lights are industrial spotlights on black poles, and everything is accented in wrought iron (or at least, a good imitation of it).

The instant I step through the doors, I *feel it*.

Everything I'd expected to feel when we met Topher Fletcher for the first time. The inspiration, the awe, the way my brain is set spinning with a fresh wave of ambition and ideas and *want*.

There's something magical about this space.

While the foyer isn't huge, it's partitioned off by a wall that's plain white halfway up, and then glass the rest of the way, reaching up towards the high ceiling. Through it, I spot raised walkways wrapping around the sides and leading to various rooms. The noise of machinery can be heard over the radio the receptionist is playing.

She gets up, waving to Nadja as we all pour in through the doors. 'Hang on, I'll just go fetch him. Can you have everybody sign in?' she asks.

I'm one of the first to sign the visitors' logbook, so I step away to look at the displays. I pause at the giant infographic poster showing a timeline of Arrowmile since it was first founded twenty-four years ago (although back then, they focused on regular old motorcycles and motorized scooters before pivoting into electric vehicles). It's punctuated with facts about the benefits their work has for the environment and their steadily soaring profit margins; photographs of products or the team help illustrate it. There's a giant photograph of Topher Fletcher with a quote:

Here at our labs, even our best and brightest know that to make an arrow fly, you have to pull back first – and we here at Arrowmile always strive to keep moving forward.

I must be staring at the quote a little too obviously, because beside me, there's a soft snort.

'He really loves leaning into the whole "bow and arrow" metaphor, with a last name like "Fletcher".'

I look over, only realizing a beat too late why the voice is familiar. Immediately, I feel my eyebrows knitting into a scowl, my mood darkening. *Of course* Lloyd is here. He's *everywhere*, all the damn time.

'Hello, Fletcher,' I say, nice and civil, just like I promised I would be.

'Hey.' He beams at me, and it's dazzling. Not so much the rows of straight white teeth (although sure, those too), but the brightness in his eyes, the radiance of that expression. He looks genuinely happy to see me.

No – not happy to see me. Just . . . He's happy to be here, that's all. Hanging out with everybody. Infiltrating our cohort, or whatever. That smile is all Lloyd; it's nothing to do with *me*.

'What're you doing here?' I ask.

'Dad always sends me along for this; he hopes I might learn something.' Lloyd rolls his eyes. 'Like

I don't already spend a good chunk of my time here – getting underfoot and in the way, he reckons.'

Lulled into a false sense of companionship by his tone, I almost say something like, *That sucks*, or maybe, *Why do you come here so often?* But Lloyd checks himself before I can decide what to say – reminding me that whatever we are now, it's a far cry from the night we met.

He gives a wide smile that doesn't quite reach his eyes. 'He's probably not wrong, huh? Anyway, it's a great tour. Always something new to learn! Plus, I get to hang out with you guys, so that'll be fun, too.'

Oh, sure. I can't think of anything more fun than spending the day with a guy who kissed me then treated me like dirt. But I bite my tongue – because we *did* promise to be civil, and I don't want the others suspecting anything is off between Lloyd and me, asking questions I can't answer.

'I missed that,' I tell him, turning back to the infographic. Something uneasy has swelled in my chest and I tamp it down quickly. 'The whole Fletcher, arrow thing.'

'Wanna know a secret? I didn't make the connection until I was, like, twelve. I was reading some high fantasy book where they talked about this guy being a fletcher and making arrows, and it was a total light-bulb moment.'

My lips start to twitch up in a smile, but I catch it, pull it back and hide it away.

'I don't need to know any more of your secrets. I don't think that's a very good idea,' I say, very quietly.

He starts to reply, and falters. I feel the shift in his mood: it's like the sun moving behind clouds, every-thing feeling a little greyer, a little *less*, than before. I feel a little flare of resentment at him for wearing his heart so much on his sleeve that the change is so obvious. Can't he keep a lid on it, like the rest of us?

'Sorry,' he mumbles.

He takes a step off to the side, putting more space between us. It makes some tiny, irrational, too-loud part of me want to snatch at his arm and pull him back in, or turn and smile at him so *he'll* smile again.

I try my best to pretend I don't notice, going to join the others instead, and leaving him alone in the corner.

Our tour guide for the day is a scientist. An *actual* scientist. A 'not *that* kind of doctor' kind of doctor. Dr Paulson has salt-and-pepper hair and a pep in his step, and the more he tells us about the work in the labs, though it's clearly a well-rehearsed spiel he's delivered dozens of times before, the more enthusiastic his voice gets.

This guy clearly *loves* his job.

It makes me love it, too.

Although most of the more technical details do go a little over my head, hard as I try to grasp them. Dr Paulson is approachable enough that I do ask a few questions, but after Tasha scoffs when I ask what an electromagnet is, I stop.

It doesn't escape my notice that after I resort to furtively googling things on my phone instead, Lloyd, who's managed to position himself just behind me in the group, mumbles brief explanations to me as Dr Paulson goes animatedly through his talk.

I don't have to *like* him, but I do appreciate the help.

While most of the others look politely interested and a bit overwhelmed, it's clear that a couple of them are absolutely in their element here. Izzy – a biochem student – is full of curiosity and hangs off Dr Paulson's every word; Dylan has no end of precise, intricate questions – so much so that Nadja laughs and says maybe he'll need to spend a couple more days here with Dr Paulson, or we might never get through the rest of the tour. Dylan flushes, though he looks more pleased than offended.

There's a quick break for lunch at the cafe on site. Nadja leaves us to take a call, and Dr Paulson returns to his desk for a while.

Lloyd stays with us, though. Sitting between Monty and Elaine, telling some funny story about how he broke a display scooter when he was seventeen, complete with exaggerated expressions and demonstrations that have him half-stood up, arms flailing as he acts it out and makes a spectacle of himself.

'Thing is, I didn't realize it wasn't even a real prototype – it was just a mock-up of what it was *going* to look like. It was just a regular scooter, but it wasn't even put together solidly. Because it's just for display, right? So I'm checking nobody's looking – reception's empty – and I grab it to go for a quick spin around the room. Just as I take off, in walks my dad and Nadja with a bunch of bigwigs from Birmingham City Council so they can show off what they're working on . . . And there *I* am, on this scooter that *immediately* falls apart, and I just roll up to them on essentially a skateboard, holding this handlebar that's not attached to anything . . .'

'Oh my God.'

'No way!'

'That's *hilarious*.'

I watch as everybody hangs off his every word, all of them laughing. Monty digs him playfully in the ribs with his elbow. Izzy has actual *tears* on her face, she's creased up so much.

It puts a weird feeling in the pit of my stomach. I think for a minute it's jealousy: *this* is more like the guy I spent the night with, so maybe it just hurts to share him. I sit with it for a little while before realizing it's something worse, more corrosive than any green-eyed monster.

I resent him, for proving he *is* the guy I met after all. For showing me that I wasn't special, to have been around him like this. For making me hate his charisma and the smile on his kiss-me lips.

I resent that I'm *still* hurt over it, too. I should never have left the bar with him. I should never have indulged myself, thinking I deserved to have a little fun for once.

I need to be more careful than that. Smarter.

'Did you get in trouble?' Elaine asks Lloyd, agog at the vivid imagery of his story, and there's a beat where I know we're all picturing that: a slightly younger Lloyd, maybe one a bit more reckless and rougher around the edges, facing off against the good-humoured CEO we met last week.

Lloyd scoffs. He rolls his eyes, but somehow it turns

into a full-bodied move: his shoulders arc with his eyes, chest rising, head tipping back for the moment. 'Nah. I mean, it didn't exactly make for a solid first impression, but they all found it pretty funny. At least I didn't break the *actual* prototype. Now that might've been a different story!'

Everyone laughs again, voices overlapping as there are more Oh my God's and That's so funny's. Lloyd grins, but it turns rigid at the edges as he reaches for his bottle of Sprite, his shoulders settling into a hard line as his relaxed posture, the way he lounged so comfortably in his chair only a moment ago, is pulled taut.

And I'm back in the starless night-time under the lights of the city, and he's asking me, *Tell me something true.*

Like he can sense me staring, he lifts his eyes directly to meet mine.

He must be able to tell I don't believe him, because the tension in his jaw eases and this time, his smile is small and soft, truer than the last one; and he shrugs, a minute movement that's miles away from the wild gestures that accompanied his story just seconds ago.

But then, just like that, he slings an arm over the back of his chair, takes a swig of his Sprite, and is laughing at Burnley's story about the time he was a kid and rode a skateboard right into a lamp post, breaking his nose.

The change in Lloyd is so drastic, the moment our eyes met so fleeting, I almost wonder if I imagined it.

Almost.

By the time the minibus drops us all back at the office in Victoria, it's gone six o'clock and everyone is ready to head home. Tasha and a couple of others decide to go get dinner, and Elaine is meeting a friend.

'See you guys,' Lloyd calls to the group, and makes to go inside.

'Don't you want to come for dinner?' Tasha asks him. 'You're more than welcome.'

'Ah, thanks, but I've got plans.'

Shouldering my bag, I head for the doors as well. 'See you all later. Have a good night, everyone!' I call, mostly aiming the comment at Elaine, since she's my flatmate.

'You're not going to work *now*, are you?' Izzy asks me, aghast at the mere idea – and I realize very quickly that she's not the only one: Burnley wrinkles his face and Dylan almost shudders in revulsion. Monty and the other intern in Nadja's team, Cambridge student Verity, exchange a glance, both peeking at Nadja as if she'll expect them to go inside and do a full day's work at this time of the evening, but she's busy on her phone while looking through her bag for her pass, not listening.

Um . . . yes?

I'll check through my emails in case I missed anything today, and I should probably take another crack at that automated spreadsheet I promised Michaela I'd get finished for Monday; I'm not even halfway done with that yet.

'No!' I tell Izzy and the others, too quickly, too loudly, and pray they don't look hard enough to see right through me. 'No, no, I've just – I left something upstairs I need to go pick up.'

'We can wait for you,' Dylan offers, even though Tasha's already making her way down the street and everyone is starting to disperse before the idea of getting any work done now becomes too serious a notion, one they're all collectively guilted into.

'Nah, don't worry about it – I should probably get home anyway, I've got a few things to do.'

'Okay, if you're sure . . .' But he doesn't need any more convincing, and jogs off after the others.

Nadja, having found her pass now, holds the door open for me. She pins me with a fierce look, one eyebrow raised sharply. 'Let me guess – need something finished by tomorrow morning and haven't started it yet? Rookie error, Anna.'

'Oh! No. It's just – I wanted to check my emails and stuff, you know? Just get a head start for tomorrow.'

She nods, but says, 'Don't stay too late. We don't want you guys burning yourselves out on week two. At least let us get a little more mileage out of you before you break down.' She laughs at her own joke, and I join in – although I'm not exactly sure just *how* much she's joking.

Lloyd, not that far ahead of us, sees us coming and holds the lift. At this time of the evening, the ground floor is mostly empty: plenty of people are leaving, but we're the only three going up. In the lift, he's busy on his phone, AirPods in.

'Thanks for organizing today for us, by the way,' I tell Nadja. 'It was really interesting.'

She scoffs. 'It's always interesting. But – did you *enjoy* it?'

I'm not sure there's such a distinct difference between those two things as she obviously thinks there is, but I reply, 'Definitely. It was a real eye-opener. It's great to get a more hands-on look and a different perspective on some of the projects, since it seems like my team are dealing with it at a higher level, so some of that nuance gets missed.'

Nadja holds my eye and smirks. 'Textbook answer,' she informs me, not unkindly.

'I liked the bit with the coolants,' I blurt out. 'What you guys are doing to find more effective ways to prolong the battery life, and stuff. But that might just be because all the test tubes and everything look kind of cool.'

There's a beat before she lets out a brash bark of laughter. '*Cool*. For the coolants. *Cool*.' She laughs again to herself for a second before shaking it off as the lift pulls to a stop on the eleventh floor, where both of us get out. She reaches to hold the door and look back at Lloyd. 'Topher's gone home, if you were looking for him.'

'Huh?' He looks up from his phone and pulls out one of his AirPods, startled and confused. Then he smiles at her, shaking his head. 'Oh, no. I just left a couple of things upstairs I need to pick up.'

It's only later, when I'm back in the lift at gone eight o'clock to head home, that I realize why his words sounded so familiar.

Chapter 10

The next day, I'm so bogged down in spreadsheets that when I look away from my screen, the pale grey outline of cells swim in front of my eyes. My brain is stuck in a series of SUMIF statements, until the jarring *ping* of a message on Teams disrupts me from this god-awful task.

> **Lloyd Fletcher**
> Is Craig at his desk? He's not online.

I open the message, wary and confused. The fact Lloyd is messaging me about *anything* is weird. I know he's been quite chatty with some of the other interns, but we haven't spoken one-on-one outside of our few less-than-great conversations so far.

It's so weird, in fact, that I message back the first thing that comes to mind.

> **Anna Sherwood**
> What, not even a 'hello Anna' first? So much for agreeing to be polite and civil, Fletcher.

Lloyd Fletcher
You last-named me? Ouch.

Hello, Anna.

Is Craig at his desk? He's not online

> He just got back from a meeting, so yes. I'm sure he'll be online in a minute if you need to ask him something.

Lloyd Fletcher is typing . . .

And then the little message disappears, and there's no reply from him. Not so much as a thank you. A moment later, his status changes to 'away'.

Well. Fine. If that's how he wants to be, fine.

I return to Excel, but now the numbers swim on the screen and I can't quite remember what I was supposed to do next. I'm still replaying the last few minutes of my work and trying to block Lloyd's weird messages out of my mind when I hear someone calling, 'Craig! Hey. Alright?'

As Lloyd walks to the bank of desks across from mine, he catches my eye and nods, half a greeting, half thanks.

Well, still. He might have at least had the time to message *thanks* before rushing on down here. It's not that difficult.

I wrench back around to face my monitor, teeth gritted . . . eyes drifting over to watch the two of them rather than focusing on my work. Craig, one of the older members of the team, who wears cufflinks and a tie without fail, stops plugging his laptop back into the dock to look up with a ready smile for Lloyd.

'Hiya, Lloyd. Haven't seen you around much lately!'

'Ah, you know me. Always keeping busy.'

'Always chatting someone's ear off,' Craig quips, and it's with a stern sort of look that a parent might give their kid – but then he rolls his eyes and settles into his seat, pushing it out from the desk to face Lloyd better. 'My turn now, is it?'

'Yep, your lucky day. It was just about the latest updates on the Phoebus IV . . .'

My ears prick up. Phoebus IV is the newest model in Arrowmile's car range; Craig looks after the project for our team, and I asked to get involved a bit since I know it's an important one.

But then I hear Craig say, 'You might be just as well to talk to Anna, actually. I asked her to pull together the report ahead of next week's meeting, so she'll probably have more up-to-date information than me.

I've got to jump on a call in a few minutes anyway. Anna,' he calls, and they both turn towards me. I blush; it's *so* obvious that I've been eavesdropping on the whole exchange. Crap. I sit up straighter and do my best to pretend I'm only just noticing them.

Lloyd's posture stiffens, and he looks less than thrilled about this development.

Yeah, well, that makes two of us.

The last thing I want is one-on-one time with Lloyd. I don't need more reminders of our night together or the kiss, or how one wrong move could ruin my entire summer.

'Anna, are you alright to take Lloyd through some of the Phoebus IV stuff?' Craig asks, completely oblivious.

'Of course.' My response is automatic; I don't want to be a 'no' person, not here. I can't afford to be. Lloyd says a quick thank you to Craig then makes his way towards me – and perches right on my desk, leaning with his hands braced against it, just inches away from me. Close enough that I can smell him. Not the cologne, this time – something softer, rich and familiar and just on the tip of my tongue, though I can't quite place it. I edge my chair back a little, and breathe through my mouth.

'So you probably already noticed, but Phoebus IV is coming in *way* under budget right now. I'm trying to work out why. Something feels off.'

There's something off about his *voice*, I want to say. Although it's steady – casual, even – it rings with quiet authority, a confidence that feels more like arrogance. He waits patiently, expectantly, for me to cough up the information he's after. I count to three before Lloyd gives me the dazzling smile I'm beginning to think must be his trademark expression.

With a smile like that and a name like his, it's no wonder everyone falls at his feet to give him anything he asks for.

I lean back in my seat a little. 'What do you need it for?'

He blinks, visibly startled. I wonder if this is the first time he's been questioned about this kind of thing, which only makes me dig my heels in further, enjoying messing with him a little too much. I cross my arms and raise my eyebrows, waiting for him to answer.

Lloyd rolls his eyes, amused. 'Because, like I said, something's not adding up, but I can't work out what. I know what happens in these kinds of projects – the lab team are so deep in the details they miss the big picture, and someone in charge tries to sugar-coat it for whoever's in charge of *them*. Someone else is always focused on protecting the investment . . .'

'And what, it's *your* job to get to the truth?'

Lloyd shrugs. 'Maybe. So – are you gonna let me look at those files, Annalise?'

I'm loath to be another person he can walk all over, but I also know that everyone will know if I don't play ball. If I'm a 'no' person, not a team player.

'Just this once, then. Go get a chair, Fletcher. I'll give you twenty minutes, and that's your lot.'

He bounces up from his spot against my desk, grabbing a nearby empty chair and swinging it into place beside me, settling low into it with his elbows on his knees. He gives me that smile again, slanted and swaggering.

'That's all I need,' he says.

It's not that I'm *avoiding* the other interns. I'm not. I spend a bunch of time with Elaine and Louis (admittedly, because we live together, but still – we take turns cooking dinner, or hang out sometimes in the evenings to watch something on Netflix). I even went to Tasha and Verity's flat the other night when they decided to do a girls' night, while all the boys went to hang out with Burnley and his PlayStation. So, I'm not avoiding them when I turn down lunch invitations – I'm just busy. And when I decline another dinner out, it's more out of paranoia for my bank balance than because I don't want to spend time with them.

When I sneak out at six in the morning, it's only so I can get into the office early to catch up on work. I know the others have an intense workload, too, but I seem to have bitten off more than I can chew.

Maybe this is why they only take second- and third-year students for the internship? Maybe that extra year or two they've got on me gives them a wealth of experience that means they aren't drowning in reports and spreadsheets and meetings like I am.

The morning is cool and pale; London is already wide awake, even if rush hour is still an hour or two off yet. I join a string of other commuters out of the Tube station at Victoria, feeling just like one of them in my blazer and sensible Marks & Spencer shoes.

Sometimes, on the rare nights out I went on at uni, it was a reminder of how young I felt. Surrounded by crowds of kids, all of them fresh-faced and barely out of school, with no inhibitions or responsibilities . . . Not like these people on their way to work. These people *matter*. They have important things to get on with, lots to do, complex lives to take care of. They don't have to worry about mean flatmates or trying to fit in.

And now, I'm one of them.

The office is quiet, the receptionist and security guard chatting lazily over steaming mugs of tea. Hopefully, my team won't be in yet and I can get a solid hour or two of quiet time to focus on the current bane of my life: this automated spreadsheet I 'volunteered' to create.

I swipe my pass, but when I go to step through the barriers, I collide straight with it.

I swipe again.

The usual *blip!* sound is more of a *BWOOP*, an aggressive indication of something wrong. Across the room, the security guard looks over with a frown, setting down his mug to make his way towards me. A red light flashes on the sensor and I clutch my pass, chest tightening. Is this it – my paranoid nightmare from my first day come to life? They know I'm not cut out for this, that I'm too young and too inexperienced and don't even know how to create a pivot table, and –

A voice slices through the ringing in my ears, just as I'm about to start hyperventilating.

'You won't get anywhere with that.'

Lloyd plucks my red lanyard out of my hands, which doesn't exactly relax me. Is that his way of telling me I'm fired? *Is* this a nightmare? It must be. Where did he even spring up from? Why is *he* here so ridiculously early?

'This is a visitor's pass,' he says. 'Didn't you get a proper one last week?'

I shake my head. I think, if I open my mouth, I might

vomit all over his shoes. *Visitor's pass*. Of course. I'm not being sent away in disgrace. As I get a grip on my racing heart, I follow Lloyd over to the desk as he chats to the security guard and receptionist, then ushers me over to stand against the wall.

I'm too busy berating myself for being such an idiot that I forget to smile when the receptionist takes my photo, but too afraid of making even *more* of a scene this morning to ask to do it again. I'll have to put up with a mug shot on my new lanyard.

'Michaela didn't say anything about getting a pass,' I finally manage to tell Lloyd, who has decided to wait with me. 'I didn't really think about it, I guess.'

'She probably just forgot. Could've been worse – what if you'd stayed late, and gotten stuck? I know you were really keen about this internship, but getting locked in and having to sleep at the office? That's a little *too* far.'

I laugh, and Lloyd smiles broadly. I notice his shoulders relax and wonder if that's because of me. Like he was worried about my reaction, or something.

'Nope. Just here so obscenely early that this, apparently, was a sign I should've stayed in bed.'

Just then, the receptionist interrupts, handing Lloyd my new pass. 'Here you go.'

Lloyd looks at the photo, smiling – small and

earnest, not like the way he does around the office all the time. He offers it to me. 'Nice picture.'

The lanyard is blue this time – Arrowmile cobalt – with my name and photo printed on the pass instead of VISITOR. As I take it, my fingers brush against Lloyd's, and I shiver at the contact, the heat of his skin – the memory of his hand in mine, and how it felt when he kissed me.

He's staring at me like he's thinking the same thing. Both of us hardly daring to breathe, both still holding the pass with my fingers against his. His lips part, like he wants to say something – something part of me wants to hear.

But before he can, I snatch my hand back, the pass with it, and blurt, 'Thanks, but it's really not. Look at me – I'm grumpy as anything.'

I hold it up and, to ruin the moment even more, mimic the face I'm pulling in the photo. But Lloyd just cocks his head slightly to one side, mouth tilting up in a lopsided smile that makes my heart lurch.

'You're not grumpy,' he says, and somehow it doesn't feel like he's only talking about the picture. 'Just a little fierce.'

I look at it again, preferring the sight of my own miserable, grainy face to the endearing expression on Lloyd's face that makes me long to touch him again – to trace the line of his lips with my thumb, brush his fingers with mine as I draw myself close.

I stare determinedly at the photo, until Lloyd steps backwards, towards the barriers, and says, 'Shall we go up?' and the moment is finally broken.

He's not wrong, though. I do look a little bit fierce in the photo.

I like that.

This time, I get through the barriers no problem.

'So why are you here obscenely early?' he asks over his shoulder as I follow him to the lifts.

Mind your own business, Fletcher. What's it to do with you?

I debate my response for a minute before deciding that if we talk about work, it should stop things getting tense like they did just now. So I admit, 'I'm having some Excel trouble. Knowing which formula to use and getting them to work properly. Currently my whole spreadsheet is just a bunch of "#VALUE" errors. It's probably a super-easy fix if you know what you're looking for, but . . . I don't.'

'Been there.' Lloyd nods sympathetically, but doesn't miss a beat before smiling and saying, 'I can help you out, if you like? I had some stuff I wanted to get through this morning ahead of a few meetings, but it'll keep.'

'You'd . . . do that?'

I'm surprised he's willing to help me, after I was so difficult about helping *him* just yesterday when he wanted some info about the Phoebus IV. After I've been difficult, full stop. I know we said we'd be polite, but I don't think I've exactly been nice and friendly towards Lloyd so far.

'Sure. Why not? Wouldn't be the first time I've helped out an intern. Plus, I do know my way around the sheets.'

He winks, making a big joke of it – then seems to realize what his corny joke is implying, and *who* he's saying it to. Embarrassment colours his face and his hands start to gesture wildly. I shrink back, feeling like I've just been punched in the gut.

'Spreadsheets. *The spreadsheets*,' he amends quickly, but it's too late.

Even if I were willing to accept help, it's a good reminder of why Lloyd is the last person I can ask for it.

The lift stops at the eleventh floor, and I get out.

'That's okay,' I tell Lloyd. 'I wouldn't want to add to your reputation of *just* being the guy who "helps out" the interns.'

'Annalise . . .'

I wait, but he doesn't have an excuse to offer. He just sighs, dejected, and we part ways.

At my desk, I check my phone as I wait for my computer to come to life, and there's another gut-punch moment when I see a text notification on my screen.

> Hi sweetie! Saw your fab news about the internship. How's it going?! Which company are you at? If you ever need a little business advice, you know where to find me!

Scowling, I clear the notification off my screen.

It's a bit rich that after all the years Mum dropped off the face of the earth, *now* she wants to talk – to give me business advice, imparting all the pearls of wisdom she learned while she was out there being a boss instead of being my mum. What a warm and fuzzy reunion I bet that'd be.

Well, I don't need it. I don't need her help, or Lloyd Fletcher's help, or anybody's. I can do this all by myself.

Correction: I *will* do this all by myself, just like I've always done.

Chapter 11

Sunlight streams through the windows in wide yellow stripes, casting a glare on computer monitors and a pall over the mood in the office as the day wanes on. People would rather be anywhere but shut up in the office, dashing between meetings in stuffy rooms or tap-tap-tapping away at their keyboards with a steaming cup of coffee beside them and sweat beading on the back of their necks. Somewhere, a few banks of desks away, someone has a playlist of pop songs murmuring out of their computer. It makes heads bob distractedly and feet tap lazily, and adds insult to injury that we're not basking on picnic blankets enjoying cold ciders and ice creams somewhere.

It's the end of June and almost a month into the Arrowmile internship.

Things have ramped up *a lot* in the last two weeks. I told Dad it was like riding a bike with the stabilizers on at first, but now it's more like being pushed out of a plane with a thumbs up while trying to remember which cord deploys the parachute.

Some of that, I know, is my own fault. When someone asks if I can do something, the answer is always an unhesitating 'yes'. Or sometimes I overhear things my team are working on and ask if I can help out, in an attempt to prove myself.

After all, I'm not here to coast through. If I'd wanted an easy summer, I would've stayed at home.

So the answer is always yes, I can do that. And the question is always, can I get involved in that?

This is nothing new, though. I'm used to pushing my limits, tiptoeing just along the edge of being too burnt-out to function. I make sure to put in the effort with the other interns, going out enough that they keep inviting me, missing enough dinners and drinks that I can catch up on sleep. Or work. Whichever needs my attention most at the time.

It's a delicate balance, because they're always making new plans – heading out to posh cocktail bars or chic Instagrammable restaurants they stumbled across on some influencer's TikTok . . .

As much as the others are constantly hanging out together and enjoying themselves, whenever we all talk about work, it's clear that everybody is trying to suss out the competition. They all want one of those coveted full-time roles when they graduate; they need to know that they're not just doing *their* best, but doing better than everybody else. I wonder if I'm the only person downplaying how hard I'm working – although while I'm scared of them calling me 'boring', they might be doing it to lull everyone else into a false sense of security. More than once, someone has joked about outright sabotaging another intern over something so silly, it's obviously a joke – but still. It adds to the pressure, a little more.

I honestly don't know where they find the energy to socialize as much as they do – or the money. Clearly, they're not too concerned with saving as much as they can ahead of their next term at uni, and would rather enjoy the moment.

Today is payday, and tonight, they're going to the Shard for drinks. It's eye-wateringly expensive, so I made some excuses to avoid joining them.

Distracted by the nagging worry that they'll start excluding me if I don't go out, and listless in the heat, I take a break from an email I've been trying to write for the last ten minutes and open up the internet browser instead. A brief respite before I get back to the grind, that's all. One of the open tabs is the Zara website, where I have a basket full of pretty, office-appropriate outfits that I'll never buy, but like daydreaming over.

There's a sudden weight against the back of my chair, hands that startle me out of my daydream, and a voice too close that says, 'Working hard or hardly working, Barbie?'

I click hastily to another tab – although that one's not much less embarrassing: a step-by-step tutorial on VLOOKUP IF statements in Excel, which I still haven't figured out. (I might have ultimately succeeded in my automated report for Michaela, but now the whole team seem to think I'm a whizz and keep asking me to rebuild their spreadsheets better.)

Near my ear, Lloyd laughs. 'Don't worry, I won't tell on you.'

I crane my neck to look around just in time to see him wink, and scowl at him. 'Can you let go of my chair, please? And did you just call me *Barbie*?'

He lets go, allowing me to swivel my chair to face him. His usual bright smile is spread across his face, and he seems undeterred by my frown or the way my arms are crossed, my spine stiff.

Instead, he just gestures at me with one hand. 'Yeah. Because of the bright pink. Or were you going for more of a *Legally Blonde* thing?'

I cringe.

He doesn't need to know it was very much originally a *Legally Blonde* thing – or that I decided to retire this dress after taking stock of what everybody else wore to work during my first week here. It hadn't taken me long to notice that the bubblegum-pink dress I initially loved so much was . . .

Well. It was *loud*.

Everyone else is always in blues and browns, beiges and whites, blacks and greys. There's the occasional splash of colour in a floral blouse. I saw someone in olive green, once, and it felt like they might as well have been in neon.

So, I decided not to wear the pink dress again – until today, when everything else was in the wash, and this was a last resort.

But at Lloyd's 'Barbie' comment, my bright pink dress suddenly feels like a blinding beacon. Immature, like a kid playing dress-up – and not in the cool Margot Robbie *Barbie*-movie kind of way.

I fidget with the sleeve, readjusting it on my shoulder. 'Was there something you needed, or are you just here to make a nuisance of yourself?'

He clasps both hands to his chest. 'Annalise, you *wound* me. To think I would be trying to misuse your precious time by simply being a pest, rather than having a worthwhile reason to be here . . .'

I give him a flat look.

And, as he's done several times over the last couple of weeks, he drags a spare chair over, plonks himself into it, scoots it so close that the wheels of our chairs get caught, and leans over my desk before asking me about one of the ongoing projects.

'How's the budget looking on the Vane engine?' he asks.

With a sigh, I close Chrome and pull up the documents for Vane, pointing out the places it's over budget right now. I'm all too aware that my tone is clipped and irritated, but I can't help it.

The rest of my team are usually so busy that they ask me to help Lloyd out, and I can hardly refuse – but I hate that they all expect me to immediately drop whatever I'm doing because whatever Lloyd Fletcher wants *must* be more urgent and more important than anything else I'm doing. It grates on me – and while I can't take it out on my team, I don't mind letting Lloyd know just how much of a pain in the arse he's being.

So, *okay*, he had a point about something being missed in the Phoebus IV reports – some rounds of testing were overlooked, so while everything looked pretty good on paper, it was actually behind schedule.

Trust Lloyd to be heralded as a hero for catching it.

For the next half hour, I go through the updates on the Vane engine, and although I like to make it *abundantly* clear to Lloyd that whenever he does this to me, it's a great inconvenience – it actually *is* quite helpful today. I get to treat it as a little practice run for when I actually present this on Monday, which is a pretty big deal. It's my first time *giving* a presentation, not just compiling it or sharing with the rest of the team.

'What happened here?' he asks, pointing at the screen, the red bar signifying 'cost of component materials' that is way higher than its accompanying grey line for 'projected costs'.

'*That* was your experimental coolant.'

Lloyd gives me a funny look, and not just because I sound like I'm accusing him personally. 'That's accounted for under Phoebus IV.'

'It's *supposed* to be. But when I tried to bring that up, it didn't go down very well.'

'Who'd you talk to?'

'Well, Fiona in R&D wouldn't reply to my emails, so Dylan said he'd speak to her, but *she* said it was one for Finance to deal with, and *they* told me it was down to the project manager in the labs, who told me it would have to be handled by R&D if it needed to be re-allocated somewhere else, so . . .'

Lloyd's mouth twists downward and his eyebrows scrunch up, an expression full of sympathy. *Been there*, it says, just like when I told him about my battle with Excel a couple of weeks ago.

And I pounce, turning sharply towards him and lifting my index finger to him in warning. He's leaning so close that I almost poke him in the nose. 'No. I know what you're thinking, and *no*. Don't you dare.'

'But if you'd just –'

'*No*.'

'Listen, I'll just drop by Fiona's desk before I go back upstairs, and –'

'Well, I could do that!'

'So why don't you?'

'Because – because . . .' Because it seems *rude*. Because she might be busy and have more urgent things to deal with, and I don't want to 'stop by' with something so important. She'll want facts and figures, all the things I put in my original email to back up what I was trying to explain, which she already *ignored* . . .

I get embarrassed just thinking about it, squirming in my seat.

'You think she won't make time for you?' Lloyd guesses, too accurately.

'I don't need *you* to swan in and fix my problems. It's – it's not even a problem! In fact, I'm going to bring it up at the meeting next week. Fiona will be there, and so will Simon from Finance, *and* the project manager. Someone will have to own up and take responsibility, if they're all put on the spot.'

I hope.

God, I hope. I don't have a backup plan, otherwise.

But Lloyd looks – sort of *impressed*, actually. He hums quietly, nodding, and clicks onto the next slide to scan that one. I feel a little flicker of warmth in my chest, and have to suppress a smile before he notices and has one more thing to feel smug about.

We finally wrap up when my computer dings, a reminder popping up on screen that I have a meeting in fifteen minutes.

Lloyd starts to get up, and does that thing where he only stands halfway, one hand braced against the desk and the other on the arm of his chair.

'Does that thing', like I know all his quirks and habits by now. I don't.

But I do know this one.

'Can you –'

'Yes, Fletcher, I will send you the slide deck, so you can give me copious notes which I may or may not choose to take on board.'

He grins at me. I should be used to it, but I'm not. It's no less heart-stopping than it was the first time.

This time, he winks, and I think my heart actually *does* stop for a moment. He should have no right to look so bloody good all the time.

'You're a star. Thanks, Annalise.'

'I've *told* you it's just Anna.'

'Whatever you say, Barbie.'

'You call me Barbie one more time, I'll report you to HR.'

'And risk them bringing up your file and realizing you're only a first-year?' he asks in a low, teasing voice that draws me in closer against all my better instincts. He smirks and pushes away from the desk – from me. 'Sure thing. *Barbie.*'

'Oh, piss off already, Fletcher.'

With Lloyd's notes on my presentation landing in my inbox at four o'clock that afternoon, I push away from my desk and decide to take a breather. Loath as I am to admit it, he's made some good points. I don't want Lloyd's help, but he *is* the font of all Arrowmile knowledge – I've grudgingly come to accept that I'd be silly to ignore that.

The first time he sent me back a pile of notes, I was mortified. I wasn't expecting them, and immediately messaged him to remind him in *no uncertain terms* that I did *not* need his help and did not *want* his help, either.

Lloyd was quick to point out that he's pretty well known across the office for giving notes and feedback on things – I wasn't getting any kind of special treatment.

Anyway, I'll tackle this latest batch of notes this evening; I'll only stress about them all night otherwise. I don't mind staying late, but I *do* think I should take a break.

Outside, I take a gulp of fresh air. It's somehow cooler out in the blazing sunshine and still city heat than it was in the office, and the sun feels good on my skin, breathing a little life back into me. I walk to one of the nice coffee shops a few streets over to grab myself a Frappuccino and a snack.

I'm not paying very much attention as I go back into the office; my mind is already on the details of the Vane engine and Lloyd's notes. There's a mass exodus underway as people escape a little bit early to go and make the most of the summer afternoon. I have to wait for a break in the tide to find an empty barrier to swipe my way through, and then wait for the lift, which seems to stop on almost every floor on its way down.

But finally, the lift makes it to the ground floor, and I wriggle past the group of people on their way out. I reach for the button for the eleventh floor.

'Sorry, do you mind pressing number twelve as well?' says a voice behind me, and I jump out of my skin, choking on the Frappuccino I just took a sip of; I hadn't realized there was anybody else in here.

Coughing into the back of my right hand, I jab the button with my left.

'Thanks. I've been stuck in here ages trying to get out. But you know our motto – at Arrowmile, we always *strive to keep moving forward*,' my lift-mate jokes, and there's something familiar about the way he speaks . . .

I'm already rolling my eyes, turning to face Lloyd with a wholly unimpressed look.

'I'm surprised you didn't just command your legions of adoring subjects to step aside for you to –'

Oh.

'Oh.'

Crap.

'You're . . .'

Not Lloyd, but . . . I have to pause to take a better look, feeling like my brain has stalled. The guy is a bit older than me, with thick dark hair and brown skin like Lloyd, green eyes and a lean stature, but he's decidedly *not* Lloyd. His hair is cut shorter, his nose is smaller, and he's skinny where Lloyd is slightly more built.

Also, he's dressed very casually in green shorts, a faded band T-shirt, and a pair of brown-framed glasses.

So, no, not Lloyd.

His mouth pulls into a wide smile, and while it's uncannily similar to Lloyd's, it's *not quite* the same. It's not as all-consuming, as infectious, as Lloyd's smile.

'Wrong Fletcher,' not-Lloyd tells me. He sticks out a hand towards me. 'I'm Will. His –'

'His brother, right, yes, God, I'm – I'm so sorry, I just, um . . .'

Just made an atrocious first impression on the CEO's other son. Brilliant. Well done, Anna, gold star.

I trail off helplessly, cheeks burning, and then look at Will's outstretched hand and gesture with my own hands: Frappuccino in one, brown bag of cake and panini in the other. Will grimaces and drops his hand back to his side, trying to laugh it off.

I almost ask what he's doing here, because it's been a month and this is the first time I've seen Lloyd's brother around the office. Actually – nobody's even *talked* about him. The only reason I know Will exists is because Lloyd mentioned him that night by the river. Why isn't he hanging around the office like Lloyd, making a nuisance of himself? He's clearly not as arrogant as his brother, but is he invested in the goings-on at Arrowmile like him?

Has he hooked up with interns in the past, too?

No – I can't ask that. That's a bad route to go down.

'Hi,' I say again, getting more of a grip on myself – and giving him a proper smile, this time. 'Will. I'm Anna. I'm on the internship programme. Sorry about that . . . I just –'

'It's all good.' The smile he gives me this time is sincere, but small and fleeting. Where Lloyd takes up so much space, Will leans against the back wall of the lift and seems to shrink into it. I'm not sure what to say – what kind of polite small talk will carry us through the next twenty seconds without being cut to a sudden, awkward end. Instead, we lapse into silence until the lift eases to a halt and the doors slide open.

'Well, see you,' I say.

I get out, and only make it a short way when I hear a hand catch the doors and Will hurrying after me. I stop and he tries to fall in step, but ends up bumping into me and has to stumble around me to prevent us both from crashing to the floor. He flings a hand to my shoulder to steady me. My coffee and snacks survive – Will's pride, not so much. I can't help but laugh at the flustered, embarrassed look on his face.

'Sorry,' he says. 'So, you're on the internship programme? How's it going?'

I think he's only asking to be polite, but say, 'It's tough, but I'm really enjoying it. I'm guessing you had more exciting ways to spend your summer than working here with us?'

'Ah. Um. Yeah. Something like that.' He lets out a breath of laughter that I think is supposed to sound nonchalant, but is more of a self-deprecating snort. He reaches up to scrub a hand through his hair a few times, making it stick up at odd angles.

'You didn't take a year out like your brother, then?'

'Oh, definitely not,' he says. 'So, you know Lloyd, huh?'

I look at him for a long moment, confused. I settle on an answer that's honest – maybe, judging by how dry my tone is, it's a little *too* honest. 'Doesn't everyone?'

Will laughs. 'Right. You're not his biggest fan, I take it.'

To put it mildly.

Suddenly, I wonder if Will knows about *me*. Would Lloyd have told him about our kiss? Would he have talked to his twin about how angry I was when I realized who he was? It had sounded like they were close when he talked about Will before, but . . . Well, a lot of things sounded different to the reality that night.

'What gave me away?' I ask Will.

'Well, you looked a little bit like you were going to either throttle me or dump your coffee over me when you thought I was him.'

'I would *never*,' I inform him, 'waste such a good coffee on him.'

'Oh, I don't know. I probably would.' Will laughs, and I warm to him a little more. He opens his mouth, second-guesses whatever he wants to say, but then blurts in a rush, 'Everyone normally fawns all over him around here.'

'They don't fawn over you?'

He's visibly surprised by the mere idea of it, and I suddenly feel kind of bad for him. I should have guessed Lloyd would be *that* sibling: the one stealing all the limelight, pushing his twin out of the picture because he can't share. I mean, this *is* the same guy who let his brother get a tattoo of SpongeBob SquarePants on his bum but bailed out of getting his own.

Not to mention the guy who pretended not to know me to save his own reputation.

'It's kind of like you said,' he tells me at last, 'I don't hang around here much. I'm just here to drag Lloyd away – we've got plans with some friends soon, and I know what he's like.'

I scoff before I can catch myself, thinking – *yeah*, he's pretty egocentric, and don't I know it. But Will starts to say something, then reconsiders, and I realize that's not what he meant at all, and I've messed up – again.

His mouth closes into a smile that at first I think is fond, but there's a sadness to the edges of it that seems to weigh it down, and he lets out a quiet sigh. He pushes his glasses a little further up his nose and then finally tells me, 'I know my brother can seem like a prat sometimes, but try not to hold it against him.'

'Don't you have to say that? You're his brother.'

'That's exactly why I *don't* have to say it. Anyway – I'd better go find him. I'll tell him you said hi?'

'Sure. Nice to meet you.'

'It was good to meet you too, Annalise.'

Will smiles broadly at me, stepping around me to head back to the lifts. He raises a hand in farewell, and it's only after he disappears behind the doors on the way to the twelfth floor that I realize what he called me.

Maybe Lloyd did tell his brother about me after all.

Chapter 12

On Friday night, the office is dead and I've been hunched at my desk for so long that the motion-sensor lights have turned themselves off.

Elaine texted earlier asking where I was, since I wasn't back at the flat; I told her I'd gone to meet some other friends – much easier than explaining I'm still in the office at midnight because I'm struggling to keep up with the immense workload I've taken on.

Being a 'yes' person is seriously backfiring on me.

A tiny hammer is pounding against the inside of my skull and my eyes are feeling the strain of staring at the screen so long. I save my work and close the laptop, getting up to stretch. The lights flicker back to life; it's so quiet I can hear the low whirr of the bulbs.

It's probably time to call it a night, but first, I need a cup of chamomile tea to unwind, or a big glass of water. Hopefully there are some snacks left in the kitchen I can grab, too . . .

I have no luck on free food in the kitchen on my floor of the office, but there was a big board meeting upstairs this afternoon, so there's every chance there's something left in the fridge on the twelfth floor. Worth a shot, anyway.

Upstairs, I make a beeline for the kitchen area, lights sputtering on in my wake.

And through the silence that blankets the entire floor, a voice cries out –

'*Bloody hell*, you scared the life out of me!'

I jump back with a shout. I think I might even black out for a second from the fright, but that could just be a side-effect of exhaustion. Gulping down a breath, I straighten back up, eyes adjusting again in the new light to see someone (very literally) lying low on the sofa in the nearby break-out area.

Lloyd's head peeks up, barely visible over the back of the low sofa. His knees hook over the arm, feet dangling to the floor. Papers and files are splayed out on one of the tables nearby, and his face is illuminated by the blue light of a laptop screen resting on his chest.

It reflects off his glasses, which is when I realize aloud, 'You're wearing glasses. I didn't know you wore glasses.'

Lloyd grimaces. He puts the laptop aside, on top of his sprawled collection of papers, and then he gets up in the same kind of way I just did – stretching out his neck, his back, fingers working under his glasses to rub his eyes. He doesn't seem to notice the smudge he leaves behind on one of the lenses.

He looks ... different, somehow. Same pair of smart-casual trousers and same shirt with the sleeves rolled up as he normally wears around the office, but now it looks rumpled. Softer. Some of his curls spring up around his temples, unruly and tousled, and others are squashed flat where he's been lying on the sofa. The glasses are large, squarish, with thick black frames; they suit him, complement the lines of his high cheekbones and jaw, and make him look older – more sophisticated. A few butterflies cartwheel around my stomach, but I can't bring myself to look away.

He looks disoriented, oddly vulnerable, and more like the boy I first met.

'What're you still doing here?' he asks me. His voice is thick, a hoarse quality catching on the consonants; not quite sleepy, but more from disuse. 'It's gone midnight.'

'I could ask you the same thing.' I finish making my way into the kitchenette and Lloyd follows. I set down a mug to make myself some tea and silently offer him one too. He nods. 'I had to make a few changes to my presentation, and it's easier to rehearse when you're not worried about people overhearing.'

Lloyd looks – for once – guilty. 'You're not here this late just because of me, are you? I didn't think my notes were *that* drastic.'

'It's not all about you,' I say, surprised when it comes out more like a joke, and even more surprised when he smiles in a soft, unguarded way that makes me smile back. 'It turns out I'm too much of a people-pleaser and can't manage my workload as efficiently as I thought I could. *And* I'm too proud to tell my manager I've taken too much on.'

'Ah,' he says gently. 'That checks.'

'What about you? I didn't realize you had to work overtime to terrorize staff with feedback nobody asked you for. I thought that was just a natural talent.'

Lloyd gives me a withering look, but he's still smiling. 'I had some things to catch up on. Lost track of time.'

'Wow. *Wow*. You realize how super vague that sounds, right?'

'You don't say?' Lloyd chuckles as he collects the milk for me. He stays crouched in front of the fridge before pulling out a plate with a quarter of a chocolate cake on. The letters 'Ha' and 'Bir' are written on it in pale cream icing. My stomach growls at the sight of it.

'Think anybody's going to miss this come Monday morning?'

'I hope not.'

As I make the tea, Lloyd unwraps the clingfilm covering the plate of cake and finds two forks. I expect us to go back to his sofa, but he heads for one of the tall tables in the kitchen instead. I take a fork and dig in unceremoniously, scoffing down mouthfuls of slightly dry fudge cake like it's the greatest thing I've ever tasted. And after a self-imposed sixteen-hour work day, it kind of is.

'Big plans for the weekend?' I ask him, defaulting to the usual 'Friday' office small talk.

He shrugs, humming noncommittally. 'How about you? Hopefully you're not going to be chained to your desk all weekend.'

'No. A bunch of us were going to order some pizzas and watch a movie tomorrow night. Burnley and Izzy organized it. I'll have plenty of time to catch up on the sleep I'm missing tonight,' I joke, but even I can hear how exhausted I sound. I try – and fail – to stifle a yawn.

'You know, you can just tell your boss you need extra time to work on things. Or say "no" when they ask you to do something,' Lloyd says. There's more gravity to the conversation now; it prickles along my skin and sits leaden in my stomach.

'Yes, *thank you*, I am aware.'

'Oh, so you're just incapable of doing so.'

I want to bite back, but he's not wrong. I shrug instead, conceding the point.

'Can I ask you something?'

The cute guy sat across from me, wearing glasses and rumpled clothes, carefully picking up a large scoop of buttercream icing on his fork, meets my eyes for a moment. The harsh lights of the office are softened somehow by the darkness that pours in from the large window behind him. And just like that, in five words, I'm back to having a strange and unexpected and beautiful night cloaked in the midnight magic of the city with a boy who asks me, *Tell me something true.*

I'm still not sure which version of Lloyd Fletcher is true.

I tell him, 'I get the feeling you will anyway, so sure. Go ahead.'

'It's just ... The way you talked about this internship ... And now, overworking yourself like this ... I've just gotta wonder – why?'

'Why? What do you mean, *why*?'

'You know. Why it's so important to you. Why you act like it's the be-all, end-all. Like everything is hingeing on this and if you don't kill yourself for it now, it's not going to be worth it. I know you're the kind of person to "work hard, play later", but . . . I mean, you don't think it's a little extreme, burning yourself out for a job you'll be leaving behind in another two months?'

'Okay well, *one*, I'm not burning myself out.' Yet. Not quite. Please ask again later. 'And *two*, you know what a big deal this is. If it goes well . . . An internship like this could change my whole future. It could guarantee me a job when I graduate, or at least improve my chances of getting a really good one somewhere else.'

'What does that even mean, "a good job"?'

'Well. It's . . . You know.'

Lloyd fixes me with a look as if to say no, he doesn't know – but really it says that he *does* know, he just wants to make me say it. There's an edge to it, and no hint of a smile on his face anymore. The light tone of conversation as we considered if the leftover birthday cake would be missed is suddenly long gone.

A good job is *money*, but not the kind that buys nice handbags or shoes with red soles like Mum would wear. The kind that sits there for a rainy day, just in case, that means not having to worry. The kind that means I don't have to worry if buying that hideously over-priced textbook means I'll be living on baked potatoes and toast for the next month. The kind that means opportunities, being able to choose my future. Possibilities.

It's security, the kind I have to work towards now so that later, when I have my own family, I won't feel the need to walk out on them in search of something *better*, the way Mum did.

Instead of giving Lloyd the answer he thinks he already knows, I say, 'Maybe to you, it's only three months, so that means it's not worth the effort. But to me, this is *only* three months – and if I use that time right, it might change the next thirty years of my life. I don't want to waste it.'

'Yeah, I see that. But . . . I guess what I'm asking is, what does Annalise Sherwood want to do with her life that *this* internship is what's going to make all the difference?'

'Now you sound like the guy who interviewed me for this role.'

A dry smirk flits across Lloyd's mouth. 'Humour me.'

It would be easy to tell him to bugger off, to snatch up the plate of cake and stalk off with my head held high. I could tell him, again, that I can't expect Topher Fletcher's son, CEO-in-training, to understand.

But the chocolate cake tastes a little bitter and after I finally manage to swallow a mouthful, I fidget with my fork for a minute before setting it down. I can't quite meet Lloyd's eyes, but imagine he's still the person he was that first night we met. It was easy to bare my soul to that Lloyd.

I want him to understand so he'll stop asking – but more than that, I find I simply want to *tell him*.

'I guess . . . I guess I don't know how *not* to work hard or give my all to things. And – so my dad's a teacher, I think I told you that, but he really loves his job. It's less like *work* for him and more . . . purpose, I think? I kind of want to find that. And if I have a good job, that sets me up, you know? Opens doors. Gives me a leg up, or whatever. It means I get to find something like that for myself, if I want. And like I said, I'm a people-pleaser, so, that's kind of a factor.'

'What about your mum? She's . . . not around much, right?'

'No,' I tell Lloyd. 'She's not around much. She hasn't been since I was little. Dad met Gina – my stepmum – not long after though. Mum was . . . She's . . . It's like life was a series of tick-box exercises, and she had to make sure she got them all. Keep pushing to be the best.'

One of Lloyd's eyebrows goes up slightly, his mouth tilting with it. 'Three guesses where you get that from, then.'

'That's different. *I'm* different.'

'If you say so.'

'I am. I'm – I don't want to stomp all over everybody else just so that *I* can succeed. Throw them under the bus while I focus only on myself. I want . . . I want to do it *for* other people, if that makes sense. For whoever I am in the future. Whatever family I might have.'

'Is that what she did with you – threw you under the bus? Why you don't want to talk to her when she gets in touch?'

'Remember you told me your mum used to make costumes for you and Will for school plays and stuff? I don't have those kind of warm, fuzzy memories. Mine never did anything like that. She lived to work, and having a family was . . . an inconvenience, I guess? Like we could never stack up against her career. That's how it always felt, anyway. She definitely didn't fight for custody after she and my dad split up. I barely even got a birthday card on time until recently.'

I say this mostly to the kettle, looking off to the other side of the kitchen and keeping Lloyd only in my periphery. I notice the way his face crumples in sympathy, the judgement there a moment ago easing away in an instant.

'And besides,' I confess, before I can talk myself out of saying it out loud, 'my work ethic is . . . kind of an escape. I know how sad that sounds, okay? So you don't need to tell me. But if I'm busy with studying or after-school clubs or a job or something, then it's just . . . easier, to pretend that's why people didn't invite me to do things. You know I said my ex called me cold and unlikeable when we broke up? It's because I *am*. I've never been good at making friends. I'm not good at making people like me – but here, I don't have to be likeable. I just have to do a good job.'

The noise Lloyd lets out is sad and whisper-quiet, something that might be a sigh or might be my name. I keep my gaze far away from him; I don't need to see the pity on his face, or – worse, that he understands because, deep down, he doesn't *actually* believe I'm likeable. Then I square my shoulders, bracing myself before I turn to face him again.

'So, to answer your question, I don't know what I want to do with my life, exactly. But I do know I want to give myself all the advantages I can, so I can choose when I'm ready – and working hard is something I *can* do. Not all of us have that silver-spoon life with the whole world at our feet, swanning around aimlessly in our millionaire father's offices on our *gap yah*.'

Lloyd has the good grace to wince, discomfited. 'It's not . . . exactly a gap year. And I don't *swan around*. I've got a job to do.'

'You absolutely do swan around,' I say, latching on to this excuse to move on from talking about myself. I desperately, desperately do not want to talk about me anymore. 'And what *job*, exactly? Nobody even knows what you do! You're always here, there and everywhere, getting stuck into all sorts ... You probably have some gimmicky title and a nice big salary, and it's all an excuse to act like the big man, and go on some ridiculous power trip.'

'Okay, I'm *definitely* not on a power trip. And not that it should matter, but I'm not on the payroll, either, and I don't have some fancy job title.'

'Then what *do* you do around here?'

'Act like the big man, apparently. I must be compensating for something,' he jokes before laughing at himself, and it's infectious enough that I crack a smile too. It breaks some of the tension, and I let go of the worry that I'll be faced with his pity or his judgement from what I just told him about myself. This Lloyd, I feel like I can trust.

Simply curious, now, I ask, 'What *are* all those papers for, keeping you here so late on a Friday night? Don't you have, like, I don't know, plans to lurk in bars spying on your interns?'

'Oh, *ha-ha*. My dad's a big-picture guy, so I ... make sure the details don't fall through the cracks. Keep an eye on things. See that it runs smoothly. Old habits, I guess.' His smile is wide, his tone flippant, but there's an undercurrent to his words that I don't quite understand. Before I get a chance to ask him about it, though, he takes a deep breath and says, 'So I hear you ran into Will the other day,' and digs into the cake again, taking a giant mouthful.

Lloyd's never been shy about throwing his weight around in the office before, though admittedly always with a smile. It's weird that he's suddenly avoiding talking about whatever he's working on right now – but maybe it's above my pay grade.

'Yeah. Will seems great. Really friendly.'

Lloyd cuts me a look, laughter dancing in his eyes. 'Not like me?'

'Oh, you're polar opposites for sure.' There's a beat, and then I can't help but ask, as casually as I can, 'So . . . did you tell him about us?'

I expect him to say, *There's nothing to tell*, or maybe try to fob me off by saying, *Why would I do that?*

I'm surprised when Lloyd's face scrunches up, bemused, and he says, 'Why wouldn't I have told him about you?' like it's that simple.

Maybe it was, for the boy with his kissable smile who falls in love with someone new every week, giving his heart away so freely.

'He called me Annalise.'

'So?'

So, what did you tell him? Were you disappointed by the kiss, embarrassed by me, do you think I was an idiot? Did you feel guilty after I confronted you, and ask him for advice? Did you regret playing games with me, did you like me the way I liked you that night?

'I don't go by Annalise. You're the only person here who calls me that.'

'Well, now Will does, too.' He grins at me, wide and warm, eyes crinkling at the corners. It makes his glasses slip down his nose a little; I want to push them back into place and trace the shadow of stubble along his jaw, following along the curve of his smile.

Except I don't, obviously, because this is the same guy who pretended not to know me and claimed that he was 'doing me a favour' by sparing my reputation from rumours of hooking up with the boss's son. And anyway, I've got more important things to concentrate on this summer.

I grip my fork tighter, poking at some of the cake. 'Will isn't around here much though, is he? Definitely not like you. Nobody's ever really mentioned him, which, the more I think about it, is *weird*. Unless he doesn't want to spend his summer hanging around here? Or –'

'He doesn't. I mean, he's just . . . you know, it's not his thing so much.'

'But it's yours.'

The pause before Lloyd says, 'Yeah. It is,' goes on just a little too long.

It doesn't seem fair that I gave him such an honest response when he wanted to know about me, but his own answers are still vague half-truths, cryptic and leaving me with even more questions. I suppose I haven't really invited much openness from him, but that's not just *my* fault. He's the one who preferred to act like we were strangers instead of just talking to me; he can't really blame me for being stand-offish.

I want to know what he's hiding. I want to know all the complex, messy truths he's glossing over. I want to know which Lloyd is the real one.

But I can tell, tonight is not the night for that. The mood has shifted; Lloyd's earlier vulnerability has vanished, and the look on his face now is more akin to the shiny, self-important one he usually wears around the office. I see it in the slant of his mouth, the slight upward arch of his eyebrows, the way he stretches his legs out and slings an arm over the back of his chair to take up more space than necessary. Our conversation's run its course; I can't help but feel disappointed.

There's an unspoken mutual agreement to pick up

our things and head back to our work. Lloyd scrapes the last crumbs of cake into the bin and takes my now-empty mug from me to wash up.

'Are you staying much longer?' he asks.

'No. I think I've run out of steam for the night.'

He nods. 'I've still got a couple of things to get through. I can walk you to the Tube station though, if you want?'

'Thanks, but you don't need to. It's fine. Don't stay too late, okay?'

When I get back to my desk downstairs, I click my laptop back to life to double-check all my documents are saved before I log off properly, and see a new Teams message.

Lloyd Fletcher
Goodnight, Annalise. Thanks for the chat.

PS. Don't tell anyone how late I was here – it'll ruin my devil-may-care reputation.

Anna Sherwood
I'll add it to the list of secrets I'm keeping about you. Night, Fletcher.

And when I finally close my computer and head out for the night, I'm almost looking forward to maybe running into Lloyd on Monday.

NEW EMAIL DRAFT

Dear Lloyd,

I don't want to spend time getting to know you. I don't want to spend any time at all with you, but you seem to be making it impossible to do anything else. It'd be a lot easier if you weren't always popping up and asking me stuff about projects. (Why do you do that, anyway? Does it have something to do with whatever you were working on tonight?)

But I am getting to know you, and it feels like the more time I spend with you, the less I actually do know you. I don't know if I'm supposed to be looking for the guy who kissed me, the golden boy of Arrowmile, or someone else. I resent that you occupy enough space in my brain that I keep wondering. I resent how much I want to like you.

Who are you, Lloyd Fletcher? And why do I want to know you so badly?

So much for not letting anything distract me this summer. Consider me suitably distracted.

Sincerely Yours,
Anna Sherwood

Chapter 13

Sitting squashed between some of the girls on a sofa, bloated from eating too much pizza, and with a bad action movie on TV that nobody's really watching, is much more fun than I was expecting it to be. Everyone is lethargic – a combination of a month of intense work and the summer city heat; voices are slow and hazy, bodies limp and cosy.

My flatmate Louis tells us about a date who ghosted him, and the date he's got lined up for Monday after work. Quiet Freya talks dreamily about her cousin's wedding in Greece next weekend. There are in-jokes that skip over my head, references that I'm left wondering about, and I realize how much I've been missing out on – which is nobody's fault but mine.

Although we try to talk about anything *but* work, it's not very long before conversation turns that way. Monty and Verity have seemed a bit funny with each other all evening – it turns out it's because they're both constantly trying to one-up each other to impress Nadja, to the point where they're cutting each other out of meetings or emails; Burnley overslept a few days ago and gave the first 'sorry, I had a doctor's appointment' lie of our cohort; Elaine is still humiliated after forgetting her team meeting had been moved to lunchtime, while she took a break at a nearby gym and missed the whole thing.

'Ugh, *please*, enough,' Elaine groans, while we're still laughing at her. She grimaces, then nudges Monty with a foot and gestures for him to pass the veggie pizza over. 'I can't keep reliving it. I should've *known* something was up when I got back and everyone's desks were empty, but did it twig? *No*. And now, I'm going to have to make up for it like hell so that it doesn't get held against me. What about you, Anna? You've got that big presentation coming up, right?'

'Huh? Oh, yeah.' I peel myself out of the opposite corner of the sofa, wriggling into a slightly more up-right position as heads swivel towards me expectantly. 'It's my first proper presentation. It's about the latest stuff on the Vane engine project, to some senior managers and heads of department.'

'Oh!' Freya says suddenly. 'I'll be there, too. Topher

forwarded the meeting to me; he thought it'd be a useful one to sit in on with him.'

'With – I'm –' I choke a little on the words, struggling to breathe for a second as I twist around to look at Freya. *'With him?* As in . . . Topher Fletcher's going to *be there* when I give my presentation?'

'You didn't know?' Dylan asks, cocking his head to one side. 'I thought that's what you and Lloyd were talking about the other day.'

'What? When did –' I want to say: *when did you see us?* But that sounds weird, so I correct myself abruptly to say, 'I didn't see you around.'

'I had to talk to Craig about some stuff for Phoebus IV. I waved, but you guys were so busy talking that you didn't notice. I figured I'd just leave you to it.'

'We were just going through my presentation. He was being nosy. Curious, I mean.' It's true, and it's not a big deal, because that's the kind of thing Lloyd does with everybody, except then Tasha scoffs from her spot on the floor, where her long legs are stretched out and her hands are braced behind her, her back to the TV. When we look towards her, she tosses her hair over one shoulder and gives an exaggerated eyeroll.

'Please. He's always hanging around at your desk. I see him there *all* the time. If you thought you were being sneaky, you're not. It's an open-plan office, babe.

I can see you from where my team sit. Does he fancy you, or something?'

His body shifting closer to mine, his hand on my cheek and breath on my skin, the way he murmured my name and teased his tongue along my bottom lip . . .

I hope to hell I'm not blushing.

'Of course he doesn't! It's – he's just –'

Pretended I didn't know you . . . I was doing you a favour . . .

'He's always loitering around asking for updates on projects and stuff, that's all.'

'He does that with us, too,' Dylan says – and honestly, thank God for Dylan. 'I think he just likes to know what's going on. It's kind of *his* company too, right? Everyone says he's being groomed to take over when his dad retires. I think it's cool he takes a real interest. He's always in the labs if any of us are there.'

Tasha rolls her eyes again, but even as the others carry on talking about Lloyd, her gaze lingers on me, and it's . . . not nice. Judgey, somehow. Suspicious, maybe a little bit, too.

I feel like there's something she's not saying. I don't think I want to know what it is.

It quickly becomes clear that Lloyd's been hanging out with some of the others over the last few weeks, too, which is a saving grace. Dylan and Monty have gone for lunch with him a few times, Elaine chats to him when he drops by the Finance department . . .

'He's been to a couple of client meetings with us, hasn't he, Monty?' Verity says, smug – although I'm not sure if it's her natural inflection or if she means to brag. 'He's *such* a nice guy, don't you think? And *so* good-looking.' She giggles and some of the group murmur agreements; I'm trying hard not to react, in case I blush.

Tasha asks, 'You've talked to him lots, Monty – does he have a girlfriend? You should find out for Ver. I bet you'd have a chance if you went for it. Not like you'd be off limits or anything – he dated an intern last year, I heard.'

I look at Verity, who's classically beautiful with her heart-shaped face and honey-blonde hair, with her small, upturned nose, and boobs in perfect proportion to her waist. And I immediately picture them kissing, wrapped in each other's arms, and there's a flare of something sickening and corrosive in my chest. I grit my teeth and shove the image away.

I'm *not* jealous.

I'm not.

'Oh, no, babe, it's not even on the table,' Verity says – and though she tries to sound upbeat, it falls a little flat; she's obviously disappointed. She's squished in the middle of our group on the sofa: Freya and Izzy, either side of her, reach to rub her arm or pat her leg sympathetically. Even *I* feel a little bad for her for a second. 'I asked him for drinks last weekend, but he made some excuses. Didn't give off very "interested" vibes.'

'Maybe he's just being polite,' Izzy suggests. 'You know, because of the whole being the boss's son thing.'

Yeah, it was real 'polite' when he pretended not to know me.

'I don't think so. No offence, Ver,' Dylan adds quickly, offering a smile to soften the blow. 'He mentioned a thing with some girl he used to date – they went out for a drink, like, a week ago. He didn't seem too keen to talk about it, so I didn't wanna pry too much, but I wouldn't want to get in the middle of all that if I were you.'

'Well, *definitely* not on the table in that case. I don't need to be the other woman!' Verity giggles.

I laugh, too, because everybody else is, but my mind is spinning. Was this other girl on the scene when he kissed me? An ex from a long time ago, maybe, one he's just friends with these days? Is she a newer development – the girl he lost his heart to last week, maybe?

More importantly: *Why do I care?*

I don't. I *don't*.

The others start speculating – is there someone in the office? Someone from his uni course? An intern from years gone by, maybe, if not *the* intern, the one he did date. Most likely, he met her on a dating app. Dylan suggests maybe she's a friend of his brother's – which is when basically the entire rest of the group find out about Will.

'I knew there was another one, but I thought he was, like, way younger, or something,' says Monty.

'You should hear Topher talk about Lloyd. It's like the sun shines out of his arse,' Freya says, then blushes and adds hastily, 'but obviously, Lloyd's great, and it's super cute his dad is so proud of him and stuff. I just mean, I could count the times he's mentioned Will on one hand. I get the vibe Will just doesn't care about Arrowmile. It's kind of weird, right? He's probably *really* up himself, or something.'

'Now if *he's* single . . .' Verity jokes, but I get the impression she's at least halfway serious.

'Maybe we'll meet him at the summer party?' Elaine suggests.

The summer party is an annual company event, an excuse for a friendly piss-up under the guise of being an all-office meeting with updates on how the company is doing so far that year, with a team-building exercise or two sprinkled in. There's lots of food, lots of booze, and 'always' (so I'm told) lots of fun. An excuse for everybody to let their hair down, a reward for their hard work.

I'm looking forward to using it as a networking session. It sounds like a perfect opportunity for it.

I guess it's not beyond the realm of possibility that Will could be there. Thinking about his self-deprecating, quiet humour and his awkward, natural clumsiness, I tell the others, 'I ran into him once. He was at the office looking for Lloyd. He's really lovely, actually. Kind of . . . quiet, I think? More introverted than Lloyd is, anyway. But he seemed really nice.'

'Surprise, surprise,' mutters Tasha, but it's so quiet that I wonder if maybe I imagined it – especially when nobody else seems to notice. I must have misheard, I decide; it's a weird remark, and I can't figure what she means by it. Anyway, the others are already busy grilling me on exactly *when* I met Will and what that conversation was like.

'You'll have to find out if he'll be at the summer party,' I tell Monty and Dylan, trying to distract the attention away from myself. 'Ask Lloyd next time you see him. Let us know in the group chat.'

'Or *you* can ask him,' Izzy says, nudging me in the side and smiling. 'If you see him first.'

Tasha scoffs, and I definitely didn't mishear it that time. Some of the others notice, too.

Does he fancy you or something? she'd asked me. *If you thought you were being sneaky, you're not.*

Shit. Does Tasha think there's something going on between me and Lloyd? Something serious and more than just a kiss from before the internship started that nobody even knows about?

I don't care if she sees me talking to Lloyd around the office, but I *do* care if she honestly believes there's something between us. The others all seem to like her well enough, but she's the very last person I'd want leaning into some kind of office-romance rumour. She gives every indication she's the kind of person who drags others down to try to boost herself up.

Maybe I was too harsh on Lloyd for pretending he didn't know who I was that first day. It's clear now that he *was* doing me a favour; I really don't want to risk anything undermining the work I do on this internship.

Maybe I owe him an apology after all. *Maybe.*

Tasha, thankfully, keeps her mouth shut, and nobody calls her out on it. I don't either, because I can't bear the idea of dragging this discussion out any further and digging myself into a hole. Everyone returns to idle chatter and the movie, but it's a long while before I feel myself relaxing back into the sofa to enjoy the rest of the night.

I smooth my hands over my skirt, making sure my blouse is tucked in neatly for the umpteenth time. My laptop sits open in front of me, the presentation mirrored on the large screen behind me. I'm glad I booked this meeting room out for the half hour before my big presentation; it took me ten minutes to figure out how the projector worked.

The whole thing is nerve-wracking, but the waiting is worse. My adrenaline builds with each passing minute. I watch the clock in the corner of my laptop screen like a hawk. And I know, I know, a watched pot and all that, but . . . *God*, why can't this be over already?

It's not that I'm not used to public speaking. But this is *different* from anything I've done at school or university. This is *important*. The next hour could be the thing that makes or breaks my future at Arrowmile – my future *anywhere*, depending on how well (or how horrendously) it goes.

And besides that, this is serious, grown-up, real-life stuff at stake. If I mess it up, it could set back projects massively. What was the worst thing that would happen if I flubbed my lines in the school play, or got my facts a bit muddled up in a school council meeting?

My brain immediately goes into a full-on spiral. I imagine having the wrong numbers in my presentation or having completely misinterpreted things, and the project being shut down when it shouldn't be, and everybody blaming me, and having to hand back my laptop to Michaela in shame while everyone stands at their desks judging me. Or, God, what if I've misread the meeting invite somehow, and I'm not supposed to be presenting on the Vane engine at all? I'll waste everybody's time and they'll be wondering how in the hell I got a place on this internship in the first place, and Illustrious Leader/CEO Topher Fletcher will be shaking his head in disappointment and that look will haunt me in every job interview I ever have after this . . .

And all of a sudden, they're here.

The glass door is opening, people starting to file in, chattering away. I desperately try to put names to faces I've only seen once or twice, or only on their little profile picture attached to their email contact. Freya gives me an encouraging wave when she takes her seat, but it only makes me feel worse – a fellow intern here to bear witness for the rest, if I crash and burn.

Michaela is one of the last in, walking in with Dylan's boss Fiona, and Topher.

She cuts herself off mid-sentence to say, 'Hi, Anna! All ready to go?'

'Yep.' My voice comes out reedy and thin. I clear my throat as I plaster on a smile, hoping they can't see through it. I also hope they can't see the sweat beading around my hairline.

'Great! Big responsibility, leading this one. Don't let me down!'

Aw, Michaela, did you have to put it like that?

I want to melt through the floor. My throat is dry and my mouth full of sawdust and – *crap*, I left my water bottle at my desk. Is it too late to duck out and grab it? I don't want to look unprepared or make a bad impression. That was the whole point of being here early, wasn't it?

I try to wet my lips, pretending to fidget with my laptop as I do a quick head count. 'It looks . . .' My voice is so quiet only two people look up. I try again, and wince when it comes out too shouty. 'It looks like everybody's here, unless we're expecting anyone else . . .?'

Heads swivel, then shake.

Michaela smiles at me. I think it's supposed to be encouraging, but I could swear she's just grown fangs, turned into some monstrous harpy sent here to torture me. 'The floor's all yours, Anna.'

I pull up my pre-prepared script in my mind, getting started. I launch into my 'Thanks for making the time for this' spiel and run through the agenda for the meeting, but I don't get much further before Michaela gently clears her throat.

'Maybe before you go any further, you could give everybody a quick introduction, Anna?'

'Oh, well – that's my next slide, actually.'

Was she not listening to my agenda? Did I imagine saying it at all?

'I meant introduce *yourself*,' she says. 'I'm not sure everybody's had the chance to meet you.'

'Great idea,' booms Topher amiably, from a few seats down. He nods, as enthusiastic as the Churchill insurance dog. 'Tell us a bit about you, Annie. We're always keen to know how our interns are getting on!'

'It's . . .' *It's Anna*, but is it also rude to correct him? Shit. *Move on, Anna, move on.* 'Okay, great – well, I'll keep it quick, I know we've only got an hour to get through everything . . .'

I know what Michaela's doing – she's making sure I 'use my platform', 'get myself seen'. She's trying to help me so that I have a better chance of securing a job here after I graduate.

But my quick, stilted list of Things You Should Know About Anna Sherwood (namely, my degree and where I'm studying) means that when I turn back to my presentation, I have no idea where I was. I try to pick up the thread of my script, wishing I'd made some flashcards. I dive in head-first, hoping I'll figure it out soon enough and they won't notice, but I don't think it works. I'm very aware of how fast I'm talking, how heavily I'm breathing, the way I stumble over some of the numbers and have to correct myself.

It's not going well.

It gets worse when the door opens, and someone slips inside. I notice it in my periphery, trying so hard to focus that I'm doing a terrible job of making eye contact with my audience like I know you're supposed to, and irritation curdles through me. I thought everybody was here? Who else can *possibly* need to be witness to this car-crash of a presentation? And why are they showing up more than fifteen minutes into the meeting, late by anybody's standards? Even the CEO got here on time.

I have to pause in the middle of a sentence about spending to gulp down a breath. I also need to stall to remember why it's so far over the projected budget – because God, why is it way over budget? I knew this. Why don't I know this? I let my eyes flicker to the end of the table, to the seat that was just pulled out by the interloper.

And . . .

It's Lloyd. I know I shouldn't be surprised, but I am.

'Sorry,' he says, loud enough that he seems to be addressing everyone. 'Sorry, don't mind me. I didn't mean to interrupt. You were talking about the development budget – the coolant?'

The coolant!

I let out a sigh of relief, my heart calming down considerably – which is ironic, since discussing the new Arrowmile coolant leads to a heated debate around the table, getting someone to take responsibility because it was meant to be allocated to a different project. I don't really know why that's so important, only that everyone's so difficult about it, it *must* be. When I talked to Elaine about it over breakfast, she suggested it was maybe a tax thing, or linked to investors somehow.

As a couple of the managers bicker between themselves about who takes the blame and who needs to fix it, I get finally get a chance to ground myself and breathe. It's enough to remember my script, figure out what's next.

I catch Lloyd's eye and mouth, *Thank you*, wondering if he's aware of how much he just saved me from total humiliation.

He grins back, bright and friendly, an anchor.

My heart gives a little skip, and damn him, it takes more effort than it should to pull my attention back to the ongoing debate in the middle of the table.

Still. I'm glad he's here. Especially when I falter a couple more times and he pipes up with a leading question to pull me back on track, since he knows my presentation as well as – or, I guess, better than – I do. And especially when he smiles at me with an encouraging nod; it's a little easier to make eye contact with him in the room. I find I keep glancing his way for reassurance rather than to Michaela, or anybody else.

This boy with his unfaltering smile, who carries the sunshine with him wherever he goes, with summer in his eyes.

Damn him. And damn me, for being so drawn in by it – *again*.

Chapter 14

It's approaching five o'clock on Friday and I have big plans tonight. Huge. They involve switching off for a couple of hours with whatever thriller Netflix recommends to me, a frozen pizza I'll buy on the way home, and maybe a pint of Ben & Jerry's. I feel like indulging. It's been a long week, especially after all the stress of that presentation on Monday – which mercifully, I salvaged so I didn't make a total fool of myself. Mostly thanks to Lloyd.

Speak of the devil . . . My computer pings, a little purple box appearing in the bottom corner.

Lloyd Fletcher
Working hard or hardly working? TGIF, Annalise Sherwood.

Anna Sherwood
Fletcher. Hi. How are you?

I always have to re-orient the conversation. Well, I suppose I don't *have* to, but he never says hello or anything that amounts to a remotely *normal* greeting, and this has become our pattern. So, predictably enough, his next message is –

Hi, Annalise. I'm very well thank you.
How are you?

What are you doing tonight?

Why?

Trying to figure out if I'll run into you at midnight again and you'll scare the shit out of me, popping up out of the darkness all 'LET THERE BE LIGHT!' while you steal someone's birthday cake out of the fridge

That's not how that happened. And no, I'm about to log off actually. You just caught me.

. . . You're not staying here all night again, are you? Don't you have better things to be doing?

I am so glad you asked.

And then the chat goes dead. His status switches abruptly to offline, leaving me staring, bewildered, at the screen. What the hell was that all about?

I wait to see if he'll come back online, and half expect him to suddenly pop up behind me. When he doesn't, I huff, muttering under my breath, determined to forget that whole conversation – if that's even what you can call it. He's so bloody infuriating.

When I pack up a couple of minutes later, I glance over to see if Tasha's ready to go – it seems rude to just *leave*, since we're going the same way. But she's preoccupied at her desk chatting with Verity and two women I only vaguely recognize (I swear I only ever seem to look over when she's stopped to chat to someone or check her phone), so I leave them to it, secretly relieved I don't have to endure a journey home with Tasha.

I join the steady trickle of people leaving the building. The weather's a little cooler this week, which makes this whole commute thing less painful.

I don't know how people do this every day, *all the time*. It must get so exhausting. I know I used to get the bus back and forth for school, but after a year of uni, that feels like a distant memory. And so much for days that didn't start until an eleven a.m. lecture, or where I could trundle home at two in the afternoon. After just five weeks away, uni feels like a distant memory, too.

Is this what it means, being a grown-up? Will this be my whole life after I graduate – steeling myself for the trip home and daydreaming of eating pizza on the sofa?

There's a pang somewhere deep in the pit of my chest, something tight and fierce and hot. A life like that – it's what I want, isn't it? What I've been working towards, wishing for. But thinking of it like *this*, realizing that it'll be just an extended version of how I'm treating this summer, it feels . . .

Small.

So very, very small.

Swiping through the barriers, I try to push the thought to the back of my mind. Somewhere far, far away where I can squash it down underneath everything else and it won't come crawling back out again and spark fresh waves of self-doubt.

I don't even notice the person falling into step beside me until there's a hand on my arm to catch my attention, and Lloyd is suddenly there saying, 'So, I thought we could hang out. Maybe *buy* some cake this time, instead of stealing leftovers. Or we could get some chips – I won't even judge you if you get gravy on yours again, I promise. What do you think?'

'Wait, what? What are you talking about? What's . . .?'

I stop, immediately causing a bottleneck in the flow of people leaving the building. Lloyd's hand is still on my arm, his touch hot through the sleeve of my cardigan, and he draws me out of the way.

'I thought we could hang out. Outside of the office, I mean. Stop each other burning the candle at both ends, or whatever.'

He beams at me, so wide that his nose crinkles a little. It's unbearably cute.

And I am unbearably confused.

'Fletcher, we don't . . . We don't hang out *in* the office.'

'Sure we do.'

'No,' I say slowly, frowning. 'You show up at my desk asking about projects, and interrupt me halfway through my first big meeting. We talked *once*, because we both happened to be around late. Twice, I guess, if you count when you helped me out with my new pass. But that's it. If that's your definition of "hanging out", then you seriously need to re-evaluate your social life.'

Lloyd raises an eyebrow. 'I thought you said you were *glad* I showed up at your meeting?'

'I was. But you still interrupted it. And that's still not hanging out.'

'Okay. So, let's hang out. Full stop.'

'I don't . . .' Warily, I shift back half a step, teeth catching the inside of my bottom lip as my frown deepens. I can't help the way my eyes flit around, as if expecting to see people – people we *know* – stopping to stare at us. Nobody is.

But I think about Tasha, probably leaving the office any moment now, and how I can't afford to give her any more fodder for whatever rumour she might be inclined to invent around us.

'I don't think that's a good idea, Fletcher. I – we said we'd be civil. Polite. *That's it*. Remember?'

He rolls his eyes, but he's still smiling – like he thinks this is all so amusing, like he knows me *better*, somehow – and that rattles me far more than any worry we might be seen hanging around together like this.

'Come on,' he cajoles. 'I'm not asking you on a date. We *are* civil. Friendly, right?'

'Right . . .' I mean, I *guess* that's what you could call it – at a stretch.

'And friends hang out. Right?'

'Fletcher,' I say, very seriously. 'Do you not have any other friends – *real* friends – to spend your evening with? Literally anybody.'

'Why? Worried you won't be able to resist my charms and you'll be trying to snog me again by the end of the night?'

I almost lunge forward like I can clap my hands over his mouth and hold the words in. Thankfully, it doesn't seem like anybody overheard; nobody's paying us any attention at all, actually.

Even so, my jaw clenches and I press my outstretched hands over my eyes before letting out a shaky, agitated huff. '*Lloyd.* You can't just say things like that.'

He does, to his credit, look a bit sheepish.

'Besides,' I say, 'what about your girlfriend?'

He pulls a face, baffled. 'What are you talking about? I haven't been on a date since –' He stops abruptly, eyes darting away from me. *Since you.* Even if it wasn't technically a date, it was still *something*.

'Oh. But I thought . . . Dylan said you went for drinks with someone a little while ago. An ex, or something.'

A muscle ticks in Lloyd's jaw when he tries to smile to dismiss it; it doesn't quite reach his eyes, but he laughs like that'll make up for it. It doesn't.

'That? Nah, that was . . . It doesn't matter. And anyway, this isn't a date, so you don't have to worry about making anybody jealous.'

'That's not – I'm not – I just thought you might be seeing her, that's all.'

'Well, I'm not. Free as a bird. Unless you have better plans?'

Literally, anything.

'Yes, I do,' I tell him. 'Goodbye, Fletcher. Have a nice weekend.'

I leave before he can try to convince me to stay.

But *damn it*, he makes it impossible *not* to think about him, especially when I'm trying so very hard to forget about him. I keep replaying the conversation, the smile on his face – the flicker of hurt in his eyes before I stalked away.

Maybe he really *doesn't* have a lot of friends, I wonder; I can sympathize with that. And he really did seem to just want to hang out, no ulterior motives – I don't think Lloyd is capable of ulterior motives of any kind, quite frankly – he's too earnest and open.

Elaine and Louis are both out tonight, so I can't rely on them to distract me. Instead, I end up stalking Lloyd's Instagram – which is basically just an advert for the young, rich and famous. It's pictures of him at fancy bars, in fancy clothes, or pseudo-advertisements for Arrowmile, or doing *actual* brand deals for gadgets or expensive hair products. There aren't many pictures of him with friends, though he must clearly be *with* people in most of them. There are hardly even any photos of him with Will, which I think is a little odd.

Worst of all – it's *familiar*, because it's a glossier version of my own social media: except mine consists of lonely coffees or family dinners, attempts to show people I *do* have a life . . . even if the reality is pretty lonesome and ordinary.

Oh, bloody hell.

Fine.

Fine, he wins.

I scroll through my work emails looking for one from Lloyd, and find his phone number from his email signature.

> So, theoretically, if we were to go buy cake instead of stealing it, where would we go for that at eight o'clock on a Friday night?

I get a read receipt within a couple of minutes, and then his reply is immediate.

> Annalise?

> Do you invite a lot of people to eat cake on a Friday night?

And here I was starting to worry you didn't have any friends

I'm just realizing that 'eat cake on a Friday night' sounds like a euphemism for something

It's not

Or at least, it better not be.

Hahahaha def not a euphemism

As you know, I am deadly serious when it comes to food

There's this cool late-night cafe place I know near Southbank. It's kind of like a bar, but they only serve coffees and soft drinks and stuff

They have live music sometimes too

Can meet you there in half an hour?

He sends me a link to this not-a-bar-cafe, Keye & Shore. It's much more up my street than an actual bar as I've never been a big drinker, and I agree to meet him in half an hour before I can think better of it.

I get changed out of my leggings and University of Leeds Netball Club T-shirt, and try not to think too much about my outfit. It's not like it's a date. It's not like I care what he thinks, or that I even want him to notice how I look.

Except maybe I do? Just a bit.

No. *No, I don't.*

Still, the place looked kind of cool and fancy on the website, so I pull on my one good going out-out dress, a black short-sleeved one. I pair it with my trainers and denim jacket, not wanting to show up *too* overdressed, or have Lloyd think I made any particular effort for his sake. Because I didn't. Obviously.

It's not for his sake that I put on some lipstick and a little mascara, either.

I mean, if anything, the lipstick should be a deterrent. I'm not putting it on just for it to get all messed up, after all.

By the time I'm leaving the Tube station at Waterloo and following Google Maps, I start to think that I've had a horrible lapse in judgement. It's still light out and the city is bustling with people, though there are hints that night is sweeping in: the crowds gathering near bars, the outfits that have shifted from office-appropriate to distinctly-not, the tendrils of purple and pink dusk creeping up through the clouds. Looking up to check my bearings against the map, I catch a glimpse of the London Eye. For a moment, I see it lit up against a midnight sky; but I blink, and the memory is gone.

I can taste Lloyd's kiss, phantom lips against mine.

I almost talk myself out of meeting him. The closer I get to this late-night cafe, the more adamant the nagging voice in the back of my mind becomes – although right now, it's very prominently at the forefront of my mind.

What are you doing? This is the worst idea you've ever had. This is a sure-fire way to get fired, you absolute idiot. Screwing around with the boss's son. There's no way people won't find out . . .

'Annalise? Hey! You okay?'

My snippy internal voice is easy to shut down when Lloyd is there, pushing off from the lamp post he was leaning a shoulder against to wave at me, his usual dazzling smile on his face. It slips a little and I see him looking me over. Not checking me out – more like something's wrong, and he's looking for what. His eyes flick down to my shoes, searching.

'Did you step in dog shit or something?'

Huh?

Oh, I soon realize. It's me that's wrong. I'm grimacing – and probably look like I just smelled dog shit. *Great*.

I do my best to rearrange my face into something more neutral. Polite. Civil, like we promised we'd be. I even attempt a smile, but think better of it when it feels too fake. I know he'll see right through me. He's . . . unusually good at that.

'Sorry. Just, um. Checking the map.' I wave my phone at him as I click the screen off, shoving it into my bag and then nodding at the cafe. It's lit up bright, just a few meters away. 'Shall we . . . go in?'

I gesture for him to lead the way, but he adjusts his pace to fall in step beside me. His arm brushes lightly against mine, elbow nudging the sleeve of my jacket. It's electric. A lightning strike that empties my head of everything except that sensation, every nerve in my body suddenly focusing on that one point of too-brief contact.

However much hanging out with Lloyd feels like a bad idea, there's one singular, crystal-clear reason why I changed my mind and agreed to meet him.

He's magnetic.

And I, like everybody else at Arrowmile, am drawn

to his good looks, easy charm, friendly smile . . . and the kindred spirit I think I recognize in him. A moth to a flame.

But then he holds the door open for me and catches my eye to wink, his grin cheeky, spreading wide across his face, and he says, 'Knew you'd cave eventually, Annalise. After you.'

And just like that, the lightning strike is a distant memory.

Chapter 15

Keye & Shore is unlike any place I've ever been before. It's a dreamy, hipster coffee shop plucked straight from Pinterest, with chipped hardwood floors and exposed beams overhead, pleasantly mismatched tables and chairs in the same mix of farmhouse and industrial styles. There are low-slung lampshades hanging from the ceiling, tealights on each table. A small, raised stage across the room has a two-piece band playing: a girl with a guitar and another with a keyboard, both of them singing indie songs I think I maybe recognize – or else, good enough that they sound like something I'd hear on Spotify mixes.

It looks like a coffee shop, and it definitely smells like one. The counter is larger than any I've seen at a Starbucks. But the hiss of steam and churn of coffee spitting out of machines, the clink of mugs – it all belies the bawdy chatter and loud laughter and the crowds standing at tall tables with their drinks, which makes the whole atmosphere feel more like a pub. I hesitate in the doorway, taking it all in, overwhelmed by the caffeine that sits thick in the summer evening air.

Lloyd turns slightly to face me, gesturing over his shoulder at the counter. 'I'll get the drinks. You find us a table?'

I'm about to protest that I'll buy my own drink, thanks. I've had plenty of his so-called 'chivalry'. But then I remember we're just hanging out. Like friends. And I'd let my friend buy me a drink, so I could buy the next one.

I nod. 'Okay. I'll take a hot chocolate, if that's . . .?'

Okay, but why wouldn't it be?

'On the menu,' I settle for saying.

I find us an empty table in the far corner near the stage, and before long Lloyd is weaving deftly towards me, a tray held high and steady as he keeps a sharp eye out for anyone getting up from their table too quickly – just as well, because he only narrowly avoids someone stepping back into him and knocking it all to the floor.

'Phew!' He sets the tray down with a victorious smile, puffing upwards to blow some hair out of his face. 'Okay, so I wasn't sure what you'd like, and I couldn't decide what looked best anyway, so I got us some options.'

'Options?' I echo. 'Fletcher, you got us an entire bakery.'

He's bought five different slices of cakes (I count them). A lemon one, a cheesecake with a raspberry swirl, a three-tiered chocolate one with chocolate buttercream, some carrot cake, and a Victoria sponge. Two forks sit in the middle of the tray, and Lloyd hands one to me with a smile.

'Dig in.'

'Remind me to send you some money for this later. Seriously, this must've cost a fortune.'

Lloyd shrugs, not quite meeting my eyes all of a sudden – making it clear that whatever it cost, he didn't think twice about it.

'Right. The whole "heir to a massively profitable company" thing.'

Frowning, he points out, 'It's a few slices of cake, Annalise. If it makes you feel better, you can send me money for the cakes. *And* your drink, so we're even. Is that why you changed your mind about hanging out? So you could . . .' Lloyd trails off, his words leaving him in a rush of sudden anger that colours his cheeks, but it vanishes as quickly as it appeared. He runs a hand up and through his hair.

'Sorry,' I say. 'I didn't . . .'

It feels awkward, apologizing; I've obviously hit a

nerve though, and while I didn't say anything that wasn't true, I don't like how quickly the night has soured. That I've done that. Will do that, if I dig my heels in and keep biting at him about this.

I snatch up a fork and carve a big chunk out of the carrot cake. A whiff of walnut teases at my nose, complementing the smell of coffee in the air. 'So *did* you buy the entire bakery, or are there some left for when it's my turn to buy the next round?'

Lloyd eyes me warily, searching for the barb in my words, but finally a faint smile crosses his face. I watch the tension lift from his shoulders and I feel a little lighter, too. He collects his own fork, along with a chunk of the chocolate cake.

'Bold of you to assume there'll be a next round,' he declares, with a little too much gusto. 'I don't know about you, but I think I'll be too full after this lot to manage *more* cake.'

'Next time, then.'

His full-wattage smile dims, but in a way that softens it into something more real. Almost tangible. It spreads through my chest, warm and fuzzy, and I realize what I just said.

'Next time,' he murmurs.

Conversation lapses into nonexistence as we sample the cakes and sip our drinks; I keep expecting

the silence to get awkward, brace myself for it, but . . .
it doesn't. We're cocooned by everybody else's chatter,
the music wrapping around us like a blanket, cradling
our little bubble into something calm and comfortable
instead of accenting it. Lloyd reclines after a while,
lounging more comfortably in his chair. I shift to lean
one elbow on the table, my left arm resting against the
wall, turning slightly to face the stage better.

My knee jostles against Lloyd's as I move, and I
get that same jolt of electricity as I did outside when
our arms touched. I determinedly don't look at him,
forcing away the curious thought of wondering if he
felt it too.

We're halfway through our drinks when we both
reach for the lemon cake, forks clashing as we each
try to get the generous scoop of icing on the top, the
tines snagging together. Laughing, he takes my fork
to untangle them – and then snags up the bit with
the icing.

I mock-glower at him. 'And here I thought you were
the very model of chivalry, Fletcher.'

He shrugs, teasing, 'Maybe if this were a date, I'd let
you have it. But it's not. Right?'

'Right.' I shift in my seat, wriggling up a little
straighter. 'Obviously.'

He helps himself to some cheesecake next. 'I was

kind of surprised to hear from you, though. Thought you said you had plans?'

I shrug. 'Guess I felt guilty that if you didn't have plans, you'd just end up lurking in the office all weekend. I couldn't leave you to such a sad and miserable fate.'

'Ah. So this is pity cake.'

'Exactly.' But I glance at him, comparing the polished guy across the table to the rumpled, distracted one I found on the twelfth floor last week. He *did* look especially cute in those glasses, too . . . 'What, um . . . what *were* you doing last week?'

He twists the handle of his mug around, tracing the curve with a fingertip. It's hypnotic. 'Just, you know. Same as you. Working on some stuff. Lost track of time.'

'Uh-huh. And the real answer?'

Something crosses over his features, distant and deep-down all at once. Like in recalling the answer, he's found it buried away in some secret part of himself. The slant of his lips turns reluctant, disappointed. It's a lot, considering the answer is probably 'looking at diagrams from the labs'.

It disappears just as quickly as I register it. I blink and suddenly discover myself on the receiving end of a playful smirk and sardonic look as he leans over the table towards me.

'Ah, *now* I know why you wanted to meet me. Corporate espionage – isn't that what they call it? Trying to uncover company secrets to sell to our enemies, Annalise?'

'*Enemies*,' I repeat, rolling my eyes. 'Jeez. You realize you sound like a bad movie villain when you say things like that, right? You sell *scooters*.'

'We're revolutionizing the industry. Careful, bad-mouth us too much and I'll have to have "my people" deal with you.'

'Colour me terrified,' I deadpan, but crack a smile when he laughs. Considering we talk a lot about ongoing projects at Arrowmile whenever he drops by my desk, Lloyd is being weirdly secretive – and making me think whatever he's doing, it's more serious than filling time by hanging out at his dad's company while he takes a break from uni. Unless . . . 'Was it about uni? Were you looking for a new course or something, because you don't like yours?'

Lloyd looks at me in open surprise, blinking rapidly while his green eyes go large. At first I think he's surprised I remembered, but then he looks away and says quietly, 'I can't say that's an option for me.'

'What? But – but you don't like your degree, right? Law and Economics? You said it wasn't really your thing.'

'I've only done one year. It's ... I might change my mind.'

'Well, yeah, but you seemed pretty sure, that –' *That night you kissed me.* 'That first time you talked about it. Why don't you just switch and do something else? Or leave? It's not like you don't obviously have a place at Arrowmile if you wanted it, so –'

'It's not that simple, Annalise,' Lloyd tells me sharply.

And *this* version of him, I think, is a complete stranger. There are glimpses of the boy I kissed by the river when I see him in the office; there, he seems like a parody of the guy I met. Rearranged into someone else, but parts of him still there, somewhere.

But right now, I don't recognize him at all. His voice is low, an undercurrent in it like a warning, and he hunches over his mug, cupping it with both hands now. This boy who's always so much larger than life makes himself smaller right in front of my eyes, and there's a wild part of me that wants to grab his hand and yank him back.

'I don't get it,' I press. 'I mean, I know it's scary starting over or doing something new – I was terrified about starting this internship – but you could still change your mind. People go back to uni and retrain to do something totally new when they're, like, *forty*, so you could do it at – what, nineteen? Twenty? It's not a big deal. I bet all you'd have to do is talk to the student services at your uni or whatever and –'

'*Anna*. Just drop it, okay? It's . . . Look, whatever I said that night, I was – I was talking out of my arse.'

That was maybe the only time I've seen you that you weren't talking out of your arse.

But I don't say that. I can't say anything at all. Retorts turn to ash on my tongue and my lungs become tight as I breathe in the pain of it – *his* pain, which seeps across the table, palpable. He hunches smaller again, scowling, not at me, and maybe not entirely at himself either. A breath shudders out of him.

And my brain stalls as all I can think is that he called me Anna.

All those times I've bugged him about calling me Anna instead of Annalise, and now he finally does, it feels wrong. Twisted.

I miss the way he says my name.

I don't know this version of Lloyd – the tightness of his jaw or the angst in his eyes, the anguish that cuts his words into sharp, cruel edges.

Deciding to back away from the topic of uni, I say more gently, 'The others were asking if Will was going to be at the party next week. I don't know if Dylan or Monty got around to asking you; they never messaged the rest of us to say either way. He's kind of upstaging you, you know – the mystery man, all elusive. Everybody's wondering about him.'

Lloyd's face eases into one I'm more used to. The corners of his lips tug up a little, a laugh chuffing out of the thin, pressed lines of his mouth. '*Mystery man*. He'll like that. Think they'll be disappointed when they find out he's just kind of shy?'

'Nah. So, he'll be at the party?'

He nods, shakes himself out, wriggling his shoulders like he can force them into a more relaxed position, before slumping back in his chair again. His leg knocks back against mine. I tuck my feet underneath my chair, out of the way.

'Yeah. Dad kind of expects him to show his face, so . . . But it'll be fun. It always is.' He smiles, and this time, it's more sincere; it sticks. 'You heard there's basically an open bar, right? So one year – we must've been fifteen, I reckon – Will and I are there, like always, and we sneak off during the presentations about the quarterly report and whatever and found this crate of beers they'd ordered. It was back at the office, then – the old office, it was way smaller. They basically just bought in booze and pizzas for everybody. Anyway, Will and I got completely *smashed*. I reckon we only had about four cans each, but, you know. We were kids who'd never really had a drink before.' He laughs, eyes glittering in the soft yellow glow of the lights. 'Will threw up. He was trying to mop it up before anybody could find out, and because I was drunk, I thought the best way to help would be to cause a distraction.'

'Of course you did. Don't tell me you pulled the fire alarm or something?'

'*That* would've been smarter. No, I go up to where the head of HR is talking to everyone about some new mental wellbeing initiative they're rolling out, take the microphone off her, and start teaching everybody yoga.'

'I'm – I'm sorry, *what?* Why?'

'In my defence,' he says, still laughing, his cheeks pink, 'she'd been saying something about the benefits of simple exercise like walking or stretching, and I just ran with that. My mum used to do a lot of yoga and Pilates and stuff, so I just copied some of the poses I saw her do. The best part was, everybody just *went along with it*. I'm pretty sure it was obvious I was drunk, but . . .' He shrugs, not looking the least bit ashamed or regretful.

Of course they went along with it. He's the golden boy, beloved by all. I bet, even then, he had everybody wrapped around his little finger. Maybe *especially* then, when he was a bit younger.

'How'd it go?'

He snorts. 'Got everybody out of their seats and having a bit of a laugh. Plus, nobody ever found out Will was sick everywhere, so I'd call it a raging success.'

'Your dad didn't even find out?'

'Ah. Well, yeah.' But he shrugs again, and takes a breath before smiling. 'We've learned to handle our alcohol better since then at least, so don't expect any yoga-related shenanigans at the party next week – but you *can* let the others know they'll see Will there.'

'I'll do that. Hey, do you want another drink? We've still got a lot of cake to finish up . . .'

And I'm not ready for this night to end just yet.

Lloyd beams, handing me his empty cup to return to the counter and clear some space. 'We've got time. This place doesn't close till, like, two. Same again?'

'Same again.'

Chapter 16

We still have cake left when midnight ticks around. I didn't even realize how late it had gotten, but Lloyd is full of fun stories and light-hearted anecdotes, and every time there's a lapse in conversation, it remains comfortable and easy until one of us thinks of something else we want to share.

I only notice the time because Lloyd ducks out to go to the loo, and now I'm left alone I check my phone, where I also see some WhatsApp notifications.

At the top of the screen, there's a message from Mum. I read enough in the preview to know it's yet another overly-enthusiastic hi/how are you/just checking in, like she has *any right* to 'check in' on my life. I delete it before it can spoil my good mood.

I see some messages from Louis and a prickle of panic curls its way up my spine. *Shit.* Louis. He's probably already home, wondering where the hell

I've disappeared off to after saying I'd be vegging out on the sofa all night, and I'll have to come up with some half-baked lie to cover up the fact I've been with Lloyd, because I *know* there's no way I'll be able to make this sound platonic or innocent and like anything *but* a date . . .

But as I read his messages properly, I find I have nothing to worry about.

> **Louis**
> Heyyyyyyy roomie, change of plans – we're heading out to a club so won't be home anytime soon. Or at all, tonight?! I am getting some SERIOUS signals, so wish me luck!
>
> 23:26

> OKAY SO NOT THAT YOU WISHED ME LUCK OR ANYTHING, BUT THE SIGNALS ARE FULL-ON ACTIONS NOW. Don't wait up lol (and yes, I realize you're probably already in bed and asleep)
>
> 23:49

Since he'll probably notice the two little blue ticks that I've seen his message at some point, I reply with a string of appropriately excitable, celebratory emojis and telling him I can't wait to hear all about it tomorrow.

I don't mention that I'm not in bed, asleep.

Lloyd slips back into his seat, hands braced on the table as he does so, careful not to disturb our shared pot of decaf tea. (I have no idea how he had *any* kind of coffee earlier – let alone how other people are still drinking it now, at this time of night.)

I say as much aloud, pointing in particular to a guy a couple of tables over with an espresso.

'Maybe this is just their first stop of the night,' he suggests. 'Setting themselves up to make it through partying till five in the morning.'

I must pull a face because Lloyd raises his eyebrows.

'Let me guess – the only time you've stayed up that late was to pull an all-nighter studying?'

'You say that like it's a bad thing.'

'Not at all.'

'I probably – I mean, I'm *sure* I have at some point. Sleepovers with friends, or something.' I pull another face though, knowing it was never actually as late as it felt when we'd stay up late at nine or ten years old. 'Maybe . . . maybe when I was a baby?'

When he laughs, I kick him half-heartedly under the table.

'Alright, Fletcher. When was the last time *you* stayed up all night partying?'

He's quick to answer – until he's not, whatever answer he had so ready faltering as soon as he opens his mouth. I watch his eyes drift to the side as he reconsiders. His mouth closes again. When his eyes drag back to mine, he rolls them.

'*Fine*. Not for a while. Probably last year, when I was at uni, I guess. Probably Freshers' Week.'

'All night?' I press, and he shrugs, looking a little less sure of himself. When he sighs in defeat, I giggle into the palm of my hand. 'It's okay, we'll just be boring old biddies avoiding the party lifestyle together.'

'I don't *avoid* it.'

'Yeah? That's why you're hanging out with someone from work at a coffee shop instead of being out with your friends living it up, or with the mystery lady who's not your girlfriend?'

He grumbles under his breath, half-formed and half-arsed insults, making a show of scowling melodramatically. I laugh, trying to ignore the little somersaults my heart is doing inside my chest.

Just because he's cute, just because it feels like it *could* be a date . . .

It's not.

'She's *not* my girlfriend, for the record,' he tells me after a beat. 'And not much of a mystery lady. She was . . .'

Unlike when I pushed him to talk about uni, I immediately want to back down from this topic, regretting bringing it up at all. What should it matter to me if Lloyd *does* have something going on with another girl? It's not like we can – not that we *want* to date each other, I correct myself hastily.

'You don't have to tell me. I didn't mean to bring it up. It's not any of my business, anyway,' I say.

It's not.

But Lloyd takes a deep breath and says, 'She's the intern I dated last summer.'

Oh.

Now, I kind of *do* want to know, but in that sick, uneasy way that will only make me feel worse in the end. I want to know what made her so special that he was so heartbroken when it ended, and why this girl made Lloyd think it was better to pretend we'd never met when our paths crossed again.

I wait, and Lloyd looks apologetic – torn – before continuing. 'Last year's cohort invited me out with them a lot, and she . . . I mean, she was flirty, and I flirted back. I liked her, *a lot*, so after a couple of weeks I asked her out. We were spending so much time together and the whole thing was such a rush, I – I fell for her, hard. And I *thought* she felt the same way, but at the end of the summer . . .'

There's a sinking feeling in the pit of my stomach, a look of such dismay on Lloyd's face that my heart aches for him.

'She liked me, but not in the same way I liked her. Mostly, she liked that my dad owned the place and I knew everything about the company, and I'd drop everything to help her out with something.'

A horrified gasp rips from my throat. 'She used you to get ahead?'

'Sounds worse than it was.' He quirks a smile, and it disappears fast, sliding away as he shrugs one shoulder then the other. 'She *did* like me. Wanted to date me. It wasn't all as calculating and cold-hearted as it sounds, but . . . she still did it. And still called things off at the end of the summer before she went back home. She's back in London now working for some consultancy firm and kept reaching out, wanting to pick up where we left off. I only met up with her to tell her I wasn't interested.'

I'm too busy reeling to say anything. So instead, I reach out to give his hand a quick squeeze, trying to convey all the things I can't say – that it sounds awful, and I can't imagine the audacity of this girl to have used him like that, dumped him, and now want to rekindle things. And that I understand, now, why he pushed me away that first week and felt like he had to protect his reputation.

I wouldn't have done that to you, I want to say, but the words stick in my throat.

Lloyd's fingers shift slightly beneath mine, not pulling away but simply acknowledging the comfort. The corner of his downturned mouth draws up a little, his eyes softening, the green flecked with the golden reflection of the lights above us.

'Kinda screwed up my approach to dating a little, though,' he announces suddenly, with a self-deprecating laugh, slipping his hand away from mine. 'I kept getting a little paranoid that girls would care more about the Arrowmile stuff than about *me*, so I haven't dated anyone for more than a couple of weeks at a time since.'

He grins, like it's all a great joke he can laugh at now, but I can tell he really believes that.

I roll my eyes. 'Fletcher, I said it once and I'll say it again – *you sell scooters*. You're not the hotshot you think you are.'

'Not with you to keep me honest, at least.' He laughs, winking at me, and I have to swallow down the smile that threatens to steal across my face. Talking about an ex, about dating . . . It feels too intimate, given our (albeit very brief) history.

I tuck myself a bit tighter into my seat, scooting back against the wall again. The band are taking a break; pop music filters out of the speakers instead, louder than it should be for a coffee shop, but quiet enough to allow for conversation without needing to shout across the table. It's still packed, although the crowd has shifted and changed, people having come and gone in the time Lloyd and I have sat here poking at our shared slices of cake and talking.

Fork poised for the last chunk of carrot cake, I ask, 'Do you mind?'

'Go for it. I'm not much of a carrot cake guy myself.' He claims the last of the chocolate fudge, which I've only nibbled at.

'Why'd you get it then?'

He shrugs. 'You like it though, so it was obviously a good choice.'

'A great one,' I agree, tugging the plate nearer to me so I don't drop crumbs everywhere. 'I, uh . . . I meant to tell you thanks, by the way.'

His nose scrunches, adorably confused. 'For the cake?'

'No. Well, yeah, obviously, but I meant for coming to my presentation on Monday.'

'Oh! You already messaged me after to say thanks. It's okay.'

'Still, I haven't properly said thanks. I . . . really appreciated it. A lot.' I hesitate, my gaze laser-focused on some of the crumbs on my plate. Lloyd waits, obviously sensing I've got more to say – and finally, I continue, 'I didn't expect to see you there.'

'I knew you were nervous about it,' he tells me.

Like it's that simple. That easy.

Maybe it was.

'Thanks,' I murmur, voice thick, eyes prickling. I blink a few times, suck down a deep and steadying breath.

At the edge of my vision, I notice his hand begin to stretch across the table. Towards mine. His fingers stretch out, open, an invitation – and curl one by one into an awkward fist. He draws it back to his side, fidgeting with his napkin instead, unaware I even noticed. Even though he never touched me, the skin across the back of my hand suddenly feels cold.

Composing myself, I look up with a small, plain smile, like nothing's amiss. Lloyd returns it, and I pretend not to notice the disappointment and relief mingling in equal measures in his expression.

Somehow, neither of us notices the cafe clearing out around us.

It's only when an employee in a dark grey polo shirt emblazoned with a cursive 'Keye & Shore' approaches us to clear our collection of empty plates and cups that I take stock of the room around us, finding other employees going around clearing tables ready to close up. The band never came back on, and it's only now I think about it that I realize people have been filtering out steadily for the last hour or so.

Grudgingly, I push my chair away from the table, gathering up my bag and then standing to pull my jacket on. Lloyd seems even more sluggish than I am – weird, since he had another latte after midnight. I'd almost expect him to be wired to the point of breaking, after that.

He checks his watch, his smile small and lopsided and short-lived. 'Well, we didn't do too bad, Annalise. We made it to two-thirty a.m. Real party animals, check us out.'

Two thirty?

I fish my phone out of my bag to confirm it, but even seeing the time for myself leaves my mind boggled. There's no way I've spent over *six hours* with Lloyd, just the two of us, and not because we were, like, trapped in a lift at the office during a blackout or something, forced to be in each other's company with no escape.

(Oh, God, please don't let that ever actually happen.)

There's no way I'm *sad* that the night's finally over, that I have to go home now.

That first night I met him, it was the most fun I'd had in a while. I'd enjoyed letting my hair down a little, making new friends and even having a few drinks. Leaving with Lloyd had been spontaneous, feeding off and into my upbeat mood at the time, the late-night magic of a new city lifting me higher, dizzier.

This hasn't been fun in the same way that was. This has been slow, temperate.

We stretch out our departure, and I'm glad Lloyd's not in a rush. If I could, I'd make tonight last indefinitely. I want to live inside this pleasant little bubble we've created over the last six hours.

It feels impossible to consider that this will end; that outside of this, there's a reality where Lloyd is a pest who monopolizes my time and distracts me from my work, where his smile is something too bright and grating, his attitude cocksure and flippant.

A pang slices through my chest, agonizing in how gradually it spreads through me, how deeply it lingers. Why can't he be more like this all the time? Why can't we *both* be? Why do I only get to see this more vulnerable, less curated version of Lloyd when the stars are sprinkled across the sky and we're alone?

It'd be different if he was horrible all the time. If he just didn't like people, or if he was so focused on his job (whatever it is) that he made no time for anybody else. That, I could understand.

But he's not. The rest of the time he's just . . . *more*. Exaggerated, emphasized. A little further away.

Outside, the air is cool and crisp. It fills my lungs in a crystalline rush, clearing away the heady scent of coffees and pastries. In spite of the deep, violent purple sky and the heavy grey clouds rolling across it, threatening a summer storm, it feels brighter out here than it did indoors – disorienting, like leaving a dark cinema to discover it's still the middle of the day.

'I guess I'd better head home,' I say. Announcing it, like it'll make some kind of definitive end to the night. Stalling, in case Lloyd has any more ideas of places to go in this not-so-sleepy night-time copy of the city.

'I'll walk you home.'

'It's a bit far to *walk*.'

He lets out a small, breathy chuckle. I catch him rolling his eyes before he fakes doffing a hat and sweeps a low, elaborate bow. 'Please, my lady, allow me to escort you home.'

I drag him back up, hands scrabbling at his

shoulders, mortified at the people who glance over. 'I take it back. You're not a bad movie villain. You're a bad movie hero. And I *don't* mean that in the good way.'

Lloyd only grins at me like he thinks it's an excellent compliment, and we make our way back towards Waterloo station, swiping our way onto the Tube. A few other people are on the platform, waiting for the next train towards Clapham. It makes me wonder where Lloyd lives – is this wildly out of his way? Will he have to come all the way back via Waterloo to make his own way home?

Selfishly, I can't bring myself to ask, because then I'll be obliged to say, 'It's okay, I can make my own way home,' and it might bring our night to an end that much sooner.

It's only once we're swaying in our seats, with the gentle rattle of the Tube that's become familiar to me in the last few weeks since moving here, the bubble we'd created around ourselves that I was so desperate to hold on to suddenly feels claustrophobic. He's too close in the seat beside mine; I could count his thick, lovely eyelashes if I tried hard enough. I'm aware of the steady rise and fall of his chest, the way it's in sync with my own, how his body is angled *just slightly* towards mine . . .

His left hand, the one nearest me, is balanced sideways on his thigh, fingers curved slightly. I want to slip my hand into it, feel the heat of his skin against mine, maybe the sweep of his thumb from my wrist to my knuckle like he did the last time we spent a night out in the city together, and . . .

And he's looking at me, really *looking* at me, seeing all the way down to the deepest corners of my soul and drawing me in to drown in the vivid green of his eyes. His breath slows. His head tilts slightly to one side and his full lips part; I can see his tongue move behind his teeth and he must know I'm staring at his mouth.

I wonder if he's thinking about that first kiss, or if he's thinking about this next one.

'Can I ask you something?'

Just like that, the spell is broken. Five words, and he's shattered a moment that I'm suddenly sure existed only for me. The tilt of his head is curious, the pressure of his gaze thoughtful. I bite my tongue and draw back, not quite sure when I started to lean in. My hand has crept closer to his and I tuck it between my knees instead.

'Sure.'

'Why didn't you ask for my number?'

My eyebrows scrunch together. 'Because we don't exactly . . . We don't talk, really. We don't hang out. Tonight excepted, obviously, but . . .'

A muscle jumps uncertainly in his cheek. The weight of his gaze lifts a little as he glances downwards for a second.

'Right. But I didn't mean now. I meant that night we met.'

'Oh.' I startle into speechlessness for several moments. I try to look away, but he makes it so hard. It's too easy to get lost in his beautiful face, and it feels like so much hinges on my answer – like it *matters* to him. I can't decide if I want it to matter to him or not.

The train pulls into Kennington. The doors open, and then close again. The train leaves.

Lloyd waits.

'You didn't factor into my summer,' I finally tell him. 'I don't mean as my boss's son or whatever, I mean, *at all*. I didn't want to muddy things for myself by having some summer fling. I had to – I *have to* – focus on this internship. I didn't need . . . distractions. You know. Romantic entanglements.'

He arches an eyebrow, and I blush, desperately trying not to picture a romantic *entanglement* with him – which, of course means it's *all* I can think about: naked legs wrapped around each other's bodies, the heat of his skin beneath my hands, the way he'd kiss my neck or murmur my name . . .

Is he thinking about what it would be like, too?

Nope, do not go down that road, Anna. Back away – quickly.

I shove him with my shoulder, glad of the excuse to break eye contact for a minute.

'Shut up. You know what I mean. It's not like you asked for *my* number either,' I say.

'Out of . . . habit, I guess. Like I told you, I haven't dated anyone for more than a couple of weeks at a time. I regretted it though. For the record. I really wished I'd asked for it, so I could see you again.'

'Except, when you *did* see me again, you ignored me. Careful what you wish for, I guess.'

That's enough to make him turn away. His body shifts to face forward. His eyes catch mine in our reflection of the dark train window opposite us and then he begins to study the Tube map overhead like he's committing it to memory.

Good. He should feel awkward. He should know how much his behaviour hurt.

We're quiet for the rest of the trip. Wordlessly, he walks beside me to where the pre-furnished rental apartments for the interns are. A few times I notice him pause to cross the road before I can lead the way, and realize that, of course, he's been here before. With *her*.

I tuck my heart down a little further into my chest, deep enough that he can't try to tease it back out again.

I expect Lloyd to leave once I get to the main doors of the building, but he follows me inside. I don't stop him. We both know this night goes no further than my front door.

Once we're there, I fish around inside my bag for my key. I start to say, 'Thanks for walking me home,' but barely get out the first syllable when he interrupts me by saying, 'You didn't factor into my summer either, you know.'

'Huh?'

'I didn't expect to meet you that night. Or like you as much as I did. I know it was shitty, the way I acted when we met again at the office, and I get why you were mad about that. I get it if you still are. I just wanted you to know, you didn't factor in for me, either.'

The sound of his heavy, shallow breathing is so loud it almost drowns out the fact I can hear my blood raging, racing, in my ears; my own breath catches in my throat at the earnestness of his voice. There's a plaintive edge to it that creeps down to needle at the heart I just tried to hide from him.

And because it's Lloyd, who wears his heart on his sleeve and is an open book so much of the time, his emotions always so plain on his handsome face, I believe him.

'I get that you don't want any . . . well, *anything*,' he presses on. 'And I'm not trying to ask for that. But, I mean, we're . . . You said this afternoon that we're not really friends, but we are, aren't we?'

Friends.

Right.

A smile tugs at one side of my mouth before I'm even aware of it. I hope I'm not as obvious with my emotions as he is, and he can't see the regret bleeding through me because 'friends' might be more painful than being nothing at all to each other.

I pushed him away, too. I was the one who said I didn't want to be associated with him, have him cast a shadow over my achievements this summer. I don't have any right to feel regret, or to want more than being friends.

'Yeah. Yeah, we're friends, Lloyd.'

He lets out a loud sigh, relaxing. I try not to let on how much that hurts, either.

'Do you want to shake on it?' I offer, and he laughs. A little of the serious mood from a moment ago lingers though, and before it's gone completely, I seize my courage and tell him softly, 'For the record, it's not just because you pretended not to know me, or whatever. I don't want everyone to think of me as just – another notch on your bedpost, or something.

It'd discredit anything I achieve as part of the internship.'

Lloyd's arms are loose at his sides. I reach out and tug at the cuff of his jacket around his wrist, the place he keeps his heart, and then take his hand in mine, giving it a brief squeeze. He swallows, audibly, and I watch his Adam's apple bob up and down slowly. A little sadness etches its way around his eyes, but it's forgiving, undemanding. There's only silent acceptance. He doesn't try to protest that it would ever have been anything different.

He only nods, understanding.

And then, our hands still clasped lightly together, he leans to kiss my cheek, his lips ghosting over my skin and searing into it all at once.

'Goodnight, Annalise,' he tells me, and leaves, his hand slipping away from mine, leaving me alone with this heady, bittersweet goodbye.

NEW EMAIL DRAFT

Dear Lloyd,

If only you'd kiss me again. It might be a little easier to let you in, then, I think. Your kiss made everything seem right with the world, like everything had worked just to bring me to that moment, to kiss you. How did you do that? Did you feel it too?

Did you want to kiss me again tonight, too?

Maybe it's for the best that you didn't.

Sincerely Yours,
Anna Sherwood

Chapter 17

Most of Monday passes without Lloyd so much as walking by my desk, and for all I tell myself, *Good, I can finally get some work done* – I feel like every nerve in my body is on high alert, waiting for him to show up. I keep recalling freeze-frames of Friday night, moments where I caught myself admiring the perfect profile of his face, or the way his lips moved as he spoke . . .

I half-wonder if he's avoiding me, but ultimately decide that's silly, because why would he? Of course he wasn't thinking about kissing me again, or anything like that. Otherwise, he wouldn't have just asked if we could be *friends*.

Mid-afternoon, I take a quick break from my day of back-to-back meetings to head down to the building's seventh-floor canteen for a real coffee, rather than the instant stuff in the Arrowmile kitchenettes.

There are a couple of other people in the lift, and Lloyd is one of them.

I'm too far away – too shy, suddenly – to say hello, but I catch his eye and give him a friendly smile. He waves back, so casual that I'm now *sure* that the tension last Friday must have all been in my head.

We're not the only two getting out on the seventh floor for the canteen but somehow fall into step with each other nonetheless. The canteen is a wide, open space with floor-to-ceiling windows that let in enough light to make up for the fact the view is obscured by another building close behind; there are dozens of tables, although only a few are occupied. The counters selling hot meals and the sandwich bar have closed, but the coffee cart is open.

I join the queue, with Lloyd just behind me. Two men in front of us, from another company, are in a heated debate. A lady behind Lloyd is on the phone, nodding vigorously and saying, 'Mm-hmm. Yep. Yuh-huh. Totally agree.'

I catch Lloyd's eye, and he pulls a face, impersonating her. I smother a giggle with my hand. The queue shuffles forward, and this time, he's standing nearer, closing the space between us, stealing a few inches from it that might as well be a mile.

And just like that, he resurrects that feeling of

privacy – intimacy – that's been present the nights we've spent together. I feel some of the day's stress easing out of my shoulders and spine, finally relaxing out of being hunched at my desk for hours.

'How was the rest of your weekend?' Lloyd asks – casual, but somehow not; his voice is too low, like he's aware of that bubble cutting us off from the rest of the world, too.

'Quiet,' I say. 'How was yours?'

He shrugs, a full-body action. 'Good. Spent some time with a friend on Friday night.'

Something mischievous gleams in his eyes. A secret that we're both in on. I smile, then duck my head and face forward before I fall for that charm, and try to ignore the warmth blooming in my chest.

It's *impossible* to keep Lloyd at arm's length.

The queue moves again, and this time, Lloyd stands close enough that I can feel the heat of his body at my back, almost inviting me to lean in, to rest my head against his shoulder . . .

Someone calls his name and shouts hello. I spot a man from Nadja's team striding in, joining the back of the queue, and feel Lloyd shifting behind me to raise a hand in greeting.

As he moves, his other hand brushes against mine, sending a sharp electric shock dancing up my arm,

225

making my breath hitch in my throat. I tense up, hoping Lloyd didn't notice, knowing it was an accident – but he doesn't move his hand away, and I feel his fingers ghosting against my skin. His fingertips trace so lightly down my index and middle fingers that it's enough to set my heart skittering. His thumb hooks just underneath them, almost holding my hand but not quite.

My lips part and my breathing turns shallow, but before I can decide to do something – to call Lloyd out on it and ask him what he thinks he's doing, or to respond to his touch the way I'd like to – there's a barista barking at me, 'Next, please!' and I have no choice but to tear myself away from Lloyd, and do my best not to think about how cold I suddenly feel.

It takes every ounce of willpower not to steal a sidelong glance to see his reaction.

Why did he do that? That wasn't just a friendly show of affection, and it *definitely* wasn't an accident. Is he trying to mess with me on purpose, somehow entertained by trying to set me on edge or distract me?

I focus on the hiss of the machine as my iced coffee is made, and study the other people in the queue. A little way off, the lift pings, the doors sliding open – and my mouth turns dry when I see two of the interns step out: Verity is chatting away, looking stressed and distracted; Tasha nods along sympathetically, and notices me immediately. I spin around quickly, heart hammering, hoping she doesn't see Lloyd and think we're here *together*. It's bad enough that I notice her staring at us from her desk whenever Lloyd comes by my team to ask about things. I don't know if she's jealous or suspicious, but whatever it is, I'm glad she wasn't here to glimpse Lloyd's hand on mine just now.

The other barista calls him up next and he stands beside me again. I clutch my purse with both hands, arms tucked tightly to my sides, and as far out of Lloyd's way as possible.

'How's your afternoon looking?' he asks, after ordering. 'I saw you were in calls earlier, but I could really do with going over some stuff about Phoebus IV, and you're –'

'I'm busy,' I say quickly – too quickly. His easy smile slips, my tone too sharp. I add, 'Sorry,' but even I can tell how insincere it sounds.

I can't keep him at arm's length – but I can't keep letting him get this close, either. It's too close. It's too much. All-consuming in that dangerous way that it would be so easy to sink into, let it block out everything else.

He's a risk I can't take.

I suddenly imagine a reality where I come back in a couple of years to work full-time, and *he's* still around, too. Maybe he'd even have a real position, instead of floating around and lording it over everybody; maybe I'd even have to report to him. I cringe at the idea.

When Lloyd and I were total strangers, I resolved not to let him interfere with my summer; this internship means too much to me. That shouldn't change now, I know – but I'm not used to this. To feeling like this, or feeling so *much* for someone. I've never had close friends, and I was quick enough to prioritize my degree over my boyfriend last year after that failed midterm and the ensuing breakup. I'm used to feeling on the outside of things and a general, background-noise level of discomfort.

I don't get that, around him.

This would be so much easier if he didn't make me feel so . . .

Accepted. Liked.

Like myself.

Lloyd doesn't try to call for me to wait up when I take my iced coffee and hurry off, making me think he got the message.

And the next day, when I see him coming my way around midday, no doubt purely to ask me whatever questions he has about the Phoebus IV car, I do my best to pretend I don't see him and jump up to chase after Tasha, Izzy and Monty on their way to lunch instead.

It's the sensible thing to do, I tell myself.

It's best for both of us.

Chapter 18

The neat rows of chairs under the marquee have been long abandoned, and while some people have dropped to the ground around the handful of picnic blankets that were provided, most are standing around nursing cool drinks or plates of food. The presentations are over, team-building activities wrapped up, Topher Fletcher's grand middle-of-the-year pep talk having segued seamlessly into the arrival of the food and opening of the pop-up bar. Now, the well-organized all-team meeting has dissolved into rowdy games of boules, one game of tag started by a tipsy Marketing department, and plenty of lounging around.

It's a total change of pace from the stern, focused faces always hurrying around the office or bent intently over their computers.

I lean back on my elbows in the grass, head tilted up towards the sun. Burnley's head rests on one of my thighs as he sprawls out flat, bemoaning how full he is after scarfing down three burgers and two hot dogs in practically one go from the barbecue. For such a petite guy, he sure can eat.

Elaine is sat delicately next to him, legs folded beneath her, with Freya on her other side. Louis and Dylan are sat back-to-back, playing some silly game Louis just invented that seems like a mix of Bullshit and Rock, Paper, Scissors, busy arguing over the non-existent rules (which I swear Louis changes every time he's challenged on them, or losing the game). Monty ambles back over with a plate laden with vegetable skewers, and Burnley doesn't hesitate to take one.

I jostle my leg to get his attention. 'If you're sick on my lap, I'll hold it against you forever.'

His defensive retort is mostly lost through a mouthful of chargrilled red pepper and halloumi, but I'm pretty sure it's something like, 'What, me? I would *never*. You wound me, Anna.'

Across the lawn, standing with a group of people I've come to recognize as interns from way back when, Tasha laughs. It's a high, grating sound that carries; I pick it out of the sounds of the party, my ears pricking up before I look over at her. She tosses her hair to some guy from HR. Izzy and Verity are with her, too, and one of the guys from our cohort. Again, I have to wonder if it's only me who dislikes Tasha – if *I'm* the problem.

With any luck though, we'll never see each other again after this summer. Even if that means I get offered a job here (I hope) and she doesn't (I also hope).

Turning away from her, I spot some of the other interns scattered about in different groups. A few – mainly the more viciously competitive ones, who apparently care much less than I do about appearing 'unlikeable' – prefer to keep to themselves, and stand around now with their teams from the office. My own team are similarly scattered, so I don't feel obligated to spend any particular amount of time with them beyond the tower of marshmallows and spaghetti we built earlier as part of a teamwork-building exercise. (We came second; I figured losing to the team of real-life scientists from the labs plus Lloyd was as good a win as we could get.)

I like the venue for the party. I'm told it's not as glamorous or exciting as other years and the catering is less impressive, but I think it's pretty great. There's a pond with a large water feature reaching up out of it in the middle of the lawn, a collection of young trees in the two far corners, a pretty tangle of ivy behind some flowerbeds covering up an otherwise imposing and ugly brick wall. It's a spacious garden out the back of some museum I've never heard of, and it seems weird to find it between a collection of buildings in the middle of the city. I'm not used to thinking of London as somewhere with much greenery, not like where I'm from, until I stumble across pockets of it like this. It seems wrong, somehow, that they should be shut away, hidden like this.

It makes me miss home.

I should probably try to go visit. Maybe next weekend?

No. That's no good. Dad and Gina are taking the boys on holiday next weekend, now school will be finished. But another time, I promise myself. Soon.

It's just . . . kind of hard to talk to Dad, lately. Every time I speak to him on video call, I see his face crumple into a frown and he asks, 'You're not working too hard now, are you, Anna?' because he knows how much I pushed myself to get here in the first place. He'll ask about plans with the others I don't usually have, and I know what he's thinking. I know what it makes me think.

That I'm sacrificing too much. That it's not worth it. That I'm doing what Mum did.

It doesn't help that he'll always end our conversations with, 'You know, your mum would like to hear from you, Anna. She's really proud of you and how well you're doing.'

If I wanted her to know how well I was doing, I'd tell her myself.

Besides – I'm almost afraid to leave the city. There's some irrational, panicky part of my brain that says if I leave, I'll come back to find my key to the flat doesn't work and my pass for the Arrowmile offices has been deactivated. They'll decide I wasn't much good at my job anyway and kick me out, or find out I lied about my age and kick me out because of that.

Which is *ridiculous*, because if they were going to do it, they'd do it regardless of whether I was here or back home with my family. But still. What if I jinx it?

Soon, though. I'll go home soon.

'Hey!' Monty suddenly calls out, lifting a hand high in hello. 'There he is! C'mon over here, mate.'

Conversation dips as we all turn to see Lloyd making his way over, having changed direction after Monty called out. He's dressed more casually today, a pair of aviator sunglasses propped up in his curly hair and the short sleeves of his plain white T-shirt accenting the toned muscles of his arms, sending a flurry of butterflies through my stomach.

Beside him is Will. Side by side, I see Will is the taller of the two by about an inch and his face is slightly longer, oval where his brother's is angular. His hair is cropped even shorter than the last time I saw him, but other than that, I'm startled by just *how* alike they look for non-identical twins. It's no wonder I mistook him for Lloyd initially. The main difference seeing Will this time is the way he's dressed: it's a far cry from the band T-shirt and shorts combo he wore last time, more like something Lloyd would wear to the office. His shoes are polished, too.

'Alright, guys?' Lloyd nods around us all in greeting. His eyes skim right over me and – no, I'm not hurt. It's fine. For the best.

I've been successfully avoiding him all week. I probably deserve to be ignored – if anything, I should be glad about it.

He introduces everyone to Will, and pauses at me before saying a bit too quickly, 'And you know Anna.'

Anna. Why doesn't it sound right, when I've been trying to insist on him calling me that for weeks now?

'I know Anna,' Will confirms, and gives me a shy, stilted wave but warm smile.

Lloyd finishes up introducing him to Monty and Burnley and then hesitates. Now, he looks at me. It's a furtive, awkward look, more towards my elbows than my face, but he seems to be weighing something up.

Whatever it is, he's too late to decide either way – Will takes a seat, expanding our little circle. Lloyd follows suit, striking up a conversation with Freya, apparently a topic from some earlier discussion they've had.

'So what do you do, Will?' Elaine asks him. 'Are you at uni?'

'Yeah. Edinburgh. Classics.'

'Edinburgh! God, you couldn't have gotten much further away, could you?' Monty says, laughing, and Will glances at Lloyd before smiling along with the joke.

'Tell me about it. Means I don't get back much during term time, but I like it there. Nice part of the world, you know?'

'Oh, for sure.' Monty nods with authority, although I remember him saying the other week he's never been to Scotland. I decide not to point that out.

'Classics?' Elaine asks then, smiling politely. 'That's so interesting. So different, too!'

'Different?' Will asks. His mouth quirks up, one eyebrow lifting, in a look that's uncannily like Lloyd. 'To what?'

'Well. Just, um. You know.' She gestures around vaguely, but we all know what she means. *Different to Arrowmile*. A blush starts to creep up Elaine's neck and face as she stammers, 'I just haven't met a lot of people studying it, I suppose. Ended up in a bit of a STEM bubble, with a Maths degree.'

'Inevitably.' Will nods, not unkindly. And then he

tells her, 'The science thing was never really my forte. Lloyd's the geek.'

His twin pins him with a deeply unimpressed look. It'd be borderline threatening if he weren't obviously trying so hard not to smile. 'Says the guy who tried to teach himself *Latin*. For *fun*.'

Will pushes his glasses up his nose. 'It *was* fun.'

'I didn't realize you were a science nerd, mate,' Dylan says, speaking across to Lloyd now. His game with Louis is abandoned; I'm not sure who won, and don't think they know either. 'Thought you were more into the business side of things and that was why you were always hanging around the labs. Checking in on investments and progress and stuff.'

'Yeah. I mean, yeah, obviously.' Lloyd's shrug is easy, his smile blasé. 'I was just pretty good at science in school. Picked up a few things, hanging around at Arrowmile over the years.'

I don't miss the look Will cuts him, or the way Lloyd pointedly ignores his brother. Will sees me looking and his mouth twists into a curl that seems to say: *What can you do?*

It slots something into place. Another piece in the jigsaw of who Lloyd Fletcher is, one I didn't know I was curating. The whole exchange, seeing this new dynamic, feels meaningful in a way I can't quite pinpoint. It's a corner piece in the jigsaw, anchoring something – I'm just not quite sure what yet.

'Bet you're proper jealous of him,' Burnley tells Lloyd, jerking his head at Will. 'He gets to enjoy a summer of freedom while he's home from uni, and you're stuck working.'

Lloyd laughs it off, and the conversation slides quickly into the subject of summer holidays. It's a frequent one among the interns so nothing new, but I let myself get carried along the familiar rhythm of it, with Will's occasional comments sparking new interest.

Lazy in the afternoon sun, cosy with friendly company, my mind wanders to how Lloyd told Will about the night we kissed. Did he tell him about last Friday night, too?

Not that it matters. Obviously. We can't be anything more than colleagues.

Friends. As challenging as that is.

The party shows no sign of ending anytime soon. The venue is booked until ten o'clock, with the intention of people sticking around a while longer picking at leftover food or continuing the morale-boosting bonding experience of lawn games and free drinks.

The heat of the day is just starting to abate and I'm at the pop-up bar to get a drink. I hadn't wanted to get *too* into the party spirit at what is predominantly a work event, so I've been sticking to soft drinks all day.

One Pimm's won't hurt, though.

As I order, a body sidles up beside me, heavy and unbalanced. An arm presses into mine before they right themselves.

'Can you make that two, please?' Will flashes me a quick smile, pushing his glasses up his nose. 'Hiya. Sorry, I didn't mean to crash into you like that.'

'Had a few too many beers?'

'Just naturally woefully uncoordinated,' he corrects me.

'Well, better than sneaking beers out of a crate and being sick in the office.'

His eyes blow wide. 'How did – *oh my God*. That arsehole. He's never let me live that down, you know, after I told Dad what happened and he got in trouble. We *both* got drunk, you know. We both had the bright idea to go find that crate of beer.'

'Don't worry – from what I heard, Lloyd's end of that story was *way* more embarrassing than yours.'

'The yoga.' He scoffs. 'Kinda wish I'd been there to see it, you know.'

'I didn't realize he got in trouble over it.'

Will sighs, fidgeting with the laminated menu on

the bar counter. 'Yeah. Yeah, I guess I shouldn't be surprised he missed that part of the story out.'

'I can see what you meant,' I tell him, thinking about the last time we spoke. 'About him not always being a total prat. Well – he probably was a bit, stealing the spotlight to run a drunk, impromptu yoga class, but I mean the part where he was trying to help you out. I can see why you defended him.'

Will smiles softly to himself. His fingers drum absently against the menu. 'I heard you guys hung out last Friday.'

He says it quietly enough that I know he's conscious of people overhearing; whatever Lloyd *has* told him, he's obviously aware it's not common knowledge. It does something funny to my insides. Guilt? Excitement?

'Yeah,' is all I reply.

By now, our drinks are ready. Beads of condensation sweat along the outside of the glasses already. I poke the black paper straw around and take a sip, revelling in it. Pimm's was the first drink I bought after I turned eighteen. My birthday isn't until the end of the school year so I'd been left behind with soft drinks whether I liked that or not, while my friends got to flaunt their new IDs at bartenders and bouncers. But a bunch of us went to a beer garden when it was finally my birthday, and even though it poured down with rain and we had to huddle under the parasols, they were adamant I'd get to enjoy my first 'proper' taste of summer in a beer garden – which they unanimously decreed was Pimm's. It was a proper, grown-up, *cosmopolitan* kind of drink, they insisted. Appropriate, now we were all officially real adults.

I'm not sure I like it very much, but I like the memory of it enough to make up for the taste.

Will and I drift to the fringes of the party, watching everybody else in companionable silence. A game of boules is wrapping up in the middle of the lawn near the pond, a crowd gathered around. A laugh peals out from the centre, hearty and infectious; someone shifts enough that I can see Lloyd there. He's collected up some of the boules and is juggling with four of them, launching them higher and higher, to the amazement and delight of Arrowmile employees and interns. Topher is there, too, having collected up the other boules, laughing as he watches. He nudges Lloyd, trying to get him to demonstrate how to juggle so he can join in.

'Does it ever get on your nerves?' I blurt.

I don't know Will. A couple of brief, polite conversations and some second-hand stories from his brother don't amount to *knowing* him. But he's oddly easy to be around – not in the way Lloyd is, but in a calmer, more present way. I know a few conversations don't make a friendship, but I feel a weird sort of kinship with him, not unlike how I did with Lloyd that first night we met.

So I'm not altogether surprised when he doesn't need to ask what I mean.

Instead, he just says, 'You've seen *Hamilton*, right? I mean, have you?'

'Of course. I'm not a monster.'

He chuckles. 'Well, you know how Hamilton's always super obsessed with his legacy? Can't stop going on about it, bases all his decisions around it?'

'Sure,' I say, although I have no idea where this is going until Will looks back at his brother and dad, gesturing slightly with his glass.

'Dad makes Hamilton look like he doesn't give a fuck about his legacy.'

'Oh.'

Oh, indeed. It's another few pieces of the jigsaw. Unprompted, Will carries on.

'And, I get it. He started up this company a few years before we were born, and start-ups are always rough at the beginning. Especially when he had to sink so much of the original funding into development that wasn't going to pay off for a while. It was tough. He worked hard. Poured his heart and soul into it. And . . . I respect that, I do, but I just wish he hadn't expected *us* to do the same thing. Everything was always about Arrowmile when we were growing up. I think I learned what a profit and loss statement was before I even finished learning my times tables. After we finished up Year Seven – I remember, because when other kids went back to school and we had to talk about "what I did on my summer holidays" in French class, ours was always way different to everyone else's . . .

'That summer, we spent a lot of time at Arrowmile. Mum had just died, and I don't think Dad knew what to do. With himself, or us. He threw himself into work and I guess he thought if it helped him, it'd work for us, too.'

'Oh,' I say again, and it's all I can manage, not sure how else to voice my sympathy. I'd never made the connection of Lloyd talking about when his mum died to the same summer he started spending so much time at his dad's company.

'It wasn't too bad,' Will says affably, with a fleeting but sincere smile. His weight shifts from one foot to the other as he gets more comfortable. 'It was nice to have some familiar faces around – we knew a lot of the staff already from odd trips into the office – and it was definitely better than being home with this big empty presence where Mum used to be, you know? But it became habit, and Dad started . . .'

He sucks a breath through his teeth, uncertain.

'You don't . . . I didn't mean to pry,' I tell Will, feeling equally awkward all of a sudden. 'You don't have to tell me about all this.'

It's not like I have any right to this information. I'm curious about Lloyd, but I'm not owed answers. Certainly not from Will, who I barely know.

But I get the impression he wants to talk about it, that there's some relief in sharing it with someone who might understand, so I wait patiently after he nods that it's okay, until he's ready to carry on.

'I want to say Dad spiralled, but that's not fair. It wasn't quite like that. I think, maybe, after putting so much of himself into the company, he didn't have that separation anymore. What was Arrowmile, what wasn't. We'd become part of that, too. Hanging around during half-terms, getting to know how everything worked. After a couple of years it just started to get . . . intense, you know? *Dad* got intense. Started talking about legacy, and how this would be ours one day, trying to insist on us putting in the effort to know *everything*. Wanted us to know how to run the place like he did before we even finished school.

'I say "we",' Will says on an inhale, a frown slipping onto his face, 'but I mean me. I'm the oldest.'

'You are? I – I mean . . . Lloyd didn't tell me that.'

'A whole thirty-eight minutes. It used to be this great big joke when we were little, but then Dad started piling on the pressure, and it just . . . It wasn't for me anyway, but it *terrified* me. I started imagining this life where I'd just follow whatever path he laid out, become some carbon copy of him, and . . .'

'And you didn't want that.'

Which, knowing the little I do about Will, is more than understandable. I can't quite picture this shy, modest guy in Lloyd's place, schmoozing and soaking up the entire spotlight.

'Yeah. It all came to a head when we were picking out our A levels. I picked History, English, French, and you had to get your parent to sign off on it. Dad refused. Said there was no point, it wouldn't help me in this industry. We had this blazing row, but . . .' He smiles faintly, watching where Lloyd is clapping a boules teammate on the shoulder for their throw. 'Lloyd has a better mind for business than I ever did. He's better with numbers than me. And he likes all the science behind it. He always took the brunt of it when we had work shovelled in front of us to do for Dad, and he did it again. Stepped right up to Dad's side and said it didn't matter what A levels I was doing. *He* was doing "useful" ones. We didn't both want to be vying for Dad's job one day anyway, and he'd be the better fit for it.' Will sniffs, but it's dismissive rather than upset. 'Dad and I weren't exactly on great terms for a while, but Lloyd started spending more time getting involved at Arrowmile, and eventually Dad didn't care that I didn't want to be.'

It's not just a few pieces this time, but a whole section of the puzzle that gets revealed. Suddenly, Lloyd's shiftiness about his degree when I asked why he doesn't just swap to a different course makes so much sense. Will's absence from Arrowmile and the way people only talk about Lloyd – even the way he hesitated after Monty joked that Edinburgh University couldn't be much further away.

I stare at Will for a few minutes, but he doesn't seem angry or agitated about any of it. He just looks . . . *peaceful*. Content with his lot in life. Grateful for it, even.

I follow his gaze to where Lloyd is taking his turn at boules.

'Now I feel bad for giving him so much flack about being the golden boy and always swanning around the office, sticking his nose into everything,' I mumble.

Will laughs, nudging my arm with his elbow. 'At least someone is. Wouldn't want him getting too big for his boots, right?'

'Right.'

But – God, I can't *believe* I didn't know any of this. Lloyd was being cagier than I realized. And it kind of explains why I've seen such different sides to him away from everybody else, too.

'It's been driving me crazy,' I admit. 'Trying to work out why he seems like a totally different person when we're alone compared to . . . this. The whole parading around like a prize pony thing. Turning the charm up to max, being the prodigal son and whatever. I guess now I know.'

'Like I said – I know he seems like a prat, but don't hold it against him. He's a good guy.'

'What would he be doing if he didn't have your dad pressuring him? At uni, I mean. Something science-y?'

'Oh, for sure. I caught him looking at Chemical Engineering courses a few times.'

My brow furrows. 'So, what, like . . . the kind of thing where he could figure out how to create new experimental coolants for an electric vehicle? I would've thought that was right up the Arrowmile street. Enhancing the legacy, or whatever. Did your dad really have a problem with it?'

Will pulls a face at me as he sips his drink. 'Dad doesn't know. Lloyd never brought it up.'

'Why?'

His face falls even as his mouth remains upturned. He's not easy to read in the way Lloyd is, but I'd put my money on him feeling ashamed.

'My guess is he didn't want to rock the boat by deviating from the plan. Didn't want to drag me back into the firing line and another argument.'

I think about the different facets of Lloyd I've seen, and the common threads that link them all. The endless optimism and his ever-ready smile, the charisma he wields so effortlessly and how he hides so little of his emotions. The single-minded determination I've seen him display.

I picture him standing between his brother and his dad, and never complaining or lording it over Will, just accepting it for what it was with that quicksilver smile, his charm like armour. Guilt squirms in my stomach, tying it into knots, and my mind replays a ruthless montage of all the times I've tried to knock Lloyd off his pedestal in the office.

I glance over at him now. Topher is there, clapping a hand on Lloyd's shoulder as he says something to a few other people.

And again, all I can say is, 'Oh.'

Chapter 19

Will and I end up hanging out for most of the afternoon. There are a few more glasses of Pimm's. By the time evening is drawing in, the crowd thins and the drinks flow a little more freely. Most of the interns are still here, although Elaine, Freya and Burnley went home a while ago. Lloyd has been busy charming his audience of Arrowmile employees. I wonder if it's starting to wear on him, if it ever does. There's a chance he's so used to it that it's become second nature and he doesn't even notice he's doing it anymore.

'You know,' Monty slurs, clapping a hand on Will's shoulder and giving him a playful shake, 'you're a really cool guy. Like, *proper* cool. We thought you were gonna be some really stuck-up weirdo.'

'You thought he was, like, twelve years old or something,' Tasha points out with a scoff, just as I think 'stuck-up' is rich coming from Monty, with his uber-posh accent and lofty attitude.

'Well, *yeah*, but that's only cos nobody talked about him much. Our man of mystery here, huh?' He ruffles Will's hair now before slinging a heavy arm around his shoulders enough to knock the wind out of Will.

He coughs, trying to recover, but manages, 'Uh, thanks? I think.'

'Say something in Latin again, mate. Go on.'

Will rolls his eyes, but it's good-natured. He's flushed, a little sweaty, and even less steady on his feet than usual, but he seems to be having a great time. Enjoying a little spotlight for once, maybe.

He thinks about it for a moment then lifts his glass, declaring, '*In vino veritas!*'

'*In vino veritas!*' we all chorus, lifting our own glasses, sloppily clinking them together in the centre.

'Technically, I guess it's "*in* Pimm's *veritas*",' he tells me afterwards in a low voice, snorting at his own joke and dissolving into giggles. Monty, not even hearing what the joke is, joins in the laughter. Tasha gives a thin 'Ha-ha' so as not to be left out and stands impatiently, her gaze flicking over her shoulder as she debates leaving. I wouldn't be sorry if she did. I'd love to know Will's take on her.

Verity and Izzy come over to join us, arms linked

and eyes bright. They lean on each other slightly for balance. They're chatting animatedly about something and flag us down, though we aren't going anywhere.

'Settle a debate for us,' Izzy calls. 'What's the best tree?'

'And you can't say Christmas tree,' Verity says, levelling us each with a stern look in turn. 'Because that doesn't count.'

'It absolutely does,' Izzy grumbles, pouting, but everybody is suddenly too busy debating different kinds of trees – the most inane thing turning very quickly into an intense discussion. Tasha rolls her eyes, but is quick enough to lay down her argument for lemon trees.

Behind her, I notice Lloyd stepping away from a few people. Taking a breather, maybe. He rolls his shoulders, stretching a little, rubbing the back of his neck before taking a swig of his pint. His face tilts up towards the last of the sunlight before it can vanish completely behind a nearby building.

While the others are distracted ('Who's ever actually *seen* a fig tree?' Verity wants to know) I excuse myself and slip away. Lloyd doesn't seem to notice me until I'm almost within arm's reach. He blinks in the golden, hazy summer evening light, turning to face me. A toothy, lopsided smile peels across his face. Each move is leisurely, deliberate. He's a bit drunk, I realize.

Same.

'Saw you hanging out with your new bestie.' He nods to where I left Will with the others.

'Yeah. He's going down a storm – everyone loves him.'

Lloyd's face splits into a fond smile. 'I'm not surprised. Once he gets chance to come out of his shell a little, he's a real social butterfly.'

'How about you? Having fun?'

'Always do.' He takes another drink. 'You?'

'Sure am.'

Somewhere nearby, there's a loud, booming laugh. It's jolly, spurring on a few other people to laugh too. I start to look around, although I already know the source of it – I've heard that laugh plenty today. It's Topher. In front of me, Lloyd cringes.

'Can I ask you something?' I say.

'Hopefully it's not about my secret to winning boules, because that's all natural talent, baby. Can't be taught.'

'It's not. It's just . . . That first night we met, you said your dad never smiles anymore, since . . . since your mum passed. So I'd pictured this grumpy, sullen kind of guy with a face like thunder who always looked pissed off at the whole world, but . . . I mean, he *does* smile. A lot. He's always smiling around the office. I guess I just don't get it, is all.'

'Oh. Right,' says Lloyd quietly, and then he falls silent. His mouth presses into a downturned line, a muscle jumping in his jaw. A small pucker appears between his eyebrows and I regret asking at all, if it's made him look like this.

But after hearing some of the truth from Will, understanding Lloyd better, I'm even more curious than before. He's never sounded like he resents his dad, but I wonder what else I don't understand about him.

Glancing around, Lloyd says, 'Let's go somewhere to talk.'

Our options are a little bit limited, but nobody pays us any attention as we wander to the far side of the garden near the trees in the corner, disappearing into the small grove.

It's cool here, dark beneath a thick canopy of leaves. There's a greenish glow to the shadows that makes Lloyd's eyes glitter that bit brighter, a freshness in the air that feels sobering as it fills my lungs. The ground is soft, the grass longer and patchier than on the main lawn. The noise of the party feels muted, but maybe that's more to do with the fact that Lloyd has so much of my attention right now than our perceived privacy.

Lloyd finds a spot against the brick wall that the trees are so artfully disguising, leaning against it with a heavy sigh and pushing his sunglasses further up on top of his head. He offers me a small, half-hearted smile that pulls at one side of his mouth and then the other, disappearing as soon as it shows itself, and then he slides down to sit in the grass, setting his half-finished drink at his side. Heavily, he pats a hand to the empty spot beside him, head lolling back to rest against the wall. I join him; I sit a bit closer than I meant to, and our legs press flush against each other. It sends a little fizz of warmth through me, but Lloyd doesn't seem to react, and I worry that it'll make things weird if I make a big deal out of moving away.

Eventually, Lloyd draws an uneven breath and tells me, 'It's different. It doesn't reach his eyes anymore. It's his . . .' He scoffs; it's barely audible. 'We used to call it Dad's "showroom smile". The one he'd put on for investors or at presentations and stuff. Mum would tease him about it all the time, do this great impression of him – chest all puffed out, oozing charisma, putting on a bit of a voice . . . It used to just be this kind of amped-up version of himself for work, but now it's just . . . who he is.'

'Sounds kind of like someone else I know,' I say before I can think better of it.

Lloyd, for his part, doesn't look offended. He just tilts his head in acceptance. 'I always took more after Dad.'

'For the record, I like who you are when you're just being yourself.'

A little of the tension seeps out of his shoulders. 'Me, too.'

He looks me in the eye as he says it though, speaking so softly that I understand he's not talking about himself – he means that he likes who *I* am, but . . .

'I don't try to be anybody else.'

Lloyd gives a quiet chuckle, amused but not mocking. He reaches out to place a hand on mine, resting on my thigh. His fingers link through mine, bare arm brushing against my skin, and I'm so dizzy with the abrupt realization that maybe he was protecting *himself* when he asked if we were friends, I can't quite remember why being this close to Lloyd is a bad idea.

'You let me in that first night,' he murmurs, his voice so low, so intimate, that I find myself subconsciously tilting my head closer. Lloyd's thumb brushes gentle arcs across the back of my hand. His head tips a little further towards mine and I feel his breath tickling at the base of my neck.

It's intimate in a way that the midnight kiss by the river wasn't.

'You put up so many walls, like you're so used to pushing people away, but . . . you didn't with me, that night. I keep trying to find that girl again.'

Do I really do that?

But what I say, in a voice equally quiet and soft, is, 'Well, we can't all wear our hearts on our sleeve.'

He seems as struck by that idea as I was about not letting people in, and I can't help but smile a little: it's hard to imagine that Lloyd is such an open book and doesn't even realize it. He feels so deeply, how can he not know that it spills out for anybody to see?

Leaves rustle overhead, the sun filtering down in dappled pools of gold. Laughter and chatter drifts towards us from the party, but here, tucked away from it all, the sound of our breathing is loud: slow, and even, and measured.

'I guess not,' he says. My head angles towards the sound of his voice; a shiver runs down my spine when his mouth grazes against my temple as I turn to face him. 'But you let me in when I ran into you that night at the office. And when we got coffee, last week . . .'

Of course I let you in, I think. He'd been a stranger, and seemed lonely and lost just like I felt – I was drawn to him, by some invisible connection that stole the fear of being judged for a few precious hours. I recognized something in Lloyd that I saw in myself, and I want to explain that to him – but I can't. It feels like saying anything at all would detract from this, from him, and I can't bear to do anything that might mean he'll stop staring at me like the rest of the world has stopped existing except for the two of us, like everything hinges on what I'll say next. I lick my lips, heart racing, trying to prolong this moment as long as I can, and Lloyd's eyes flicker down to my mouth. They're dark, the green of his irises barely visible.

I don't know who moves first. Whether it's his hand slipping out of mine to skim up my arm, leaving a trail of goosebumps in his wake, or whether it's my free hand reaching up to cup his face before my fingers thread through his tousled curls. I don't suppose it really matters either way; it all feels so inevitable when we both lean the rest of the way into each other, to kiss.

That first kiss was the best of my life. It was languid, confident. New and exciting, enhanced by the dreamlike night and the way I had bared my soul to this total stranger, both of us swapping secrets while the stars lurked out of sight. And I'd be lying if I thought I hadn't built it up in my memory to be more than it was.

This, though.

This . . .

I didn't build up that memory at all.

It's different this time. Fierce, almost, and electric. There's a hunger in it, his hand strong between my shoulder blades as he pulls me in tightly against him. It tugs me off balance and I fall against him, the hand that was holding his until a few moments ago now braced against his chest; a gasp spills out of my mouth before he swallows it in another kiss, his own mouth curving into a smile against mine.

Lloyd nips gently, playfully, at my lower lip, and I deepen the kiss in response. A low groan rumbles in the back of his throat, reverberating through his chest, and when his hand slips from my back to my ribs, skirting up to cup my breast over my bra, it pulls a breathy, keening noise out of me, too.

His kisses become more fervent and I match them with a passion of my own. Why have I wasted time pushing him away when we could have been doing this instead? It feels so intense, so *right*. I like the way his hands feel on me, the way I can feel his heart thundering in his chest just like mine. I like that this is the guy I've spent quiet, friendly nights getting to know, and how real this feels.

I like that he coaxes my heart out onto my sleeve, too.

He cups my cheek in one hand and while he doesn't quite move away, it gives us both chance to catch our breath. Lloyd's nose nuzzles against mine and my eyes flutter shut again.

'You have no idea,' he whispers, 'how long I've been wanting to do that.'

And there's a loud thump nearby, someone running towards the trees in peals of laughter – an abrupt and glaring reminder of where we are, and what a mistake this is.

I jerk away from Lloyd's embrace suddenly and sharply, the gravity of what just happened sinking in. I'm sure the deafening pounding of my heart is going to give us away.

What was I thinking? Anyone could have seen us! I will *not* be the girl who had a fling with Lloyd Fletcher during her internship – especially when they might think that I've been *using him* to get ahead, like his ex from last summer.

We shouldn't have snuck off together in the first place, even just to talk. I wonder if anybody has noticed yet that we're both missing, if they've made the correct assumption that we've vanished *together*. Tasha would have a field day, if she knew.

Someone tramples around nearby, on the other side of the trees, collecting a rogue boule. 'Got it! Honestly,

Craig, what the hell kind of throw do you call that? You're meant to knock the *other* team's balls out of the way, not your own!'

They retreat back to the party. My breath rushes out of me in a loud huff, and I hunch to wrap my arms around my knees, unable to believe what a lucky escape that was. I'm aware of Lloyd straightening up next to me, rearranging his arms and legs like he's unsure what to do with himself now.

Suddenly, it's so hard to make eye contact with him. Even just seeing his face out of the corner of my eye is difficult, a weird mix of guilt and want knotting in the pit of my stomach.

'We shouldn't have done that,' I say, although I'm not sure if I say it more for my benefit or his. 'We can't do that again.'

Lloyd raises the back of his hand to scrub his nose, where a little of my makeup has rubbed off, a faint dusting of pale powder against his dark skin – a dead giveaway of what we've been doing, if ever there was one.

My lips are bruised with the impression of his kiss. My skin tingles where I can still feel the warmth of his body next to me. I press my fingers to my mouth, finally managing to peer up at Lloyd – who, for once, is impossible to read. The party on the other side of the trees seems to get louder; the tang of panic is heavy on my tongue.

'Did you hear me?' I ask, worry sharpening my whispered voice. 'That can't happen again. It shouldn't have happened *this* time. We both ... We just got carried away. Right? Had a couple of drinks, forgot ourselves.' Yes. Yes, that's all it was. Swept up in the celebrations and the party atmosphere. 'It didn't mean anything.'

'Ah,' he murmurs – but this isn't the intimate, husky tone from a few minutes ago. It's unrecognizable, almost: it's *bitter*. 'There it is.'

'There what is?'

'You. Pushing me away. *Again*. Blowing hot and cold with me, constantly.'

'I'm not –'

But, I am. He's right. As determined as I am to *not* get involved with him, I keep being drawn back to him, and it's not made any easier by his constant presence at work, his happy-go-lucky attitude like nothing can ever get him down. But *he's* the one who invited me to hang out; *he's* the one always making so much effort to be friendly, to . . .

To pull down whatever walls I have, and find his way back in.

'You are,' he says, so definitively that I don't even

try to argue. 'I like you, Annalise, but that doesn't mean you get to walk all over me like this. Last week, we said we were friends – but then you spent the whole week avoiding me. Treating *me* like I was a total stranger.'

'Well, now you know how it feels!' I exclaim, shame squirming through me at the realization of how callous I've been with Lloyd's feelings.

'So, you were doing it to spite me? To get back at me? You thought you'd . . .' He trails off for a moment. 'Were you, what, luring me back in, acting like my friend, *flirting* with me – just to get revenge? I *told you*, I know I made a mistake. I panicked. I thought you understood.'

'That's not – Of course I wasn't –' Disbelief that he might actually *believe* that rattles me so hard I have to take a moment, concentrate on forming a coherent, whole sentence. 'Maybe *I* panicked, too. But come on – we both know that if anybody found out about us, *I'm* the one who'd take the flack for it. You said you wanted to protect your reputation, but that's not true – you just don't want to get your heart broken again. Nobody cares if you hook up with some random intern! But they'll care if they think I used you to get ahead. Nobody's going to tell Arrowmile's golden boy that his work doesn't hold any weight, that he didn't earn anything. Everybody *loves* you – you can't put a foot wrong.'

Now, Lloyd's gaze cuts sharply to mine. It hardens when he realizes I mean every word I say, and seeing *him* so serious in return makes me feel uneasy. His jaw clenches tight, eyes flashing in defiance and anger; there's something he wants to say, snarling words in his defence to take the sting out of mine – but he swallows it all down, settling for a derisive scoff and a resentful curl of his lip.

This reaction is worlds apart from the boy who just held my hand and told me he'd been waiting to kiss me again. It's worlds apart from the boy who asked me if we were friends last Friday night.

He opens his mouth to say something – but cuts himself off with an agitated sigh, turning sharply away. He snatches up the beer he set aside earlier and takes a deep drink.

I want to know what he was going to say, what kind of argument he would've made in his defence. The more I've gotten to know Lloyd in those quiet, lonely nights together and with the things I've learned about him from Will, I feel like I'm underestimating him – selling him short in ways I don't understand.

I want him to prove me wrong, now. Prove that he *is* the guy I thought he was that first night, after all.

To say something, anything, that will keep me from shutting him out again.

But in the end, he doesn't say anything at all.

So I leave, going back to the party. I fetch a new drink and rejoin my friends, who are tipsy and too excited by my return to ask where I went in the first place.

And when Lloyd appears a few minutes later, he's the life and soul of the party once more.

Chapter 20

I'm so wound up from everything that happened with Lloyd that I feel like a woman possessed for the rest of the party. I lose track of how many glasses of Pimm's I drink – only knowing that it's enough for me to stop tasting them. My filter, and my sense of worry that I'll say the wrong thing to people, vanishes. I make dry remarks that cause the rest of the group to howl with laughter; I even tell Tasha at one point to get over herself and stop being such a snob, which makes the others shriek and giggle – but it's not satisfying in the way it should be. It feels mean and twisted, and not like me at all.

'Are you okay?' Will asks me later. We're back at the pop-up bar, and I lean against him a little for support.

'Fine! Totally fine. Why wouldn't I be?'

'I don't know. You just seem . . .'

Off. Because I am. Trying to bury the shame of my flagrant disregard for the heart Lloyd wears on his sleeve, and the sting of him having no defence when I pointed out that my reputation was the only one at risk if people found out about us.

Will waits, giving me an uncertain look, concern knotting his brow, but I give him a playful shove with my shoulder and tell him, 'I'm just having fun! Don't be such a party pooper.'

I'm not having fun.

I want to go home, and bury myself in my duvet and sleep through the entire rest of the internship. I want to find Lloyd and tell him I'm sorry for icing him out and for kissing him – it's not his fault I got caught up and forgot myself.

I want to tell him I'm sorry for being so prickly all the time and putting so many walls up; I didn't even realize I did that. They must have been there for so long, maybe a consequence of never having close friends and Mum walking out on us, that they've become so much a part of me I don't know how to take them back down and let him in. That I'm not even truly aware when I *do* let him in, because he makes it so easy.

But after I snapped at him like that, I don't think Lloyd will let *me* in so easily next time; he doesn't owe me anything, not really.

For his part, you'd never know anything had happened. He's mingling with different groups of Arrowmile employees, getting involved in games and cracking jokes. He laughs brightly, smiles broadly like nothing's wrong, looks relaxed and casual as ever.

I fare worse and worse the harder I try to have fun. The booze makes my brain sluggish and my tongue heavy; it's tricky to keep up with conversations, as hard as I try. There's a nagging voice in the back of my mind that I should be sensible, sober up, that above all this is a *work event* and I should be trying to impress people – but I tune it out, thinking that if that's how I sound to Lloyd, no wonder he thinks I act coldly towards him. No wonder I've always had such a hard time making friends.

I drown it out with another drink.

But I'm not used to alcohol and even less used to any kind of partying, so it's not too long before I have to step out for a break: my stomach is churning and I can't trust myself not to throw up over the boules. I go inside to the toilets to close myself in a stall, sitting down with my head between my knees for a few minutes and focusing on my breathing, only emerging when I'm sure I'm not going to be sick.

I stumble out of the stall, unsteady.

'Anna? Are you okay?'

Verity's face swims in front of me. She's in the queue for the toilets, but reaches for my arm. Her hand feels hot against my clammy skin.

'She's *drunk*,' says another voice from next to her. This one is snide and superior; Tasha's smirk cuts a bright red line across her face where she's reapplied her lipstick. 'God, Anna, can't you handle your drink?'

How pathetic, I think she says but then I decide I must have imagined it, because Verity doesn't react, even to laugh.

'I'm fine.' I don't *sound* fine. My words all run into each other. Neither Verity nor Tasha seems very convinced, but I stand up straighter and say something like, 'I should probably just get something to eat. I'll be okay,' and Verity nods and they let me leave.

Back outside, I head straight for an empty bench. The warm evening air is sticky and stifling, but there's a cool breeze that fans over my skin and helps me feel less queasy.

I get my phone out to pretend to scroll, so that at least I look occupied rather than drunk. There's yet another text from Mum – how would I fancy meeting up soon, maybe? *Uh, not at all, thanks.* She'd like to see me! *Well, she should've thought about that thirteen years ago before cutting us out of her lives.*

A body sits down next to me on the bench – so close and familiar I think it must be Lloyd; or maybe uncoordinated Will – but I'm hit by the smell of expensive cologne and after a split-second I realize that it's Monty who's sat beside me.

He drapes an arm across the back of the bench, behind my shoulders, and hands me a pint of water with a grin.

'Thought you looked like you could do with this.'

'You're not wrong.' I take a sip, the taste cool and grounding. I drink slowly, worried of unsettling my stomach further. I go back to scrolling aimlessly through my phone, surprised that Monty doesn't leave.

'You don't have to stay,' I tell him.

He shrugs, a gesture I feel as his shoulder moves against the back of mine. 'S'okay. I needed a break, too. Kind of full-on, isn't it? I can't decide if I'm supposed to be networking or challenging Topher Fletcher to a game of beer pong. Makes me want to see what they do for their Christmas party,' he goes on. 'Now I bet *that's* a riot. Bet they go all-out for it.'

'I guess if this summer goes to plan, we'll find out.'

'Here's hoping. Wonder who'll make the cut. Present company excluded, obviously.' He gestures at both of us, and I'm oddly flattered that Monty thinks

I've got what it takes to get offered a permanent position when the internship ends. Looking around at the others, scattered in small groups around the lawn, he says, 'Tough competition.'

'Uh-huh.'

'Be good to see a few friendly faces back next year though, won't it?'

'I don't graduate next year,' I blurt, brain too sluggish to stop me – but luckily, Monty misinterprets it.

'Oh! I didn't realize you were doing a master's. Nice. Well – the year after, then.' He grins at me again, and I drink some more water rather than having to respond and outright lie about my degree.

After a little while, when I've finally finished my water and sobered up a bit, Monty asks if I'm feeling better and I'm relieved that I am. He doesn't mock me for not handling my alcohol like Tasha did, like I expected he would – I know rugby lads have a pretty heavy drinking culture, and Monty's been no exception to the rule so far this summer.

Instead he just says, 'We should go get a bite to eat, that'll help. The others are probably hungry, too.'

'Good plan. Thanks for looking out for me.'

'Hey, it's all good. What are friends for, right? Come on – let's go get dinner.' He slaps his thighs before standing up, and it takes me a beat to follow suit, too surprised that Monty – cool, popular Monty – considers us *friends*. It's a good feeling.

He mistakes my hesitation for being wobbly and drunk still, so offers me a hand up. His skin is cool and coarse, and I can't help but compare the sensation to when I've held Lloyd's hand.

As if thinking his name summons him into existence, the hairs on the back of my neck prickle and I'm suddenly acutely aware of a pair of eyes on me. Glancing in their direction, I see Lloyd and Will standing not too far off, and Lloyd's green eyes lock onto mine. A myriad of emotions flicker across his face before Will nudges him and says something; I can't get a handle on what's going through his mind, exactly, but I know it's nothing good.

After what happened between us earlier, I can't blame him. He must really hate me.

I feel Lloyd's gaze following me all the way over to the others, and even after we leave as a group to get some dinner.

Chapter 21

The sound of my phone buzzing violently on the nightstand wakes me up. The blueish glare of the screen is blinding in the complete darkness of my bedroom and I wince, fumbling to yank the charger out of my phone and then squinting at the screen. My stomach gives a nervous flip as I worry that it's Dad or Gina, that something's horribly wrong – because obviously, something *has* to be horribly wrong to call at almost three o'clock on a Saturday morning, and who else would be calling me?

My brain struggles to understand that the name on the screen isn't Dad, or my stepmum, but Lloyd.

Why is Lloyd calling me?

It rings out, and as the missed call notification appears on the screen I see a string of messages from him. I only get a glance at them long enough to understand that he's apparently been drunk-texting me, before he's calling again. This time, I answer.

My voice is thick with sleep when I say, 'Hello?'

It sounds like I don't know who it is. I probably should've just gone with asking, *What's wrong?* After what happened at the party earlier I sort of assumed we'd go back to ignoring each other around the office next week, but here he is – ranting down the phone to me in the middle of the night.

'You don't get to *do* stuff like that,' he snaps down the phone, agitated – but there's a sadness in his words that takes some of the edge off his anger, makes his voice wobble just a little. 'You know? You can't kiss me like that – *look at me* like that, say it doesn't mean anything, and then go out with Monty. Fucking *Monty*.'

'*What?*'

'Let me guess – that didn't mean anything either, right?' He scoffs, and I still have no idea what he's talking about. There's an electronic beep, muffled, coming from his end of the line. 'Somehow, I'm not buying it. What floor are you on? Six?'

I sit bolt upright, holding the phone tight to my ear, eyes wide as my room comes into focus, a landscape of familiar shadows.

'Fletcher. Please tell me you're not in the building right now.'

'Six sounds right,' he says, mostly to himself.

I'm on the eighth floor, but Burnley and Freya's flat is on the sixth. God, what if Lloyd hammers on their door? What if they answer, and he says he's looking for me? There's no way either of them would keep that a secret.

'I'm on eight,' I correct him, already hurtling out of my bed to meet him outside.

I tiptoe past the others' bedrooms and then ease the front door open as quickly as I dare, praying they don't hear the lock click shut after me. I allow myself a small moment of relief when I find I've gotten there before Lloyd: I had a horrible feeling I'd come out to find him knocking on random doors looking for me – worst-case scenario, waking up Tasha just down the hall.

The lift doors open a moment later and Lloyd strides out, faltering to a stop when he sees me. He's obviously been out all night – there's dirt on one knee of his jeans like he's fallen over, and his T-shirt is rumpled, his dark hair tousled. He doesn't seem to notice what kind of state I'm in: hair in French braids and mussed by sleep, barefoot and in a mismatched outfit of pyjama shorts and a too-big Freshers' Week T-shirt I got on a rare night out.

For a moment, he stands there, and I hear his breath hitch, see the misery on his face, his lips parted and gaze plaintive – pleading.

Then he steels himself before approaching me; his face is cast in shadow from the dim automatic lights in the hallway, and his eyes so dark I can hardly see the green of them.

'Fletcher,' I tell him. 'You can't just show up here like this.'

'Tell me,' he demands, chin jutting out. 'Tell me it didn't mean anything when we kissed.'

There's a steadiness and determination to him that makes me realize he isn't here in some kind of drunken stupor – however tipsy he might have been to text me earlier. It's plain old emotion clouding his judgement now.

And it makes him loud in the otherwise total silence of the hallway, his voice reverberating off the walls. I immediately panic that it'll wake the others and hiss, 'Keep it down!'

It's obviously not what he was hoping to hear because Lloyd's face crumples. He steps even closer, coming right into my personal space; I move back instinctively, bumping into the wall.

'Tell me,' he insists again, voice rough and heated. 'And I'll go. I'll let it go, and we'll just keep things professional around the office, and we can pretend none of it ever happened. That first night, the kiss earlier . . . That's what you want, isn't it?'

Yes, that's what I want. That's exactly why I spent this whole week before the party avoiding you, pushing you away, and . . .

And how can I tell him it didn't mean anything?

If that was truly the case, things wouldn't have gotten so messy. I would've been able to stay away, tuck the memory of that first night into a distant corner of my mind and not let it bother me when I saw him around the office. If it didn't mean anything, we might've even become good friends this summer, late-night cake and coffees a regular occurrence.

How can I tell him that it meant . . . *everything*?

I hold Lloyd's gaze and swallow the lump in my throat. His eyes burn, jaw tightening – although he seems apprehensive more than anything else, now, and when my lips part, I hear him catch his breath.

Words fail me though, and I can only shake my head.

Slowly, he lifts his hand to cup my cheek, his touch searing into my skin and making me lean into him until my chest brushes against his; he's close enough that I feel the length of his erection pressing into my hip, and heat rushes to the pit of my stomach. The thumb he drags over my lower lip sends a shiver through me. I'm alive and dreaming all at once: brought to life by his touch, made so delirious by it that it surely can't be real.

Finally, I manage to say something.

'Please,' I whisper, desperate for him to touch me – kiss me. For *more*.

Lloyd lowers his head to kiss the sensitive skin of my throat, just below my ear, that light touch alone electric enough to pull a small, needy sound from me, make my back arch in an attempt to get even closer to him.

'What about your date?' he murmurs at my ear – and I remember his bizarre ramblings on the phone, pushing him away slightly.

'What date? What are you *talking* about?'

'With Monty. I saw the two of you together, at the party. He invited you to dinner.'

Oh my God. I'd laugh, if every nerve ending in my body weren't on edge, willing Lloyd to kiss me again. 'We *all* went to dinner. That wasn't a date. He was just – being a friend. Making sure I was okay.'

Lloyd's eyes glaze over as he realizes he completely misread the situation. I can't even find it in me to tease him for being jealous. No wonder he was so upset, or really believed our kiss meant so little to me.

There's a beat, and I find my hands fisting tightly in Lloyd's T-shirt like I can anchor him here, suddenly worried that he'll leave.

But then his lips crash down on mine, demanding and relentless, and I moan into his mouth, something taut unspooling in the pit of my chest. Lloyd presses his hips hard against mine, sending a thrill of want through me. My hands move from his T-shirt to cord through his hair, grasp his shoulders, follow the planes of them and travel down his back. Lloyd's hand, which had been at my waist, travels underneath the hem of my T-shirt, stroking up past the waistband of my pyjama shorts to settle at my ribs, hesitating as if waiting for permission to go two inches higher to my bare breast.

When I slept with my ex-boyfriend, there was a clumsy sort of restraint to it, awkward exchanged looks as we each worried we weren't doing it right, somehow, or that it wasn't good enough. And it *was* good enough, I always thought.

It pales in comparison to what I feel with Lloyd right now, even with both of us fully clothed. This burns through me, ignites every nerve in my body. I'm hyper-aware of everywhere he's touching me and everywhere he's not yet, but that I want him to. I don't worry about where to put my hands or what my tongue is doing as we kiss, and it doesn't feel awkward to whisper, 'Let's go inside.' And it feels so completely natural to unlock the door, to take his hand, and lead him quietly inside, to my bedroom.

Lloyd takes a seat on the bed, and I look at the small, gentle tilt of his smile as he reaches out to draw me nearer, the earnest openness in his eyes as they glow almost cat-like in the darkness of my room, and I know that whatever this is, he feels it too. It means something to him, the way it does to me.

So I let him take my arms and pull me in to stand between his legs, relaxing at the feel of his hands firm on my hips, the gentle arc his thumb traces on one side. He holds my gaze for a moment longer, then tugs me a little closer, making me stumble and catch his shoulders for balance. A quiet laugh rumbles through him, but I don't feel embarrassed.

It's impossible to be embarrassed with Lloyd. It feels like he already knows the best and worst of me.

I want to know all of him.

I start to use my hold on his shoulders to make him lean back, so I can get on the bed with him, kiss him again, take it further than we could outside in the hallway. Lloyd resists though, glancing up to give me a cheeky attempt at a reproachful look, one that makes my heart skitter and pulse pick up, and curious enough to wait to see what *he* wants to do.

Lloyd starts with my T-shirt, finding his way underneath it once more – with both hands, this time, pushing it up and letting me pull it over my head. I drop it to the floor, my breathing shallow as his fingers trace a path over my stomach and up to my breasts, his mouth following with soft, open-mouthed kisses. I arch into his touch, and gasp when his tongue flicks over my nipple. My eyes flutter shut and I lean more heavily on him, losing myself in the sensation.

His hands skim lower, thumbs hooking my pyjama shorts and underwear before he takes them off me, too. He draws back slightly to look, to pay attention as his hands roam along my thighs, my arse, my hips, with a reverence that feels like worship.

And somehow, it's still not enough.

'Fuck, Annalise,' he mutters, and I bring one knee up onto the bed, half-straddling him, fumbling with his T-shirt. I give up to focus instead on palming the bulge at the front of his jeans, excitement sparking through my veins when a groan stutters out of him and his hands tighten on my legs, fingers biting into my flesh.

There's no resistance this time when I press against Lloyd's shoulders for him to lie back, so I can lower myself down with him to kiss him. His hands are everywhere, and his teeth catch my lip like they did when we kissed at the party and yet, nothing like it at all. This is hungry, not playful, but I like it. He slips a hand between my thighs, snatching the air from my lungs, and I feel his lips curve into a smile against my collarbone.

His other hand toys with my breast and his lips find mine again, tongue ravishing my mouth as my hips rock helplessly, needily, against his fingers.

It's still not enough. I want to feel the heat of his skin flush against mine, the weight of his body wrapped up with mine. I want to see him come undone; I need to hear him moan and say my name like that again.

I start to move off him so I can undo his jeans, finally get him out of his T-shirt, but Lloyd grabs my hip to hold me in place, a smirk on his lips and challenge in his eyes when I try to wriggle away again – and buck against him, when his thumb finds a particularly sensitive spot. Like he's almost daring me. There's part of me that's tempted to see what happens if I push him, see what delicious way he'll find to tease me, but his thumb circles again and I lose the battle, back arching and a moan catching in my throat as I remember the need to be quiet, to not wake up my flatmates.

Lloyd kisses me again, tenderly this time, and I'm pliant as he turns us around for me to lay against the pillows. He undresses as I catch my breath, and I stare as he bares the smooth skin of his back, then turning and giving me a glimpse of the coarse, dark hairs on his chest. His jeans come off, and then his boxers.

I drag my eyes back to his face as he gets back on the bed with me, kneeling between my legs as he rolls on the condom he just took out of his wallet. I cup his cheeks to draw him in for another kiss, languid and soft, and I shiver at the toned, hard lines of his body as he lowers himself down against me, enveloping me. Lloyd groans, low in the back of his throat, as he slides inside me, one of his hands fisting in the sheets for a moment. His forehead leans against mine.

'Annalise,' he murmurs, and that's when I know.

It means everything to him, too.

Chapter 22

Lloyd sneaks off to use the shared bathroom down the hall, borrowing my dressing gown for a little modesty, and I lie in the rumpled bedsheets, dizzy and breathless and elated. When I hear him coming back a couple of minutes later, I suddenly feel cold and exposed, sprawled naked on my bed like this, and grab the sheet, tucking it around myself.

Lloyd, for his part, shrugs off the dressing gown, hangs it back on the door where he found it, and slips back into bed with me. I don't hesitate to burrow into the warmth of his embrace. He reaches for his phone on the nightstand, clicking the screen to life.

'Half past four,' he says, turning back to me.

'Somewhere to be?'

'Just wondering how late we made it this time. Beats our record, I think.'

I remember our conversation about all-nighters

from Keye & Shore and smile. 'I'm not sure it counts when I went to sleep for a few hours.'

'I . . . Yeah. Sorry, for waking you up. Although hopefully,' he adds, grinning, 'I made up for it.'

I know it'd be easy to go along with his teasing, but there's something about the comfort of his arms around me, the cocoon of night-time that seems to cut us off from the real world, that makes me feel it'll be harder to burst our little bubble this time – safer, to say the things I should.

'I am sorry, for the record,' I tell him. 'For the whole . . . blowing hot and cold, like you said. It wasn't fair of me. I was mad at you for not just talking to me that first week, but then I did the exact same thing, and I'm sorry. I didn't mean to make you feel . . .'

'No. No, I – *you* were right. What you said yesterday. That this would – look worse for you than it does for me, if people knew.' He pauses, a frown tugging at his face, a tension prickling at the air I can't quite place.

It takes me a minute to figure it out.

I push up on one elbow slightly, to look him in the eye better.

'People *can't* know,' I say quietly. 'I'm not trying to push you away again, Lloyd, I promise I'm not. But – you understand, right? I don't want this internship to go to waste because people think I only achieved what I did because you were helping me, or whatever – just like you don't want them thinking you made the same mistake twice.'

He's unnervingly quiet and still, a stark contrast to the larger-than-life attitude I'm so used to seeing from him.

Then Lloyd reaches for my hand, lifting it so he can press a lingering kiss to my knuckles, his fingers squeezing mine as he lays our hands back against his chest. He smiles at me as he says, 'So I should probably sneak out now while everyone's asleep, huh?'

I don't argue, and I kiss him goodbye at the front door.

But there's an uneasy feeling curdling in the pit of my chest, and I can't help but think that smile didn't reach his eyes.

I'm not sure whether it's weirder if I text Lloyd throughout the rest of the weekend, or weirder if I don't. In the end, I decide against it – he doesn't text me, either, and we'll see each other soon enough anyway. There are butterflies in my stomach as I envisage more stolen touches in the queue in the canteen like last week, or maybe another late night working long past when everyone else has gone home, a quiet place for another kiss, maybe being able to sneak him back into the flat again after the others are in bed . . .

On Monday morning, when I join a few of the others for our usual early-start commute to the office, Tasha falls into step beside me to ask pointedly, 'So how was your weekend, Anna? Did you get up to anything *fun*?'

She does this all the time, asks when she *knows* I didn't have any exciting plans or skipped out on something the rest of them had planned. She probably thinks I spent the whole weekend nursing my hangover from Friday, after that comment about how I couldn't handle my drink.

She reminds me of every bully from school. The people who thought they were so much better than me and that I didn't deserve their time of day. The nasty, catty girls from my uni halls who were always quick to put me down and make me feel so silly and insignificant.

And I'm so, so sick of it.

I remember all those pep talks about 'not stooping to their level', or not giving people like Tasha the satisfaction of knowing she's got to me, but I so badly want to bite back at her, knock her off the pedestal she's placed herself on.

She sneers at me, and whatever retort I might've come up with falters on my tongue.

And that's not because I'm the bigger person.

It's just because she makes me feel so small.

It's Tuesday before I see Lloyd again. I get back from a meeting with Laurie and some of the Finance team, laptop and notebook tucked into the crook of my elbow, nodding along as Laurie asks me to write up some actions and then give an update (aka 'send an email with some bad news') to the project team for the Vane engine.

Butterflies erupt in my stomach at the sight of Lloyd, and I fight to keep my expression neutral, not to give anything away. For once, I hope he's here with some work-related excuse to talk to me.

Next to me, Laurie says, 'Ah, there he is! Heard I missed some incredible juggling skills at the party last week – you'll have to give us a repeat performance sometime!'

Lloyd pauses his conversation with some of the rest of my team to reply, 'Absolutely. Hey, how was Disneyland?'

As she tells him how 'harrowing' it was, a story I've already heard her tell, I have to bite my tongue again to refrain from saying how much I'd like to go, how fun it sounds. Somehow, I don't think that will make me sound like the sort of competent grown-up who would be offered a permanent role here when summer ends.

Laurie returns to her desk in her usual spot opposite me. Lloyd, lounging against my desk with his hands braced against it and legs stretched in front of him, straightens up and moves out of the way when I approach to put my things down. He's usually wilfully ignorant of my personal space; I can sense tension crackling in the air between us now. Like maybe he's worried if he's too close, he won't be able to keep from touching me.

'Alright?' he says to me, and maybe I'm imagining it but his smile seems strained, not quite reaching his eyes.

'Yeah,' I say, clearing my throat when it comes out too breathy. 'Great.'

'Have you taken lunch yet?' he asks me, which is a ridiculous question when it's only just a few minutes past twelve.

'No. But I have some stuff to write up from that meeting, before I forget any of it.'

He nods, but then, more loudly, he says, 'Michaela, you can spare Annalise for half an hour, right? I just wanted to follow up on some questions about the Phoebus IV before I drop by the labs tomorrow.'

Weird. He's going a little overboard to cover up us spending time together at the office. Lately, he just drags a chair over to my desk without asking my manager permission to interrupt my day.

'Hmm?' My manager looks up, Lloyd's hundred-watt smile blinding her to the confused face I'm pulling right now. She smiles back, waving a hand. 'Absolutely. That's not a problem – is it, Anna?'

'Sure,' I say, not having much choice either way now. 'No problem.'

'Meet me downstairs at half past?' Lloyd says to me. 'We can go grab a coffee.'

'Okay.'

A mix of nerves and excitement fizzes through me as he strolls off, leaving me to write up my notes. He's invited me out for lunch. Is it like a date? A little privacy away from the office?

At half past, I find him waiting just outside the lifts on the ground floor. His smile seems a little too wide, too casual, and we swipe out of the barriers in silence.

We end up a couple of streets over, at a cafe far enough away that I don't think anybody from the office is likely to stumble across us here. At least if they do, we can pretend it's about work. Like we're just two normal people on a normal lunch break. Not people who can't seem to stay away from each other . . .

Lattes in hand, we pick a table in the corner by the window. I face the door so I can be on the lookout just in case anybody we know comes in. Namely the interns. Namely, Tasha.

Hands clasped around his caramel latte, his shoulders hunched, Lloyd seems tense. Nervousness traces its way around the frown that furrows his brow, and it catches me off guard. I assumed he was acting weird because he was compensating for trying to be so normal around me in front of everybody else, but . . .

But.

Why do I feel like I'm about to be dumped?

'I've been thinking. About what you said the other morning. About how people can't know.' He lifts his eyes to mine. 'I don't want to feel like some dirty secret. That's how I ended up feeling last summer, and it was *shit*.'

Oh, my God. I *am* being dumped. He slept with me, and now he doesn't want anything else to do with me, and –

'I want to go on a date with you, Annalise. A real one, not some weird, covert one involving stolen cake or late-night lurking while your flatmates are busy.'

Yes.

Where? When? Anytime, yes, I'd love to.

My mind flashes with a montage of how this summer could be, if I let it. It's sweet, enticing . . . And it sours quickly, when I imagine how people at Arrowmile might react, how they'd assume the worst of me.

'Lloyd . . .' My mouth is dry and I swallow, hard. I catch myself fidgeting with the napkin beside my coffee and snatch my hands into my lap instead. 'I can't. You know why.'

But Lloyd's body language shifts in the blink of an eye. He relaxes into his chair, reaching a hand across the table to me, an invitation, his eyes brightening as he smiles at me, optimistic and resolute – not just hopeful, but completely convinced of whatever he's about to say.

'I know you're worried what people will say, but you're halfway through the internship already! They've seen what you're capable of. They know what kind of person you are and how hard you work – dating *me* isn't going to change that.'

'You can't know that,' I say, and my voice comes out as a whisper, scratchy and thin. I feel shaky, hollowed-out. It's no longer a creeping sense of dread – more like a solid, leaden doom, in the face of his optimism.

'Nobody has to know we met before the internship, or anything else. We could just go from here. I just think . . .' He trails off, but only to chuckle, his smile stretching even wider. 'Whatever we have, Annalise, it means something. And that's worth a shot, isn't it?'

Of course it means something. It means so much.

But – does it mean *enough*?

My mind starts careening through what *actually* dating Lloyd might mean, and it heads straight for disaster. Whispers behind my back about the times he's stopped by my desk and how maybe I was too busy flirting to do my job, vicious murmurs laced with truth. Not getting a permanent job offer because nobody thinks I earned it. *Getting* a job offer, and having people wonder if it was only because I'm with the boss's son. Interviewing at other places only to have them find out about it when asking Arrowmile for a reference . . .

I spent years at school knowing that when I was grown up, everything would be better. Focusing so hard on making sure my future would be something worthwhile, successful, important. At uni, that felt close enough that I could reach out and take it.

Is whatever I have with Lloyd worth risking the future I've been working so hard towards?

Immediately, I know the answer.

Just like I knew it after I failed that midterm because I'd been paying more attention to my relationship than my degree.

'I don't want you to feel used,' I tell Lloyd, wondering if I can talk him out of it. He seems so determined, but he's right. We *do* have something. Surely he can't want us to just throw it away? Isn't this a negotiation, not an ultimatum? 'You know that's not what I'm doing. What's so bad about . . . the way things are?'

A muscle ticks in his cheek, his smile stiffening. 'You mean where you kiss me, and look at me like you do, then panic and push me away again? Put your walls back up, act like someone else? Because that makes me feel pretty shitty and used, Annalise.'

Like you're so great at letting me in all the time? Like you don't do your own version of that, hamming it up around everybody else in the office?

Not a negotiation after all, I guess. Hurt bleeds into his voice and I know how awful I felt the first week at Arrowmile, when he acted like we'd never met; he must've felt the same way every time I rebuffed him.

He told me he wanted me to let him in, that he kept looking for the girl he met that first night. Someone more honest and vulnerable and real. Someone warm, and likeable.

I'd like to be her. I really would.

But I can't. I'm this person, who has to be pragmatic and do the sensible thing, who doesn't get swept away on the tides of a summer romance.

'I don't mean to make you feel like that,' I tell him honestly. 'And I'm sorry. You make it so easy to be around you, even if . . . Even if it's a bad idea. You want to think the best of people – and I admire that about you, really, because it's not something I've ever been able to do. But you can afford to do that – everybody at Arrowmile practically worships the ground you walk on. You've grown up there, know it inside out, and they all know you'll be running the place someday. Nobody has a bad word to say about you. Why would they? You go around with that smile, chatting to everyone, charming them, making them feel like – like they're so special, as long as they have your attention. Like they deserve to feel that way. It's impossible *not* to like you, Lloyd.

'But it's not like that for me. It never has been. I can't coast along on my dad's name and legacy. I'm cold and unlikeable – remember? You've had everything handed to you, so maybe you really *can't* understand where I'm coming from, but I've worked too hard to get here to risk throwing it away now, not when there's only six weeks left to go. If that's really how you feel about us, then maybe we can be friends, Lloyd, and if you need someone to hang out with every once in a while, then maybe that can be me, but I can't be more than that. I can't mess this up. It's too important to me.'

More important than you are, than you could be if I let you.

Lloyd's confident attitude finally vanishes. I watch

the hope dim in his eyes, the glitter of it replaced by something dark and wounded as he lowers them, watching the steam curling off his coffee instead. He turns the mug so the handle is at a ninety-degree angle to him then traces a warp in the wooden tabletop with his fingertip.

'Well,' he says. 'I guess that's it, then.'

'I – I guess so.'

There's a beat, and the world seems to stop for a moment, hinging on our next decision. Me: waiting to see if he'll say it's okay, we don't need to make a big song and dance about dating all of a sudden and can carry on as we are, he understands. Him: waiting to see if I'll realize what I've just done – what I've cost us both – and if I'll blurt an apology, change my mind.

I don't, and neither does he.

Lloyd pushes to his feet, abandoning the latte he hasn't touched. He's does a good job of trying to conceal his hurt. A heroic effort, really, because somehow even with the pain of rejection heavy in his eyes he musters up that charming smile I'm so used to seeing, and it seems real enough.

'See you around the office, then. Civil and polite, right?'

That's what I asked for, weeks ago, when I thought it would be easy to stay out of each other's way.

'Right.'

I watch him leave, trembling, reeling from everything that just happened. What I've done.

But I had to. It's what's best. This internship could shape the rest of my life. How can that compete with a boy I've known for only a few weeks?

It can't.

It didn't bother me when I broke up with my ex-boyfriend. That was the smart, sensible decision then, too, just like this is. But this leaves me uneasy, full of regret, wishing things had been different.

In a daze, I head back to the office. I'm swept into meetings for a couple of hours, peppered with questions and asked to take notes, kept blissfully busy and distracted for the rest of the afternoon. It doesn't leave space for heartache.

I manage to not think about it, or him, until that evening. Louis is out on another first date with someone he matched with on an app, and Elaine gets home late from the office to find me sniffling and teary-eyed on the sofa, huddled under a blanket despite the warm evening.

'Anna! What happened? What's going on?' She hurries over, perching on the edge of the sofa near my knees and putting a hand on my arm, rubbing it through the blanket. With her other hand, she reaches for the box of tissues and hands me a fresh one; the one I'm crying into is sodden. 'Did something happen at work? Back home?'

I shake my head. But now she mentions it, I miss home. I miss Dad and Gina and my brothers.

I miss a time when I wasn't falling for Lloyd and forced to push him away, again, once and for all.

Elaine keeps rubbing my arm, all sympathy and compassion, ready to listen and help as best she can. I even miss *her*, and she's right here; I'm mad at myself for all the times I haven't hung out with the others when they've asked me because I was more interested in putting in overtime for work I'd agreed to, just to prove myself, or because I baulked at the idea of spending a small fortune on some cocktails. It's not just Lloyd I've been keeping at bay this summer, but people who could be friends, too.

'It's just –' I sniffle, and a hiccup spills out of me as fresh tears trickle down my cheeks. 'There was this boy. And now . . . there's not.'

'Oh, sweetie,' Elaine sighs. She kicks off her shoes and tucks her feet up beneath her on the sofa. 'Do you want to talk about it?'

No. I want to bury it deep, deep down and far away and forget these feelings ever existed. I want to blot the memory of kissing him out of my mind, ready to act like this was

never even a thing in the first place once the summer's over.
I don't want to wallow, because then it makes it real, and I'm
supposed to be better than this.

But instead, I tell her. I tell her about the sweet, funny guy I met who made me laugh and swapped secrets with me, and the best kiss of my life. I tell her that I need to focus on the internship and I can't be the person he thinks I am, and how he puts up a front most of the time, too, oddly secretive for someone so open. I tell her about his big heart and easy smile, and that even though I know it's right to call it off, it still hurts.

Elaine gives me a hug and hands me more tissues as I cry, and tells me I'm worth more than a boy who'd mess me about and be so careless with my feelings anyway.

I don't correct her, and she promises not to mention anything to the others about my little breakdown.

'It's just embarrassing,' I say.

Elaine squeezes my hand. 'Been there. Heartbreak's a tough bitch, Anna, but so are you.'

It's the first time I think I've ever heard her swear, and it's enough to make a laugh bubble up out of me.

'Thanks. I think.'

'You're welcome. God, that was a rubbish way to comfort you, wasn't it, calling you a bitch? I promise you're not. Sorry. It wasn't –'

'It was a great way to comfort me. Thanks, Elaine.'

She smiles, looking a little relieved to hear it. 'Hey, some of us are doing an escape room on Thursday evening, if you wanted to come?'

I was planning to stay late on Thursday. I have meetings until six and figured I'd have some stuff to write up afterwards, and I'd promised to help Laurie with a spreadsheet which she needs back by Monday, and . . .

And I smile at Elaine. 'That sounds great. I'd love to.'

I told Lloyd I can't afford distractions, and I meant it. But maybe I don't have to sacrifice having a life *completely*.

Just one that involves covert dates, and stolen kisses, and him.

NEW EMAIL DRAFT

Dear Lloyd,

When we met, you asked me to tell you something true. I told you I didn't believe in love.

I meant it then, but I think it's become a lie, now.

Here's something true: you've made me believe in love. It's a cruel joke, considering I can't accept it. A horrible twist of fate. I must have scorned someone in another life, I think.

This isn't what the movies promised. Summer romances are supposed to be a montage of fun dates and carefree afternoons and whispering secrets in the dark. We did that last part, but instead of carefree afternoons we've tiptoed around each other, and instead of fun dates you've just sent me feedback I didn't ask for on my research reports.

I wasn't wrong, when I told you I think love is overrated. It is. Nobody tells you it's supposed to hurt this much. And it doesn't automatically make everything fall into place, either. Relationships are something you have to put work into, like I said that first night. I can't give you that kind of effort and attention this summer, and I don't think you'd know how to.

I wish things were different. That you weren't you, maybe.

But then, I don't think I'd love you if you weren't you.

So instead all I'll say is: I'm sorry, that I'm me, and that this is how it has to be.

Sincerely Yours,
Anna Sherwood

Chapter 23

In an attempt to distance myself from how things imploded with Lloyd, I use some of my precious few days of leave to take a long weekend, visiting my family at Gina's parents' place in Devon. As cathartic as it is, the weekend is over too quickly in a blur of good food, card games, long walks and baking.

I feel an unfamiliar twinge of regret when I'm back in London and setting my alarm for the morning, but it's not because I'm worried about running into Lloyd – it's because I realize *how much* I needed that time with my family, away from any and all thoughts of work. It's unnerving to see how quickly I've let Arrowmile consume my life, and I think: is this really what I've spent my whole life waiting for, barrelling towards head-first? Is this really what I want the rest of my life to be like?

I do, at least, get a small reprieve when Tasha is

absent from our usual little commuting group the next morning. Monty and Dylan ask about my weekend with my family, in peals of laughter when I tell them how I helped Gina's mum bake a cake for her book club. They're reading *Twilight*, and she insisted that she couldn't make the very-predictable red velvet cake . . .

'*Because*, she said, and I quote, *there's a vanilla man if ever I saw one.*'

I don't think they fully believe me until they see the photos on my phone of our sparkly, broody Edward Cullen portrait painted in icing onto a vanilla sponge.

Dylan's laughing so hard he's nursing a stitch in his side. 'I can't believe your gran's reading *Twilight*. Has she watched the films?'

I shrug. 'I didn't ask. I haven't seen them. I haven't read the books either – although I don't really feel I need to, now. She practically gave me a TED talk on it.'

'They're iconic,' Dylan declares. 'The films, at least. I mean, that baseball scene? Amazing. Chef's kiss.'

I laugh, and put away my phone. Glitter on the back of my hand shimmers in the glare of the lights on the Tube. I don't know what that stuff was made of, but it's as stubborn as all hell, and has been stuck there for two days straight now.

Next to me, Monty gives a soft, thoughtful huff.

I look up to see him frowning at some far-off point on the train. He's holding onto the overhead rail for balance, arm stretched up in such a way it pulls his shirt up slightly, baring a sliver of toned, pale skin.

'I don't get it.'

'What, grannies going gaga over vampires?' Dylan asks. 'They *are* a similar age. I think Edward's, like, ninety, technically.'

Monty rolls his eyes. 'No, like, the romance stuff. The books and rom-coms and that. All the soppy stuff with flowers and chocolates and big gestures. I don't get the appeal. It's not like it's anything like real life, is it? Nobody *acts* like that. And I bet if you had someone do all that stuff, you'd get sick of it soon enough.'

'Wo-o-o-ow,' says Dylan, pulling a face. He's on the verge of laughing again. 'Who broke your heart to make you such a cynic?'

'I just mean, it's not a realistic standard. Relationships are about compatibility and co-operation. Not a big dance number or standing outside someone's window with a boom box.'

Dylan snorts. 'Oh, man, I'd pay good money to see *you* do a big dance number to win some girl over. Maybe that's why you're single, mate, because you haven't done that yet!' He nudges me to laugh along with the joke and join him in the teasing, but . . .

Well, I agree with Monty, which isn't something I thought I'd ever find myself admitting. We're very different people and I don't think we'd be friends if it wasn't just convenient because we're in the same group, but – he's got a point. An excellent one.

Isn't that more or less what I told Lloyd that first night we met? Love isn't like it looks on screen, rosy and golden and impassioned. Relationships are about work. Compromise.

Something Lloyd and I, apparently, couldn't do.

'Anna?' Dylan prompts, and I've clearly been silent for too long.

I shake it off. 'I'm kind of on Monty's side here.'

Monty looks down at me in surprise, eyebrows shooting up high. 'Huh. Really?'

'Really.'

He pulls a face, and for a second I think he's amused, that he's laughing at me and is going to mock me – but just as I'm about to scowl and tell him this is the last time I defend him against Dylan's banter, I realize he's simply surprised. He's not the only one; maybe I was a little too quick to judge him at the start of summer.

I smile back at him, and Dylan's mumbled argument about how we clearly just haven't seen a good rom-com is lost to the Tannoy announcement that we are now approaching Victoria. I'm not very sorry to have it end the conversation.

After all, if I'm going to be a bit more careful with my heart, maybe getting into deep conversations about romance and relationships isn't the best way to do that.

Before long, I've settled back into the familiar rhythm of reviewing spreadsheets and studying slide decks to write up a report. My team add a few things to my to-do list without asking if I have time to pick it up for them, but I don't complain.

Being here, among the bustle of Arrowmile, reminds me why I'm doing this. The glow of pride I get when I send someone an email and see my fancy little sign-off at the bottom of it, the way everyone treats me like a grown-up and not a kid who needs coaching. *This* is what I want. *This* is what's going to make all the difference after I finish my degree.

This is why I pushed Lloyd away.

I have to turn down a lunch invite from Elaine and Verity because I'm stuck in meetings, but later in the afternoon, I take a break, heading up to the twelfth floor for a change of scenery, and to stretch my legs a little. Maybe I'll do a quick wander by Monty and Verity's team to say hi, or see if Freya's at her desk for a quick chat for a few minutes.

A fresh cup of tea in hand, I wander along the open stretch of office that serves as a corridor. The Marketing team are all standing around a whiteboard, noisy and animated. Topher Fletcher's glass-walled office is on the right-hand side of the floor, near the Client Management team; the HR department sit just beyond them, in the far corner.

Some of the desks in this section of the office look a little deserted, and the muffled voices in a nearby meeting room suggest that's where everyone is. The blinds are shut over the glass walls for added privacy.

I spot Verity at her desk, but she's got a headset on and is nodding seriously along to something – presumably in a meeting. She catches my eye and gives me a quick smile and wave, but carries on with her call. In the seat beside her, Monty's also wearing his headphones, although he's got the microphone attachment twisted up and away from his mouth and is slumped, swivelling side to side in his chair while he pays more attention to something on his computer than their meeting. Verity's greeting catches his attention and he looks over too, offering a nod in my direction.

A few desks away, Freya is talking to Topher's PA, both of them looking at something on the PA's computer. Freya's holding her phone like she might be taking notes, but I'm not sure. They're both chatty and smiley, so I can't be sure if this is a serious conversation or they're just looking at an article about the new *Love Island* bombshells who entered the villa last night. I linger for a moment, trying to work it out, not wanting to interrupt just in case.

'Looking for someone?'

I jump, almost spilling my tea.

In front of me, less than arm's length away, is Lloyd.

My heart gives a little somersault in my chest, the traitor.

There's something off about Lloyd, and it takes me a second to realize – it's his smile. This one is smaller, gentler, close-lipped. There's something cautious and guarded about it. It's not the kind of smile I'm used to seeing from him, and would never expect to see when he's hamming it up around the office.

'Not you,' I blurt, and cringe at how nasty it sounds. 'Um, just, uh – I thought I'd say hi to the others. I missed them at lunch.'

Lloyd nods slowly, a knowing gleam in his eyes. His mouth twists slightly into more of a smirk, like he wants to make some comment about me focusing on my job over everything else. I feel a prickle of annoyance, a flush creeping up my neck, at how easily he sees through me.

I thought *he* was supposed to be the open book, not me.

'Looks like they're busy though, so, I'll just . . . go,' I say.

And yet, my feet don't move.

He nods again, and when I still don't move, he says, 'You weren't in the last few days. I didn't realize you were . . . You didn't say you were going somewhere.'

He noticed. Was it because he tried to message me on Teams and saw I was away? Did he try to email me and see my out-of-office? Had he come by my desk to pester me with some Arrowmile-related questions? Had he missed me, when he realized I was gone?

My mind spirals through the questions, my heart rate picking up slightly, and I force myself to stop, to calm down. I'm not going to get giddy over the fact that he simply noticed I wasn't here. Anybody could've; it's not a big deal. And it's not like I *wanted* him to notice; I'm not trying to play games with him.

Haven't I made it so clear already that we can't be anything more to each other?

Polite and civil, though. Like colleagues, and colleagues would have a casual conversation and say: 'Yeah. It was kind of a last-minute decision. Some of my family are in Devon at the minute, so I went to see them. My stepmum had to work so she couldn't make it, but it was nice to see my dad and my brothers.'

'Right – perks of being a teacher, having all the holidays off.' I shouldn't be so surprised that Lloyd remembers what my dad does. He smirks, looking more playful – more like himself, now. 'And here we are, wasting our *actual* summers off school, stuck here.'

'More fool us.'

There's a beat, and it's too long. Like my words have more meaning than I intended. Like I'm talking about something bigger than a summer spent at an internship instead of home with friends.

Maybe I am.

The pause seems to solidify, calcifying around us with a tension so thick it feels harder to breathe than it did a second ago. It's a clear sign that I *do* need to go, before things get too weird.

I barely shift back a step when another voice suddenly says, 'Not haranguing the poor interns are you, Lloyd? He's not making a nuisance of himself is he, Anna?' It's Nadja – Senior Client Partner *and* Monty and Verity's intimidating boss. She's standing just behind us with a large hardback notebook and laptop tucked against her chest. Her lipstick is deep mauve, her lips pulled into a teasing sort of look as she arches an eyebrow between us, the smirk taking the edge off her naturally stern gaze. I'd normally be glad of someone else thinking Lloyd is a nuisance, but it's clear she's joking, a fond affection under her admonition.

It's only at her interruption that I become aware of the fact that the meeting going on in the nearby room, behind the blinds and the closed door, has just finished. People are spilling back out into the office, chattering among themselves. Nadja, I guess, was one of them.

I look back at her and deadpan, 'He really is.'

Nadja laughs. I notice that Lloyd's usual 'office' smile is back – mouth stretched wide and open, showing off straight rows of bright white teeth, oozing charm. He rolls his eyes as if in on the joke.

'Says you, loitering around up here – it's not even your part of the office.'

'Says *both of you*, loitering in the middle of the room,' Nadja snips back, but she gives a dry chuckle. Her eyes linger on me a moment. 'Cute necklace.'

I touch it instinctively. It's a gold one with pressed flowers Gina bought for me on the recent family holiday to Spain I missed out on. 'Thanks.'

'How'd it go?' Lloyd asks her, nodding in the direction of the room behind me that's just emptied out. He looks serious, suddenly, a sharp look of concentration he gets from time to time when I talk to him about updates on some of Arrowmile's projects.

I guess it wasn't just some run-of-the-mill management meeting, then – and *must* have been important if he wasn't allowed to sit in on it. I want to ask what it was about, but I don't want to seem rude. I'm sure if it's *that* important, it'll filter down as office gossip at some point.

'Promising,' is Nadja's reply. 'Looks like we're moving on to the next stage, anyway.' Then, turning to me, she explains, 'We were approached by a company about a bit of a partnership. Did you know most safety tests are done with male specs?'

'Um . . .' I hesitate.

'I'll take that as a no. There's a great study about it, I'll send it to you. You'll love it.'

Add to to-do list: read this study Nadja is going to send me, in case she questions me about it next time I run into her.

'Typically, offices are set to temperatures more comfortable for men. Things are sized to the average male body. Male safety dummies are used in tests for things like vehicle safety. Outrageous, isn't it, Anna? Well, we'll be – hopefully, not official yet, of course – doing a limited run of electric cars specifically tailored to the average *female* body, using safety dummies based on the average female body instead. It'll be part awareness-raising campaign –'

'Part cash grab,' Lloyd adds, sounding less than impressed. 'It's just some eccentric CEO who wants to be seen doing something, rather than because they actually *care*.'

Nadja pinches the bridge of her nose and lets out a long-suffering sigh. *'Just some eccentric CEO.* Honestly, Lloyd. She's a TIME 100! She was on *This Morning* with Alison Hammond for International Women's Day this year! Anna, don't pay him any attention – this woman's the real deal. Absolutely incredible. Real powerhouse. First female CEO at some furniture company, then she went on to some high-profile role with a media company and now she's got her own consultancy business. She runs a collective of networks for young female entrepreneurs, too. She'd love to meet you, I bet! Oh, we should see if she'll do a bit of a meet-and-greet with all you interns, actually. I'm sure she will. Remind me to set that up, Anna. Come on, let me introduce you.'

It's all said so rapidly, with such force and excitement that I'm too overwhelmed to respond, and can't get a word in edgeways anyway. She grasps me by the elbow and whisks me around, frog-marching me a few strides along to where Topher Fletcher is stood with his usual approachable smile, talking to a tall woman with red hair.

Even though her back is to us, the highlight reel Nadja just gave me sinks in and brings with it a curdling dread that tingles up my spine. My heart is in my throat and all I can do is stare at the back of this stranger, hoping against hope that when she turns around . . .

'Sorry to interrupt! Kathryn, I just wanted to introduce you to one of our interns, thought it might be a good opportunity. This is –'

And the woman turns around, pleasant surprise quickly replacing the open shock on her face.

And Mum interrupts Nadja to say, 'Annalise!'

Chapter 24

The last time I saw Mum was on my sixteenth birthday, the summer before I started my A levels.

The further back I go, I have more memories with her, but they get a little fuzzier. I remember her taking a phone call during Sport's Day when I was six and then disappearing, and someone else's mum had to take me home. I remember her insisting to Dad that he just didn't understand, and how tired he looked. I remember a Christmas when I was very small and she let me eat chocolate in bed early in the morning, with her and Dad squished either side of me and *Home Alone* on the TV.

And then she showed up out of the blue on my sixteenth birthday, having conspired with Dad and Gina behind my back to meet us at the restaurant we were going to. I remember the big, happy smile on her face and the warm hug she'd wrapped me up in while

I stood stiff as a board, fury building in my stomach. She pulled me into a seat beside her, tucked my hair behind my ear and peppered me with questions about school and friends she didn't know and summer plans she'd seen on my social media.

She got me a posh, expensive bag I didn't have a use for and posh, expensive earrings that weren't at all to my taste. She asked if there was anything else special I wanted for my birthday, and I was so rattled I just asked to go home, without her in tow. The five of us had a nice evening eating Chinese takeaway and watching a so-bad-it's-good disaster movie, and I tried not to let Mum's sudden reappearance overshadow it all.

She looks different to the last time I saw her.

I suppose that's not *that* surprising, but as I stare at her, so out of place in the Arrowmile offices, the blood draining from my face, I catalogue the ways she's changed since my birthday almost three years ago. There are some more lines around her eyes and neck. Her usual outfit of smart pencil dress and heels has morphed into a fashionable jeans-and-blazer combo, and she's wearing trainers.

Trainers? Am I sure this is *my* mum?

She's dyed her hair, too. She always has, but this is a bold change. Instead of the soft orange that matches my hair, she always used to dye it more of a honey tone

315

that looked strawberry blonde in a certain light. Now it seems she's leaned into being ginger, to the extreme: it's flame-red, like Black Widow or Karen Gillan. Probably, she thinks it makes her look younger, or cooler, or both.

I keep staring at her, too stunned to even blink.

Standing next to Topher Fletcher like that, I realize suddenly that it's not Mum who's out of place at Arrowmile. Her smart-casual look and natural confidence match Topher's – they make her belong.

It's me who's out of place, in clumpy patent shoes that have rubbed blisters into my heels and a boring trousers-and-blouse combo that me and Gina picked out in the Next sale, both of us sure it would be appropriate for such a corporate environment. Me, who had to lie on my application to be here in the first place.

Mum beams at me, clearly much happier to see me than I am to see her.

'You know each other?' Topher Fletcher asks, smiling between us.

Barely at all.

'Know each other?' Mum trills a laugh. 'I should say so! Anna's my daughter.'

It's a knife-sharp pain searing through my chest, though I'm not sure what hurts more: her blasé tone insinuating she knows anything at all about me, or the way she calls me her daughter like it *means* anything.

There's a choked noise somewhere just behind me, which I register as being from Lloyd.

Somewhere, in the back of my mind, I also register that as a problem. That I don't want him to know the 'eccentric CEO' he was just so dismissive of is my mum. That I've told him things about my (non-existent) relationship with her I didn't think would ever matter, because he was never supposed to run into her – let alone *here*.

I'm starting to think this entire summer is one giant cosmic middle finger.

I don't have the capacity to think about Lloyd right now though, my mind too busy racing ahead to assess the situation and see if I need to do any damage control.

I haven't told Mum about Arrowmile (I didn't post explicitly on social media where my internship was for that exact reason) and she *does* look surprised to see me . . . But is she surprised I'm here at all, or just in this particular spot at this particular moment? Could Dad have told her? Is she here because I am, or is this some horrible, cruel coincidence?

'You don't say!' Topher exclaims. He clicks his tongue at me, grinning like this is such a great joke.

'Anna, you didn't mention your mother was *the* Kathryn Jones!'

'You didn't mention she was a CEO,' Lloyd says behind me. There's a bite in his voice, an undercurrent of anger that makes my stomach twist. I can't process why. I don't have the space in my brain for it right now.

Mum laughs again. '*She-EO*, thank you very much!'

'Ah, and Kathryn, this is my son, Lloyd. I know he's taken a keen interest in this partnership we've been discussing.'

Lloyd makes a sound I think might be a scoff, but it's covered by him clearing his throat. He steps forward, hand outstretched and his usual smile firmly in place. 'Great to meet you, Kathryn.'

She shakes his hand, then nudges Topher with another broad smile and a giggle, pointing a finger at the two of us. 'Isn't that funny, Topher! The next generation of both our companies, and just after we were talking about building legacy! If you ask *me*, this partnership is going to be in good hands.'

Lloyd winces a little.

I think I'm going to be sick.

Then she says, 'Darling, I'm making some time to be back here tomorrow to iron out some details. Let's do lunch. My treat.'

There's so much wrong with that statement, I don't know where to start. 'Darling' is bad enough, but 'let's do lunch' is truly grating. Are we on *Made in Chelsea*, now, or something? Part of the in-crowd?

And mostly, it's a terrible statement because it's a *statement*, and Topher and Nadja are looking at me like this is such a nice thing and of course I'd see my mum for lunch, why ever not?

'I, um . . .' My voice sounds scratchy and high, and not at all like mine. I try again, saying, 'I'm actually a bit busy with . . .'

Oh, bloody hell, what am I working on? What's that engine project called? I need to say something, *anything*. Why can't I remember a single thing I'm doing in my internship right now? I'm going to make a fool of myself in front of Nadja *and* Topher.

'Don't be silly, Anna – I'm sure whatever it is, it'll keep. Not every day Kathryn Jones is available for lunch!' Topher claps me on the shoulder. Another great joke. Ha-ha.

Nadja jumps in, seizing her chance. 'While I've got you a second, Kathryn, I was thinking it'd be great if we could pin down some time for you to talk to all the interns? You'd be such an inspiring story for them . . .'

In a blur, goodbyes are said, and we all peel apart.

It's like I blink, and I'm suddenly standing in front of the lift with a now-lukewarm cup of tea still clutched in my hands, not quite sure how I got here.

The lift arrives and I step in.

I press the button for the eleventh floor and step back.

Before the doors close, Lloyd appears on the other side of them. His face is serious, stony – angry.

'You had such a problem with me being the boss's son, having things *handed to me*, but what about you? I mean . . . Is *anything* you told me true?'

'I . . .'

I what? I don't know. I'm still reeling.

'You're such a hypocrite, Annalise,' he tells me, his voice tight – fraught.

The doors slide shut with him glowering at me.

When I get to the eleventh floor, I cut a path to the toilets instead of my desk.

Whether it's Mum, or Lloyd, it doesn't matter, because whatever it is, it makes something inside me snap.

I cave. I become the girl who cries in the toilets at work.

Chapter 25

'I cannot *believe* your mum is famous!' Elaine gushes, wide-eyed and absorbed in her iPad. She's been looking up articles about Mum for the last half hour, with Izzy and Freya leaning over either side of her to see the screen. Occasionally, they'll read out a snippet in awe, or ask me excited questions.

Have I met Alison Hammond, too? What about Adele, from that event they were both at? How cool it would be if I'd gotten a selfie with Adele! Why didn't I work at my mum's consultancy firm for the summer? Did I know she was collaborating with Arrowmile? Is it true that she's going to fill in for Karren in some episodes of the next season of *The Apprentice*?

I hate this. I hate it so much I want to scream. I want to smash the entire dish of pasta bake I've just taken out of the oven on the floor of the kitchen and then smash Elaine's iPad too.

I do my best to tune them out.

This isn't Elaine's fault. It's not Izzy's or Freya's or anybody's, except Mum's.

It's not mine. Definitely not. I don't *have* to tell people. I'm entitled not to, I think, all things considered.

'Why didn't you say anything?' Elaine presses now, twisting from the sofa to look at me, head tilted to one side and a confused smile on her face. I keep my back to her as I plate up the food. I think we must eat variations of pasta bake about four times a week, but it's always so easy to cook for a group.

'I don't see her much,' I say, wondering how careful I need to be with my words. This is never usually a problem, as I just don't tell people about my mum. When I talk about my parents, I mean Dad and Gina. 'She and my dad split up when I was six, so . . .'

So she didn't want to be around us anymore. So she was finally free from the burden we so obviously were and flitted off to indulge in her fancy career. So she doesn't care.

'Oh,' Freya says, not unkindly, 'well that's not surprising you don't see her very much. She's a busy lady. I can't believe how successful she is. She's done so much!'

Yeah. Tons. But 'mother' doesn't feature in her list of accolades.

'You must be really proud of her,' Izzy says.

322

Am I?

In another life, I think I would've been. If she'd *tried*, I could have been. But when I think about her spectacular career, all the exciting things she's done, there's only resentment – and even that has faded, after almost thirteen years. At some point, I stopped caring, just like she did. Maybe it's a trait that runs in the family.

I shrug, and answer as honestly as I can. 'I guess it's impressive. I just don't know her all that well. She's not the kind of mum you call to tell about your day.'

'I bet she's so cool,' Izzy sighs, missing my point.

Elaine obviously picks up on it though because she says, a little more gently, 'That must be hard, with her being so busy and not being able to see you very much.'

Immediately, my eyes well up and I have to squeeze them shut and bite the inside of my cheek before a sob breaks out. I've been on edge since I let myself cry in the toilets this afternoon; I'm sure if someone had forgotten to say 'thanks' to me for holding a door, I'd have broken down crying again. I swallow the lump in my throat and take a breath, not answering until I'm sure my voice won't shake.

'Sure. But if I had the choice between hanging out with me or Adele, I'd want to hang out with Adele, too.'

The girls laugh, not seeming to notice when I don't quite join in, still needing a few seconds to get a handle on my emotions.

This is getting out of hand. I told myself that first day that Lloyd wasn't going to ruin this internship for me, and now, I can't let Mum ruin the rest of my summer. This was supposed to be a cute evening in, just hanging out while Louis is out on another first date, part of my resolution to not waste this summer and have a little fun. I *won't* let her ruin this.

I won't.

By lunchtime the next day, I have a better grip on myself. My tears turned to righteous anger by last night, and today I've woken up determined and immovable.

Or at least – I *will be* determined and immovable.

I'm wearing one of my favourite office outfits: a plain navy A-line dress with short sleeves. It goes nicely with my new necklace from Gina.

I've agreed to meet Mum downstairs in reception. Replying to her message about when and where to meet made me notice the handful of messages I've mostly ignored over the last few weeks. They leave a sour taste in my mouth.

She strides through the lobby twelve minutes late, with a smile and no apology.

'Alright, darling? All ready to go?'

No, I'm just waiting here with my bag and cardigan, standing around doing nothing for no good reason.

I am immovable. She won't faze me, not today. I won't let her.

'Yes. But I don't have very long, now.'

She starts to dismiss me before realizing I'm deadly serious, so instead puts on a forced smile and says, 'Well, we'd better be off then. Come on, I've booked us a table at a lovely little place around the corner.'

It's a brisk seven-minute walk to the restaurant Mum's booked for us, a cute and airy Italian with a delicious aroma that envelops me as soon as I walk through the door. The decor seems purposeful, chosen with care. It's the kind of place I'd normally avoid, where starters probably cost as much as a main course anywhere else.

A man in a crisp black uniform shows us to a table and hands us menus, asking for our drink orders. Mum gets a raspberry lemonade. I have tap water.

When he leaves us to peruse the menus, Mum immediately sets hers down. She perches her elbows on the table and folds her hands together under her chin, leaning forward with a smile.

'I'm so glad we got the chance to do this, Anna. I wasn't sure if I'd get to see you.'

'Well, you've seen me.' I bite my tongue for a moment, but then decide I need to know. 'Did you *purposely* come to Arrowmile just to see me?'

Mum sighs, looking a bit sheepish. 'No. This has been in the works for a while now, but your dad told me where you were doing your internship. I hoped I might bump into you. If the meeting yesterday went well, my plan was to let you know I might be around so we could have a bit of a catch-up.'

'A bit of a catch-up?' I can't help but gape, incredulous, almost on the verge of laughter. 'What, like you're a friend from school I haven't seen since we set off for uni last year? You're not my friend, you're *supposed* to be my *mum*.'

'Darling, I have been trying –'

'Is that what you call it, when you text me once in a blue moon?'

Her lips purse, and she draws a breath before saying slowly, in what must be *the* most patronizing tone she can muster, 'Anna, I know you took it very hard when your father and I divorced, but you can't begrudge me my own life. I've been trying very hard to reconnect with you –'

It's selfish. It's mean and patronizing and selfish. It makes me feel eleven years old, with Dad telling me apologetically that Mum can't make it for Christmas.

It takes me back to the school play in Year 12 and how even though I didn't want her there, even though I knew she wouldn't be, I still strode out to take my mark on the stage and looked out into the audience of parents and friends and siblings, searching for her like she might have made it after all.

It makes the back of my eyes prickle, the threat of yet more tears. I force them away, aware of how hard and loud my breathing has become and that I'm not even listening to her anymore, annoyed by just the tone of her voice – when the waiter interrupts with our drinks.

'Are you ready to order?'

'Gosh, sorry! I haven't even looked yet! Do you mind giving us a few more minutes? Thanks ever so.'

Thanks ever so. What does she sound like? Her voice has taken on some kind of affected air over the years; maybe a side effect of all the fancy, high-profile people she rubs shoulders with. I swear she didn't sound like this when I was little.

'I don't want to fight,' Mum says now, putting on another smile. She reaches over to give my hand a squeeze. 'Let's just have a nice lunch, shall we? You can tell me all about this internship of yours! I've heard only good things about it. It's supposed to be terribly difficult to get a place on,' she adds, eyebrows raised. 'I'm surprised you managed it!'

Maybe she wouldn't be, if she bothered to show up for parents' evening or took an interest in my life to know how well school and uni were going.

I don't reply, my throat tight. I don't trust my voice right now; I don't trust myself not to scream, if I do open my mouth. And I *don't* want to cry – I don't want her to think she can comfort me. She doesn't get to do that, swan in and act the hero when it's all her fault in the first place.

Mum isn't deterred by my silence, though. She draws her hand back but keeps on beaming at me, persistent with her 'questions' and making the most of this sickeningly sweet mother-daughter bonding session she's cornered me into.

'Your dad says you've been doing a super job of it though. Working hard. Like me!'

Not like you. Never like you.

'And he said you've made some good friends, too? Better than those nasty girls you were living with last year in halls, always cutting you out, or putting you down for no reason.'

What do you know? Don't act like you know about anything in my life, with this second-hand information Dad's fed you.

'The interns sound like a good bunch though. Hard workers, too. Ambitious! I bet that's nice, to make some new friends in different places – you're never too young to start building up a bit of a network, Anna, so that'll help you heaps when you graduate, I bet ... Your dad said that girl you live with is very nice? You did an escape room together?'

Maybe I should treat this conversation like an escape room. Find a codeword on the back of the menu I have to shout so someone lets me out of here.

'And that boy yesterday. Topher's boy – what was his name?'

'Lloyd,' I churn out through my teeth.

'That's it! He seems great, doesn't he? Ever so polite. Topher said he gets really stuck in with all the business. Now *he'll* be a good contact to keep hold of when you graduate.'

'I'm not collecting business contacts like Pokémon, Mum. They're my friends.'

'Well, yes, I know that. I just meant –'

'I know what you meant.'

She frowns, her too-wide smile finally starting to slip. That little give is a chink in her armour. Her forehead crumples, sadness tingeing the creases around her eyes and the edges of her mouth.

'I don't think you do, Anna. What I mean is, I know

you're very ambitious, like I am. You really apply yourself, and give it your all when you take on something. You practised your golf for weeks for your role as Jordan Baker in the *Gatsby* play at school, for heaven's sake, and you didn't even need to play any golf in the performance!'

How does she know that?

How much has Dad been telling her, behind my back?

'And while it's lovely you're making friends, it's also good to keep them in mind for the future, especially if they end up being only short-lived friendships because it's convenient while you're on the internship together. I didn't suggest you were *using* them for their future networking potential!' She laughs, an obvious attempt to lighten the mood again. It doesn't work.

This time, she takes a bit more notice when I stay silent.

'Anna? What is it, what did I say? You look grumpy as anything. You look like your dad when you pull that face, you know.'

'I'm not ambitious like you are.'

'Oh, darling! Don't be so hard on yourself. Of course you are. Look at all the clubs you did at school! And that programming module you did last year at uni. You got onto this internship programme, didn't you? I'd say you're very ambitious. Just like I was at your age, wanting to get stuck into anything and everything –'

'I mean, not like *you*. I'm not doing this to be selfish, and I'm not doing it without caring what it's doing to other people. I'm not doing all this stuff just so I can boast about it to everyone and make myself look better than them.'

Just so I can boast about it to people who might give me a job. But that's different.

'I'm ambitious so I can get a good job and do everything right and so *I* don't have to abandon my family like you did. Not so I can sit in for Karren Brady on *The Apprentice*.'

She whispers, in a very small and faraway voice, 'That's not quite confirmed yet.'

'See? You just don't care! Do you? You never did! But, what, now you think I'm successful *enough*, you want to take the credit for it? Boast about how you've got an ambitious daughter *just like you* to make yourself seem even better in the papers and stuff?'

I've always secretly hoped she'd notice the things I posted online and see how well I was doing without her – in spite of her. But this isn't satisfying like I thought it would be. It just makes me resent her.

Mum stares at me, aghast. 'Anna!'

The waiter has approached our table again but I notice him hesitate, thinking better of stepping into the middle of this right now.

I gather up my bag and cardigan, hands trembling as they ball into tight fists around my things. 'If you were thinking of giving me an early birthday present, I think I'd like the same as I had for my sixteenth birthday – for you to *leave me alone*.'

I'm shaking as I stand up, doing my best to hold my head high as I storm out without even ordering my lunch. Mum calls after me, standing, too, but I ignore her. She ignored me for long enough, didn't she? Maybe she should know what that feels like.

I'd never speak to Gina like this.

But what good is having an absentee mother who suddenly wants to treat you like a grown-up if you can't talk back to her?

Chapter 26

It's Friday night, so I should be doing something fun and exciting. I should be out at a club with my friends, sipping cocktails while I flaunt my ID to a bartender, having fun and enjoying the summer before I have to go back to uni.

But the last year hasn't offered up any evidence that I enjoy clubs, so I made some excuses to avoid a big night out with everybody tonight. Plus, they're still hung up on the exciting reveal of who my mum is, and I don't think I can stomach another round of questions about her. When I check Instagram Stories and see some of the other interns having a fun night in a dark place with flashing lights, packed with sweaty, shouting bodies, I'm relieved I'm not there having to pretend I'm having a better time than I actually am.

Instead, I'm in a place that's much more comfortable.

When it's empty at night like this, the Arrowmile offices remind me a bit of the library at uni. Sometimes I stayed late to prep for an exam or test, but most of the time I went just so I didn't have to deal with the party girls I lived with. Between nine o'clock at night and around two in the morning, when I'd normally find myself there, it was always almost empty, with a few other lone souls or insomniacs wandering the stacks or settled down in a booth with their feet up and earbuds in. There was a camaraderie between those of us in the library that late, even if we never spoke and rarely exchanged eye contact.

Once or twice, I fantasized that I'd see a cute boy there, and we'd meet each other's gaze and smile, and share a little moment, and then maybe after a few more times of seeing each other around we'd start a conversation, and he'd be someone like me, someone who understood me, and it'd be a sweet, romantic connection that would spark a real relationship.

Those kinds of daydreams were only in my most exhausted and sleep-deprived moments, though. More actual dreams than daydreams, really.

I must be in a similar state tonight to be thinking about it, and to find myself drifting away from my desk and the work I've somehow let pile up *again*. It really is never-ending; I don't know how anybody here does it.

I head for the lift, my empty mug in hand. When the doors open and I step out onto the twelfth floor, my eyes are already seeking him.

And he's there.

Somehow, I think I knew he would be.

Tonight, unlike the last time our paths crossed late at night like this in the office, the lights are on. I see Lloyd in the kitchenette, filling the kettle up; he doesn't seem to have noticed the sound of the lift or my arrival, but when I hesitate, suddenly not sure what to say or do or why I even came up here looking for him, he looks over.

He looks . . . not pleased to see me.

To put it lightly.

A frown settles on his face and a muscle ticks in his jaw.

But at least he doesn't tell me to go away. Instead, he sighs, like he was almost expecting this too, and adds some more water into the kettle, gesturing for me to set my empty mug beside his on the counter.

His shirt today is a little more casual, a lightweight blue flannel over a white T-shirt. The sleeves are rolled up again but now they're lopsided, one of them coming loose. A stray curl falls over his forehead; he's wearing his glasses again. There are bags under his eyes, a weariness to the slope of his shoulders. He looks as exhausted as I feel.

For perhaps the first time, I'm not sure what to say to Lloyd. I've never been short of words with him before. But right now, I replay our last interaction – the look in his eyes and the venom in the way he called me a hypocrite, and I can't even find it in me to demand an apology. I think he was probably right.

Lloyd takes a deep breath, and relief washes over me. Thank God, he's going to speak first.

'So, your mum.'

But then he doesn't say anything else.

'That sounds like the start of a bad joke, Fletcher.'

A smirk flits across his face. It's quickly replaced by his more serious frown, and a heaviness settles on my chest, pressing down on my lungs.

'How was lunch the other day?' he asks instead, as the kettle finishes boiling.

'Oh. Fine. Thanks.'

He pauses pouring the tea for a moment, but it's so brief I wonder if I imagined it.

And suddenly I want to tell him everything. I want to spill it all: how horrible lunch was and that I felt press-ganged into it, that I told her what I *really* thought and still feel a bit sick about it, how she spoke down to me and that she's apparently been collecting my life's story off my dad when she couldn't get it from me, but I don't want to confront Dad and end up in a fight with him, too. I want to tell Lloyd all the gory, grimy truth in the way we've done with each other before.

But there's something off between us tonight, a distance *I* created by saying I couldn't date him, and I swallow the words back down.

Lloyd pushes my mug towards me. He takes a step back, like whatever is between us right now requires physical space, too. If anything, it just makes my chest feel a little tighter again.

He lifts his cup of tea to his lips to blow the steam off it, and eyes me over the top of it, almost wary.

'You're not here to tell me off for calling you a hypocrite, then?'

He's right. This is where I push back with a sharp, haughty retort because I think I have the moral high ground and he, with his generous humour, teases me for it.

What I should do, is say sorry. Regardless of whatever my mum's career is – all those comments I've made about Lloyd throughout summer have probably been needling at him this entire time. He's just been too nice and too easy-going to call me out or tell me it bothers him.

But instead all I can do is mumble, 'I'm not a hypocrite.'

Before, I was scared that people at Arrowmile would judge me for being too closely associated with Lloyd. That's how I feel now: terrified, that my mum will tarnish whatever Lloyd thinks of me.

'I never lied to you about my mum,' I tell him. 'I told you we don't have a relationship. She's never done *anything* for me, not even paid for a school trip. She's practically a stranger. Most of what I know about her is stuff anybody could read about her online. Do you have any idea how sad that is? That I only know what my mum's up to if someone reports it in the *Sunday Times* or updates her Wikipedia page?'

He doesn't answer, and I don't really know what I'm expecting him to say anyway.

Then I make the mistake of saying, 'At least your dad wants you around, and wants you to be involved.'

Lloyd scowls, cutting me a glare – knowing I've said the wrong thing should make me feel sympathetic towards him, but this isn't like all the other nights we've spent together. This is twisted, tense and agitated, a crumbling precipice that threatens to send us spiralling the second one of us puts a foot wrong.

Which, it seems, I just did.

'Oh, right, because that's such a fucking gift,' he snaps, with a venom that I wasn't expecting. 'Always living in his shadow. Always being expected to be more like him, and *never* living up to expectations, never doing anything *right*. You act like I've got it made because of him, but it's a poisoned chalice. You have *no* idea . . .'

He's never been this upfront about his dad or being at Arrowmile, and I take a stab in the dark. 'Is it about your uni course? How you stepped up to follow in your dad's footsteps so that Will didn't have to?'

Lloyd flinches. 'How'd you –? Fuck. *Will*. He had no right to tell you about that.'

'I didn't ask him to.'

'It's *none* of your business. And whatever you think you know . . .' He shakes his head. 'You don't understand anything about it. Alright?'

'So tell me! *Make* me understand.'

But Lloyd refuses, gritting his teeth. He sets his tea down and leans against the counter, shoulders hunched, hands balled so tightly into fists that I can see his arms taut with the strain. I want to reach out and stroke them, hold him until he relaxes. But I forfeited any right to do that when we broke things off, so instead, all I can do is try to reach for whatever parts of himself he's trying to bury, that are making him feel like this now.

'You can't be mad at me for not telling you something, then do the same thing to me and be mad I don't know what you're hiding,' I tell him. 'I'm *trying* to understand. I'm not the only one putting up walls and keeping people at arm's length, you know. I mean, you won't even tell me what you actually *do* here – or what's so important that you stay so late on a Friday night. You act like everything's always so great but never actually feel anything *real* – just like you said your dad does.'

I must hit a nerve, because the scowl is back, as quick as his smile usually is.

'Would you *stop*, already?' he says, and this time, his voice isn't angry, or upset. It's steady and even, and . . . cold, in a way that Lloyd isn't. He straightens up, running a hand through his hair. His eyes burn like a forest fire when they catch mine again.

'I didn't –'

This isn't how I wanted this conversation to go. I just wanted him to know I hadn't lied to him. I thought he'd understand. I thought . . . he knew me well enough to understand. And I thought if I could just understand *him* better, we could fix this. Be friends again. But none of the words are coming out right, and I just keep making it worse.

'You act like you're so above it all. Annalise Sherwood, working hard but never hardly working. She earns *everything* she gets. She's worked for it in a way that puts everybody else to shame.' His words fill the space between us, bloated and poisonous, twisting my stomach into knots. 'You've made enough comments about *me* having everything so easy because of my dad – being the "golden boy", right? But what about you? Like you're any better, with your "She-EO" mum? Looked like she was pretty happy to see you the other day. Wants you around, wants you *involved*. And you don't think that makes you a hypocrite? You don't get to lord it over me like that when you're *exactly the same*. The next generation of the company. Right?'

He sneers, and it fractures something in the remnants of my heartbreak from last week.

I didn't think Lloyd was even capable of sneering. Of looking so intentionally nasty.

The worst part is knowing that *I've* brought that out in him.

He scoffs, a soft, breathy noise of resentment. He shakes his head again, eyes focused on some point on the floor. 'All that stuff you said,' he's muttering, mostly to himself, 'about why you wanted this internship so badly, why you're giving it everything ... It was all just ...'

Lloyd trails off, pulling a face like it pains him to have to say it out loud, to have to confront some horrible new reality of who I actually am, who he now believes I've been all along.

All those times I looked at him and wondered where

the boy from the riverside was and had to play dot-to-dot to connect these different versions of him as I uncovered new secrets, new quirks . . . Now, I realize, he's doing the same thing with me.

It bruises, knocks the air out of my lungs for a moment.

For all the irresistible connection I've felt to Lloyd, all the times I couldn't help but be drawn in by him or had to fight to keep him at arm's length – he's never felt more impossible to reach than right now.

Too taken aback by how badly this conversation has gone to think straight, I blurt out the first – the only – thing that comes to mind.

'You think we're the same?' I snap. 'We're not. I meant what I said, Fletcher. I'm doing this to give myself the best future, to open doors, so I don't *have* to be like my mum.'

Lloyd looks up, meeting my eyes again at last. There's no anger in it this time, no impetuousness or darkness. His eyes are clear, and weary. His shoulders slump, all the fight leaving him as he exhales quietly, calmly.

Whatever thought just passed through his mind, it's given him the clarity he needed to connect the dots between the version of me he knows, and the stranger he apparently sees in front of him right now. I see the understanding, the resignation on his face, and it's frightening.

I don't want to be this person. I don't want to be the girl who snaps at him in the middle of the night in an empty office, all teeth and snarl and no care or compassion. I don't want to be this angry, feral thing.

I want to be the person he's seen every other time we've been together. The one eating cake late into the night, the one who found herself in his touch, lost herself tangled up with him. I want to be the girl who walked on air through a strange city with a cute boy beneath a starless sky, eating gravy-smothered chips and swapping secrets like they weren't such precious, fragile, perilous things.

'So you don't throw anybody under the bus,' he says slowly, remembering what I said last time we were here – last time I talked to him about Mum. 'Stomp all over them on your way to the top.'

And something hardens in his face, a hurt that seeps into a small, soft smile on a mouth I kissed, when I was that other girl, and I suddenly realize something, too.

'Annalise,' he tells me, before I can beg him not to, 'that's exactly what you did to me.'

Chapter 27

I stand in the kitchen on the twelfth floor until the motion-sensor lights turn themselves off, plunging me into darkness. A breath shudders out of me, too loud in the deathly silence of the office. Far from the calm, contained environment it provided earlier for me to catch up on work, now it feels tainted, treacherous.

I move enough to activate the lights, not sure how long it is since Lloyd left. Long enough that the tea he made us both is stone-cold. I pour both cups away, then debate for a moment before making myself a fresh one; I'm shaking all over, so a few minutes to collect myself is probably a good idea before I set off home.

He's right. Of course he is. He's usually *insufferably* right about things, but I wish this wasn't one of them.

It's no *wonder* he looked at me like that, or that he was so angry with me. He has every right to be. I'd hate me, too. I do hate me, a bit.

Taking my tea over to the sofas, I sink down onto one. I set the mug on the coffee table and hunch forward, head between my knees, trying to steady my breathing. My chest is tight; the argument has left me nauseated.

It's too late to apologize. It won't make any difference now, I know it won't.

But I should still say sorry. I'd want that acknowledgement from him if it was the other way around, even if it meant nothing.

Is that the kind of thing you can put in a text? I don't think he'll answer the phone if I call, and it will feel insincere if I wait until Monday to try to do it in person. He doesn't need to accept it, but I think it's better to offer an apology regardless.

When did this all become such a mess? How did it spiral so completely out of control?

Why couldn't I have just said sorry when he called me out for being a hypocrite and left it there? Why?

After a few minutes, my breathing levels out and some of the crushing weight of self-loathing has disappeared from my chest. I sit up and reach for my tea, taking a long sip and letting it settle my nerves. There's a solid chance it's just a placebo, but I don't care. It does the job either way.

Then I notice the file on the floor.

It's one of those soft, plastic-y covered ones full of poly pockets, vaguely familiar but I can't think why. It's hefty, thick with papers and marked up with neon-coloured tabs.

Someone must have left it from a meeting earlier, or it fell out of a bag.

I pick it up and take a look – in case I can tell whose it is, so I can leave it on their desk. I'd be beyond stressed if I thought I'd lost some important document. It's probably some contracts from Nadja's team, judging by the weight of it and all those sticky tabs.

There's nothing on the cover to indicate what it is, or who it belongs to. Inside, it's even more confusing. Leafing through it gently, so I don't disturb any of the neon tabs, I find sections on all kinds of Arrowmile projects. There are some with labels stuck to the poly pocket marking them up as RETIRED or something similar, and a few with names I vaguely recognize – old development projects from the last few years. There's one for the Vane engine, one for each of the Phoebus car models. There's an entire section dedicated to the new coolant that's being developed in the labs. Near the back, in what seems to be a more recent addition, there's a label marked JONES X ARROWMILE COLLAB – the project Mum's working on with them. There are only a couple of sheets of paper in that one; in contrast, most of the other poly pockets are so full the papers have started to curl.

What is this?

It's like a catalogue of everything going on at Arrowmile. I peek at the section for the Vane engine, wiggling the papers halfway out to sift through them.

Objectively, I know this is absolutely not something I should be doing. *This* is definitely snooping, not just a polite stumbling-across situation. This could be confidential information, not the sort of thing an intern should be looking at.

But then I recognize some of the papers are print-outs of emails from me. *Sincerely Yours, Anna Sherwood*, they read.

Hi Lloyd, they start.

Oh my God.

Oh, my God.

This is Lloyd's file. That's why it looks familiar – he had it with him the first time I ran into him after-hours at the office, was weirdly protective of it. He must've left in such a rush after our argument that he didn't notice it under the coffee table.

This is what he's been working on – whatever he works on, all mysterious and vague, using his name and his smile to find out anything and everything that's going on at Arrowmile. This isn't just a few reports or slide decks – this is an entire dossier, and mostly made up of handwritten notes, or print-outs of emails and diagrams and budget sheets that he's marked up in different pens. There are costs and profits he's highlighted and commented on, schematics he's stapled tracing paper over to annotate.

How long has he spent putting all this together? What's it even for?

I don't completely understand what I'm looking at, but it feels . . . significant, somehow. Like this isn't the sort of thing that should be left for people to stumble across. How much sensitive, confidential information about the company is in this thing? I suddenly imagine some kind of criminal mastermind stumbling across it, a Bond villain or the evil scientist guy in a Marvel film, using all this stuff for some outrageous, scandalous plan.

Maybe *Lloyd* is the evil scientist villain in a Marvel film.

No, that doesn't seem likely. But he *could* be the Hallmark movie foil to that – the warm-hearted, noble hero who investigates a notorious corporation and discovers that they're committing some kind of fraud or money-laundering or stealing from charities or whatever it is the bad guy does to get rich, and then the hero guy gets to uncover the whole sham and save the day.

That sounds more like Lloyd.

But I can't quite imagine Arrowmile being one of those kinds of companies. They're always celebrated for their push to be greener and more eco-friendly. Plus, everybody only has good things to say about Topher Fletcher – it's hard to picture him embezzling their pension funds or something.

So what *is* Lloyd up to?

My brain is fried from the long day and the argument; I can't even begin to fathom the answer to that question right now.

With a pang of guilt, I tuck all the papers neatly back into their pocket and take it back downstairs with me. I'll take it home to keep it safe over the weekend, and return it to Lloyd when I see him next week. When I text him to apologize, I'll let him know I found it, in case he notices it missing and panics.

And I definitely do need to apologize.

Seeing all the work he's put into this thing, even if I don't understand it, makes me regret every time I made a snide remark about him swanning around the office and sticking his nose in, throwing his weight around and enjoying the luxury of having a job without having to do any *work* for it.

I sit back down at my laptop to make sure everything is saved before I shut it down for the weekend, setting Lloyd's file down beside me. It lands with a heavy, muted *thunk* on the desk, echoing the sensation in my heart.

How do I keep underestimating him? Every time I think I've figured out who Lloyd is and respect him a little more, he *still* keeps on surprising me.

It's so unfair, especially when he's been so generously overestimating me all this time.

NEW EMAIL DRAFT

Dear Lloyd,

I don't think it will mean very much coming from me right now, but I'm sorry. I know people usually only apologize to make themselves feel better (and that probably is a bit the case here) but I still feel like I owe it to you to say – I'm sorry.

You were right. I stomped on you on my way to the top. I threw whatever was between us, or could have been between us if I'd let it, under the bus. You're kind, and good, and deserved so much better than that. I didn't think I had any self-destructive tendencies, but the way I've pushed you away makes me wonder if I do after all.

I did exactly what my mum did to me and my dad. I did what I promised myself I'd never do. I hurt someone I loved, to protect my own ambition. I'm sorry. I'm so sorry.

I don't expect you to forgive me. That's okay.

But I want you to know that I'm her – the girl you keep looking for. Somewhere, underneath all of this, I'm her, the way you're someone else behind that act you put on around the office. Just in case that counts for anything.

Sincerely Yours,
Anna Sherwood

Chapter 28

I don't really expect much of a response from Lloyd to my apology text or my mention that I found the file he left behind and will give it back to him on Monday – and I don't get one. Radio silence is the least I deserve.

I spend the weekend stewing over all the things I wish I hadn't said to him, how things could have gone differently if we'd both just been a little less on edge – how it should have been a friendly heart-to-heart instead of such a fierce argument. I keep wondering about how angry he got when I mentioned his dad and his work at Arrowmile – Lloyd always seems so upbeat, I never stopped to consider he might just be making the best of a bad situation. Even after what Will said about why Lloyd didn't do the degree he really wanted, I don't think the full reality of his situation had really sunk in.

Is that what the file is all about? His way of making the best of a bad situation, somehow?

All those things he said about living in his dad's shadow, calling it a 'poisoned chalice' . . . And I was too busy with my own selfish and self-righteous attitude to listen to him.

When Monday finally arrives I'm one of the first at the office – but there's no sign of Lloyd anywhere. Throughout the day, I make so many excuses to leave my desk – so that I can scout around for him – that Laurie asks me if I have an upset stomach or a UTI – she has remedies in her desk drawer for both.

I figure he must be around somewhere, and that I just keep missing him, so gather my courage and find him on Teams.

> **Anna Sherwood**
> Hi, Lloyd. Just wondered if you were in today?

Lloyd Fletcher is typing . . .

Lloyd Fletcher switches his status to 'do not disturb', and doesn't reply to my message.

I go home late, hoping that I might run into him – but another circuit of the office around seven o'clock shows that it's nearly empty, and he's nowhere to be found. My bag feels heavy with the weight of his lost file as I tote it home once more.

Tuesday, I have better luck. I leave a meeting with Dylan's team downstairs and find Lloyd standing around by the lifts, holding a coffee and talking to a couple of people. I hang back until they're done talking, watching his wide, exaggerated gestures and the unfaltering smile on his face, and it makes me regret the way we argued even more.

Finally, the others filter off in different directions, and I seize the opportunity to corner Lloyd before he can storm off. Up close, I see he's looking a little frayed around the edges. There are bags under his eyes, a twitchy edge to his stance.

His smile freezes in place, eyes darting about as if noting who's around to witness if we fight again. His voice is tight when he says, 'Anna. This isn't a good time.'

'I've been trying to catch you. It's just – I – I texted you, and I wanted to apologize, but –'

He rolls his eyes, cutting me off. 'You said enough on Friday night. Now I know you think I don't do anything important around here, but I actually have a meeting to get to right now.'

'That's what I –'

'I'll see you round, yeah?' he says loudly, with a casual dismissal that probably sounds friendly enough to everybody else, but feels fake and cutting when he won't even look at me. He strides off, like nothing's wrong, and I wish I'd had the stupid file with me so I could just give it back and not have to keep chasing after him.

Does he really hate me more than he wants to get his pet project back?

I send him another text, trying to explain, but it, along with my message from Friday night, remains unread.

I spent weeks trying to keep Lloyd at arm's length, pushing him away every time I feared I was letting him get too close – and now that it's finally happened, it's bittersweet.

It makes me wish we'd never met that night, never kissed.

At least then, we might have been friends now.

I'm persuaded to take a break from VLOOKUPs (which I've finally got the hang of) to join Verity for her very late lunch on Thursday afternoon, glad for the excuse of a coffee break after hours of yet more spreadsheet automation for my team. I regret it when I realize Tasha is joining us, too.

Verity has a fancy home-made salad packed for her lunch, but queues up with us to get herself a smoothie from the coffee cart to go with it. It must be a mid-afternoon rush: the place is unusually busy. She and Tasha are chattering about some internet drama between influencers they both follow and I'm trying to keep up, when Lloyd comes into the canteen.

He looks like hell.

Lloyd moves agitatedly, one hand bouncing rapidly against his thigh as he walks. He doesn't seem to notice that one of the laces on his trainers is undone. His thick, dark curls are sticking out at all kinds of angles. He looks stressed in a way that hollows out the area beneath his eyes and lends a frantic look to his face.

He's a far cry from the polished guy who normally swaggers about the office, and I cringe to see him like this.

Verity and Tasha notice, too.

'He looks terrible,' Verity whispers, voice heavy with pity. 'He's been all over the place all week. I wonder what's wrong?'

Is this because of our argument, or is it more than that? Has something else happened?

'I should go talk to him,' I blurt, then correct myself – 'Um, I mean, I have to talk to him about something, so I should . . . catch him, while he's free.'

Tasha makes a small, scathing noise in the back of her throat. 'Don't you *always* have something to talk to each other about? I swear, it's like every time I look over at your desk, there he is.'

He's just being a nuisance, would be my usual retort.

'It's just work stuff,' is what I tell Tasha now.

She pulls a face, a sly smile that lets me know she doesn't buy that for a second.

Verity, however, gives me a little shove. 'Go, Anna – we can catch up another time!'

I duck out of the queue, and back into it again about ten people back, popping up right in front of Lloyd. He startles when he sees me – then frowns, looking around for an escape route, or maybe just trying to figure out who else is here, and if it's worth it to shout at me to go away.

'I know you don't want to see me, or talk to me, and I get it,' I say in a quiet rush, hoping that the general hubbub will cover up our conversation from any eavesdroppers. 'I don't expect you to forgive me. You've been so kind and patient with me all summer, and I've taken that for granted. You don't owe me anything. But I'm still sorry. And I'm sorry for all that stuff I said about you being the golden boy, and your dad, and . . . I've been thinking about what Will said, about how you took all this on so he wouldn't have to, and how you're stuck on a uni course you don't want, and all that stuff in your file, the research and project plans and things, and –'

Lloyd throws a hand out, grabbing my arm tightly, a manic look in his eyes.

'You've seen my file?'

'Yeah. Yeah, I found it after you left on Friday night. It's back at the flat, because I was worried people might ask about it if I kept bringing it into the office, and you seemed really secretive about it, so –'

'Oh my God.'

The air whooshes out of Lloyd's lungs all at once, and he seems to buckle, the hand on my arm now feeling more like he's holding on for support. A little colour returns to his cheeks, a weight lifting from his shoulders – and I realize, foolishly, the state he's in isn't about our argument at all. It's about the file.

'Didn't you see my texts?' I ask him as he recovers, collects himself.

'Your carefully worded apologies? I saw enough.'

'Obviously not, or you'd have seen that I picked your file up and told you I'd bring it back in for you on Monday. That's why I tried to talk to you the other day, and have been chasing you around all week. It looked important. I figured you'd want it back.'

His eyes narrow, shoulders squaring, but far from annoyed – he looks *worried*. 'You read it?'

'Only a bit. I was trying to figure out who it belonged to. I saw you had . . . emails, from me. Stuff about all the Arrowmile projects.'

It's a leading comment. He doesn't take the bait.

He just stares at me, deadly serious. 'I need that file back, Annalise.'

'I'm not holding it hostage. I'll bring it in for you tomorrow.'

'That's no good – I'm out at the labs tomorrow. There's a thing with – uh, with your mum's company. Looking at the facilities and how we'll do testing, and stuff.'

'Oh.'

He seems to be waiting for more of a reaction – like maybe the mere mention of my mum will restart our argument from the other night. Or maybe, because it's Lloyd, and he's a better guy than I give him credit for, he's just worried about upsetting me by talking about her.

'Are you around this weekend?' he asks tentatively. 'Saturday?'

I consider it – Sunday would work better for me, but I don't *really* have plans until later Saturday evening, and I don't want him to think I'm making excuses or anything. I appreciate that he's trying to make the effort of meeting me halfway.

Polite. Civil.

So I bite my tongue and say, 'I could meet you in the morning. Nine o'clock, at Waterloo station? I'll meet you under the clock.'

He nods, and doesn't joke *It's a date*, like he might have done before.

Instead, I just politely let him know that his shoelace is untied, and I wonder if these awkward, stilted conversations are all we'll salvage from the wreckage of everything we've said and done this summer.

Probably, it's more than I deserve.

Chapter 29

When Saturday finally arrives, I'm resolved to try and repair things with Lloyd as much as I can – and, if he doesn't want to, I'll have to respect that and give him whatever space he needs. I get ready as quickly and quietly as possible but when I leave my bedroom, Louis is on his way out of the bathroom. He looks a little grey and his eyes are bloodshot; he yawns widely as soon as he tries to say 'hi'.

'How's your hangover?' I ask. Everybody went out to a pub for dinner last night; half of us came home early, but Louis, Burnley and Monty were among those who stayed out late.

'Hangover? Pfft. I'm just dandy, Anna.' His voice is croaky, probably from shouting along to music at the club he ended up in last night, but he's not so sleepy or hungover that he doesn't notice my outfit, or the bag slung over my shoulder. 'You off out? Bit early, isn't it?'

'I'm, uh, meeting someone. A friend. For breakfast.'

(I might get something for breakfast when I get to Waterloo, so it's not technically a lie, really.)

'Oh, cute. Have fun! We still on for tonight? Izzy's making a cake.'

'Yes! Definitely.'

I'm glad he's at least too tired to interrogate me like he usually would want to – he doesn't even try to tease me if this 'friend' is a date. He stumbles back down the hallway to his bedroom, and I make my escape before Elaine can wake up and question me too.

It's a grey day, the sky completely overcast with thin layers of pale cloud; it's muggy, too, like it might storm later, the air thick with summer heat. By the time I'm down on the Tube platform, I've already shed my jacket.

Waterloo station is busy, but it's easy enough to spot Lloyd waiting underneath the large clock suspended from the high ceiling, standing in place while the crowds shift and merge around him.

I'm relieved when he looks more like himself than he did the other day – like he's finally gotten some rest, at least. Wearing jeans and his glasses, his hair a little unruly as if from sleep, it feels like I'm seeing *my* Lloyd: the version of him who knows where to get late-night cake and coffee, who spills secrets and draws out parts of me I didn't even know existed. He even smiles when he sees me approaching – small and reserved, but sincere.

'Hi,' I say, when I get close enough.

'Hi.'

I swing my tote bag from under my shoulder, taking out his file and handing it over. Lloyd is careful not to let his fingers brush against mine; I try to ignore the way that stings. He starts flipping through it, a frown tugging at his brow, almost like he thinks he'll find whole sections missing. Maybe he thinks I'll have graffitied them with crude drawings of penises like the boys at school used to do in textbooks.

'It's all there,' I reassure him. 'I was careful with it.'

'You shouldn't have looked at it at all,' he mutters. He's still too busy examining it to look at me beyond a quick, reproachful glance. 'It wasn't yours. You shouldn't have snooped.'

'Like I said, I was just trying to figure out who it belonged to. But . . . this is . . .' I glance at all the neon tabs, watch the file bend with the weight of all the papers in there. 'Lloyd, what *is* all this?'

He tries to play it off – a playful scoff and a full-body shrug, and a too-casual, 'What did you expect? I told you. My dad wants me to know how everything works, know the company inside out, ready for when I take over one day. I've been making notes, that's all.'

But Lloyd can't quite meet my eyes, and this time it feels purposeful rather than simply distracted. I shift a little closer so I can drop my voice, and the sudden proximity seems to resurrect the little bubble we've created on nights in each other's company before, muting the noise of the rest of the world around us and granting us some illusion of privacy.

'Notes? This is way more than just a few *notes*. It's –'

I trail off, trying to find the right words. I think about all the diagrams he'd redrawn and annotated, the notes he'd left. Costs he'd highlighted. The way he dismissed the collaboration between Arrowmile and Mum's company. Will, saying that he'd seen Lloyd looking up courses for Chemical Engineering at uni. The way he tried to play it cool when he tagged along to our labs visit, but was so obviously interested in it.

Something slots into place, and I take a guess.

'It's all the things *you'd* do differently, isn't it?'

Lloyd scoffs, starting to protest, but he falters quickly. A breath shudders out of him and he meets my gaze this time, green eyes shining, looking so oddly vulnerable for a guy who's always been so sure of himself. His shoulders hunch as he draws his file closer to his chest, shrinking in on himself until he looks physically smaller. Without the big smile or the swaggering attitude, he looks so young. More like his age.

He looks like a kid who's been under way too much pressure for way too long.

'You can't tell anybody,' he says quietly. 'You have to *promise me*, you won't tell them about this. They can't find out. Especially not my dad.'

'But I thought you and your dad talked about everything going on at Arrowmile? I thought that was, like, the whole *point*. That he wanted you to be involved?'

'Not like this. Not . . .'

Lloyd drags a hand through his hair, rattled and unsure – and entirely unlike himself. The closeness that's built up between us since the start of summer suddenly seems so much bigger than the recent distance, than the lingering tension from our fight – and I don't think twice when I take him by the elbow and gesture for us to leave the station. Lloyd relaxes, breathes a little easier, at my touch, looking at me like he's thinking the same thing: whatever else has happened between us, we know each other in a way other people don't. And that still means something.

'Come on, Fletcher,' I tell him. 'Let's get breakfast, and talk.'

Lloyd and I manage to get a quiet corner table inside one of the restaurants along the South Bank. We both place orders for some breakfast without really paying much attention to the menu, and then Lloyd starts talking, the words spilling out of him in a rush. He trips over his words and fidgets with the cutlery, occasionally losing himself in the excitement of talking about something he loves, or else abruptly turning to quiet, stilted stammering as he tries to explain himself.

He explains that this file is something he's been working on for a couple of years, but he's really been focusing on it in earnest while spending his gap year at Arrowmile. It started out as just a fact-finding mission, something to help him prepare for the inevitable day his dad decided he should get involved in the company in a more real way, with a more concrete role. It was part pet project at the beginning, too – he had a real interest in the development work going on in the labs, did some research in his own time for fun, occasionally found something from one project that could be used somewhere else, ways to make things more efficient.

'Like with Phoebus III,' he tells me, fishing some diagrams out of the file to show me. I notice the one on top is a patent application for something, but I couldn't even begin to guess what. 'They were applying tech from racing cars to try and improve the battery life of our electric vehicles, but the technology wasn't quite there at the time so it got expensive and then Dad cut off the funding and it got scrapped – but *now*, see, if we used that in the new car, in the Phoebus IV, there's a real chance it could work! But nobody's even considered it – or if they have, they're too scared to try to approach my dad about it after it failed the last time.'

Sometimes, he explains, it was more of a revenge mission. Rooting out all the rotten parts of Arrowmile, debunking some of their eco-friendly claims or the positive 'spin' they'd put on something.

'The thing they're working on with your mum – it's a nice idea, but it's all just to get some good publicity. They'll pour *millions* into it, for nothing. They don't plan to actually *do* anything beyond a few prototypes they can show off, you know? They don't care enough. Maybe your mum does, I don't know, but Dad definitely doesn't. It's a gimmick.'

Whatever this research project is, it's been his outlet. Something to channel his frustration and passion and determination into, all this time.

He pauses to take a breather when our food is brought over.

Lloyd's eyes are shining again, but this time not with the threat of tears. Now, it's pure exhilaration. The shallow heave of his chest isn't anxiety, it's adrenaline.

I can't help but admire him, even as I'm still getting my head around this.

And I can't believe I ever thought he was just throwing his weight around, enjoying exerting his authority as the boss's son and never actually doing any real work, when all this time he's been dedicated to *this*.

'I still don't understand,' I say, pulling my poached egg and avocado toast towards me. 'Why don't you want your dad to find out about all this? Wouldn't he be proud? I mean, if this is stuff that could help the company . . .'

Lloyd scoffs. 'Some of it would. Some of it wouldn't look so great if the press got hold of it, or shareholders found out, I bet.'

'Which was why you were always nagging *me* to find out what the updates to all the managers were. So you could see how people were talking about stuff, or what kind of spin they put on it.'

'Yeah. Besides, I've *tried* talking to my dad. He doesn't care.'

'He – what?'

'He doesn't care,' Lloyd repeats, and pulls a face, his mouth twisting up on one side as he shrugs, all, *What can you do?* 'I've tried to talk to him about everything in this file, but he's never interested. Just says, *Leave it to the grown-ups. Don't worry about it, it's all in hand*. Or he tells me he'll deal with it, but he never does. You said a while ago that nobody would tell me that my work doesn't hold any weight – but as far as my dad's concerned, it doesn't. He reckons I don't understand what they're doing in the labs, but I understand a lot more than he does. I've been living, sleeping, breathing this stuff since I was little. I *like* the science of it, so I've learned about it – unlike Dad, who just defers to the experts.

'If he knew just how much stuff I've collected on Arrowmile . . . I mean, this whole thing –' Lloyd lets out a short chuckle, gesturing at the file. 'This is basically a catalogue of everything he's done *wrong* for the last couple of years. He'd be furious if he found out. And . . . And I don't want to put that on Will, you know? If Dad loses it with me, he'll just start trying to rope Will back into Arrowmile, and . . .'

Breakfast forgotten, all I can do is stare at this boy who wears his heart on his sleeve, who loves so fiercely and fully and is so full of compassion, and wonder how I ever thought so little of him.

I kept calling him golden boy, not realizing he had a heart of gold to match.

Reaching across the table, I take Lloyd's hand.

'You should do something with all this, though! If it could help your dad's company, and do some good in the world . . .'

'What? What can I do, that'll actually make him sit down and listen and understand I'm not trying to sabotage his life's work? Round up all the Arrowmile teams and tell *them* instead, hope they can make him listen?'

'Actually ... Actually, Fletcher, that might not be such a bad idea.'

He snorts, giving me a sardonic smile. 'It's a nice thought, but not gonna happen. He'd find out and shut the whole thing down before I got chance.'

'Maybe. But ... I think I've got a way to help.'

We stick around for a while after finishing breakfast, sharing a pot of tea and talking the plan through, Lloyd telling me a little more about some of the parts of his research he's most excited about. They're always the geeky, science-y ones from work going on in the labs, but he's patient as he explains it all in terms that I can understand.

'Thanks,' he tells me quietly, 'for helping me with all of this.'

'Thanks for telling me about all of this,' I reply, nodding towards the file. 'And – and like I tried to say before, I really *am* sorry about the way I've been treating you. And all this stuff with your dad, and the company – I never really realized how tough it must be for you.'

Lloyd shrugs, shuffling in his seat. 'It's okay. It's not like I let on, I guess. I know that makes *me* kind of a hypocrite – like you said, I was mad at you for not letting me in, when I was busy keeping you out, too, but . . .' Then his eyes dart up to mine, and he cringes. 'As long as we're apologizing, I'm sorry I called you a hypocrite.'

'It's okay. I didn't . . . I really didn't mean to have a go at you. I was just trying to explain I'd never lied to you about who my mum was, that it wasn't like it looked. And I don't expect you to forgive me, but . . . I'd like it if we can be friends again, maybe? I'm still here for another few weeks, so, it's just . . . I mean, I don't want things to be awkward, and I *do* like spending time with you, and –'

'Annalise,' he says softly, and flashes me the quicksilver smile that's held a place in my heart since the first night we met. 'I forgive you. Friends, yeah?'

'Yeah.'

I smile at him, happy – relieved.

Even if I shouldn't have been so quick to dismiss my connection with Lloyd or shut down the possibility of anything romantic going on between us so I could focus one hundred per cent on the internship, it doesn't change the fact that there's only three weeks to go until this is over, and then I'll pack up and move back home.

And come October, we'll both be at uni, in different cities, and didn't last year already prove to me that I couldn't manage to study *and* maintain a long-distance relationship? Or probably *any* relationship?

This summer was always a finite stretch of time. It was always going to be this self-contained little pocket.

So there still can't be anything between me and Lloyd; it wouldn't be fair to either of us. And Lloyd deserves better.

Friends, though. Friends, I'll happily take.

Because I can't lose him. Even if we can't be together, I can't lose what I have with Lloyd completely.

My phone buzzes on the table, for like the twentieth time. Lloyd eyes it with an amused smile.

'Again? Someone's popular. Or is there some gossip going off in the group chat?'

I turn my phone screen-up to check; I'd silenced it and turned it face-down to talk to Lloyd properly.

'It's just my mum.' I snap the screen off again.

'Oh. What does she want? Lunch, again?'

'Um . . .' Suddenly awkward, I feel my cheeks beginning to heat. 'She wanted to wish me happy birthday.'

I glance up in time to see Lloyd's jaw drop, the sympathy over my tricky relationship with Mum replaced instantly by a blank expression, and then again by guilt.

'Annalise! You should've told me!'

'It's not a big deal. I don't normally make a fuss about my birthday anyway. And,' I joke, 'I didn't get much chance, what with you demanding I hand over your Top Secret Project file.'

Lloyd laughs. 'Yeah, that's fair. Sorry for highjacking your birthday. And, obviously, happy birthday.'

'Thanks. And that's okay. I didn't really have plans this morning anyway, beyond FaceTiming my dad and everyone at some point. A bunch of us are going out for dinner tonight though, and Izzy's making a cake. You could – I mean, you could . . . join us, if you like. And Will. I'm sure nobody would mind.'

Surprise colours his face, his eyebrows shooting up towards his hairline.

'Are you sure *you* wouldn't mind?' he asks.

'Honestly? I can't think of anything I'd like more,' I tell him, and I mean it.

We finish up breakfast, but neither of us suggests parting ways just yet. We wander along the river, another pair of people in the Saturday morning bustle, and conversation is easy: we talk about birthdays from our childhood, what plans Lloyd and Will have for their birthday at the end of August and how rubbish it's always been to have a birthday in the school holidays like this. We talk like we did the first night, and that time at the late-night cafe, and I have to try hard not to follow Lloyd's lead and wear my heart on my sleeve around him, when we can't be more than friends.

We leave each other around lunchtime. I text Lloyd the plans for tonight so he can meet us with Will at the restaurant, and call Dad when I'm on the bus home to chat to everybody.

'I wish you'd come home for the weekend!' Gina tells me, when she manages to wrangle the phone back off Oliver and Christian once they descend into bickering. 'We would've paid for your train ticket! I didn't get to see you with the others in Devon the other week, and I miss you! But at least you've got plans with all your friends – I'm sure that's much more exciting than seeing us lot. I know I sent you some nice new clothes and a few bits from us all, but your dad's sent you some money, too, so you can treat yourself to a little something!'

I miss her too. I miss all of them.

It must just be this homesickness for family that makes me feel a little bit guilty when, back at the flat, I find a birthday card from Mum with some money inside, too. And she *does* sound contrite in her earlier text, when I finally read that properly – like she really *is* trying.

It's hard to let her.

I don't want to give her the chance to disappoint me again.

Either way, I find myself thanking her for the card, the money and the birthday wishes, and I even apologize for being so short with her at lunch. Maybe, I say, if she's still around in a couple of weeks, we can try again before I leave.

On my terms.

The evening arrives suddenly, all at once, with a group of us piling out to a restaurant Elaine found nearby. There's a little initial surprise that Lloyd and Will are joining us, but I just mention I'd invited them 'a while ago' and they're swept easily into the fold, and come back to the flat with us afterwards to enjoy the cake Izzy made – a giant vanilla sponge with lashings of buttercream that is truly mouth-watering. We stuff ourselves with cake and play charades, and when Will and Lloyd make a move to leave, I walk them out. They both fit seamlessly into the group, but I feel a new sort of warm glow at bringing some friends together; I bask in the feeling of being surrounded by people I feel are genuinely my friends, and not just because we're in the same club together at school or something. For once, I enjoy being not just included, but the centre of attention.

And it's nice to know that Lloyd and I really can spend time together this way, without it being weird or tense.

'Thanks for the invite,' Will tells me, and gives me a quick, one-armed hug. 'This was fun. And I'm glad you two are speaking again.'

Lloyd shoves his brother, rolling his eyes. Will steps away to call the lift, granting us a tiny, fleeting moment of privacy.

'Thanks for coming,' I say. It comes out a whisper.

Lloyd smiles at me, leaning in with a hand braced against my elbow to kiss my cheek, dangerously close to the corner of my mouth, sending a current of electric shock all the way to my toes. He smiles softly when he draws away.

'Happy birthday, Annalise.'

I watch them leave, my fingers coming up to brush against my cheek.

As presents go, that kiss was the best one.

Chapter 30

By the time the weekend is over, I feel way better than when it started. My relationship – *friendship* – with Lloyd is back on track, and I even feel okay about the fact I'm going to meet Mum for dinner next week. I think it helps that Dad looked so relieved when I mentioned it to him, and he seemed as proud of me for making the effort with Mum as he did when I got into uni.

Despite there being only a couple of weeks left in the internship, things show no signs of slowing down. On top of our usual workloads, we all have presentations to prepare for a big talk at the end of the summer. I still want to make sure I leave everyone with a good impression, so I can't suddenly start to take things easy now.

On Wednesday, Lloyd and I leave my desk, wrapping up one of our usual chats about an ongoing Arrowmile project. We both go to get a fresh hot drink, taking the opportunity to talk more quietly about our plan for Lloyd's secret project. When I head back towards my desk, alone, Tasha is striding towards me. The snap of her high heels is muffled by the carpet. She holds herself tall, shoulders squared, piercing me with such a sharp look that I stop in my tracks before she can cut me off.

'You're *always* hanging about with him.'

It's clear she means Lloyd. 'He's always hanging about. My team asked me to help him out with some stuff.'

'What *stuff*?' Tasha demands, eyes narrowing at me. She's my height, but somehow manages to look down her nose at me. I notice her eyes flit to scrutinize my hair, and I tuck some flyaways behind my ear self-consciously.

'Just some stuff about some projects.'

She scoffs, crossing her arms. 'Right, okay. Just *tell me*. I know the two of you are like this.' Tasha holds up two crossed fingers – and then, bearing down on me, hisses, 'I *know* you guys have a thing. I saw you snogging in the hallway, weeks ago.'

Oh, shit. Shit!

Weeks ago. She's known all this time, and – not told anybody. Has she just been waiting for the perfect moment to try to use it to undermine me, or . . . Maybe she didn't get a good look, and only assumed it was Lloyd? Surely she would've told everyone by now, if she was so sure . . .

I swallow the taste of bile in the back of my throat. 'I don't know what you *think* you saw, but –'

'He's been helping you out with the internship, hasn't he? I saw your presentation for the end of summer talks on your laptop. Is he helping you with that?'

How nosy has she been, exactly? Isn't she too busy concentrating on her own work to keep such a close eye on what I'm doing all the time?

'I'm sure if you need some help with your presentation, Lloyd wouldn't mind taking a look at it,' I say tentatively. 'H-how – how is yours going?'

'He is, isn't he? He's been telling you all the right things to do, and now he's telling you how to do your presentation so you can get a job after you graduate, isn't he?'

'No! That's not –'

Tasha smirks, shifting her stance slightly. Somehow, she manages to look more casual and infinitely more intimidating all at once. Maybe she's been studying Nadja's body language, or maybe this is just a natural talent.

'I really didn't think you were capable of it, you know, Anna?'

'Capable of what?'

'Pretending to be interested in him just to use him to do better at your job. Sleeping your way to the top. Honestly. Good for you. I'm kind of impressed.'

My whole face starts to burn, something raw and angry igniting in my chest when she smirks wider.

'That's not – I'm – You're *wrong*. That's not what I'm doing.'

'*Please*. We both know you're not qualified for this internship. I mean, you don't even *dress* right for it. You look like some frumpy mum, or something. It's embarrassing. Especially when you're barely even nineteen – a *first-year*, and not technically even qualified for this internship.' She pouts, pulling a mocking baby face expression. 'Did you get Lloyd to pull some strings for you there, too? Or maybe you got your famous mum to do that?'

The blood drains from my face and the breath is snatched from my lungs.

Tasha's head cocks to one side, triumph glinting in her eyes.

'I – I didn't – that's . . . You've got it wrong, I'm . . . I've . . .'

I've lost the ability to form a whole sentence.

'Aww, don't worry, babe. I won't tell.' She lays a hand on my arm and squeezes. '*Mum's* the word, right?'

I wait for the inevitable blackmail, or some more cruel comments, but none come, and I realize she's not telling me any of this for any reason other than to one-up me somehow. To stand on my shoulders to make herself look taller. I know we're different kinds of people, but I always thought we got on okay *enough*. Or, put up with each other, at least. I didn't think she'd be this vindictive for no reason other than, I guess, pure spite.

Tasha lets go of me, laughing, and strolls away in the direction of the kitchenette, empty water bottle swinging idly from her fingertip. I stand for a moment before deciding to chase after her, catching her arm to yank her back around in the empty stretch of corridor.

'Listen, I don't know *what* your problem is, but I earned this internship all by myself. Not with my mum's help, not with Lloyd's, not with anybody's. And for the record, I don't care if you think my clothes are frumpy and embarrassing, because at least I'm doing a good job. I earned my place here. I'm *still* earning it. Just because you've been coasting along, don't take it out on me now you realize it won't get you a job when you graduate.'

I say it in a last-ditch attempt at self-defence more than any real knowledge of how much of a grafter Tasha actually is when she's at her desk – but her face pinches and I can tell I've hit a nerve.

She snatches her arm away from me and is deathly silent as she whirls around and strides off, leaving me to shuffle back to my desk, shaken and not really sure who won.

Tasha stays out of my way and none of the other interns say anything, so she's obviously not shared her accusations with anyone. She's just done it to be spiteful. One of 'those' girls, Gina would say.

But the next morning, I should know something's up.

It's one of those days. My phone is dead – I fell asleep watching TikToks and never plugged it in to charge – so there's no alarm to wake me up, only Elaine knocking on my door to check on me because she hasn't heard me up yet, and she knows I'd normally be out of the flat by now. I drop jam down my white blouse when I scarf down some toast, but I'm still ready in record time and out of the door before Elaine or Louis. And then, to top it off, there's a delay on the Tube line.

People seem to show up at Arrowmile any time between eight and ten in the morning, but it's almost nine by the time I'm hurrying towards my desk, ready to apologize to my boss Michaela for being an hour later than usual.

There are papers taped up around the office. They're tacked to blank stretches of wall and the lockers at the ends of desks, to computer screens where people haven't shown up yet. They're print-outs of text and a couple of dark, badly-designed posters so grainy I can't see what they're promoting. I wonder what that's all about – maybe some weird phishing email warning? Maybe a scavenger hunt, some fun team-building activity; I bet the Marketing team would come up with something like that.

Whatever it is, I'll take a proper look after I've logged on and sat down.

There's someone waiting at my desk, though. More than one someone. *People*.

Michaela is standing there, some papers in her hand. Illustrious Leader/CEO Topher Fletcher is talking to her, frowning, looking ... concerned? Angry? Whatever it is, it makes my stomach clench and my palms sweat. There's Nadja, too, busy scowling at something on her phone, teeth bared.

I falter, dread creeping over me.

They know. Tasha's told them I lied about my age on my application. They've found out and they're going to make me pay back the salary and they'll kick me out before I can finish the summer here and they'll send me home in disgrace and next year when I apply for summer jobs this will follow me around and –

I wonder if I can run away before they spot me.

I barely take half a step back when I hear someone behind me – 'Anna! There you are! Shit, did you see? Are you okay?'

There's a hand on my shoulder, pulling me around. Monty.

His face is creased in a worried frown and he's grimacing, and – why is he worried? I've never seen Monty look worried about *anything*, much less about someone else. Does he know I lied on my application, too? But why would he care?

There's a stack of crumpled papers in his hand. Some of them are a little torn.

'We tried calling you earlier, me and Verity and Dylan – we got in early and found them – but you weren't answering. We're trying to gather them all up before ... well, I mean, everyone's going to see anyway, but ...'

My mouth has gone dry. My heart beats a furious tattoo.

'See what?' I whisper, but I'm already figuring it out in the few seconds Monty hesitates before answering.

I look down at the papers in his hands more closely. They're print-outs of emails. As if in slow motion, I turn to look at some stuck on the wall nearest me, finally focusing on the text.

Dear Lloyd,

they say.

And they end:

Sincerely Yours,
Anna Sherwood

Oh, fuck.

And the poster, the dark, grainy image – it's a photo, blown up to A4 size.

Of me, my orange hair in messy French braids, barefoot in my pyjamas in the hallway, with Lloyd's hand up my shirt and our faces attached at the mouth.

Fuck.

'They got sent out to everyone this morning. I guess they were scheduled, or something? It came from your email, but *obviously* you didn't send it out yourself. How bloody embarrassing would that be, putting this stuff out for everyone to – well, not that it's *embarrassing*, you see, just . . . And obviously, you didn't print out a bunch of copies and tape them up around the office, or take that photo. Dylan's got the tenth floor, and Ver is doing upstairs. I came down to get the ones here. We only just got in, like, fifteen minutes ago . . .'

Oh my God.

Sent out to everyone.

All my emails to Lloyd, the letters I penned him and saved as a draft, just trying to muddle out my own thoughts and feelings about him . . . Talking about the kiss before the internship started, how irritating and awful I found him, the way he broke my heart. All those deep, dark secrets. Sent to everyone. Taped up, for all to see.

I feel exposed in a way that has nothing to do with my legs on display in that awful photograph.

Monty's still talking. His hand is on my arm, warm and heavy, in a way I think is meant to be comforting and reassuring. It makes me feel trapped, rooted to the spot. The group at my desk have noticed me by now and are coming over, too.

Nadja steps forward first, and the sympathy on her stern face is strange to see. 'Anna, are you alright? We're trying to get IT to see if they can recall the emails, but it probably won't make much difference for anybody who's already read them.'

Like it'll matter. The internet is forever, isn't it? And the people who don't get chance to read them will hear about them from someone else anyway. Who wouldn't gossip about this?

'And we're obviously going to be checking who could have hacked into your email, or printed them out. It shouldn't be too hard to find out who's behind all this. Unless you've got any ideas?'

Any ideas?

Oh, God. When I left my laptop unlocked yesterday, after my chat with Lloyd. Being confronted immediately afterwards.

Tasha.

I guess now we know who won.

But I can't say anything, can hardly remember to breathe. This is so much worse than them finding out I'm too young for the internship, or kicking me out. This is completely humiliating. It'll follow me around, haunt me, overshadowing everything I've achieved this summer exactly like I worried it would when I called things off with Lloyd.

And now everyone else will think just like Tasha did, that because of how close I am with Lloyd, *he's* the only reason I've done well here at all.

Nobody would believe I earned this, after reading those emails. I wouldn't.

I hear Topher muttering, 'That boy, honestly. Like we didn't go through this already last year . . .'

I shake my head vehemently. *No, it's not like that*, and I try to draw a breath to say something, but instead some weird high-pitched squeak comes out of my mouth, and I realize I can taste salt – that my face is wet, and I'm crying.

I'm not even the girl who cries in the bathroom, anymore. I'm the girl who cries in *public*. Like this all wasn't mortifying enough already.

'Let's go upstairs, Anna,' Nadja is saying, her voice ringing with its usual brusque authority, which is oddly comforting. 'Just while we sort all this out, okay? Monty, you can carry on gathering all this rubbish up, can't you?'

'Sure, yeah.'

'But – but I've got a meeting at half past nine. I'm supposed to –'

'Don't worry about any of that now, Anna,' Michaela tells me. She crouches slightly to look me in the eye, to smile and nod, and it makes me feel like a child who needs taking care of – not the grown-up we've all been pretending I am for weeks.

Monty leaves to collect more of my emails of shame and Michaela rubs my arm reassuringly before going back to her desk; Topher Fletcher declares he's off to speak to IT, and then HR.

Shit, he's getting HR involved. They're definitely

going to fire me. Is Lloyd in trouble, too? Topher didn't seem exactly happy with him either . . .

Numbly, I let Nadja usher me into a small meeting room where she draws the blinds down for privacy and then fetches me a cup of tea, and lets me weep and babble at her about exactly what happened this summer between me and Lloyd so she doesn't think I really did use him to get ahead. I beg her not to kick me out of the internship because of this or because I kissed Lloyd or because I lied and I'm only in my first year of uni or because I left my laptop unlocked and I know we're not supposed to, because I don't know what I'll do if they sack me and send me home.

Although at this point, I'm seriously considering abandoning it all on my own.

I alternate between desperate apologies and frantic hyperventilating – even as Nadja assures me that I'm not in trouble, and this won't jeopardize my place on the internship.

Dryly, she adds, 'Although it will jeopardize *someone's*, I'm sure.'

Two cups of tea and several bouts of crying later, I finally feel a little calmer. They aren't kicking me out, so my summer hasn't been wasted and my whole future isn't in ruins from that regard – but I'm still not sure how I'll ever live this down. Whatever Nadja tells me, and whatever the truth is, I know there will be people at Arrowmile who think the credit for my work here should go to Lloyd, and that I don't really deserve it.

Not to mention, everyone will have seen all those things I wrote.

Including –

Oh, God. *Lloyd* will have read them. He'll have seen those things I've said. How he had everyone fooled, that I didn't want to get to know him – that I fell for him, and he made me believe in love after all.

I wish the ground would swallow me whole.

There's a sharp rap on the door, and it swings open.

Mum stands there, harried and concerned in a way I've never seen.

Her face crumples when she sees me.

'Oh, Annalise.'

And I break down crying all over again.

Chapter 31

'Topher called me,' Mum tells me, smoothing back some of my hair. Through the taxi's window, London trundles past us in fits and starts; we zoom down wide roads, weave through lanes of traffic, move in short bursts near traffic lights and crawl along seemingly endless lines of cars and taxis. A few raindrops patter against the windows. 'He thought, under the circumstances . . .'

I make a noise that's neither assent nor disagreement.

On the one hand, even if my relationship with Mum has been non-existent for most of my life and tedious for the last couple of years, having her there to comfort me while my world fell apart was exactly what I needed.

But there's also the fact that my mum coming to pick me up makes me feel even more like I've been sent home from school like some unruly child, adding to my embarrassment.

'What . . .' My voice is raspy, throat sore from all the crying. My tongue feels thick and awkward in my mouth. I swallow, and try again. I can't quite meet Mum's eyes. 'What did he tell you?'

'Enough.'

Now I do cut her a look, not in the mood for this vague, misguided attempt at being the protective parent. It doesn't suit her, and it's not helping me right now either.

She sighs slightly, but says, 'That you've obviously grown very close with his son and some rather personal emails you'd written him had been distributed to the office, along with a, er, somewhat intimate photograph of the two of you. *And* paper copies had been taped up everywhere this morning, so obviously it was a nasty little prank and not some silly accident. Although honestly, Anna, using a professional email for that sort of thing – I *really* thought you would know better . . .'

'Yeah, alright, thanks, Mum. That's not helping.' I scowl, turning back to the window. That feeling of safety and comfort she'd provided not ten whole minutes ago, hugging me in that little room at Arrowmile, is suddenly long gone.

'Well,' she says, more lightly. 'Let's just count ourselves lucky you weren't using your email to sext him, or send anything naughty.'

'*Ohmigod, Mum.*'

And to think I thought this whole thing couldn't get more humiliating. My cheeks burn – though I'm not sure if it's more to do with the fact my mum just said the word 'sext' or the mere idea that I might've written that kind of thing to Lloyd at all. I sink a bit lower in the seat, smothering my face with my hands.

'I didn't realize the two of you were an item,' she says after a few moments. Her statement is curious, open.

'We're not.'

I wonder, if things had been different, if I would've gossiped with her about boys. Would I have been FaceTiming her throughout my internship like I had been Dad and Gina, but instead of telling her about friends or the work, gushing about the cute boy I'd met? Would I have confided in her about whether I should give Lloyd a chance or focus solely on the internship?

Would it have seemed less black and white, if things with Mum had been different?

Several beats pass; Mum looks like she wants to ask

me more, but is clearly biting her tongue, conflicted. Like she's afraid that pushing me too hard, trying too much to be my mum or my friend or whatever, will burn whatever bridges I have tentatively agreed to start building.

She looks hurt. Hopeful. Scared.

I've never seen Mum look like that before. When I was little, I remember her being exasperated and exhausted from time to time. Mostly, I remember the fire in her eyes – that look of barely contained excitement she'd get when she was particularly driven about something, which was most of the time. In all the photos and videos of her online in more recent years, she's always been so composed. A funny little half-smile, like she knows the secret to having it all, a confidence in her posture.

But right now, there are lines pinched around the edges of her mouth, ageing her. Her hair isn't as smooth as it normally would be and there's some eyeliner smudged beneath one of her eyes, like whatever time she would've normally taken to fix it wasn't worth it in her rush over to Arrowmile after Topher's call. Her eyes are downcast; there's a deep furrow between her professionally maintained eyebrows. Uncertainty threads through her made-up face, cloying in the air around her.

She didn't even look like this either time I asked her to leave me alone and stormed out on her.

Realizing that, something softens in the hard angles that have spiked up around my heart. The ache in my chest eases.

And I break the silence by telling Mum, 'We might have been an item, if . . . It's complicated. Or, it didn't have to be, I suppose, but I made it messy. I kept making it messy.'

'Do you – do you want to tell me about it?'

I expect a sharp retort ready on my tongue, out of habit if nothing else – *No. Don't pretend like you care. Don't think that being here for me now, just because someone else involved you and you had to save face by showing up, makes up for anything.*

But it never comes.

I just hunch smaller into the corner of the car and take a deep breath.

'It started months ago, the weekend before the internship . . .'

The taxi takes us to Mum's hotel suite. A *suite*, I notice, not merely a room. It has its own designated sitting area. The bathroom must be bigger than my entire bedroom back home at Dad and Gina's, I think, measuring it up mentally before I splash some cold water on my face, using one of the luxurious white facecloths branded with the hotel's logo, and some of Mum's expensive-looking products, to scrub my mangled makeup off my face. I borrow her hairbrush to tidy up my hair, too.

In the harsh spotlights of the bathroom, in the humongous mirror above the double sinks, I can't help but stare at the girl in the reflection. She looks like she just had her whole life ripped out from under her; she's strung-out. Wrung-out. Exhausted. Her white blouse is a remnant of her school days, the pencil skirt awkward and frumpy. Her pale face is hollowed, ashen – young. She looks like a kid playing dress-up.

Who have I been kidding all summer?

I *am* just a kid playing dress-up. I'm not the #GirlBoss millennial stereotype I've always secretly looked up to and was trying so hard to emulate all summer, smashing glass ceilings and climbing the corporate ladder, with her houseplants and her whole life together. I'm not a grown-up. In America, I'm not even old enough to drink.

I've been so focused on making sure my life is set when I *am* older, I think I forgot somewhere along the way that I'm not actually there yet. That I might not be for a while. That it might be okay, to just . . . be a teenager, and kiss a cute boy on my summer break.

By the time I return to the sitting room, Mum is fussing about with the little kettle. I wonder how many times she's re-boiled it, waiting for me to come out of the bathroom.

'I – I wasn't sure how you took your tea, Anna.'

'Oh. Um, milk, no sugar.'

'How much milk?'

Again, she looks so uncertain. This isn't the mum who met me for lunch a few weeks ago. This is . . . this is someone who realizes that, as my mum, she should know how I take my tea, and how much milk to put in.

'Just, like . . .' I try to gesture. 'A tiny splash.'

A faint smile crosses her face. 'Your dad always liked his tea strong, too. Like the milk barely touched it, I used to say.'

She finishes making it, handing it over while I take a seat on the plush sofa, and sets to the toggles and buttons on the fancy coffee machine to make herself a drink. 'I've got some biscuits here too . . .' she mumbles, and sets an open pack of chocolate bourbons on the coffee table. I almost expect them to be some posh brand, too, but they're just regular Tesco ones. Nothing special.

Exactly like the ones that used to live in the bear-shaped biscuit jar in the kitchen at our old house, back when Mum was part of the family.

I reach for one, nibbling at it. It tastes like being five years old and sitting at the kitchen table, legs swinging under my chair, blathering on about school while Mum paid half a mind to me, and half to her computer. It tastes like innocence, and ignorance.

I'm only able to manage a little of it; the stress of this morning has stolen my appetite. Even for chocolate biscuits.

Mum sits on the sofa by me, dunks a biscuit in her tea and eats it whole.

I've already told her all about Lloyd. Our accidental meetings in the empty office. The late-night cake, the kiss at the summer party. That he came to the flat and stayed the night (although that's all I mention on that one). I tell her about how I struggled to figure out who he was and how I thought he was probably some arrogant, entitled guy beneath it all because that was how he seemed around the office ... That I pushed him away, because I chose the internship over him.

Now, I realize I'm not quite done.

'I just feel like such an idiot. All this time, he was exactly who he said he was. He was never anybody different, that was just ... in my head. But I kept thinking the worst of him, even when he kept giving *me* the benefit of the doubt. I – I *liked* him. I really liked him. I could've just – had that, you know? Let myself like him. But I didn't, and now I've ruined it, and it doesn't matter anyway.'

'Oh, Anna, sweetheart.' Mum tucks an arm around me, only seeming to think better of it afterwards. I feel her freeze a little, but she relaxes when I don't shrug her off; I might have done if I didn't feel so completely, wretchedly sorry for myself.

Across the room, my phone starts going nuts. I asked Mum if she could put it on charge for me, and I guess now it's finally come back to life. I can bank on some of those notifications being missed calls and messages from my friends – Monty and Verity and Dylan, desperately trying to get hold of me this morning; the others, probably, after they found out and thought they should check in. Maybe some of them are teasing me about it in the group chat, trying to make light of it. I dread to think what the other notifications might be.

I wince. 'How am I meant to go back there, after this?'

'People will understand. Things like this – well, they don't happen *often*, but they'll know it was someone being vicious. I'm sure it won't even be all that bad, Anna, really. It'll blow over.'

I try to say something, but all that comes out is a wobbly groan. I feel queasy again; I might actually bring up the biscuit and my breakfast this time.

'Do you want me to . . . I mean, I could take a look at the emails. See how bad it is. Isn't, I mean.'

I look up. 'But Nadja – they said IT were going to retract it. That they did. It won't be there anymore.'

'It'll be in your sent folder. It came from your email, didn't it?'

I cringe to know that somewhere, there's still a concrete record of those emails. But I nod, and wave Mum over to my phone, telling her my passcode so she can look for herself. She stands upright, the phone lifted so she doesn't hunch over it, manicured fingers swiping efficiently. This looks more like the version of Mum I'm used to seeing online: cool, calm, confident.

Finally, she pauses, her index finger pulling slowly at the screen as she reads.

I sip my tea and try to eat the other half of my bourbon biscuit. I don't want to see, but can't take my eyes away. It's like stopping to watch a car crash. Some warped, mortal part of my soul is compelled to witness the destruction.

Mum's face is a mask as she reads – until finally, it's not.

There's a small gasp that sounds so fragile and raw I don't know where it's come from, not until Mum presses a hand over her mouth and I see her eyes fill abruptly with tears. The blood drains from her face, turning her ghostly pale beneath her makeup. Slowly, she sets my phone back down and blinks rapidly, but I don't know whether it's to cover the tears or if she's just trying to get her head around something.

My stomach drops.

I didn't think they were that bad. Were they? Unless I've forgotten something truly awful I wrote about Lloyd, or Arrowmile . . . Unless Mum's seen something else. Maybe there's something horrible on my phone that she saw, or they've kicked me off the internship after all, or –

'Is this . . .' She swallows, hard. 'Is that really what you think I did? Chose my ambition over you and your dad? Stomped all over you?'

Oh.

Oh. That.

I stare at her, not sure what to say except, 'You did.'

Mum stares at me. A few tears fall onto her cheeks.

I carry on, my voice steady. It's all fact. It's been fact for years; this is one thing, today, I don't need to get emotional over.

'We were always secondary to you. To your life. The glamorous businesswoman and self-declared "She-EO". You left us because we couldn't compete with your career and your ambition. You chose to go out there and be Kathryn Jones, instead of my mum.' I shrug, starting to feel a bit uncomfortable by how upset she looks. 'I remember you used to skip out on school things with me because you had more important things to do at work. Even when you were at home, you weren't really *there* most of the time. After you left . . . Well, you'd left. You were gone. It's not like you came back, is it?'

Mum flinches. After a moment, she shuffles to the armchair furthest from me. When she sinks into it, she looks small. Frail. So . . . not like Mum.

'Dad says he knew when he married you, he couldn't compete with your ambition. That he used to admire it about you, until it eclipsed everything. I obviously couldn't compete with it, either.'

'Oh, darling – no, that's not . . .'

'It is. It's fine.'

It's not fine. It's never been fine. But it's the truth, and I can't change it. I'm not trying to.

Mum shakes her head, hunching forward to press her hands over her face. She smudges her makeup when she drags them away.

'Me and your dad had other problems. Mainly mine, I'll be the first to admit that, but there were other things . . . It wasn't the only factor in our divorce. I knew I couldn't look after you, but he was so angry with me – much like you are now, I suppose – that he suggested I stay away until I decided I was "settled" enough to be part of your life. It wasn't fair on you, we agreed, if I kept flitting in and out, or not showing up. I . . . Anna, I wasn't ready to be a mum when I had you. I thought I was, but – when it came to it . . . I had awful post-partum depression, you know. I turned into this husk. Your dad had to take care of both of us, for a long while. When I started to get better, it felt like I'd lost this huge part of myself. Work was the only thing I could cling to that made me feel like my old self. I – I suppose I threw myself into it a little too far, is all.'

I stare at Mum. At her pale face and smeared makeup, the tears flowing down her cheeks and her trembling hands. At this strange, aching creature I've never seen before.

And I whisper, 'I didn't know you were depressed.'

She looks startled. 'Didn't your dad mention it?'

'I – I mean . . . He said you had a rough time, after you had me.'

The corner of Mum's mouth twitches. '*He* had a rough time. I was like a ghost. It wiped out a whole

403

chunk of my life. I think, by the time I was better – it's like you said, I let work eclipse everything else. Your father and I agreed I'd let you both have some space – some stability – and I don't think I ever felt ready to come back into your life. I thought it would only be for a couple of months, but every time – I put it off. *After this merger's finished*, I'd think. *After I've got through this probation period*, or, *Once this deadline's out of the way.* There was always something.'

She draws a shaky breath, and gives me a watery smile. When her eyes meet mine, it's a vice around my lungs, wrapping them in barbed wire and drawing a sharp gasp out of me, prickling tears into the corners of my eyes.

'The plain and simple truth is that I was scared. I didn't know how to be a mum. I loved your dad, and it hurt me that I'd lost him. I didn't want to hurt you both more by coming back if I ended up leaving again.'

'But . . .' I pause, taking a breath to steady myself. 'But you did come back. On my birthday, three years ago. You showed up suddenly wanting to be involved, pretending like you'd never left, like everything was fine.'

She turns her hands palm-up on her knees and looks down at them, lost. 'I miscalculated my approach, and I apologize for that. I always wanted to be part of your life, Anna, I just didn't know how to be. I realized that if I kept putting it off and staying away, I might never know you. I didn't want that. And I'm – I'm sorry, that I never stopped to consider if you might want to know me. You were old enough – *are* old enough – to make that decision. I should have let you.'

I'm speechless.

All I can do is keep staring at her, turning her words over and over and over in my mind. Slotting my own memories and opinions of Mum through this new filter she's just given me, trying to make sense of it all.

She looks at me, nervous, waiting for me to say something.

All I can come up with is –

'I didn't realize you were so human.'

Mum laughs. It's a wet, snotty sort of sound and she sniffles, wiping tears off her face even as she smiles. 'That sounds like something a child would say. What was that I just said, about you being old enough?'

'No, I just – I mean . . .'

Well, yes, I did mean it like that, a bit.

'You always look so in control of everything,' I try to explain. 'It's weird to know you're just – normal, underneath it all.'

'Oh, darling. We all are.'

She moves over to the sofa again, but this time is more hesitant to hug me. So I turn towards her, hugging her back. She strokes my hair, pressing a kiss to the top of my head. My throat is thick, and I squeeze my eyes closed.

I think about how often Dad's told me I'm like Mum, and maybe he was right after all. We're like ducks: working so hard to look like we're floating along, and kicking hell for leather under the water where nobody can see how much effort it takes.

Normal, underneath it all.

Chapter 32

Mum takes me back home to the flat later that afternoon, despite my insistence that I'm alright to make my own way, and the cost of a taxi. She doesn't bat an eye at the meter; I wonder if she ever does.

I can't help but mention it. I think about the lavish hotel suite, the fancy products lined up in her bathroom, the extravagant use of taxis, and remember my argument with Lloyd about how she never contributed while I was growing up. It's not that I want *compensation*; I just can't work out why, if she did want to be involved like she said.

She frowns, but it's confused more than anything else. 'What are you talking about?'

'I heard Dad on the phone to you, once. He said we didn't need your money. He works as an exam invigilator and stuff sometimes, too, for the extra money.

I'm not supposed to know, but I heard him talking to Gina about it once.'

Mum squints, trying to piece it together, then pulls a face at me.

'I think he probably meant, he and Gina were coping alright without me contributing. He wanted me to set the money aside for *you*. We used some of it to buy you a car, when you were learning to drive.'

'What? No, but – that was from Gina's friend. They were getting rid of it.'

'Yes. But we paid them for it, obviously. They could've gotten a decent price at a garage for it. They weren't just *giving* it away.'

'Oh.'

Did I know that? I must have known that, at least a bit. But Dad and Gina had never made a big deal of the car, so I'd never thought very much of it. I definitely hadn't known Mum was involved.

Now, she picks up her phone, tapping at it almost absently. There's an email open on the screen. Whatever it is, it's so second-nature she's only got half a mind on it. She tells me, equally casually, 'The rest of it is in your trust, Anna.'

'My – the – what?'

'The trust fund,' she clarifies, although that doesn't really clarify anything at all.

'I thought those only existed in, like, movies and stuff,' I blurt. 'Like in that one episode of *Derry Girls*.'

She laughs. 'Think of it as a protected bank account I've been paying into for you over the years. It's yours when you turn twenty-one. Your dad and I – and Gina – agreed it was money better set aside for you, to help you set yourself up when you finished uni.'

I gawp, not sure what to say to that.

She smiles at me, apparently oblivious to the fact my brain seems to have stopped working. 'Anyway! It'll be a nice little nest egg for you, when you're a bit older! Something to put towards a house deposit. I gave your dad some to put away for your brothers, too. Gina was a bit resistant at first, but – call it guilt money, I suppose. I know you're close to them, so I didn't want it to turn into a source of resentment down the line somewhere.'

'Holy shit.'

'Language, young lady,' Mum says – almost teasing, like she's mocking her own un-mum-ness.

But I just say again, 'Holy shit,' and she starts laughing, and hugs me close.

There's someone lurking in the corridor outside my flat.

I startle to a stop, only halfway out of the lift. Lloyd's head jerks up at the same time.

He's sat against the wall with his knees tucked up, and now he scrambles to his feet. The lift doors start to slide close, squeezing either side of my arms. I wince as they automatically bounce back open, and step into the hallway towards him.

'Annalise, I'm so – I don't – I had no idea . . .'

The words pour out of him in a rush, like his mouth can't keep pace with his brain. He stops, takes a breath.

And another.

And another.

I realize I'm holding mine, counting the heartbeats while we stare at each other, trying to put an entire summer of heartache and want into words. A little curl of dread coils up my spine when I consider – maybe it's not that, for him. Maybe he's angry, more upset with me now than when we fought, maybe he's embarrassed and bitter.

But . . . he's not.

This is Lloyd, after all. Heart on his sleeve. An open book.

Wide eyes, green like the first rush of grass in a new spring, plaintive and hopeful. His full lips parted slightly with a hundred things to say on them – too many, making it impossible to know where to start.

I don't know how long we stand in the hallway.

I don't know who moves first, either, only that we come together in a collision of outstretched arms and trembling hands, my face buried in the crook of his neck; the familiarity of Lloyd's embrace, the way he holds me so tightly, eliminates the need for words.

He's here, and that's enough.

For as long as we stand there, clinging to each other, I *know*, can feel in my bones – that it'll be okay. That the disaster of the emails, of everyone finding out about us, won't be the calamity it felt like this morning. The steady rise and fall of his chest against mine, the warm flush of his skin beneath my fingers, the way he makes me feel so suddenly and completely grounded – so wholly myself – feels so much bigger than any internship.

How could I ever have convinced myself that *this* was worth so little? That it in any way compared to my last relationship, which had been so easy to put behind me in favour of 'the big picture' stuff?

Lloyd draws himself upright, ready to say something. A tiny, adorable crease puckers between his eyebrows; I reach up to smooth it out, revelling in the lopsided smile that replaces his focused expression, and my fingers trace a path along his cheek, my palm settling against his jaw. His head bows until his forehead is pressed to mine; it's tender, a stark contrast to his grip on my elbows, anchoring me close, like if he lets go I'll slip through his fingers for good. I know how he feels. This is so perfect – so right – that I'm half-afraid it's not real. Like if I say something, I'll jinx it somehow, and this will disappear.

I tilt my head up towards his, our noses brushing against each other. His lips are so close to mine, but the few millimetres of space that parts us feels cavernous.

Just when I think he's about to kiss me, Lloyd finally breaks the silence.

'I wrote you poems, you know.'

'You – what?'

There's a *ping* behind us, the lift doors opening, animated voices slicing through the tension in the air. We've stood too long; we've lost our moment.

Lloyd lets me go, inch by inch, reluctance in his every movement.

The voices stop before I can turn, and then there's a cry of, 'Annalise!' and I'm being wrenched into a hug, a pair of thin arms wrapping tight enough around me that it crushes all the air out of my lungs.

'Ohmigod,' Elaine says in a rush, 'we were so worried all day! You weren't answering your phone! Are you alright? What happened? Verity said you left with your mum. Are you okay?'

She steps back to hold me at arm's length, scrutinizing me like she can expect to see the after-effects of this morning's events written all over me. She probably can, in all fairness. I must look like crap.

Behind her is Louis, along with Monty, Dylan and Izzy. They're all looking at me with concern, and pity.

They've all read the emails, I'm sure of it.

I fumble to reply, trying to shake off the heady intimacy of the moment Lloyd and I just shared – the one they've ruined.

'Sorry. My – my phone died, and I haven't really had chance to check it since . . .' I trail off, not really sure what to say – they're all looking at me so expectantly. My first instinct is to ask how their days have been, if they've all got plans together tonight. It doesn't seem right to say something so normal, when it's been such a screwed-up day.

'Let's go in. C'mon, I'm gasping for a cuppa,' Louis says, ambling down the hallway with his keys out.

Izzy says tentatively, 'Or if you want some space we can leave, Anna. I mean, we don't want to get in the way.'

Are they all here to gossip about me?

Could I blame them if they were?

Right now, they simply look sorry for me, and like they care. They're just being my friends; I want to let them.

'No! Don't let me stop you. It's fine, honestly. Come on in.'

Behind me, Lloyd clears his throat, seeming to draw everyone's attention to himself for the first time. (Which would be funny, under other circumstances – that he has, for once, managed to fade into the background.)

'I'll get out of your hair, guys. See you round the office, yeah?'

Dylan starts to say, 'Mate, what're you talking about? Stay! You're –'

But Monty elbows him in the rubs, with a sharp and very obvious jerk of the head in my direction. 'Dude.'

Dylan flushes, deferring to me awkwardly.

'Um, it's . . . okay,' I tell Lloyd. 'You can stay, if you want.'

He can't leave. We haven't even had a chance to talk.

Was he going to kiss me again? Or did he just get caught up in the moment and is relieved he didn't?

Stay. Stay, please.

But he's already shaking his head. 'Nah. Seriously, I'll leave you guys to it.'

414

He smiles around at everyone – his usual hundred-watt smile. He claps Dylan on the arm as he passes by and calls the lift, and the rest of us file into the flat, the chatter starting back up. I turn to look over my shoulder at Lloyd, and he offers up a shrug and a small, sorry sort of smile.

It's okay, he seems to say. *We lost our moment.*

So I let him leave, and join the others in the flat. Louis offers some tea to everyone – Elaine, only half-joking, asks if I want something stronger.

'I'm kind of sick of cups of tea today,' I laugh, having lost count of how many times one has been placed in front of me like it will fix everything. 'Just some water is great, though.'

'They tell you about Tasha yet, Anna?' Monty says.

This time, Dylan elbows him. 'Dude!'

'What? *What?* She's gonna find out eventually! Wouldn't you want to know?'

'I haven't checked my phone, like I said . . .'

Izzy searches my face. 'You knew it was her?'

I shrug. 'It wasn't hard to figure out. She . . . said some things yesterday, that weren't very nice.'

'I can't *believe* it,' Izzy sighs, looking genuinely upset – but not on my behalf this time. 'She was always so lovely! I can't imagine why she'd do something like that! You must've really upset her.'

Monty scoffs. 'Or she was just a bitch. Which is definitely the more likely of the two.'

I stare at him in surprise. Who'd have thought Monty was such a kindred spirit all this time? A fellow non-believer in great romances *and* not taken in by Tasha's sickly-sweetness.

'Thanks, by the way,' I tell him and Dylan. 'For this morning. Collecting all the emails, and stuff. It's . . . It means a lot to me. Thanks.'

'Course,' Monty says, in his usual bolshy tone, like I said thanks for buying some shots when it was his turn for a round, like he didn't go out of his way to do me such a massive favour and look out for me. He shrugs, clearing his throat. 'It's nothing.'

It wasn't. It really wasn't. Not to me.

But I just smile, and tell him, 'I owe you a pint.'

'Yeah, you do.' He smiles back, a little more gently this time.

'So what happened? They found out Tasha was behind it?'

'Oh my *God*, Anna, you should've seen it! Well – not – obviously, it was awful, but still. *Total* drama,' Elaine gushes, returning from the kitchen to fold herself into the corner of the sofa next to Dylan – and I wonder if maybe she wasn't very fond of Tasha all this time, too, because she's normally so good at taking the middle ground. 'She got called up to Topher's office, and the Senior HR Partner was there, *and* Tasha's manager, *and* yours, *and* Nadja – and they really let her have it. Nadja really went for the jugular.'

Izzy says, sounding a little reproachful, 'Monty and Verity were helpful enough to message us all to let us know what was going on, so we could all come and listen.'

'You could've heard a pin drop,' Dylan tells me, eyes wide with the excitement of the scandal. 'Everyone was listening in.'

'She got in *soooo* much trouble,' Elaine goes on. 'For messing with your work computer and snooping through it when she knew it could be, like, a breach of confidential information and stuff, but also because it's just rude. For sending the emails, because it was vindictive. Even wasting company resources, printing out hundreds of copies to stick up everywhere!'

'What did they say about it?'

'Well it *looked* like she was going to get away with a slap on the wrist, just a telling-off and be kept tabs on a bit for the next couple of weeks . . .'

'But *then*,' Louis tells me, coming back over with a couple of mugs of tea, handing one to Izzy. '*Then*, Tasha lost it. She'd just been standing there taking it, crying, apologizing, all that – and then when Nadja kept berating her to make her understand how much she'd fucked up, she just started screaming. Started yelling at *them*, defending herself and trying to drag *you* under the bus, saying they were just looking out for you because you were shacking up with the boss's son and how everybody ought to know if you were sleeping your way through the internship.'

I'm very, very glad I wasn't there to witness all this.

Even hearing it second-hand from someone who obviously doesn't believe it to be true, it's crushing. I knew people might think it when they saw my emails to Lloyd, but having someone yell it for everyone to hear . . .

'So Topher's trying to say that's not true, and your manager is defending you,' Dylan says, picking up the story. 'And then Nadja just held up a hand, waited for Tasha to finish, and told her to go pack her things. Literally, there and then! Said they'd dock her final pay cheque for the cost of printing, and everything! Threatened to call security to "forcibly remove her from the building" if she didn't comply!'

'Oh my God,' I whisper, reeling. I figured they'd throw the book at Tasha and tell her off, but I never imagined . . .

I guess I thought it was nothing she couldn't wriggle her way out of. Not when I'd come out of it all looking so bad, anyway.

'Right?' Elaine says, nodding bug-eyed at me. 'It's *wild*. She's had to move out to go back home and everything. *And* she's left the group chat. Didn't say a word! Just left!'

'Oh my God.'

'I thought it all seemed a bit harsh,' Izzy says quietly, and blushes when everyone looks at her. 'Making her move out like that, and stuff, I mean. Making such a big deal out of it in front of everybody like that.'

'What, like she didn't deserve a taste of her own medicine?' Monty scoffs. 'She had it coming. Karma's a bigger bitch than even Tasha.'

I laugh.

For the first time, all day, I laugh. It sputters out of me so suddenly that I clasp a hand over my mouth – but it bubbles up, hysterical, filling my chest until another laugh spills between my fingers and I crease up, yet more tears forming at the corners of my eyes – but this time, the good kind.

I think, maybe, I'm supposed to feel guilty. That I should feel inclined to reach out to Tasha and apologize, but – I don't. I don't really know what I should have to apologize for. Monty's right: it's a taste of her own medicine. If she'd just left me alone, this wouldn't have happened. I can't bring myself to feel sorry for her; I've wasted all my pity on myself.

Before long, Elaine carefully, as tactfully as she can, says, 'We didn't realize . . . You and Lloyd . . . Has that been . . .? Is he that boy you told me about, when –?'

And Louis interrupts to ask me more bluntly, '*Are* you shagging?'

'No! No, we just . . . Well, *once*, but . . . I mean, I kissed him, before the internship started. I didn't know who he was at first, and then . . . We tried to just pretend it never happened, and then I kept seeing him around –'

'When?' Elaine asks, curious.

I squirm in my seat. 'The office. On Friday nights, sometimes. We hung out, one night – outside of Arrowmile, I mean.'

'What were you doing there on Friday nights?' Dylan asks, incredulous.

And I have to tell the truth – there's no point in little white lies to make things easier for everybody now. 'I had a hard time keeping on top of everything at work. And then I'd keep saying yes to extra stuff, trying to go above and beyond, like Nadja said right at the start . . . I stayed late sometimes to catch up. I'd – I'd tell you guys I was meeting other friends, or you'd all be out and assume I was just at home. Lloyd was, um, doing some work for his dad. I think it was easier to do when people weren't around all the time. You know what he's like – total chatterbox. Doesn't get anything done when he can talk to people instead.'

It's *near* enough the truth, anyway. A stretch, on Lloyd's part – but that's not my secret to share.

Elaine looks sorry for me; Monty stares at me like I've lost the plot, and so does Louis.

'Anyway,' I barrel on. 'We spent some time together, and . . . I liked him. But I said I wasn't interested in anything serious because I wanted to focus on the internship, and I didn't want to be that girl who was dating the boss's son. I thought people would . . . say stuff like Tasha did. That all the work I'd done this summer wouldn't mean anything.'

'This is the most romantic thing I've ever heard,' Elaine gushes.

'It's tragic,' Izzy says – not unkindly. I think she means in the Romeo and Juliet sense. She looks genuinely sorry for me, not scathing.

'I don't know what the big deal would've been,' Louis adds. 'You could've had a great summer sneaking around to hook up with him!'

Elaine swats at him, so viciously he almost spills his tea. 'No! Louis! Didn't you read the emails? It wasn't just *sex*.'

'Yeah, we can't all have a string of dates and

hook-ups that don't mean anything,' Dylan scoffs, grinning across at him.

'They liked each other!' Elaine goes on, impassioned. Her cheeks flush, eyes shining. 'They had real feelings for each other! Anna was clearly heartbroken over the whole thing! She cried over him! You should've heard the way she talked about him!'

'So?' Monty says, nudging me. 'Did you tell him?'

'Tell him what?'

He rolls his eyes.

And then Elaine says, 'That you're in love with him.'

Chapter 33

Lloyd finds me at the top of The Mall at Buckingham Palace, near an entrance to St James's Park. It's bucketing down with rain, a welcome respite from the stifling summer heat. Raindrops thunder against the ground and ricochet off the top of my umbrella, which is barely holding up in the downpour. The weather has driven away anybody who harboured ideas of a lazy summer picnic sprawled on the grass in the park or reading a book under the shade of a tree, but a walking group of tourists strides past me, led by a man with a neon orange flag sticking out of his rucksack and talking into a microphone.

The relative lack of people mean it's easy to spot Lloyd arriving.

His trainers splash through puddles, his jeans damp; the hood of his raincoat is pulled up over his head and his hands are buried tightly into his pockets.

A couple of rogue curls have been caught in the rain and are plastered, wet, against his forehead. He reaches up as if to push his hood down as he approaches me, but seems to think better of it and turns the gesture into a wave instead.

'Hey,' I say, when he's near enough.

'Hi. I got your text. Thanks for . . .' He gestures vaguely – between us, around us. Then, he jabs a thumb towards the park. 'Shall we go for a walk?'

I nod, and we fall in step near each other, arm's length apart. It's close enough to talk without feeling like we're intruding on one another's space. There are thick, purplish clouds overhead; the park stretches out in front of us, so far that I can't see the other side of it.

I texted Lloyd last night, asking him to meet me here. *I think we both have some things to say that are better said in person*, I told him.

His reply was short, simple. Straight to the point.

I think you're right.

It was too exhausting to even contemplate looking at the other messages that were waiting on my phone after the emails leaked. Lloyd had sent a *lot*. He left some voicemails, too, but I didn't have the energy to listen to them.

424

It's nothing he can't tell me in person today, anyway. This is the conversation we never got to have last night. One that, I think, we should've had a long time ago.

'How're you doing?' Lloyd asks after a minute. 'After . . . yesterday.'

'Better, I think. I heard Tasha got fired over it.'

'Yeah. I knew she didn't like you, but bloody hell, that was . . . Who does something like that?'

'What do you mean? How'd you know that?'

Lloyd pulls a face, shrugging one shoulder. 'Just some of the things she said sometimes. I talked to all the interns when I was around the office. She said she thought you were really up yourself.'

I can't help but snort at that. Tasha's resting face was looking down her nose at people.

'I kind of got the impression she was all talk. That she hadn't really been doing much, and not doing a stellar job at the stuff she *did* do,' he adds.

Huh. Somehow, I'm not too surprised. It adds up with her reaction when I accused her of coasting along. But I don't want to talk about her anymore.

'I should've tried to speak to you properly yesterday,' I say. 'I was never going to send those emails. They were just – cathartic. Helping me work through my own stuff, which I realize, now, I kind of took out on you . . . I don't even know *why* I . . . Anyway,

I'm sorry they got out and I dragged you into this mess with me. I know your dad was . . . He didn't seem too happy about the whole thing.'

He scoffs, but it's resigned more than anything else. 'You could say that.'

I wait, wondering if he wants to tell me – wondering if I have any right to ask, or if that's unfair of me, after everything.

He catches my eye as if hearing my unspoken question anyway, then tells me, 'He was furious to think I'd been screwing around with the interns – *again*. All he really knew about my ex from last year was that she broke up with me and turned down a job offer from Arrowmile a couple of weeks later – I was too embarrassed to tell him what really happened between us. He said I was putting our name and reputation on the line. How I should know better – but it's like I told you, I never meant . . . That night we met . . . I was never supposed to . . .'

'I'm sorry it got you in trouble.'

Lloyd sucks in a sharp breath, drawing to a stop in front of me. Rain trickles off the end of my umbrella and onto his face, slaloming down the slope of his nose. A frown puckers between his eyebrows, but when his eyes fix on me, they're so serious it makes the rest of the world fall away.

'I was never supposed to fall for you the way I did,' he tells me.

Me either.

My breath hitches, a reply sticking in my throat. My heart starts racing, doing somersaults – doing a whole damn decathlon.

When I don't say anything, Lloyd rushes on.

'We had something, that night we met. I know you laughed at the idea of love at first sight, but *I* believed in it. I believed in that with you. We had something, and the smart thing to do would've been to stay away, but . . . Every time I saw you, I'd fall a little harder. I knew – I mean, I *thought* you didn't feel the same way, especially after you said the internship meant more to you than *me*, so I didn't want to make a big deal of it. But the stuff you said in your emails . . . Annalise . . .'

Lloyd trails off; his breath shudders out of him, washing across my face. I can taste it – faintly like coffee, and something sweet. It makes me want to lean in to kiss him, drag my tongue along his lips.

He stands there, jaw tight and chest rising and falling heavily, his gaze locked on mine.

The frown is still there, but his eyes are wide and earnest, a glimmer of hope against hope illuminating them, stark against the grey world around us.

Raindrops continue to land on his face, trickling down from his temples, his nose, along his lips and jaw, down his throat where they disappear beneath the raised collar of his coat.

Lloyd shifts forward slightly. Just an inch, maybe two, and hesitates. Terrified of being too sudden or careless with this brittle, barely-there moment that engulfs us, so breakable. Irreparable.

He'd prefer this limbo of longing for each other, doing nothing about it, so long as we got to stay in each other's lives, than risking it all for the chance of more.

And I should be thinking that, too. I had been, up until recently. None of this should change anything: I'm still leaving soon, and we'll spend the next year at different universities, in different cities, living totally different lives. We'll part ways, and we'll both be heartbroken.

It shouldn't have changed anything.

And, yet.

I step closer, feet crunching on some loose stones on the path. It sounds so loud, even with the rain rippling onto the pond nearby and bouncing hollowly off the leaves of the plants around us. I step close enough to bring Lloyd just under the cover of my umbrella, close enough to feel the heat of his body radiating out.

His eyes flit to my mouth, but then he looks firmly back at my eyes.

And I raise my eyebrows, a smile playing at my lips.

'You really wrote me poetry, Fletcher?'

I feel the tension sliding off his body, shed like an extra layer of clothing. He's lighter for it, and the frown finally disappears from his face. He gives a breathy chuckle, rolling his eyes as he turns his head away – but I lift a hand to cup his cheek, warm and damp beneath my palm, turning him back to me.

'Can I read it?'

'Maybe one day,' he says, and then – then, he kisses me.

He wraps an arm around my waist to pull me flush against him, pressing his lips to mine in a delicate kiss – barely a kiss at all, lasting only a heartbeat, our breath mingling as we stand wrapped up in each other – and then another kiss that's so fierce and desperate he must be pouring an entire summer's worth of want and heartache into it, or maybe that's me, or both of us all at once.

I'm vaguely aware of the rain drenching me when I drape an arm over his shoulder, my umbrella sliding out of my fingers to dangle from the rope handle looped around my wrist so my hand is free to slide into Lloyd's hair. I'm not even sure which of us pulled the hood of his coat down.

I'm only aware of every place our bodies are touching, the searing heat of his kiss, the arms wrapped firmly around me to anchor me against him like if he lets go, if this ends, I'll vanish.

It's everything, and I'm delirious.

Chapter 34

The final week of the Arrowmile internship arrives all too quickly. I receive a few curious or pitying looks from people in the office after the email leak, but nobody really brings it up; and when it becomes common knowledge that I'm only a first-year and technically not eligible for the internship, they only comment that my application must have been very impressive, and I take that as a win.

As the other interns wind down and enjoy long lunches, I work at breakneck pace trying to finish things I started rather than hand them over.

Old habits die hard.

But I haven't been staying so late anymore. Elaine and the others are determined not to let me; and I'm easily swayed when Lloyd is there to tempt me away to enjoy summer evenings in the city with him, packing three months' worth of dates into a couple of weeks with trips to museums, the zoo, art exhibits neither of us really 'get', ice-cream shops, and even a trip to the theatre. I spend a good chunk of the money I was trying so hard to save all summer, but can't bring myself to regret a penny of it – not when it means these memories with Lloyd.

But there are still the final presentations to focus on, showing off everything we've done during the internship to managers and board members. It's meant to be a final chance to get seen, to push us outside of our comfort zone one last time. Something to add to our future job applications, or, hopefully, to impress the folks at Arrowmile enough to secure ourselves an offer when we graduate.

Izzy has a full breakdown the night before, and when Louis and I go to check on her, we find Monty pacing the hallway and muttering to himself as he recites his presentation from a series of flashcards, looking stressed-out for once. Dylan keeps sending pictures of his slides to the group chat and asking if they make sense or are too technical, or if we think he's included too many jokes.

The big day arrives whether we're ready or not though, and the entire twelfth floor has been dedicated to the Arrowmile interns showcasing our summer. Desks have been pushed aside and chairs lined up in haphazard rows, facing a large screen standing near the windows.

Everyone has ten minutes to present, plus ten minutes for questions afterwards. Nadja warns us to keep to our time limits – because she *will* cut us off, if we go over, which isn't a terrifying concept *at all*.

I take a seat with a few of the others near the back. It's alphabetical, which means me, Elaine and Dylan are among those who get to torture ourselves with nerves and adrenaline waiting for our slots in the afternoon.

For all our nerves though, the day runs smoothly, and nobody has too much to worry about beyond tripping over their words slightly or fumbling to answer a question coherently. Freya has technical issues when her laptop decides not to connect to the projector, but gamely starts without a PowerPoint behind her until someone fixes it, and Verity talks so fast her presentation is done in five minutes flat, but then she dazzles during the questions afterwards.

When it's my turn, my heart is in my throat and my mouth feels fuzzy, like it's been stuffed full of cotton wool. I've rehearsed plenty, but as I stand there in front of this huge crowd of important, influential people in this impressive company, knowing this could be what my future hinges on, the entire thing suddenly turns into an out-of-body experience.

I smooth out my Elle Woods-confidence-infused pink dress, take a breath, force myself to smile, and say, 'Hi, everybody. My name is Anna Sherwood . . .'

And the next thing I'm sitting down with my laptop on my lap and Elaine is squeezing my arm, whispering, 'You did so great! That was amazing!' and Dylan is on my other side saying, 'Bloody hell, Anna, when did you have time to do all that? Talk about a tough act to follow . . . Wish me luck!' Then he gets up to take my place at the front of the room.

I tune him out as he sets up and starts talking, trying to filter through the static that's taken over my brain. I recall my steady voice talking methodically through my slides and the surge of panic when Nadja cleared her throat for my two-minute warning, and making everyone laugh at my reply when one of the managers asked if I felt like I was too much of a people-pleaser.

I think . . . No, I *know*, it went well.

I relax, the mood in the room helping to set me at ease as people chuckle at Dylan's dorky jokes or hum with interest. Finally feeling back to normal, I twist to look over my shoulder, spotting Lloyd standing a few rows back, his shoulder leaning against a wall and arms crossed over his chest.

He looks nervous, too, but gives me a thumbs up – *good job*.

Thanks, I mouth back, then nod at him and give a reassuring smile. He puffs out a breath, blowing some of the hair up from his forehead, but smiles back. Still nervous, but ready.

The last presentation wraps up and the applause is louder this time – for all of us, and because it means this long day is over.

Nadja begins to move out of her seat, but I beat her to it, bolting from my spot in the front row with the other interns presenting this afternoon, and standing to face the crowd once more.

'Hi, everyone, sorry – if you could just all stay seated for a second . . .' I look around them with an expectant smile, clasping my hands in front of my torso so nobody notices them shaking, trying my best to exude an authority I most definitely do not possess.

But people hesitate, and stay where they are.

'Thanks. So, um, as I think most of you are probably aware, up until recently, there were fifteen of us on the internship programme. But, um, due to some, um, unfortunate, um, circumstances . . .'

I'm saying 'um' too much. I look like an amateur. I'm losing them. I'm screwing this up.

I notice Monty near the back – looking at me like I've lost it, or like he's hoping I'll announce a round of shots. He pulls a face as if to say, *fuck if I know*, but then gives me two thumbs up anyway. Next to him, noticing, Verity gives me an encouraging nod.

I've got this. I can do this.

'I thought there was someone else here who could use that empty slot, now that other intern has left.'

Nadja purses her lips, frowning at me, but doesn't try to stop me. Topher is whispering something to her, looking a bit less eager to see where this is going.

But I look away from them, over at Lloyd – and wave him over to take his spot at the front. Heads turn and whispers rush through the crowd. Lloyd says a quiet thanks to me as we pass when I return to my seat, and plugs his laptop into the projector before anybody has really had chance to get their head around this change in the programme.

He looks at Nadja, though, as if waiting for permission.

Topher looks irritated, and more than a little apprehensive.

Nadja shrugs, and tells Lloyd, 'Well, it's un-conventional, but . . . Why not? You know the drill: ten minutes to present, ten for Q&A.'

He nods once. 'Got it.'

'Floor's all yours.'

This wasn't the original plan. When I met Lloyd on my birthday and found out exactly what his file of secret projects was all about, I offered to give up my slot today. I felt like I'd made a solid impression on my manager and some other people (before the whole emails/photo horror show, anyway) and I could send my presentation to people after the fact. I'd probably get another chance to show off what I'd done here.

Lloyd hadn't had that chance – ever.

It was his idea that I keep my spot, and he take Tasha's instead – everything fell so perfectly into place.

Now, he steels himself, and I watch as he shakes off his nerves and trades them for a more muted version of his usual, charming smile. He looks less like the Lloyd Fletcher who swans around his dad's office, and more like the one I've fallen for.

And he starts talking. Oozing charisma in a way that holds everybody's attention, and diving in quickly to one of the projects he picked from his file to talk about. He goes into an incredible amount of detail on how much it's cost the company so far and the truth of just how 'eco-friendly' it is under all the layers of buzzwords and corporate varnish, backing up his suggested changes with other Arrowmile projects or existing initiatives from other companies. There are cost projections and calculations and animated diagrams, and even a model he got one of the scientists in the labs to create for him.

People hang off his every word. A couple take notes, or murmur to each other, but nobody takes their attention completely off him for even a second. The attention they give him now is different to the usual deference because he's the boss's son – it's respect, because they realize how keenly he understands all of this.

He clicks onto a final slide that reads THANK YOU FOR LISTENING and looks around his audience, unsmiling but relaxed, and confident.

'Any questions?'

A couple of hands shoot up. A few people start speaking.

Topher shoots out of his seat, marching up to Lloyd. He doesn't raise his voice, but the room has fallen quiet enough that I'm sure everyone hears when he hisses, 'What the hell are you playing at? How many times do I have to tell you to stop interfering and wasting people's time like this? I have *real* employees to do this kind of thing. *Qualified scientists* to put together proposals like this, if there was any real value in them. When are you going to learn to leave well enough alone? This isn't your playground, Lloyd – this is a business.'

The edge of Lloyd's mouth twitches, and his jaw sets before he gives a thin, sardonic smile that doesn't belong on his face.

'Gosh, Dad. It almost sounds like you don't *want* me involved in what you're doing here at Arrowmile.'

Topher grits his teeth, hand bunching into a fist at his side.

Lloyd steps sideways, away from where his dad blocks his view of everybody, reclaiming the audience. The spotlight here has always belonged to him, and now he's finally using it.

'I've spent my whole life here. Some of you have known me since I was small. Some of you celebrated my exam results with me from school. You've seen me around here every summer, elbow-deep in everything Arrowmile. I'm not wasting your time. I've checked these things with *you*. *You've* run the models for me, answered my questions, helped me do calculations or understand where things went wrong in the past, what we could do differently. I've just – consolidated all that information. I'm not saying I know better,' he adds, and turns now to his dad, speaking directly to Topher. 'But I've been taught to step back and look at the bigger picture, and that's exactly what I'm doing.'

Topher stands there, mouth agape, speechless.

'*So,*' Lloyd presses. 'Nadja, if you can start that ten-minute timer – does anyone have any questions?'

After the allotted ten minutes of question time wraps up, it's clear that some people – Topher included – aren't quite done with Lloyd, but Nadja steps in to wrangle back control. She resumes her closing speech to thank all of us interns for our hard work and everybody who attended the presentations, then swiftly sends us away. Lloyd and some of the managers disappear into his dad's office, all laser-focused.

We linger for a little while and the others pepper me with questions because they had no idea Lloyd had been working on that kind of stuff all this time; he's the man of the moment, and they want a piece of him, too. But it isn't my place to share his secrets, even if there aren't very many left to keep for him: it must be obvious to everyone from the way Topher spoke to him that there's some underlying tension in their relationship, and that he hasn't given Lloyd's ideas the time of day before.

When Lloyd doesn't reappear after fifteen minutes, Monty suggests we all make the most of the early finish and head to the pub. Nobody argues, and I text Lloyd to let him know where to find us later, if he wants.

I hope he does; I hope it's going okay, and he's not in trouble.

Everybody forgets about Lloyd's surprise presentation as they fall to dissecting how their own went. Conversations start to overlap, making it hard to focus on any one of them, so I sit quietly with one eye on the door until, finally, Lloyd arrives. He spots me instantly and makes a beeline for our table, looking a little drained and a little wired. Coming down off an adrenaline rush – although I'm not sure yet if it's the good kind or not. His shoulders slump and he scrubs a hand through his hair, but when he reaches us, he breaks into a grin.

'What're you all sat around staring for? I thought we were celebrating! Anybody need another drink?'

'How'd it go?' Dylan bursts out, and Elaine shuffles over to make space for the extra chair Burnley is bringing over for Lloyd.

Freya asks, 'What happened?'

And Louis wants to know, 'Did they oust your dad and declare you the new CEO of Arrowmile?'

Lloyd laughs, bracing his hands on the back of the chair Burnley leaves for him but not sitting down yet. He looks more relaxed now than he did a moment ago – and definitely lighter than he did throughout his whole presentation. The weight of the world off his shoulders, for a little while at least.

He fills us all in on what happened after we left. A couple of people from the labs or Dylan's R&D team were there and could back up the science and data Lloyd used, and several managers wanted to back his proposal, see if it really did have legs.

Encouraged, and not knowing if he'd get a chance like this again, Lloyd told them it was only the tip of the iceberg. He showed them his file with all the notes he'd been collating over the past few years, other Arrowmile projects he wanted to work on in more depth. Apparently, one of the guys from the labs – the not-that-kind-of-doctor scientist who'd taken us on a tour right at the start of our internship – suggested Lloyd would be better placed pursuing some kind of science degree instead.

He had, apparently, a natural aptitude for it.

Lloyd catches my eye as he says that, fighting back a smile and failing.

'Is that what you want to do?' Verity asks him, surprised.

'I mean . . . Kind of, yeah.' He shuffles awkwardly from one foot to the other, then braces himself and announces, 'Yes. It is.'

'What did your dad say?' I ask.

He shrugs one shoulder. 'Not a whole lot. There wasn't much he *could* say. Even he had to admit it was worth hearing me out. We've set up some time next week to go through everything in more detail.'

'Mate!' Monty stands up to clap him on the shoulder. 'That's great news! Definitely deserves a pint – you smashed it. Anyone else?'

'We should do shots,' Burnley says, and is met with a resounding and unyielding chorus of 'No!' from half the group, which makes everyone laugh.

'I'll get a round in,' Lloyd tells Monty, prompting him back into his seat. 'This one's on me – to say thanks to you all for letting me highjack your day like that.'

'Well, *most* of us weren't clued in,' Dylan points out, but he's grinning. 'I'll have another G&T. Make it a double, if you're buying!'

When Lloyd leaves to join the queue at the bar, an elbow digs sharply into my side.

'Ouch! What was that for?' I turn to face Elaine, who's looking at me wide-eyed and urgent, jerking her head in Lloyd's direction, which is about as subtle as a foghorn. So I mumble that I'll go help, and ignore the sidelong looks and cheeky grins the others exchange as I follow Lloyd to the bar to steal a few moments alone.

I stand close, my fingers brushing against his elbow. It's still strange – thrilling – that I can touch him like this. It's a far cry from the stolen, secret touches in the canteen – and infinitely better.

'How're you feeling?' I ask.

He blows out a long puff of air, leaning on his elbows on the countertop before straightening up and angling his body towards me. 'Honestly? Kind of relieved. I'm glad I did it. Dad will come around, now he can see there are other people on board and I'm not just full of hot air, or trying to undermine him. And I think – I think I'm going to try to change my uni course. I was talking to Will about it the other day; he thought it was a good idea. Said he'll back me, if it causes trouble with Dad. Apparently, I've had his back enough times that he owes me.'

Lloyd looks tired, worn down, but his smile is earnest and there's a gleam in his eyes. My hand slips up his arm to his shoulder and he draws me in a little closer, his hand settling on my hip. His thumb brushes in slow arcs over my dress, sending tingles through my whole body.

'Thanks, Annalise.'

'I didn't do anything.'

'Yes, you did. I couldn't have done this without you.'

'You sure about that, Fletcher? I can't imagine you having a hard time using that inflated ego of yours to get your way eventually.'

He smirks a little, but the look in his eyes is more serious. 'I mean it. I was playing it safe. Too busy being "the golden boy" to rock the boat. Thanks for reminding me who I am. Who I want to be.'

'And who's that?'

Instead of replying, Lloyd smiles at me – close-lipped and full of mischief, because the answer to that question is a secret we both know, and he kisses me.

And it's wonderful.

Epilogue

Thin stretches of cotton-wool clouds drift across the sky. Reclined on a blanket in the patchy, hazy sunshine in Hyde Park, I close my eyes, enjoying the warmth on my face without the full glare of the sun. Beneath my head, Lloyd's chest rises and falls so steadily I wonder if maybe he's fallen asleep.

But then his body shifts, and his fingers trail through my hair instead. I hum, enjoying the sensation. It's so soothing that *I* might fall asleep.

It's so good to be back with Lloyd for a while. We have the whole summer stretched out ahead of us, not just stolen weekends in between our uni courses, taking turns to visit each other, or finding time together alongside seeing our families during the term breaks.

I have my graduation next week. Despite being a year older, Lloyd still has two more years of his course to go, since he dropped out of studying Law and

Economics as his dad finally encouraged him to pursue something that interested him more: Chemical Engineering.

He likes it, a lot. He turns into a real nerd when he starts talking about it. It's unbearably cute, just like almost everything else about Lloyd. He's thinking about pursuing a PhD part-time after he finishes his master's, balancing it alongside work at Arrowmile. Nadja's even been inspired to set up a new programme, sponsoring students through university courses while they work at Arrowmile.

Not that Lloyd will need to get one of those coveted places. Perks of being the CEO's son, and all. I still tease him about it.

Now I'm graduating, Mum offered me a job working alongside her in the network she runs for young female entrepreneurs. As good as our relationship is these days, I wasn't interested in having her as my boss as well as my mum.

'Sorry,' she'd said, after I pointed that out. 'I'm good at being a boss. I'm still figuring out the "mum" thing.'

Besides, even if I have learned to let my hair down a little over the past couple of years and give myself some breathing space instead of letting my studies or worries about the future consume everything, I'll always fundamentally be that girl who wants to work hard and earn everything she gets.

Instead, in September, I start a job in a company that works alongside government-sponsored environmental projects.

Lloyd's passion for science and sustainability has kind of worn off on me.

I walked through the interview, with the Arrowmile internship behind me. Dylan works there, too – he was the reason I heard about the job in the first place.

I'm still in touch with some of the Arrowmile interns. We have a group chat, and some of us have met up a few times. Elaine and Monty are both working at Arrowmile; they're meeting us for dinner tonight, along with Will.

'What're you thinking about?' Lloyd asks. The words rumble through his chest; his fingers keep stroking my hair.

'Just about how everything worked out. Uni. Work. Us. All of it. It really fell into place, didn't it?'

He lets out a small breath of laughter. I can *feel* him grinning. I don't have to look to picture his mouth stretched into a smug smile, that little glimmer in his eyes as they crease around the corners.

'Don't tell me I overthink things, or try too hard, or worry too much,' I tell him before he gets chance to speak. 'We don't all waltz through life like you, Fletcher.'

He nudges me, so I roll over slightly to look at him. Propped up on my elbow, I push my sunglasses up on top of my head so he can feel the full effect of my challenging glare, but he just keeps grinning. His hand comes to rest on the back of my head.

'I was *actually* going to say, of course it all worked out. You put everything into making it happen – how could it not? It fell into place because you made it happen.'

'Oh.' I bite my lip. 'Well, you're right.'

'I know. I usually am.'

I shove him half-heartedly in the shoulder. 'Good to know you're still as insufferable as ever.'

'Annalise, you'd despair if I were anything but,' he tells me, and his grin stretches even wider. Smug, and over-confident – and agonizingly attractive. My heart does a little flip, and whatever snarky reply I might've made gets lost somewhere between my brain and my mouth.

Lloyd pulls me down towards him, the hand on the back of my head drawing me in close so he can kiss me. Our lips slot together with familiarity, habit, and even now, it sends a spark fizzing through me. He's still smiling, mouth curved upwards as his lips press softly, sweetly to mine. I smile back, my hand bunching in the fabric of his T-shirt as I lean closer into him.

He tastes like summer. Like first love and reckless abandon and secrets beneath a starless sky. It's a kiss that's full of memories, and full of the promise of what's next.

Acknowledgements

This book is a bit of a love letter to tropes; to first love and finding yourself; and a little bit to London. I suppose these acknowledgements are a bit of a love letter as well, to all the wonderful people around me. There are always so many people to thank for everything that goes on behind the scenes, and throughout the whole writing process for a book, so I'll try to keep it as brief as I can!

First up, even if she's not here to read this any more, thank you, Becca, for so often being on the receiving end of texts about my random book ideas. I told you about this one in May of 2022, before I could forget about it, and you were on the other end of the phone while I stayed up until two a.m. writing sample chapters. I wish you could have been here to see it published. And to the Cluster: thanks for being so bloody brilliant, for the laughs and support and everything in between. Hopefully this one makes it across the pond to you all soon!

Next up, to the rest of my friends. Thanks to Lauren (nobody gets my love for the last-naming trope quite like you); to the Gobble Gals; the Physics gang; and Amy and Aimee for always being there and cheering me on. Specifically, to Lauren, Jen, Hannah and Ellie – we all made it through the other side of grad schemes not too dissimilar to the one that Anna goes through on this internship, and I'm forever grateful you're much more than just work-friends.

Big thanks to my family, as always, for their support! Mum, Dad, Kat, and my auntie and uncle – and especially thanks to Gransha, a true champion of my books and publicist extraordinaire no matter where you are.

And last, but by no means least, thank you to the whole team at Penguin and Darley Anderson! Clare, you're a rockstar as always; Sara, I couldn't ask for a better editor to work with; and Naomi, Katie, Shreeta, Chloe and Chess, you're all too fantastic for words. I couldn't do it without you!

IF YOU ENJOYED

Sincerely Yours, Anna Sherwood

WHY NOT READ MORE ROMANCE BY BETH REEKLES?

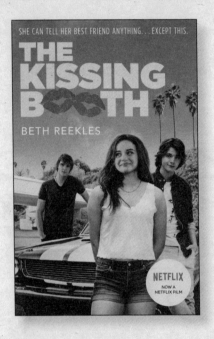

THE KISSING BOOTH

When Elle decides to run a kissing booth for the school carnival, she never imagines she'll sit in it – or that her first ever kiss would be with bad boy Noah.

From that moment, her life is turned upside down – but is this a romance destined for happiness or heartbreak?

THE BEACH HOUSE

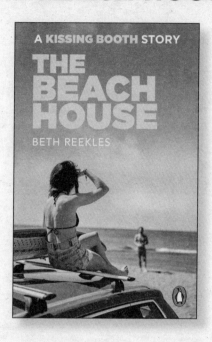

Elle is now officially dating hotter-than-hot Noah – it's amazing, but with Noah leaving for Harvard at the end of the summer their future is unknown.

Meanwhile Elle and Lee have always been BFFs, but can everything stay the same with Lee's new girlfriend, Rachel, on the scene – and with Elle now dating Lee's big brother?

Can Elle have one last perfect summer with her two favourite boys?

GOING THE DISTANCE

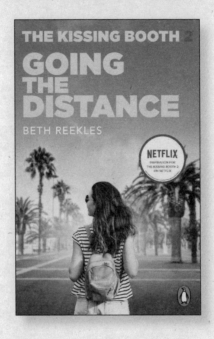

Elle seems to have finally tamed hotter-than-hot bad boy Noah Flynn, but now they're facing a new challenge. Noah's three thousand miles away at Harvard, and they're officially a long-distance couple.

Then she sees Noah getting friendly with another girl online, and a new cute boy at school shows interest in Elle.

With her heart on the line, what's a girl to do?

ONE LAST TIME

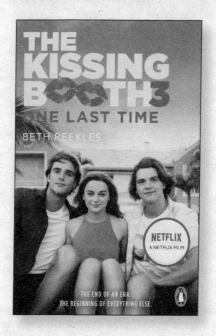

It's the summer before college and Elle needs
to make a difficult decision: go to Harvard to be
with boyfriend, Noah, or Berkeley as originally
planned with best friend, Lee.

Back at the beach house, Elle and Lee find a
bucket list they wrote as kids, and it's a great
distraction. She's determined to make this the best
summer ever, before everything has to change.

But in the end will she choose love or friendship?

THE SUMMER SWITCH-OFF

**Loved The Kissing Booth? Why not try *The Summer Switch-Off*,
a hilarious summer must-read from Beth Reekles.**

Solo travellers Luna, Rory and Jodie arrive at Casa Dorada in
desperate need of a relaxing holiday.

Luna's relationship just ended, and it feels like her old school
friends are ghosting her . . .

Rory lives for posting her art on social media, something her
sensible family just don't get . . .

And **Jodie's** life is great on paper, but she's exhausted from trying
to keep up with her friends.

When the idyllic resort turns out to be a digital detox retreat –
no phones, no internet – no one knows what to do. But with zero
distractions, maybe this will be a summer the girls won't forget . . .